That Girl

KATE KERRIGAN is a *New York Times* bestselling author whose novels have been translated into fifteen languages. They include the Ellis Island trilogy, *Recipes For A Perfect Marriage* and *The Dress*. *It Was Only Ever You* won the RNA Romantic Historical Novel of the Year Award.

Kate began her career as an editor and journalist, editing many of Britain's most successful young women's magazines before returning to her native Ireland in the 1990s to edit Irish *Tatler*. She has a weekly column in the Irish edition of the *Daily Mail* and contributes regularly to the RTÉ Radio programme *Sunday Miscellany*.

Kate lives with her husband and two children in Killala, County Mayo, Ireland.

Kate Kerrigan
That Girl

HEAD
ZEUS

9 7 5 3 2 4 6 8

A catalogue record for this book is available from
the British Library.

ISBN (HB): 9781786694157
ISBN (XTPB): 9781786694164
ISBN (E): 9781786692597

Typeset by Adrian McLaughlin

Printed and bound in the UK by CPI Books

Head of Zeus Ltd
First Floor East
5–8 Hardwick Street
London EC1R 4RG

WWW.HEADOFZEUS.COM

To Niall

1

Hanna

Sligo, Ireland, 1961

It was her first visit to Dr Dorian Black's surgery, and Hanna liked him straight away.

She had only been living in Killa for a few weeks at the time. After her father died suddenly, two years before, her mother Margaret decided they needed a new start and rented a small cottage in Killa, a fishing village on the north-west coast of county Sligo. Margaret hoped proximity to the sea would help heal their ongoing grief. Indeed, Margaret's spirits lifted as she began a new life among people who knew little or nothing about her, fitting easily into the friendly new parish. Hanna, just thirteen, had settled well into the local convent school. Their home was at the end of the pier, and Hanna developed an appetite for the fresh, salty air, spending hours sitting on the front wall reading and watching the sea. However, this time spent in the chilly air had also resulted in a nasty cough. Margaret, overly protective of her only child, had brought her straight up to the local surgery where she had been greeted by this kind, handsome Dr Black.

'Now, we're going to have to take a little look in your mouth, Hanna. Can you open wide for me?'

Hanna opened her mouth widely and he peered in. He smelt of soap and she felt strangely pleased to be in the company of a nice man, even if he was only their doctor. Most of the men they knew from home were farmers, rough and ready, smelling of manure or beer. This man was clean and gentle, like her father. She missed him. It had been two years now and Hanna had started to find it hard to call his face to mind.

'Now, that doesn't look too bad.' Dorian leaned back and took his stethoscope from around his neck. Hanna smiled at him. His accent was refined, barely detectable as Irish. She reminded him of a Jane Austen hero, handsome and dapper like Darcy, but friendly and open too, like Bingley.

'Well, young lady,' he said, 'I think you'll live.' Hanna laughed.

Then he turned his attention to Margaret. 'But, I am writing you a prescription for some antibiotics to clear this nasty cough.'

'Thank you, Doctor,' Margaret said.

'Please,' he said, smiling, 'call me Dorian.'

'Thank you, Dorian.'

Hanna noticed her mother blushing. Margaret was taken with him and, for a moment, Hanna felt pricked with possessive irritation. She reminded herself that her father was dead and it was nice, after all, to see her mother smiling.

As they were leaving, Dorian signalled Margaret to stay back for a private word. For a split second she had a dreadful feeling that there was something wrong with Hanna. After losing Liam, she knew she had become unnaturally attached to her daughter. There was just the two of them now. She couldn't face it if Hanna were sick.

'I was wondering,' Dr Black said, his eyes downcast in shyness, 'if you would do me the honour of allowing me to take you and Hanna out to dinner this evening.'

Over the coming weeks, Dorian courted Margaret. It was like a dream. This charming, erudite man had come into their lives after all the pain, hurt and shock of the last two years. She could hardly believe her luck in finding love again and, although she was as head over heels as a schoolgirl, it was Dorian's kindness towards Hanna that truly won Margaret's heart. Most men would have baulked at taking on another man's daughter, but every time they went out for a drive, to a nice hotel for dinner or to a movie theatre, he always made sure to invite Hanna. Even when they went to Dublin for a weekend, Dorian insisted she and Hanna shared their own room in the Shelbourne rather than have Hanna enduring the upset of her mother being with another man.

That, he said, was the reason for his marriage proposal just two months after their initial meeting.

'As soon as I met you, Margaret, I knew you came as a family unit. Hanna is an important part of what I love about you. I want to look after you – both.'

All the ladies of the village were delighted when it was announced that their good doctor, at the age of thirty-seven, was finally getting married. The bride wore a simple cream wool suit and her young daughter, quite a striking looking child (although clearly bashful in the face of all the attention), followed her down the aisle in a pink dress. Dorian had no family, so the day was marked with a catered drinks reception in the local hotel where all of his neighbours and patients came along to help celebrate their beloved doctor's good fortune.

'Finally,' Mrs Murphy said to him after her third glass of sherry. 'We were beginning to wonder what was wrong with you!'

He laughed then put his hand on his new wife's shoulder. 'Well, I just had to meet the right girl.'

Margaret giggled at being called a girl and slapped his arm playfully. She reached her arm out for Hanna and drew her into her side.

'Ah – or should I say, girls?' Dorian corrected himself. Everyone laughed.

A year passed and Hanna turned from thirteen to fourteen. She became more independent and began to speak her own mind. She was glad that her mother had Dorian to focus on, instead of just her, and she came to trust him. While she knew her stepfather would never be a replacement for the father she so deeply loved, Hanna grew fond of him as time went by. Dorian Black loved her mother, there was no doubt about that, and he made her happy. Hanna also understood that he had been kind and generous regarding her as well. As the nuns pointed out to her in school, 'It's not every man would take on another man's child.'

Dorian never patronised her, or talked to her like she was a poor child, as so many people did since her father died. He treated her as an equal, and she liked that. Dorian allowed her to call him by his first name. When she first did it, her mother tutted, insisting she call him father to show him proper respect. But Dorian had been on Hanna's side. 'Don't push the child, Margaret,' he said. 'I am not her natural father. There is no reason she should look on me as such. Hanna is old enough to make up her own mind about the role I play in her life.'

Margaret became worried that Hanna was moving away from her, that she was losing her. Dorian was as wise and reassuring as ever. 'Hanna is becoming a fine young woman,' he told her. 'She is not your little girl any more, Margaret. Sooner or later you'll have to accept that she's an adult.'

Margaret pursed her lips and remained silent on the subject. Hanna could tell she didn't like it but it was important that her mother understood she wasn't a child any more. Dorian was right, she was becoming a 'young woman' and her mother just had to get used to it. United in that understanding, a bond grew between stepfather and stepdaughter that felt to Hanna like friendship, or maybe even love.

Then, as Dorian and Margaret Black were coming up to their second wedding anniversary, Margaret came down with a nasty bout of flu. At first it seemed not to be serious but then her symptoms worsened with lethargy and headaches. Weeks passed and Margaret remained bedridden. With little appetite and no energy to lift herself from the bed, it appeared that there was something more serious underlying the illness. Hanna was worried and asked Dorian if there was anything more they could do. He reassured her that her mother's recovery was just around the corner.

'It's only a virus,' he promised.

But Hanna could see that despite all the tinctures and medicine Dorian was administering, Margaret seemed to get worse. One afternoon, when her mother was barely able to open her eyes and smile at her when she came in from school, Hanna asked Dorian if it would be better to move her mother to a hospital. Dorian looked at her, stricken, but also a little annoyed.

'I know you are worried, and so am I. But she is my wife, Hanna. Nobody can look after her as well as I can. Please,' he said, his eyes were wide and pleading, 'trust me. Let me do this. For you. For both of us.'

Hanna could see that this was hard for Dorian. He loved her mother too. Dorian wanted her mother back as much as she did.

So she sat at Margaret's bedside each evening and prayed for her to wake up. Dorian kept reassuring her that her mother would get better soon. But she was constantly asleep, and seemed to be fading away before Hanna's eyes.

Every few days she asked, 'Is there anything I can do?'

'Just be a good girl,' Dorian said, 'and leave your mother to the experts.' He kissed her forehead, sent her to school each day and told her that everything was going to be all right. Soon her mother would be better and they would be a happy family again.

One day Hanna came home from school and found Dorian standing in the hallway to meet her. His face was stricken. Hanna remembered the expression from when she was eleven years old and her mother told her that her father had been killed in a car accident.

She screamed out. Dorian ran across the hall and held her in his arms. She sank her head into his chest, drawing what comfort she could from the smell of soap and tobacco on his cashmere sweater. The smell of a father. He was all that was left of her family now. Hanna did not remember much of the next few hours. Dorian administered tea and comfort and, eventually, to stop the jagged sobbing that she feared would snap her body in half, a sedative to help her sleep.

Late at night or early the next morning – she could not be sure – Hanna was woken by the sound of Dorian opening her bedroom door.

'Father?' she called out in her groggy state. It was the first time she had called him that.

She could see from his outline against the light from the hall that it was Dorian, but he did not reply.

Instead he walked silently across the room towards her. Hanna was briefly warmed with a child's moment of relief that a parent is nearby. She felt the warmth of his breath as Dorian leaned down to kiss her on the forehead, as he had done a hundred times before. But he did not kiss her as he had done before. Instead, he kissed her on the mouth and bore his body down and into her.

Her body clenched as the first pain shot through her, but after that, Hanna did not struggle or scream. Her limbs, in any case, felt too weak and he was too heavy to fight. She kept her body as still as she could. Afraid to move. Terrified that any movement on her part might be read as encouragement. His body was heavy and his touch firm and confident. The same chest she had leant against for comfort when her mother was sick, the same hands that had patted her back with reassurance, betraying themselves in this appalling act. Hanna was numb, unable to comprehend if this was really happening. Why was he doing this? Had she done or said something to invite it? This man called himself her father. Although, she now realised that he never actually had. She had not allowed it. She had demanded that she call him by his first name. Perhaps if she had called him father, as her mother had wanted, this would not be happening.

After he had finished, Dorian lay down next to Hanna. She had not realised she was crying until he gently wiped her tears away with the palm of his hands. Her body flinched at the gentleness of the gesture. There was something even more terrifying about that than what had gone before. The betrayal of it.

'I probably should not have done that... but you looked so sad.'

Hanna did not know how to react. Sad? Her mother had died. Was that what you did to people when they were sad?

'You are still crying,' he said, and then he began to cry himself. It was terrible to see a man cry. Despite what he had done to her, Hanna wanted him to stop. She wanted to make his tears go away.

'I am sorry,' he said. He told her that he missed her mother and had simply acted out of grief. He said he would never do it again. He seemed so contrite, so upset by his own actions that when he said, 'Do you believe me Hanna? Please. I'm sorry. Forgive me,' she said that she did and would.

Although she knew in her heart that things would never be the same between them, she wanted to believe him.

Nonetheless, Hanna locked her bedroom door that night. Over the coming days, through the drama of the wake, funeral and burial of her mother, Dorian's actions became subsumed by Hanna's despairing grief.

The night after the burial, she heard him try the door of her bedroom. She was protected by the lock. He went away and she told herself that he would not come back again. The locked door had made him pause. She would just have to continue locking it until he came to his senses.

Over the coming days things returned to normal. As normal as they could be without her mother. Dorian opened the surgery and Hanna went back to school. Every night, she locked her bedroom door and every night Dorian came tapping gently. With no reply he left and after two weeks the tapping stopped. Hanna finally believed it was over.

The Monday after her mother's Month's Mind Mass* Hanna came home from school and met Dorian's housekeeper,

---

* Irish Catholic tradition marking the end of an official grieving period.

Eileen, at the door. She was most upset and bustled past Hanna with barely a greeting.

When she got into the house, Dorian called her into the drawing room. Standing in front of the tall bookcases in the Prince of Wales wool three-piece suit he wore for work, he had a stern expression that filled her with dread.

'What's the matter with Eileen?' she asked, trying to keep a note of fear out of her voice. It was the middle of the afternoon, a bright sunny day. Nothing bad could happen.

'I dismissed her.'

'Why?'

'I decided we don't need her any more. You are old enough to cook and clean for us both.'

Hanna was afraid, but she knew that she had to stand her ground.

'I don't cook and clean. My mother did all of that for me, as well you know.'

Dorian stood for a second, his mouth twisted into a sardonic smile, then, in one deft movement he was across the room and beside her. He felled her to the ground with a slap to the side of her head. She thought she would pass out, but then he grabbed her and, pulling her up by the root of her long ponytail, dragged her over to the grand piano. He held her neck down so that her face was pressed hard on the polished, mahogany surface. As he dragged up her school uniform, he spat, 'This will teach you to lock your bedroom door you cruel little bitch. I tried to be nice but this is all you understand. You think you're so beautiful, so alluring, but this is all you deserve.'

Hanna had never known pain like it.

She never locked her bedroom door again.

2

Four years later...

Sligo, Ireland, 1966

Hanna and Dorian lived as man and wife. In his mind, in any case, that was how things were. Even though it was still their 'little secret'.

Hanna kept the house and cooked the meals. There was no question of their inviting anyone over. They might see that the stepfather and stepdaughter now shared a bed. Hanna's academic performance started to drop. The nuns were puzzled by it. She was a clever girl and had such sterling support from her stepfather. He, indeed, was such an educated man – and so liberal – rearing another man's child when he could so easily have sent her to board in their convent after her mother died. A saint. Two years ago, when Hanna decided to leave school at sixteen, Dr Black had told the Mother Superior that, although he was disappointed, he felt confident that, before too long, she would make a good wife. He was sure that he would find a nice, respectable man to take her on.

'She's so pretty,' the nuns reassured him.

'If you say so, Sister,' he quipped back. 'I can't say I have ever seen it myself!'

'We'll get married soon,' he said to her one night, after he had made love to her. That's what he called it. Making love. Occasionally it was rough but as time went on, and Hanna became more compliant to his needs, the punishments stopped. When they were in bed together, Dorian tried to be tender. She could see by the longing in his face that he was trying to love her in the way he touched and kissed her. But no matter how tender he was, it always felt wrong. It certainly never felt like love.

Nonetheless, within the four walls of his large house, they lived like most married couples. The house was big and Hanna enjoyed making it beautiful. She polished the decorative tiles in the hallway to a glossy shine and kept the large basement kitchen, with its flagstones and large old-fashioned range, spotlessly clean. Dorian bought her French cookbooks and she taught herself a few cordon bleu dishes. He praised Hanna when she made an effort for him in the kitchen and she found that she liked to please him. Sometimes, when Dorian was sitting back with a contented smile after a meal she could believe that they were, after all, a family of sorts. Stepfather and stepdaughter enjoying each other's company. Reading side by side with an open fire, him teaching her how to play chess... if only it weren't for the other thing. For the love.

Dorian loved her. That was the problem.

'I love you.' He kept saying it. He said it every time he did 'it' to her.

She knew he expected her to say it back. So she would mumble, 'I love you.'

'Look me in the eyes and say my name,' he would beg, whining like a child. At those times, Hanna could almost believe she was in charge, but that was, as she learned from experience, a dangerous assumption to make.

So instead she looked him straight in the eyes and said, 'I love you, Dorian.' Most of the time he smiled – a pathetic half-hearted hopeful look – and seemed satisfied that she was being sincere.

But when he didn't believe her, he got angry and punished her. Afterwards he would be sorry and insist it was only because he loved her so much. It was her astonishing beauty and the power that she exuded over him with her womanly guile that sent him into these terrible fits of rage. He just wanted to be loved. So Hanna would persuade him that she loved him back. Even though it turned her stomach, she kissed him over and over again and called him her 'only love' and touched him and told him that she wanted him. They were the worst times, when she had to pretend to love him. To love 'it'. She could not just lie back and fall into the trance of emotional dispossession that made his lovemaking tolerable. But, Dorian would be ecstatic with delight. The show of love would appease him, and he would give her mind, if not her body, some peace for a while.

After one of these month-long lulls, fell the third anniversary of Margaret's death.

Hanna had been polishing the silverware in the kitchen and the domestic act reminded her of her mother. She began to cry, thinking about how Margaret used to polish the cutlery to a shine in the week leading up to Christmas every year. She would cover the drawing room table with newspaper and made a great show of bringing Hanna in to help her with this refined task, while their housekeeper washed floors and did the high dusting that her mother so disliked. Dorian had acted the great benefactor to her and her mother, but before him, when it was their father instead, he too had hired housekeepers. Even if it was only for that one special day each year. Yet, now, Hanna was living the life of a common skivvy. Quite suddenly, she found the wave of grief for her mother give way to an annoyance that Dorian expected her to wash floors and peel potatoes when he could easily afford a housekeeper.

Hanna never dwelt on the personal situation between her and Dorian. What happened between them was torture enough without thinking about it too. She shut it out of her mind. Of course, she had dreamt of escape once, but had long since realised it was hopeless. Dorian was always there in the surgery, watching. She was trapped and normally she accepted that she just had to make the best of it. However, on this particular morning, in the name of her mother, as she thought about all the work she did in this man's house, Hanna's irritation grew into a petulant anger. So when Dorian came into the kitchen, instead of finding the hot lunch he was expecting, he found her surly and pouting.

Dorian was in such a good mood he believed nothing could upset him that morning. He had decided to take Hanna away for her eighteenth birthday. In time, he planned to move them both to Dublin, where they could marry and nobody would know about their unfortunate past. But, for now he had booked them two nights at the Shelbourne hotel. He would take her shopping on Grafton Street, book her a hair appointment and take her into Brown Thomas to buy her underwear and other pretty things. Anything she wanted. What a pleasure it would be, for them both, to swan around openly. For him to show off his beautiful young 'wife' to the world without fear of being judged or misunderstood by nosy old biddies. In the evening, he would take her to the opera.

It was all very well making love to a beautiful young woman, but sometimes, lovemaking just wasn't enough. Dorian needed Hanna to converse in a more interesting way. She was beautiful, he thought, but limited intellectually. After all, she had not performed as well in school as she might have done.

'I have a surprise for you,' he said, sneaking up behind her, putting his hands around her waist and gathering her into him.

She pulled away. 'I'm not in the mood, Dorian.'

Then, unable to stop herself, she turned to him. 'It's my mother's anniversary today – have you no shame?'

His elevated mood shockingly struck down by Hanna's insubordinate attitude and insensitive cruelty was too much for him.

Dorian struck her and sent her staggering backwards towards the range.

He looked down to unbuckle himself and, while he did, Hanna was suddenly overcome with an overwhelming, unstoppable rage. Without thinking, she picked up a cast iron pan from the stove and ran, swinging the pan at him, screaming. It hit the side of his shoulder. Dorian cried out in pain as a bone cracked, fell to his knees and wailed.

'You've broken my arm.'

Hanna didn't hear him. She couldn't stop now. She knew that. There was no going back. She lifted the pan and slammed it into the right side of his face. Another crack sounded as his nose collapsed into his cheek. Dorian fell to the ground, grabbing a handful of her mother's silverware as he went.

Hanna felt sick at the sight of his collapsed body on the floor.

'Hanna?' he moaned.

So weak, so pathetic. Pleading. An urgent regret overcame her. What had she done? She should reach down and pick him up. Call an ambulance. Make him better. Make this go away. Make it not have happened.

She stood there and watched him try to lift his arms up to her. His face covered in blood, his broken nose bent to one side. Had she done that to him? What sort of a person was she?

But as sure as Hanna knew he was in terrible pain, she also knew that when he recovered, he would be furious. He would kill her. When he recovered.

If he recovered.

Hanna lifted the pan one more time. She shut her eyes and, with tears streaming out of their corners, made herself remember the night her mother died. The first time he had come into her room. Her lungs filled slowly, breathing in every time he had touched her in vile wretchedness. Finally she breathed out with a roar, swinging the heavy pan like a low tennis racket as hard as she could over the left side of his head. There was a mighty crack, then silence.

It was over.

3

Dorian was dead. His eyes were closed. His body was still. Tentatively, Hanna reached down and touched the arm he had held up to his face. She jumped as it fell to his side, arranging itself in a soft claw on his thigh. She had to be certain, so, terrified that at any moment he might wake up and grab her, Hanna knelt down and levered her fingers under the palm of his large hand and lifted. It flopped back down onto the brown gabardine fabric of his trousers. All at once she was both sickened and relieved. Then she saw the blood pouring down from the top of his head, down over his shirt, pouring, pouring from the gaping wound on his face into a gathering stream on the floor, spreading into a river, oozing over her hand. She jumped back, scraping the blood onto her apron, quickly moving her feet away from the puddle.

She had to run but felt paralysed. She had to get away but where could she go? Who could she turn to? There was nowhere – nobody. As much as she hated him, Dorian was her life. He was dead. She had killed him. When Dorian did not turn up for afternoon surgery in an hour, his nurse would telephone. Everyone at the surgery was strictly forbidden from calling to the house unannounced but if there was no reply from the phone after an hour, and with patients waiting, surely they would come here. If she didn't move fast, move now, they would find her. Even if she could lift the body she could not get rid of it in that time. Get rid of the body. It made her stomach turn. They were the sort of words you found in Agatha Christie thrillers – not words you ever uttered in real life. She looked at Dorian, as if searching for an answer and was shocked, again, to see that his nose was broken, smashed. Had she really done that?

She had to get out of here but she couldn't move. She had killed a man. A voice – of her mother, her father perhaps – suddenly spoke in her mind. *Think, Hanna, think. You can't get caught. You mustn't get caught. Remember why you did this. Dorian ruined half your life. Don't let him take the rest of it. Nobody will believe it was self-defence. You'll spend the rest of your life rotting in jail for killing a monster.* If only she could move. Hanna looked at the dead face and reminded herself of what he had done to her. Any jail would be better than the jail he had her imprisoned in. *Move, Hanna, move. Move your legs – just MOVE. Now! Run before it's too late. RUN!* She forced herself to recall some of the terrible things he had done. The beatings, his filthy touch, the repugnant things he made her do. Her eyes closed and she thought about that terrible night, the night her mother died... The first time. Righteous anger rose inside her and took hold. She was not trapped here. She would get herself free. Make it look like a robbery.

She ran through rooms upending furniture and opening drawers, concocting her story. When was the last time she had been seen in public? Mass the previous Sunday. Two weeks. The grocer had called to the house with a delivery on the Monday, but, as usual, simply left the grocery box on the steps. She had not waved at him through the window. Good. That was good. She could have been away from the house for fifteen days and nobody would be any the wiser. The beginnings of her story began to develop. She had been away. Where? Dublin? Yes. Getting papers ready to go to America. Or just abroad. No forwarding address. Disappear. She would disappear but she had to close off the trail otherwise they would come looking for her. She jacked open the desk drawer in Dorian's office with the fire tongs, stuffing all the money she could find into her apron pocket, then went upstairs and emptied the contents of every bedroom drawer onto the floor until she found Dorian's mother's jewellery. Into a small suitcase she threw enough clothes to legitimise her story that she was away, plus the jewellery, the money and her diary. She grabbed a jacket and realised she was still wearing the bloodied apron. In that moment, the truth hit her in a sudden wave of nausea, and she barely made it to the bathroom to throw up into the toilet. She had a flashback to a moment when Dorian had smashed her head against the ornate porcelain sink. She grabbed at the memory and ignited enough of a snap to haul the apron over her head, roll it up then run back into the bedroom and stuff it into the case. She could burn it later. Hanna ran out the back door, smashing the glass panel with the coal shovel as she went and upending the bin. Angry burglars. Nobody would ever be as angry as she was now. Anger and fear: that was all that was inside her. That was all she was now. That was what he had reduced her to: an animal. Adrenalin pumped through her as she ran across the fields like a hunting dog. Except she was not chasing – just running. Her small case banged against her leg, bruising it, but it didn't weigh her down. Her desire to run was too ferocious.

Hanna didn't know how far or for how long she ran. Out

across the open fields, stumbling into invisible bog holes, tripping on large stones, slipping on patches of damp, flat heather-coated rocks. She ran hard and long, until, breathless, she stopped at a bleak stretch of bog-lined road, throwing her case down beside her. She closed her eyes and rested for a moment. The heat of her body prickled against the salty sea air. She could not see the water but she knew it was beyond the horizon, where the land dipped at a cliff edge down to the wild Atlantic. Even though they lived near the sea, she had not seen it since she was a child, when she was with her mother. Dorian had no taste for nature and less still for walking, and he never let her out of the house without him. When they first moved here, Hanna and her mother stood at the cliff edge that bordered this stretch of road, looking down on the rolling waves, wondering at the magnificence of God's work. Both of them were wishing that her father was there to share it with, but they also knew that they would never have come to this wild corner of the world if he had not died. Hanna felt something jolt inside her at the memory. As suddenly as the urge to escape had come, it was snatched away by the realisation that as surely as her own father was dead, she had killed her stepfather. Dorian was a terrible man. But did he deserve to die? Hanna began to shake from the inside out. She pressed her arms around herself in a hug, to try to stop the shivering. Her body was pleading to curl itself into a ball. *I am not a murderer*, she told herself. *I am...*

What else did she even have to define her? Who was she, after all? All she had ever been was Dorian's wife. Not even his real wife. Not even by choice. Hanna had no schooling, no accomplishments – no family, aside from him. Apart from cooking, cleaning and giving her body to Dorian, there was nothing else. Now, even that was gone.

I am nobody.

Hanna said the words out loud but even as she did they were swallowed up into the vast silence of the black bog. *I am not even words*, she thought to herself. *I truly am nothing.* In that moment, Hanna wanted to die. She longed to lie down on the springy ground and gather a blanket of moss about her. Eventually the soft, ancient bog would swallow her up. She could stay here, alone, out in the empty bog, and sleep forever. Then all of this would be over. Her legs were bending to sit down when, over the horizon, Hanna saw something trundling along the road towards her. A bus. She should lie down now, disappear into the land so they would drive past and never see her. But in that moment the same voice that had called to her earlier spoke again.

NO, Hanna. Stay standing. This is your chance. Make your escape.

As the vehicle drew closer Hanna saw it was the Galway bus.

Keep running, keep going.

She flagged it down and climbed on. Her heart was banging against her chest and she kept her head down as she paid the driver. Taking her seat, she counted just three people on it. Nobody she knew. For the rest of the journey, Hanna covered her head with her coat and slept. She dreamt of her parents. They whispered encouragement to her.

Keep running. Freedom is only around the corner. Don't be afraid.

Hanna woke when they reached Galway and, despite the words of encouragement, she found that she was still afraid. The bus was filled with the smell of cigarette smoke and sweat. She wished she could stay on it. If only she had stayed and slept herself to soft death in the bog. Instead, she got off the bus and walked quickly into the train station where she bought a ticket to Dublin. As her luck would have it, the next train was leaving in only five minutes' time. She took care to find a quiet carriage. A man sat down opposite her and offered her a cigarette. When she refused, he asked her name. Trying to keep her voice from shaking she paused before answering.

'Annie.'

The man nodded and she looked out the window, closing her eyes to pretend she was asleep. Annie. That was her name now.

The man opposite her got off at Athlone. Hanna pulled her notepad and pen out of her bag and put her plan into action.

Dear Dorian…

It felt wrong writing a letter to a dead man. Hanna started to feel afraid but then reminded herself, she wasn't Hanna any more. She was Annie. Annie Austen. Like Jane Austen. Annie Austen could be whoever Hanna wanted her to be. Annie would go to London and start a new life.

… just a short note to let you know that I arrived safely in Dublin, as planned, and have been taking the necessary steps for my ongoing journey to America…

Throw them off the scent, but don't give too much information. Her pen hovered reluctantly over the page before she put down her last sentence.

Thank you for all that you did for me and my mother.
With gratitude,
Hanna

It was a lie. All of it. Hanna felt the anger rise as she read it back. Part of her wanted to write out all the terrible things he had done. The rape. The manipulation of her mother. She wanted the world to know what a nasty, vicious man he was. But, even more so, she had a desperate urge to expunge it, to get it out of her system. To get him out of her head and start life as Annie with a fresh, unsullied soul.

But that would be asking too much of God. So she left the letter as it was. Dorian would be buried as a kind, gentleman doctor who had rescued a poor orphan girl, instead of the monster he was. With gratitude. The letter would have sounded more convincing if she had said with love, but she could not write the words. Even if it might save her from ever being caught she could not use the word love in relation to him.

When Hanna arrived in Dublin she walked from Heuston station to the city centre. She knew the city from weekends spent there with Dorian and her mother. The sharp tang of the Liffey and the hops from the Guinness factory on the Quays made her heart hurt, reminding her of walking these streets with her mother, in her best coat, full of hope and happiness. She stopped first at the GPO on Connell Street to post the letter, and then took a bus along the Quays to Dublin Port. Here, she bought a foot passenger ticket to Holyhead.

The boat was busy. Queues of people lined up outside the narrow gateway. Young men wearing working boots and carrying knapsacks, ready to work the moment they hit English soil. Young women shivered in short skirts and smart jackets, dressed for London itself instead of the arduous twenty-four hour journey ahead of them.

Once through the door, the crowd dispersed into the bowels of the ship, quickly scurrying up the steep, metal steps like worker ants until the engine started and they all lost their balance. Hanna went straight up to the deck and stood at the front of the boat as it left Dublin Port. She did not look back but kept her eyes firmly on the grey expanse of water stretched ahead of her. As the engines started up and the ship began to plough forward, churning up great lines of angry white foam, her mother's voice called out again.

Keep running, Hanna. Freedom is only around the corner. Don't be afraid.

As the ship moved ahead she looked back and watched Ireland recede into the distance. Her mother's voice grew distant with it as she left Hanna, and all the bad things that had happened, behind.

She was Annie Austen now. And soon, she would be in London.

4

Lara

Dublin, Ireland, 1966

'I'm joining the priesthood.'

Lara was standing at the door of her hostel in Dublin, frantically searching for her key in the depths of her college satchel. It was nine fifty-five, and the nuns double locked the doors at ten. It wasn't exactly an ideal arrangement, especially since she had started at the National College of Art and Design nearly two years ago. It had been that long since she and her childhood sweetheart Matthew had actually managed to catch a full film. Last year they had tried to get a flat in Rathmines, but her forged marriage certificate had not been good enough. One nosy old bag had reported her to the college and living in sin just wasn't an option. It brought terrible shame on your family. Anyway, even if you were prepared to do that, Dublin's landladies wouldn't let you. The mere fact that she had been caught trying had upset her mother so much that Lara said she would move back into the hostel with the nuns until she graduated. But last week she and Matthew talked about the possibility of a no-fuss marriage service before they started their third term. They could both finish their degrees like civilised adults before moving to London, where Lara would pursue her dream of being a fashion designer, and Matthew could do a postgrad in religious art. That was their plan. Join the priesthood! Not an especially funny joke, but she laughed anyway as she finally located the key and fixed it into the lock.

'Hilarious,' she said, turning. 'Are we having lunch together tomorrow or have you got a lecture?'

'Lara.' Matthew caught her hand. 'I'm serious.'

His sky blue eyes were wide, set deep beneath a heavy brow and framed with unruly jet-black curls. Still, six years later, he was the boy she had first fallen in love with – her best friend's brother. Shy, studious, raven-haired Matthew Lyons, the most beautiful boy she had ever seen. He looked away from her confusion. Was he being serious? No. It was too ridiculous. Before she even had the chance to chide him again he continued.

'Really, Lara. I've been accepted. I go to Maynooth tomorrow.'

The words sounded rehearsed. His voice was sharp and steadier than it had a right to be. Defensive too, which she knew was just to cover the fact that he was afraid. This was no joke.

Surely, she must have heard him wrong or, at the very least, he had made some crazy mistake. Matthew was passionate, his ideas and emotions sometimes overcame him. He had an artistic temperament. Lara was the sensible one. If either of them were best suited to the cloying discipline of religious life, it was more likely to be her. This was one of his silly notions. Like the time when he was a teenager and decided to paint a Raphael nude on his parents' sitting room ceiling.

Lara had persuaded him to cover it up before they came back from their holiday. She was the one who protected Matthew from his impulsive self. He needed her.

She felt as if she couldn't speak. For a moment she just stood and stared at him until she heard herself say, 'When did you decide?'

'A long time ago, Lara. I guess... I suppose I love God more than I love you. I'm sorry.'

Sorry? What was he talking about? Where had this come from? It was so out of the blue; it had to be a mistake. He loved her. Of course he loved her – but did he love her more than God? What did that even mean?

'I'm sorry, Lara,' he said. 'I'm sorry.' He was repeating the words as if the sound of them spoken aloud might add balm to the gash he had just sliced through her heart. His face collapsed, as if this was his pain instead of hers. As if, suddenly, he had some higher conscience to answer to. God? Lara knew she should say something to persuade him. Beg. What was a girl supposed to do at a time like this? Matthew was leaving her. The love of her life. Her soulmate. Her soulmate was leaving her. For God?

She felt Sister Attracta, the night duty nun, creep up behind her and, using her presence as an excuse to escape, Matthew began to walk backwards towards the road.

'I'm sorry,' he kept saying, tears streaming down his cheeks. Lara felt a quick panic rise in her chest. Come back, come back – we need to talk about this! But the words wouldn't leave her. He picked up speed until he was out of earshot across Parnell Square, still mouthing, 'I'm sorry.'

His slim, narrow back in its shabby, grey coat melted into the drab city landscape. Towards O'Connell Street and away from her. He was nothing more than a coward. Perhaps she would have screamed if the nun had not been standing directly next to her, urging her inside.

Part of her wanted to run across the road after him and scream, 'Come back!' He could not really be going. This could not, truly, be happening.

'Never mind,' Sister Attracta said, putting a kind hand on Lara. 'You'll see him again tomorrow. I'm sure it's only a tiff and will pass over.' With that, the nun pulled the large wooden door closed on Lara's retreating lover.

Lara smiled at her. Yes. She was right. This was just one of Matt's silly ideas. He would be back tomorrow. Join the priesthood? Ridiculous. Lara kept telling herself the same thing all night, repeating the words *he'll be back* to herself until the sick feeling in her stomach subsided and, eventually, she fell asleep.

The next morning, Sister John came into the dorm and announced that Lara was wanted on the telephone. The nun woke up two of the three girls Lara shared with, neither of whom complained because they knew nobody rang the office phone unless it was an emergency. There was a pay phone in the hall but it could only make calls, not receive them.

Lara padded barefoot into the austere office with its institutional pale green walls and stood in her night attire under the huge crucifix on the mantel, the bloodied figure of Jesus looking down at her in all his glorious martyrdom.

'Jesus, Lara, it's Noreen.'

Noreen Lyons. Matthew's twin sister. Her best friend.

'I had to call you straight away. I just got the news now. The stupid eejit! I'll murder him stone dead...'

Lara nodded at Sister John, who, satisfied that nobody had died, closed the door of the office. She would be irritated to have been party to a drama that wasn't a bona fide emergency, but Lara could face that later.

'A priest?' Noreen continued. 'I mean, Jesus Christ and Holy Saint fecking Joseph.'

So, it was true. Lara's heart swelled inside her chest, suffocating her so that she couldn't speak.

'I can't believe he's actually going through with it! I thought he was joking. When did he tell you? Why didn't you call me?'

Lara felt the truth slap her across the face.

Her oldest, closest friend noticed her silence.

'Holy Mary, Lara – he did tell you, didn't he?'

'Of course he did.' Her voice sounded too light. Like it belonged to somebody else. Noreen had known before her. His parents must have known for a while. Maybe everyone knew and Lara was the last person he had told. Of course. She was just the fool who was in love with him. The fool that had believed he loved her back, the fool that had thought they were getting married. The stupid, misguided girl, dreaming and saving for a future that was never going to happen. Maybe with his new superior conscience he was trying to spare her and hadn't wanted to hurt her feelings. Well, he bloody well had.

'Oh thank God. For a moment there... I mean, when he said he was thinking about it, about a month ago now, was it?'

'That's right,' Lara said. There it was again. The voice that wasn't hers. The lie. What could she say? Your bastard brother didn't tell me until last night – I was the last to know. No. She might be the greatest fool that ever lived, but Lara didn't have to admit that to anyone else. Not even Noreen. Not yet, certainly. Maybe never.

Noreen's sing-song Cork accent trilled down the line. 'We all thought he was joking. I suppose I should have called you when he first said it but – I thought – you guys needed to work it out yourselves.'

'Of course,' Lara said. There was an awkward pause. 'Well,' Lara found herself speaking, 'it's clearly what he wants.'

As Lara made the statement, so calm, so reasoned, every nerve in her body fizzled against it with fury and shock. Was it really what Matthew had wanted all along? He had never given any hint of it, not to her. She thought he wanted the life they had planned together. They had made love, as often as any young unmarried couple might expect to, which was not very often. There had never, for either of them, been any sense of urgency. Soon, they would get married and they would have a lifetime for making love. Matthew was always reserved, yes, but he told her he loved her. Had that been a lie? Had all of it? Noreen was talking about her brother becoming a priest as if it was annoying, inconvenient, unfortunate but true. Lara couldn't help but see herself standing there on the cold convent floor, shivering in her flimsy cotton nightdress. Her feet were as cold and naked as the Jesus statue, and her toes pressed hard into the red, polished tiles with the tension of keeping her voice steady. Now that she knew for certain, Lara wasn't going to lower herself by begging. She had been right to keep hold of herself last night.

'He's no more a bloody priest than I'm a nun, Lara, and we all know that was never going to happen, no matter what Mammy said.'

'Noreen,' Lara interrupted. 'I had better go now. They are calling us down for breakfast.'

Breakfast wasn't for an hour.

'Are you alright, Lara?' Noreen's voice was full of concern.

'Of course,' Lara said.

'I honestly think he's just being an arse. He'll be out in a week and begging for you to take him back.'

Noreen always said things with such conviction that Lara

couldn't help but feel that whatever she decreed might just happen.

'If it's what Matthew wants,' Lara said, 'he should follow his heart. I just want him to be happy.'

Noreen was certain that Lara was heartbroken over her brother. No one could truly love a man and be that magnanimous when they dumped them.

But she also knew Lara well enough not to push her. There was pride at play here, and the pride of a Cork woman, especially one as accomplished and confident as her dear friend, was not something to be chipped at.

'Call me if you want to talk it through,' Noreen said.

'Thanks,' Lara said, 'I will.'

Although they both knew that was never going to happen.

When Lara got back to her room all three of her roommates were sitting on their beds in various states of undress. They stopped talking as soon as she walked in.

'Everything alright at home?' Helena Moran asked.

'Fine,' Lara snapped, going straight over to her locker. 'Why wouldn't it be?'

'No need to bite her head off,' said Elaine Tigue. 'We were just worried about you.'

Lara grabbed her sweater and pulled it over her head with more vigour than needed.

'Bertie McGrath was telling Da at the fair last week that your Great Grand Uncle Mikey Feeney is sick down there in Killaloe... we thought maybe...'

Lara saw Elaine and Helena exchange a look.

They probably knew. Not just about her uncle. About Matthew. If they didn't know now, they would soon. Everybody knew everything about everybody in Ireland. Cork might be hundreds of miles away but in gossip terms, it was only around the corner. She knew what they were thinking right now, as they looked at her. There's that Lara Collins who got engaged to a priest. She forced herself on him. She wouldn't let him go. He was afraid to tell her he didn't love her. She was the last to know.

Matthew had left her less than twenty-four hours ago. She had not even told her own family yet, but there probably wasn't any need to. Bertie McGrath (whoever the hell he was) could inform her father at the next Fair Day.

A broken heart was one thing. People poking around at it and judging you was quite another.

Lara was brushing her hair when Sister Attracta stuck her head in the door and said, 'Lara, might I have word with you? In private?'

The nun's long face was even more mournful and concerned than usual. One look in her pitying eyes told Lara that she had just heard about Matthew. Of course she had. Nuns knew everything, and what they didn't know they sensed. Lara was being called out for a 'kind-nun' lecture. She was, after all, the sort of girl who had fallen in love with a young man who wanted to be a priest. 'Cross-nun' talk was what you got by being a lawless, dirty strap who got caught having carnal relations out of wedlock. Lara would have taken the latter any day of the week. Suddenly, the truth was stark. There would be no let-up and no privacy until she left Ireland.

She would sit through Attracta's lecture, smile and nod at all her kind wisdom. Then, as soon as it was over, she would go to the bank and empty the account where she had been saving for her future with Matthew. To hell with college. To hell with family. To hell with being a good girl and doing the right thing. Lara was going to put on her shortest skirt and head for the most Godless, shocking place on the planet: Swinging London.

5

Once her parents realised there was no persuading Lara to finish her studies, they offered her the hospitality of a dozen cousins living in the north-west suburbs of London: Kilburn and Cricklewood. Favourite among these was her father's sister. 'Auntie Una says you can stay with her as long as you like. You can share a bed with your cousin Eunice.'

Lara was having none of it. There was no point in leaving Ireland to go to a version of the same thing. Her mother, of course, was not happy. 'Auntie Una just wants to help.' Help. 'Poor Lara. Her sweetheart ran off and left her to become a priest.' Auntie Una would do the opposite. She would never let Lara live it down.

So, just two weeks after Matthew left her, Lara arrived in Chelsea with nothing more than a sewing machine, a satchel containing her sketchpad and a few bits of clothes. After an exhausting boat journey and a train to Euston station, she somehow managed to negotiate the mystifying tunnels of the tube and get herself to Sloane Square. As she emerged from the grey bowels of the underground into the blistering white sunlight, Lara couldn't help but feel adventure opening up in front of her. She was here. On the most famous, fashionable street in the world. The Kings Road in London. Broad and magnificent, it stretched out in front of her – a cacophony of people, shops and stalls and a kind of cool craziness. She had read about it and yet the newspaper and magazine descriptions had not begun to capture it. Men wearing bright orange trousers, and black women in miniskirts rushed past textbook-stiff Englishmen in bowler hats. Patterns were everywhere: on shop fronts, jackets and the tablecloths of packed cafes. Everywhere people were running, smoking and shouting, the whole world crowded with colour and life. The very air was wide awake and Lara smiled. Her life would begin here. Even without Matthew.

Over the next two hours Lara tramped up and down the Kings Road looking for a job. She walked in and out of every hip boutique and some of the bigger fashion shops. The exploding fashion scene meant there were plenty of places selling clothes but also plenty of girls already working in them. Every wannabe model and It girl wanted to work on the Kings Road, in the centre of the booming Chelsea fashion scene.

The further away from Sloane Square that she went, the quieter the streets became. Near the end the number of clothes shops thinned out somewhat to make way for hair salons and food places. There were tall, ornate redbrick buildings that she assumed must contain flats and bedsits.

Her arms were aching from carrying the sewing machine so she walked into a small boutique hung with bright flowery dresses.

The English girl working there was very sweet but shook her head. 'You're out of luck, I'm afraid. We've got nothing at the moment.'

The day was not working out the way she had planned.

Perhaps she should give the Kings Road a rest and start looking elsewhere in London. Oxford Street, Portobello Road. Although Lara had set her heart on Chelsea – and now that she had actually been here, she knew it was where she wanted to stay – luck didn't seem to be in her favour.

She was tired and hungry. Across the road from the boutique was a small row of shops and a friendly looking cafe with the name FRED'S above the door. She plonked herself down in a window seat just as the rain began to pour.

As she looked out at the water streaming down the outside of the steamed up window, Lara began to panic. She would have to book into a hotel for the night. She might as well have stayed in Dublin. With no work, her money wouldn't last long and she would be with Auntie Una by next week.

Suddenly she felt lonely and exhausted.

'Just got here?'

The waitress was a middle-aged woman. Friendly.

'I know the feelin'. Bin a long time but I never forget the day I came here from Italy. Where you from?'

'Ireland.'

'Nice.' The woman nodded, although Laura could tell she didn't know anything about Ireland. Unlike Italy, with its Popes and volcanos and sunshine and pasta, Ireland had nothing of note. Just nuns, rain and potatoes. It was an unremarkable place to anyone but the Irish themselves. In fact, mostly to them as well.

'You found work?'

'Not today,' Lara said.

'Nev' mind,' the waitress said, 'maybe tomorrow.'

Lara smiled weakly and ordered a cottage pie dinner and a pot of tea, which she wolfed down. Her belly full and the longevity of the journey hitting her, all she wanted to do now was to lie down and get some rest. Auntie Una's was starting to feel like an option.

When the waitress came back and noticed the pretty Irish girl's eyelids drooping she asked, 'You found somewhere to stay yet?'

'No,' Lara said. 'Not yet. Is there a hotel in the area?'

'Rich lady.' The waitress made a face. 'Always plenty of rooms to rent on Beaufort Street,' she said, nodding to a street just across from where Lara was sitting. 'You can leave your bag here if you want to go take a look.'

It was the first bit of kindness, Lara noticed, that she had encountered since getting off the boat.

Hopeful, Lara took the waitress up on her offer and, quickly tidying her hair with a comb, buttoning and brushing down her coat, she walked across the road.

Sure enough, there were three or four ROOMS TO LET signs stuck along the basement railings.

Lara climbed up a rather steep set of steps up to the front door of the first option. She had her hand on the knocker when she looked to the left and saw a large sign in the window with large handwritten letters spelling NO DOGS. NO BLACKS. NO IRISH.

She was horrified. She had, of course, heard that the English didn't like the Irish. Not really. To be truthful, the Irish weren't crazy about the English either. They had a chequered history. But she never thought they might compare them to dogs. She understood, too, that a lot of people looked down on black people. But London was a melting pot of people from all over the world, so it hardly made sense. Surely that was what made London great? In Ireland there were no black people. Anywhere. They weren't banned or anything, they just didn't want to go to Ireland. There was nobody in Ireland but Irish people, and most of them eventually left to come here or go to New York. The Irish came to London for work, but they also came to escape the repressed boredom of living in a country where books were banned for mentioning sex, or criticising priests, or depicting anything that might be disapproved of by the grey, humourless dictates of a church-run state. The only escape was alcohol or burying oneself in the beauty of nature. Wild, alcoholic farmers were the Irish the landladies didn't want, but Lara felt tarred with the same brush. The choice was to pass herself off as English, but she wasn't sure she could do that either. Even if she had wanted to. The setback had made her too tired to check the other houses on the streets. Perhaps it was time to head to Auntie Una in Cricklewood after all.

'No luck?' the Italian lady asked her when she was collecting her bags.

'No Irish,' she said. Then by further explanation added, 'no dogs or blacks either.'

The Italian waitress, Giuliana, didn't know much about the Irish, but what she did know was that they were good Catholics. Some of the West Indians too. She felt guilty for having sent the nice Irish girl on such a disappointing and hurtful mission. Since she came here from Italy as a young girl, England had been good to her. If only it wasn't for the bloody English. They could be so cold. Unwelcoming. Her husband, Fred, was English but he was from the East End and they were nicer. Suddenly, a thought popped into her head.

'If you need work you could try Chevrons across the road. I know they're looking for waitresses at the moment.'

Shirley had been in the day before complaining that they were short staffed. Giuliana did not wholly approve of the nightclub. Its waitresses wore skimpy costumes and it had a reputation as a gambling den. Sometimes she caught Fred in there pretending to deliver lunches. But what could she do? He was English! For all their corrupting influence on her husband, however, Chevrons was run by an East End family, and the manager, Coleman, was a decent man. Always well dressed. Good looking. Lovely manners. A gentleman. Shirley – the manageress – was a bit brassy but she had a good heart as well.

Lara shook her head. 'I have no experience,' she said. She didn't come to London to wait tables. She came here to get into the fashion business.

Giuliana smiled. 'This is London. This is where you come to get the experience.'

Lara shrugged, smiled politely, and stood up to leave.

'Tell you what,' Giuliana carried on. 'You leave your bag here and go knock on that door over there.' She pointed out the window towards a black door in a nondescript building across the road. 'You ask for Shirley and tell her Giuliana sent you.'

Then, as Lara shook her head, trying to decline politely, the waitress added, 'What you got to lose? Who knows? This is London. Anything can happen. You never know what to expect.'

Lara stopped for a moment. Anything can happen. The unexpected had already happened with Matthew. Maybe it was time to embrace the unknown and see where it would take her.

After all, the alternative was Auntie Una in Cricklewood.

6

The sea turned rough as the great hulk of the boat left Dublin Port. The engines churned while young men huddled on deck, cupping their hands over cigarettes near the stairwell. As the boat gathered speed they turned their faces to the wind, looking through sea-salt tears at the country they were leaving behind. Were any of these young men, Annie wondered, running away for reasons as dark as her own? Had any of them committed a crime as well? Maybe. Although, it was more likely that most of them were going to England for work. Here, on deck, they were planning their new lives and hoping to make their fortune. In a few years' time some of them would come home, triumphant, with new suits and leather wallets, to make their mothers proud. They would marry sweethearts and build houses next to their parents. Others would never return, instead deciding to settle and rear their children as English. They all smoked together for now, gazing at the disappearing land, their lips sucking on the ends of their burning cigarettes. Annie imagined that they must be sad to be leaving loved ones behind, even though they were looking forward to the adventure of a new life. They were so different to Annie, who had no loved ones and was trying to escape an old life.

A young man standing next to her threw his cigarette into the water, looked over at the ports and gave a huge wave. She couldn't pick out who it was directed at among the crowd that had gathered there.

'Are you leaving many behind?' he asked. The roar of the engine and the wind caught his words so he leaned in closer to ask again. Annie stiffened. There was a smell of beer on his breath. Along with the boat it made her nauseous and then anxious. She must not start talking to people on the boat. It wasn't safe. Not yet.

'No,' she said, giving him an awkward smile before quickly turning back and walking down the metal stairwell into the ship. Once she got onto English soil, she would feel safe again. She had to remind herself that even running, as she was now, she felt safer than she had done since her mother died.

When Annie got to the top deck lounge, people were flooding up from the car deck, snatching seats from the rows of hard chairs and rushing towards the bar. Annie quickly sat at the end of a wooden bench. As the journey progressed, she began to feel grateful that she was not sitting on her suitcase on the floor like some of the others around her. Conditions on the boat were quickly deteriorating. Less than an hour out of port and the upper deck was covered in vomit, and a heavy rain shower carried the debris down the stairs, making the ship's population shelter below. Somebody closed the deck door and cigarette smoke clung to the ceiling in a malignant cloud. For the next seven hours, while the vast boat heaved its cargo of sickened travellers across the Irish Sea, Annie curled her body into a tight ball, put her head on her suitcase and slept as much as she could. Every hour or so she was woken by somebody sitting on her feet, the sound of men singing, children wailing or the smell of some unfortunate vomiting nearby. Each time she started awake, Annie felt only relief that she was here, in this filthy, floating no-man's-land, rather than with Dorian. Dead or alive. Although, in her half-asleep state, she was able to admit it to herself: he was worse alive. Dorian could never hurt or touch her again. She was on a wooden bench inside a boat, with only a coat and a case for bedding, surrounded by strangers, vomit and smoke, not knowing where she was going or what she was going to do when she got there. Yet she was sleeping more peacefully than she ever could at home. It was called that but it never truly was any more than a prison.

When they arrived in Holyhead the crowd shuffled in a sleep-riddled state, shoving past one another onto the train to London. Annie was less lucky in finding a seat this time and spent the journey walking up and down the train carriages, sometimes finding an empty corner where she could rest for a minute on her suitcase before moving along when a friendly Irish person tried to lead her into a conversation.

They arrived at Euston station at five in the morning. The crowd flooded off the train as quickly as it got on the boat in the first place. The empty station suddenly began to bustle as the Irish boat–train crowd surged in, their relatives arriving to collect them, or wandering around in search of coaches. Leeds, Manchester – they gathered by the entrance to the tube station, waiting for it to open.

Annie automatically followed a group of people towards the open mouth of the station. When they got out onto the wide pavement in front of the station the crowd dispersed, each individual disappeared into the London streets until Annie was left standing alone. She turned and looked back at the station front. The portico entrance, the grand Euston Arch, had been pulled down a few years ago to make way for a new, modern building. The world was changing. Out with the old, in with the new. But so far, the brave new building was just an ugly no-man's-land. A half-built concrete box scattered with scaffolding and builder boards, some of which would probably end up being worked on by some of the young men she had just shared the boat journey with. Euston station was in transition, neither old nor entirely new yet. The truth of where she was, or rather, where she wasn't hit Annie in a wave of panic. She had nowhere to go and she had no plan. So she started walking. What other choice did she have? This was not a field in the middle of Ireland. She could not simply sit down and disappear. If she started walking something would surely present itself to her, as it had when she was running earlier and decided to hop on the bus to Galway. She walked past closed shops and large buildings that could be universities, schools or libraries. London seemed a bit like Dublin but on a much, much larger scale. In Dublin you could walk in almost any direction from Stephen's Green in the city centre and, before the hour was up, you would hit the coastline or open fields. If you looked up the side roads off Baggot Street, you could see the Dublin Mountains. Here, the buildings seemed to stretch on forever. The streets were empty at this time in the morning, making it feel like a ghost town.

Finally, around nine, the streets began to fill up. Cars started to roll along the roads at a leisurely morning pace and, with them, big red buses. When Annie saw them she began to get excited. This was the London she knew from books and photographs. Her mother had taken her to the pictures when she was young, and Annie remembered seeing almost this exact scene – red buses trundling down the broad roads. So when a number 14 bus stopped in front of her at some traffic lights, she hopped on and climbed up the steep stairs. The conductor frowned when he saw she had nothing smaller than a crown to pay the tuppenny fare but he let her off with a shrug. It was too early to be splitting shillings.

From her seat on the top deck, Annie watched London come to life. Shops opened, women pushed large prams down narrow streets, men in bowler hats rushed to offices, crowds of people gathered at stairwells to the underground, disappearing down as others spewed up. Annie was happy here, observing other people. She could have sat on the bus all day if it hadn't stopped outside Westminster and Chelsea hospital. Annie felt a sort of dread in her stomach when the bus conductor shouted, 'All change here!'

Once, when she was younger, Annie thought she would like to become a nurse. She might have worked in a hospital. Like hundreds, even thousands of Irish nurses, she could be over here working. That was back when her mother had just met Dorian and she wanted to please him. With the thought of him fresh in her head, Annie got off the bus and began walking, almost running, away. She neither knew nor cared where she was any more. Annie was utterly, utterly lost. She looked around for something familiar – a face, a tree, a plant – but all she saw was busy strangers, concrete and closed windows. She could jump in the River Thames and not a soul would find her, or care or miss her. Perhaps that was exactly what she should do. How could she start a new life here? She knew nobody and could do nothing. She was no good to anyone. All she had ever known was serving the cruel man she had left for dead. Every inch of her wanted to scream out. Standing in the middle of the street, she was trapped in her own body. Imprisoned by her misery. Her heart started beating so fast and her breathing became so heavy with panic that she thought she might faint. Searching for somewhere to sit, she spotted a cafe just a few doors along from where she was standing. A homely looking woman was putting a noticeboard outside. The smell of cooking wafted towards her from the open door and, as it steadied her, Annie realised that she was hungry. She stepped into the steaming cafe and took a seat by the window. If she was going to throw herself into the Thames, she may as well have breakfast first.

7

L ara tripped, sending two glasses flying and right into her manager, Brian.

'Jesus Christ!' he spluttered, under his breath but just loud enough for her to hear. 'Clumsy bitch.'

'Sorry!' She grimaced, flinging the silver cocktail tray down on the counter and crouching behind the bar to pick up the pieces. Lara's teeth were gritted as Shirley appeared behind her. Picking up Lara's tray from the bar, the curvaceous blonde arched her eyebrow.

Lara had never tripped in her life before starting work here. She had a straight back and an elegant demeanour, drummed into her by being made to walk with books on her head by nuns in deportment classes. All the girls commented that 'Irish' glided more than walked. Lara had always been very steady on her feet, even in heels. She could have sworn somebody had deliberately tripped her up, and it didn't take much imagination to figure out who that was.

'Oops-a-daisy, Irish! I'll tidy this up for you shall I?'

This was Lara's third 'dropped' tray in as many shifts. Ethel had been shamelessly sabotaging her all week, sticking out her foot at any chance she had to trip Lara up. At first,

Lara thought the cheap, black stilettoes that they had to wear as part of the uniform were to blame, catching on cigarette burn holes in the worn carpet. But, as Ethel sashayed away to take another order, her full bottom wriggling perfectly in the all-in-one kitty costume of Chevrons and the stupid, cheap pink fur tail swaying just as it should be, Lara knew, without a doubt, that it was her. Later that shift, after Ethel had gone home, one of the younger girls turned to her.

'I see Ethel had you again earlier?'

Lara's anger rose.

'If that bitch trips me up one more time,' she said, 'I swear, I'll pull that tail and fling her out of the window by it!'

Ethel was close with Shirley (the waitress's manager), practically her right-hand woman, and did not like Lara for any other reason than she was Irish. It certainly wasn't jealousy. Lara was taller than all the other girls, hair recently cut into an asymmetric bob she knew she cut a rather manly figure next to her small, curvaceous workmates.

The younger waitresses were sweet, but they were all afraid of both Ethel and Shirley. Nonetheless they decided to fill Lara in.

'Ethel finks you're uppity.'

'And she says that the Irish ain't got no right to be uppity because they're... you know?'

'Irish?'

'Bogtrotters. A bit fick.'

'My dad's Irish and he's really fick,' said one of them, trying to console her.

'Not saying you're fick, like, it's just, you know... the Irish? Anyway, Effil can be a bit of a bully sometimes.'

'Don't take no notice of her. She'll calm dan once she knows she can't hurt ya.'

Their prejudice was shocking but not entirely unexpected. Lara was what her parents rather loftily described as Educated Irish. Despite the derogatory 'Irish' brush the girls swept her with, Lara thought they were probably only picking up on what was there. Lara had to admit to herself that maybe she was a bit uppity. She did consider herself a cut above Ethel and Shirley, with their coarse language and outdated bleached blonde bouffants. The younger ones weren't being cruel, they were just young and indiscreet and, probably, in their own words, a bit fick.

Many times, over the past ten days, Lara thought about leaving. Perhaps she could have another go at the boutiques, or even waitressing in Fred's cafe. That would be easier work than this. Her hands were already scratched from picking up broken glass from dropped trays, and her bottom was pinched red raw from 'fruity' customers. However, when Shirley realised she was straight off the boat, she had let Lara stay in the flat over the club.

'That's very decent of you,' Lara said, impressed by the kindness.

But Shirley had given her a withering look. 'I'm not being decent – I'm just desperate. Make sure you do a good job. You lose the job, you lose the bed.'

The flat was as close to derelict as it could be, but it was also large, way too big for one person, in fact. There were three bedrooms off a large living area with a small kitchenette through a counter arch. The kitchen had a sink and a small gas stove that the last tenant had obviously never cleaned. It looked like somebody had died in the place and the bed was damp and smelly, but Lara had it all to herself. That first night, exhausted though she was, Lara took the carpet up in the biggest of the bedrooms. It had six-foot-tall windows and looked out onto World's End and Fred's cafe. The light was perfect and the buzz of the city outside would give Lara just the atmosphere she needed to be creative. After her first shift in the club she gathered odds and ends of furniture from the rest of the flat, and propped an unhinged bedroom door over the top of two chairs, turning it into a cutting table. With the kitchen table commandeered for her sewing machine, Lara frantically began drawing. Over the following few days she had already almost covered the mouldy walls in swatches of fabric and sketches. With the urgent desire to create, Lara had turned the space into a working studio any designer would want within her first week in London. She spent every penny she earned from her first weekend on fabrics, patterns and haberdashery. She was determined to get her first collection started as soon as possible. How she was going to sell it and who she was going to sell it to, were questions that she must ask herself later. When her time came, Lara wanted to be ready. If she left, or lost her job in Chevrons, she would have to leave the makeshift studio and who knew when she would find a place that could accommodate her work this well again? So she would put up with Ethel's bullying and Shirley's bitchiness for the sake of her future collection. After all, it really was a very small price to pay.

Cocktail waitressing in a gangster nightclub was not exactly Lara's style, but then, neither had been dropping out of college and leaving the life she had so carefully built. The running away had certainly worked. Lara had been so busy surviving Chevrons and using every spare moment to pursue her dreams, that she had barely remembered the broken heart that brought her here in the first place.

'Shit! It ripped again!'

Flossy, a pretty, plump girl was pulling on her kitty costume, when she felt a tear along the buttock seam. Tears were threatening to spill when Lara whipped a black needle and thread out of her cosmetic bag.

'Give it to me,' she said.

Flossy began to peel the costume off, wailing. 'It keeps ripping.'

'What do you expect if you keep eating dinners in Fred's the middle of the day?' one of the girls snapped.

'Dinner...' another sighed wistfully. 'I ain't eaten a proper dinner in six months.'

'Roast chicken and gravy...' another one said.

'Stop it,' another chimed in. 'This is my third costume this year. I worked a full week last month 'cos it tore right along the side seam.'

'I hate these stupid cat costumes. I'm on a permanent diet just to stay in the wretched thing.'

'They're too tight.'

'There's no give in them.'

'And they itch like hell. I wish they'd change them.'

'Shirley picked them out.' One of the older girls frowned. 'She doesn't have to wear it.'

'But she likes them, there's no way she's gonna change them.'

Lara fingered the cheap fabric. They were cheap – nylon – and completely impractical. They didn't do the girls any favours either.

'I'll design you something,' she said.

The girls went silent.

'No, really, I will. I know about clothes. I've studied fashion. Leave it to me.'

All of them continued to eye her in silence. They were young, they didn't understand. Shirley might be a bitch but she was also a manager, Lara reasoned to herself, a working woman.

Surely, she would understand the benefit to her business in having the girls wearing uniforms they were happy with.

So, when her shift was over, Lara went in search of her boss. She found her in the back office, behind the bar, smoking with Brian, the bar manager.

'May I have a word please, Shirley?'

Shirley ignored her but when Lara hovered beside her instead of going away, she stubbed out her cigarette and rolled her eyes.

'What is it?'

'I was wondering if I might have a word with you about the uniforms.'

Shirley smirked. 'No, you may not. In fact, I wanted to have a word with you. I believe you dropped another tray earlier?'

'Ah, yes. I'm sorry but...' Lara trailed off. There was no sense in explaining that Ethel had tripped her. 'I'm happy to pay for the glasses out of my wages.'

'Oh really?' Shirley was losing patience already. Lara needed to steer the conversation back to where she wanted.

'It's just that I was talking to some of the girls earlier and they're not happy with the uniform.'

'Which girls?'

Oh God. She didn't want to get them into trouble.

'Well, um, me. I'm not happy with the uniform.' Shirley was glaring at her now. Lara needed to get it all out, explain herself as quickly as possible. 'I'm a dress designer and I was wondering if I made up a few designs you might consider—'

'No,' Shirley said. 'And if you drop one more tray you're out by the end of the week.'

Lara took a deep breath.

'Right,' she said. 'Thank you.' She left quickly before her mouth got the better of her.

It was dawn outside; everything was closed up. Lara went back up to the flat but she was too furious to sleep. She took out her sketchpad but all she could think about designing were new waitress costumes for Chevrons. Once she got a creative idea in her head, she could not rest until it was out. Her head was a mash of ideas straining to come out. But what was the point? Shirley had made it quite clear she would not even consider looking at them. In fact, Lara didn't even want to show them to her now. The worst thing she could do was give the woman another opportunity to undermine her. Frustrated, Lara paced about the flat until the sun rose and Fred's cafe, across the road, opened for breakfast. Lara was hungry and, having not yet got the kitchen in the flat into a fit state to prepare food, had been eating nearly all of her meals in Fred's.

Throwing a cardigan on over her shift dress, she made it just before the rain started. She was about to sit down when she realised that a beautiful girl with long auburn hair and pale, pale skin was sitting in her usual spot. She had to be Irish. Sad and lost, she reminded Lara of herself, just a couple of weeks ago when she was fresh off the boat, running from heartache and humiliation. The raw pain revisited her in the girl's face. It had been the loneliest Lara had felt in her life and yet, less than a fortnight later, she was busy in her new life. The last thing Lara needed was somebody else's problems but, instead of walking away, she found herself walking over and touching the seat opposite. The girl nodded, so Lara sat down.

'You Irish?' she asked.

The girl looked slightly panicked.

'The red hair and milk-bottle skin.' Lara smiled, shrugging off her cardigan to show her own pale arm. The girl nodded, obviously relieved. They introduced themselves and ordered breakfast. Straight away, it was clear they liked each other, agreeing with one another that Irish sausages were better than English ones. Annie had a refined accent – middle class – like somebody who had been to elocution lessons. Lara couldn't place her county in Ireland and when Annie didn't offer the information, she didn't ask. Like herself, Annie was obviously running from something. She didn't want to talk about what had brought Annie to London any more than she wanted to talk about why she was here herself. Lara had come to London seeking anonymity and found it – so it was her duty to help Annie find it too. They were both running and that was all they needed to know about each other. Ireland was in the past – today was where it was at. They were London girls now, part of the new, modern generation. They were the 'now' people. Coming from nowhere but going everywhere, never looking back.

Their breakfasts arrived and as Lara buttered the mountain of white toast in front of her, she felt, for a moment, as if she was back home at her mother's kitchen table.

'Is this your first time in England?'

'Yes.' Annie, despite being as thin as a whip, was stuffing the food down as if she hadn't eaten for days. Lara liked that.

'Me too, I've only been here a couple of weeks.'

'You seem like you've been here for ages,' Annie said. Then added shyly, 'You look like a London girl.'

Lara was flattered but demurred, 'Well, the girls in work don't think so. They nicknamed me "Irish".'

'That's not very nice,' Annie said.

'They're not very nice,' Lara said. 'At least, one of them isn't. Ethel is a dreadful cow. Keeps tripping me up. Some of the others are OK, but the English are different to us. Harder. Straight to the point.'

Annie looked slightly alarmed.

'Oh I don't want to put you off… it's great here, really.'

Annie smiled, self-consciously, though she hadn't smiled in that natural ordinary way for quite a long time.

'Don't worry, I don't scare easily. I'm not as delicate as I look.'

Lara thought she liked this girl very much indeed. She hadn't realised how lonely she had been, surrounded only by English girls that she had nothing in common with.

'Where do you work?'

'In a nightclub – well, it's a sort of joint you could call it.'

'Sounds like fun.'

'Hmmm – sometimes. But most of the time it's just very hard work in a short skirt.'

'Tell me about it, will you?' Annie said, refilling their teacups.

Lara confided in her new friend about all her problems in the club and Annie drank in every word of her story. Annie was happy to have something else to focus on bar her own, sordid reasons for being here. Getting involved in Lara's life felt like a relief.

'If this Shirley won't listen to you maybe you should go to her boss?' Annie suggested. Lara considered it, then agreed. It was a good idea. Lara liked this girl. And talking to her about work, she realised she needed a friend.

'Have you got a job yet, Annie?'

Annie shook her head.

'A place to stay?'

The beautiful green eyes began to fill with tears and Annie tried to apologise, hastily wiping them away. Lara knew the feeling.

'Why don't you come back and stay with me? It's not much. In fact it's a horrible place, virtually derelict. But it's home. Actually, it's not even that, not yet. I've only been there less than two weeks myself but it's a place to stay and you're very welcome.'

Annie did start crying fully then. Lara, tired and emotional could not steel herself, and joined her, until the two of them started laughing.

As soon as Annie got into the flat she went straight to the kitchen and started cleaning.

'Leave that!' Lara said, embarrassed.

But Annie had already located a filthy cloth, a scrubbing brush and a tin of Ajax under the kitchen sink.

'Tell you what, I'll leave this kitchen as soon as you have some uniform designs drawn up for that club of yours.'

Lara smiled and wrinkled her nose.

'Really?'

'Really,' said Annie.

'You think I should?'

'Absolutely.'

'Right. I will!'

In that small, certain exchange with a girl she had just met, Lara got a warm feeling in her heart that she thought might be happiness.

8

'He's dead. He's dead.' Annie sat up suddenly in the bed. Black, nervous dread filled every molecule of her body. The black fear was so overwhelming that, for a moment, she thought she was dead and hell lived inside her. As she woke to her new surroundings in Lara's flat, the mismatched sheets, a lumpy pillow, the long window in front of the bed which looked out onto the Kings Road, her head immediately came alive with the terror of getting caught. Were the guards looking for her in Ireland? They would come after her. She would get flung in prison in England or taken back to Ireland. Back in Killa, everyone would know what she had done. The life here, which had barely started, would end. Lara would be horrified to realise she had taken a murderess into her home. Had she left some crucial evidence behind? Annie was convinced that she must have done. She wanted so badly to forget. Lara had offered her the chance to do that. But Annie knew that the only way to unlock this paralysis of fear was to make herself remember.

So she got out of bed and walked over to the window to look down onto the early morning quietness of the broad street. With a deep breath, she closed her eyes and rewound the last few days.

Dorian's lifeless body. Lift his hand – check he's dead. Blind panic. Suitcase. Desk. Running through the bog. The Galway bus. Annie drew up each picture then discarded it like she was flicking through somebody else's photo album. The Dublin train. The man offering her a cigarette. GPO post box. As she quickly referenced each event she reassured herself that she had left no clues behind. By focussing on single, innocuous details she was somehow able to forget the overwhelming fact of murder. Queue for boat. Holyhead terminal. Train from Wales. Annie could feel her stress lessen in picturing each truth, covering each track. The final scene was arriving at London's Euston station in the early morning, then wandering the streets of London, in a clueless, miserable state wondering what the hell she was going to do, until Lara found her in Fred's cafe.

That was it. They had come back here and she had slept, until now.

Her suitcase was on a chair by the window. She went over and opened it. She shivered at the contents. Stolen jewellery, a bloody apron. Things she had stolen from him. She took out the few items of clothes she had thrown in and some cash, then rummaged around and found a padlock. As a doctor, Dorian kept a padlock in every bag in the house, in case he needed to lock away medicines while travelling. She padlocked it then placed the suitcase squarely under the centre of the double bed so that it could not be seen from either side. She wanted to forget about the case and everything in it. She wanted to pretend it wasn't there.

There was a tap on the door and Annie quickly jumped up.

'I made you some coffee,' Lara said, opening the door and handing her a mug.

'Instant?' Annie said, taking a sip of the acrid black liquid, laced with sugar.

'Is there any other kind? I'm afraid I'm not much of a hostess.'

'You're a wonderful hostess,' Annie replied, 'taking a stranger into your home.'

'Not much of a home, I'm afraid,' she said, nodding around the rather grim and grubby decor. 'Besides, a red-haired colleen straight off the boat? That virtually makes you family!'

Annie laughed. The fear was gone. In company, she felt safe.

'I'm happy to pay rent,' she said. 'I can start looking for a job today.'

'No need,' Lara said. 'With a face and a figure like yours, they'll lap you up in Chevrons. The pay is okay and the work is easy enough, once you get used to it. And it'll be even easier with these fantastic new uniforms.'

Lara waved a sketchpad in front of her.

'I was up early putting some ideas together – thanks to you, friend.'

'I don't know that I'd be very good at waitressing,' said Annie.

'Look,' Laura said, in a firm, pragmatic tone, 'the most important thing is that you look absolutely gorgeous – and you're a friendly person. They're the two qualifications you need to do that kind of club work. Trust me – they'll love you.'

It wasn't difficult for Lara to persuade Shirley to give Annie a try-out. Good-looking girls were always a welcome addition in Chevrons and this one, with her long legs, striking face and red hair, was a knockout. Shirley put her on the lunchtime shift, there and then sending her and Lara straight into the changing room with a spare kitty outfit. Annie's skinny limbs barely filled the ill-fitting costume and immediately she put it on Lara could see how uncomfortable she was in it. Annie kept picking at the back gusset with her long fingers to try to pull it down and make it less revealing. From the minute she hit the floor it was obvious that Annie was not cut out for the rough and tumble of nightclub work. The leering men made her visibly uncomfortable and the feisty English girls could not make head nor tail of her timid, ladylike manner. She tiptoed through the tables trying to smile politely at customers, but flinching every time one of them spoke to her.

After one hour, Shirley took Lara aside and declared, 'Where did you get her from? She an even worse waitress than you! Get that lanky freak off my floor. She looks terrified and she's upsetting the customers.'

Lara couldn't argue. Annie was clearly excruciated by the whole experience and seemed relieved when Lara said her trial period was over.

'Did I get the job?' Annie asked.

'Afraid not,' Lara said apologetically. 'I think she had somebody else lined up.'

Annie said, 'Sorry, Lara.'

She was upset at having let her new friend down.

'That's OK,' Lara said. 'I'll see you up in the flat later. Make yourself at home.'

Annie went back to the flat and busied herself cleaning it from top to toe. Then she took a lot of money out of her bag and went in search of a shop where she could buy groceries, including real coffee. She remembered, with a shudder, Dorian ordering coffee through the post from Fortnum & Mason's, nonetheless wondering if the shop was nearby. She would cook Lara a magnificent meal that evening and start again, tomorrow, looking for work. Although she had not the first clue what she was qualified to do. Clearly not working in a nightclub, but office work was out – she had never learned to type – and she had very little schooling. She wasn't creative or clever, like Lara. Maybe cleaning work? But where?

As she was thinking that very thought, she passed the door of Fred's cafe, the place where she met Lara the day before, and saw a sign in the window. HELP WANTED.

It was an understatement. A building site had opened up in nearby World's End and Fred's small cafe was suddenly thronged with workmen every morning and evening. Most of them Irish and away from their families, and late lunchtime/early afternoon was their craziest time. Fred could barely manage the kitchen on his own and his Italian wife, Giuliana, was run off her feet.

When this stunning young Irish girl appeared at his kitchen counter Fred barely had time to look at her. The place was full, every seat taken, and Giuliana run ragged taking and delivering orders.

'Excuse me?' she said, her eyes straining to follow him as he darted in and out of the kitchen opening. 'I saw a sign in the window and was hoping that…'

'Can you start now?' Giuliana appeared behind her.

'I suppose…'

The older Italian woman ran around the counter, grabbed an apron and threw it at her.

Annie caught it.

'Clear that table by the window, then get three shepherd's pies and a liver and bacon…'

'Sorry,' Annie said, pulling the apron over her head, 'what did you say – four…?'

'Three shepherd's pies and one liver and bacon – look in your pocket.'

Giuliana was already flying around to another table, four plates of steaming dinners balanced on her arms. Annie reached in her pocket and wrote down the order then ran into the kitchen with it. Fred snatched it off her, barely giving her a glance, then called her back.

'Thank you darling. We'll catch up when the men are fed.'

Annie smiled and the old cockney fry cook thought it was the sweetest smile he had seen in a long time.

For the next hour and half Annie ran, wiped, cleared and smiled at the customers. These were all big working men, many of them Irish. They were hungry and more interested in their dinners than her. When lunch was winding down a half-drunk man came in from the pub next door and made a lewd comment about her. Annie didn't hear what it was but Giuliana chased him out the door with a wet tea towel to the back of the neck.

When the place cleared out Giuliana put up the CLOSED sign and made them a pot of coffee before they began clearing up for the early evening dinner shift. It was a quieter group, then. The Irish builders had their main meal in the middle of the day. Meat and potatoes, pies and stews. The 6 o'clock shift was unmarried office clerks who couldn't cook for themselves: mixed grills, omelettes – occasionally even pasta, they had more genteel tastes.

'Did I get the job?' Annie asked. She genuinely had no idea. Especially after not having passed the test earlier at Chevrons.

Giuliana and Fred looked at each other.

'Yes,' they said in unison. Then Giuliana went over and gave her a big kiss on the cheek while Fred looked on enviously. They gave her the contents of the tips jar and said they would pay her hours at the end of the week when they totted them up.

Annie was over the moon, and so was Lara for her.

The next day Annie arrived at Fred's at 7 a.m. as promised for the breakfast shift. She gingerly put down a strange looking heavy loaf in front of Fred, who was throwing a dozen sausages onto a huge pan.

'What's this?' he said.

'I thought you might like to try it. It's soda cake. We eat it for breakfast at home. I heard one of the men saying how much he missed it yesterday. I thought – if he came in this morning we could surprise him with it. Or some of the Irish men might like it with breakfast.' Then she reached down into her bag and pulled out another one. 'This one is for you and your wife. To thank you for your kindness.'

Annie was not just a hard worker, cleaning and waiting tables with Giuliana like an old pro but, unlike his wife, she could cook, and, even more extraordinary, she cared about their customers. He called his wife in to show her what Annie had done, and they tore off and tasted a slice of the delicious, sweet bread. Both of them felt a little emotional. This Irish girl was sweet and sweet people were few and far between in their experience of London. In the moment that she presented them with the bread, the older couple made a silent vow to each other to look after her. Annie was beautiful, but more importantly, she had heart and she was vulnerable. She had not even asked what the pay was and they both had a feeling that she would work for tips, or even nothing. She wanted little more than their approval. Childless, her simple manner moved them. Within a week Fred had Annie working in the kitchen as his commie fry chef.

'I don't know who brought you up, girl, but they did a good job. Your mother should be proud of herself,' Giuliana said to her after her third day. 'Seeing my husband so happy in the kitchen doesn't just come from a pretty girl – but one that can work as well. I better watch myself with you!' The homely Italian woman was able to joke about Annie stealing her man because she could read in the girl's eyes that no such thing would ever happen. Giuliana had no child of her own, but she had the instincts of a mother. She knew that something had happened to that girl, somewhere along the line. She would never ask what. She knew enough of the world to know that terrible things happened. Knowing about them was no use to anyone so she minded her own business. Within a month Fred and Giuliana had cast themselves as surrogate parents and were calling Annie 'our girl'.

Annie loved her work, and she loved living in the flat with Lara. In less than a week her life seemed to have completely turned around. She felt more at home in London than she had felt anywhere since her mother died.

9

'Irish won't wear the costume.' Shirley barged into Coleman's office, waving her arms. 'She says she wants a word with you.'

Coleman was just out of the shower and still in the process of securing a towel around his waist. His head waitress looked him square in the eye before deliberately running her eyes down the perfect triangle of his rippling chest, still wet and steaming.

'Don't you ever knock?' he said.

'Do I need to?' she said, smarting at the rejection.

Smoke from the cigarette that was permanently carved into the corner of Shirley's full mouth disappeared into the curve of her bleached blonde bouffant. She was clearly still angry with him for cutting off their arrangement. Coleman had been sleeping with her since her divorce, six months ago, but the affair had run its course. Coleman knew Shirley was developing feelings for him and he didn't do love. He was still fond of Shirley. They were old friends and he didn't want to lead her on or make promises he couldn't keep. She deserved better than that and she would get over it anyway. In the meantime, she was glaring at him, thunderously.

Coleman sighed and reached for his shirt.

'Send her in then. What's her name again?'

'I just call her Irish. I dunno. Laura? She's only been here three weeks and ain't much of a waitress.'

'Why did you take her on then?'

Times were good at Chevrons. London was swinging and there were any number of great waitresses willing to put on a sexy kitty costume and swing. Everyone wanted to be a kitty girl. It could get rough sometimes, depending on who was in but scuffles among the punters just added glamour to the place. The money was good and Coleman ran a clean house. There was no excuse for employing dead wood.

Shirley shrugged. 'I dunno. Candy left. We were short staffed. I needed someone fast and she turned up at the door – begging for work. Fred's wife said she was hard-up. I felt sorry for her.'

Coleman shook his head. Shirley had never felt sorry for anyone in her life. She was trying to get at him.

'I put her in the flat upstairs.'

'Jesus, that dump? It's virtually derelict!'

She made her don't-care face.

'She seemed happy enough to take it. Though she'll have to leave that too,' she added, dropping her cigarette into his ashtray without stubbing it out.

'What do you mean?'

'I want you to get rid of her.'

'I never hired her.'

'Yes, but she's crap and you're so good at getting rid of people.' She gave him a pointed glare before walking out of the open door and waving the Irish girl in.

Coleman winced when he realised that the girl had been standing there all along. She must have heard everything.

Flustered, he turned his back to her to finish buttoning up his shirt and threw a 'take a seat' look over his shoulder.

He had forgotten that the sofa was still made up as a bed from the night before.

He had also forgotten that he wasn't wearing trousers.

Lara looked at the bed then across at the man with the towel around his waist and tried to decide whether it was safe to sit down or not.

Chancing it seemed like the best option. As she perched herself on the edge of the white sheet she noticed the dip in the pillow where his head had been. The sheets were probably still warm from his naked body. She shivered.

'I hear that you don't like the Chevrons uniform,' Coleman said.

'That's right.' The Irish girl nodded. 'Would you like to know why?'

'Not really.' Coleman was about to turn and tell her to simply wear the damn thing or take the door, when he realised that he was not wearing trousers. Shirley had him so flustered that he had buttoned his shirt and knotted his tie but was still basically naked from the waist down. He paused and stayed with his back turned but it was important to act normal – to keep talking.

'But I suppose I should hear you out.'

'Well,' Lara began, wondering if he was going to turn round or expected her to continue talking to his back.

'The fabric is really nasty and cheap and the way they are designed makes them chafe at the gusset. If the girls put on an inch of weight here or there, they rip.'

Coleman knew that he could not keep his back turned indefinitely. Perhaps if he argued his point (whatever that was) the Irish girl would think this was simply the way men did business in London.

'The girls aren't supposed to put on weight,' he said, turning around too abruptly. He gripped urgently at the waistband of the falling towel. 'Those costumes were very expensive.'

Lara did not know whether to be offended or amused. She had seen Coleman in the club and heard the other waitresses talking about him, but this was her first proper conversation with him.

He was a hard man, the girls said. He could handle himself, but he wasn't a greedy bully like his boss – the volatile, loquacious bully, Bobby Chevron. The girls respected Coleman but they were not afraid of him. He was clean cut and good looking with a scarred jawline, aquiline nose and blond hair kept short and square. He had remarkably old-fashioned manners and never laid a hand on any of them (although that was more often than not much to their disappointment). He called all the girls 'ladies' although several of them, Lara suspected, were anything but. Lara had been warned that even if he did make a pass, she wasn't to go near him because he was Shirley's property. In her two weeks, Lara had also heard endless rumours about these gangster boys. Apparently they tortured each other and roughed up rival gang members. Some of the girls found that exciting, but it meant nothing to Lara. While everyone seemed slightly in love with enigmatic Coleman, Lara's impression of him had been that he seemed rather outdated. Like his club. Chevrons was stuck in a 1940s time warp, with its men in Saville Row suits and waitresses wearing those stupid, cheap kitty costumes with crippling stilettoes. In the rest of London being young and free was the hip thing now. Men were growing their hair and joining bands. The sexy women were doing their own thing: wearing miniskirts and flat boots, going on the pill and sleeping around.

This situation she found herself in now epitomised that opinion. If Coleman was a modern man he'd have simply said, 'Pass me my trousers would you?' or, perhaps, dropped the towel altogether and conducted their meeting in the semi-nude. As that very thought occurred to her, Lara felt herself redden and decided to take the matter into her own hands.

She took the trousers from the arm of the sofa, and simply walked across the room and handed them to him.

'Well, Mr. Coleman.'

'Just Coleman,' he said, taking the trousers off her and, visibly relieved, stepped behind the open door of the shower room. 'I just have one name.' Then blurted out, 'I'm an orphan.' He immediately grimaced to himself at the revelation. What was wrong with him today? Why was this stupid stuff coming out of his mouth? Was he this flustered by forgetting his trousers?

'Oh,' said Lara, slightly taken aback. This guy was not the self-assured, arrogant Neanderthal she had been expecting. Nonetheless, she had a point to prove.

'Well, Coleman. I don't care how expensive your costumes are, they look cheap and awful. And let's face it, Coleman, nobody wants to be served drinks by a girl who looks uncomfortable in what she's wearing. You want the waitresses to look sexy but happy – am I right? And if they're not comfortable, they're not happy.' Lara was shocked by herself. If she had not caught him without his trousers, she wondered if she would have been as confident.

Now that he was fully dressed, Coleman was starting to pay attention to what Lara was actually saying, and he didn't like it. Of course his girls were happy! Shirley made sure of that. He paid them well. In some clubs, the girls had to buy their own costumes, which were docked out of their wages. Who did this girl think she was coming in here telling him how to run his business? He came back into the room ready for a fight, and was surprised to find her holding out half a dozen sheets of paper towards him.

'Look at these,' she said. He accepted them gingerly, thinking they might be some kind of a legal writ, suing him for making her wear an uncomfortable costume. Unlikely, but possible.

But it was just a bunch of drawings. Sexy pictures of women's figures with hurriedly drawn squiggles for their pouting mouths and big, bovine eyes. They were wearing an array of short, revealing outfits.

'What are these?' he said, immediately thrusting them back to her. The words and gesture came out harsher than Coleman intended. But he wasn't in the habit of holding somebody else's offerings and it felt unnatural. Exposing. As if he were back in school as a small child handing work in to the teacher and getting it thrown back in his face. Truthfully, he was embarrassed and uncertain of how he was meant to react.

Lara felt hurt by the immediate rejection but, equally, she believed this meeting was a chance. Not a big chance, maybe not even a chance at all. But it was something. Maybe. And even a maybe-something was better than nothing. So Lara took a deep breath, and pushed them back into his hands.

'They are designs for waitress costumes for Chevrons,' she said, keeping her voice as steady and firm as she could. 'As you can see,' she said, moving in next to him, 'they're as sexy and revealing as their current ones, but a bit more up to date. This baby-doll minidress is the most practical.' She picked out one from the middle of the pile. Lara stood a full head shorter than him. As she pointed to the pictures she could sense him looking at the side of her face, instead of the page he was holding. 'The whole costume is made in one, circular piece, so it's fluid, which gives the girls easy movement. They'll be able to walk quickly and with more confidence, which is so important when you're carrying drinks.' He coughed slightly, and she felt his breath catch the side of her neck. 'Plus, I have sourced a fabric which is water resistant and quick drying in case of spills.'

He nodded, slowly. He seemed flummoxed. 'This isn't really my thing,' he shook his head and handed them back, more gently this time. 'You need to speak to Shirley.'

'I already tried.' Lara refused to take the drawings from him and added, as diplomatically as she could, 'She didn't seem interested.'

Coleman looked at the girl. She had brown hair that fell, unfashionably straight, to her shoulders and she wore a plain dress which, while short, hung on her like a sack. Over this was a cream hand-knitted cardigan like one that Coleman remembered seeing on a postcard Bobby had sent back from a trip to Ireland. Her eyes were dark brown and hopeful, her long nose and clear white skin gave her an earnest, serious look, which made Coleman feel peculiarly sad. He noticed that she wasn't wearing any makeup and the intimacy of that fact pinched him and made him feel sadder again. The only time Coleman saw a woman without makeup these days was if they were in bed with him. Even then, they rarely spent enough of the night to take it off. 'Irish' did not look like a fashion designer to him. Did fashion designers even exist in Ireland? Wasn't it all fields and cows? Poets, writers and spectacular alcoholics, sure. But fashion designers?

She was talented. He could see that clearly from the extraordinary drawings he was still holding. She was naive, certainly. Yet she had come straight off the boat and had the hutzpah to come in here and sell to him.

He held up the picture of the baby-doll dress.

'How much would this one cost?'

'About two pounds per costume; three if you go with the marabou trim.'

Coleman sucked his teeth and paused.

'That's expensive.'

'How about I make one up for you?' she added quickly. 'I can have it by tomorrow. One of the girls can model it. You can see how it looks in the flesh?'

Coleman pushed back a smile. It wasn't expensive. He had just wanted her to keep selling it to him, keep her in his office. Because since this Irish girl came into the room, Coleman felt a peculiar sense of loss rising up in him. Beyond their harsh introduction, beyond the towel, beyond her criticism of Chevrons' staff costume and her strange request to design new ones, Coleman simply felt as if a piece of him had gone missing in her presence. He was afraid that if he gave her what she wanted, then she would leave the room and, if she did that, he might never get it back. Confused by the irrational feeling that was drawing over him he nodded.

'Bring me in something by Friday.'

Lara grinned and Coleman caught his breath at the innocence of her clean face.

'What's your name?' he said, handing her the pictures and watching as she put them back into her bag.

'Lara,' she said. 'Lara Collins.'

She held out her hand and as he took it, Coleman felt such heat in touching her it was if he had been branded.

He pursed his lips, which was as close to a smile as he could manage and, with great reluctance, nodded her towards the door.

After she had gone he stood for a moment and, finding his voice unable to reach the dizzy heights of speaking, he mouthed her name into the empty, silent room. Lara Collins.

10

Shirley was not impressed when Irish brought in the new waitress costumes for them all to try on. On the pink velvet dressing room chair was what looked like a pile of nurse uniforms – cotton fabric with a pink and brown check running through it – like something you might find on a man's jacket. She couldn't really see how this Irish girl was going to produce something sexy enough to keep them all happy. But Shirley had agreed with Coleman that she would give Lara a chance. Besides, the old uniforms were looking shabby and the girls were constantly complaining.

Standing now in front of the mirror, she had to admit Irish had done a good job. Even though Shirley was an old-fashioned girl, with bouffants, pencil skirts and stilettoes, she could see that she actually looked cool. And she liked it.

The skirt was A-line and so short that it barely skimmed her buttock cheeks. At the same time, miraculously, you could not see her panties, no matter which way she moved in it, they remained hidden beneath the artfully tailored hem. The sleeves were to the elbow and were loose enough around the top to give plenty of movement. The neck had a round lace collar that gave an old-fashioned feminine touch to an otherwise thoroughly modern outfit. The dress was London cool. And every girl, even kitty-costume waitresses, wanted to look cool these days. It was also extremely comfortable, going in and out in all the right places and somehow, making Shirley's figure do the same.

Lara watched with bated breath as Shirley rubbed the fabric on her sleeve between finger and thumb.

'It's treated cotton,' she explained. 'It's not completely water-proof but it will repel drinks and small spills. If you get to it quickly enough it won't stain.'

'Black doesn't stain at all,' Shirley said. 'I thought we were sticking with a dark colour.'

Lara wanted to tell her to get off her high horse, but didn't dare. She needed Shirley's approval to get these uniforms.

'Oh come on Shirl,' said Ethel, 'don't be so miserable.' When Shirley glared at her, the sidekick quickly added, 'You look gorgeous. Your legs go on forever.'

Shirley, despite herself, had to admit that whatever miracle Irish had worked with her cutting design, this plain-looking baby-doll was an absolute dream to wear. Reluctantly, she nodded her approval at the pile and the waitresses dived in, pulling off blouses and skirts, stripping down to their panties with the uninhibited speed of strippers.

Five minutes later Lara was looking at seven young women of various shapes and sizes each wearing her design.

'You look boss, Ethel.'

'Hot to trot, Kitty.'

'Boss, baby!'

As the girls preened and pranced in front of their dressing room mirrors Lara was so excited she started to laugh. This was the first time she had seen anyone wearing her designs other than herself, aside from the free bits she had made for

Annie. Seeing the waitresses, en masse, wearing something she had designed made it real. She was a proper designer. Plus, they all looked amazing. Even Shirley, with a grumpy head on her, couldn't take her eyes off herself in the mirror.

'Hey, Irish – where's your uniform?' one of the girls asked.

'Oh Jesus, I forgot to make one for myself!'

'Aaah Jaysus…' one of the girls mimicked, and they all started laughing.

'Well, you better get your Paddy arse in gear 'cos we're launching them tonight,' screeched Ethel, then remembered herself and looked at Shirley, 'if that's alright?'

Shirley was annoyed, she could tell, but at the same time, Ethel knew she wouldn't say no. There would be war with the girls over this, and she wasn't an idiot. Although, Ethel could tell that Shirley did not like Lara and she could be a vindictive bitch when she wanted to be.

'If Coleman approves,' she said, 'I suppose we can wear them tonight.'

The girls cheered. They all knew the boss couldn't give a monkey's what they wore, as long as they were happy and worked hard.

Later that night, on the floor, the buzz about the place was tangible. The girls were flying about, delighted with their new comfy, cool costumes.

At one point, Lara was standing at the bar, waiting for Brian to prepare a tray of drinks when Coleman came up behind her. 'Well done,' he said, into her ear, although it registered at her neck. She nearly jumped out of her skin and was glad she wasn't holding the drinks tray.

'Sorry,' he said stepping in front of her, 'I just wanted to say well done on the uniforms, and thank you. The girls seem really happy.'

'They are,' she said, beaming. When she smiled, like that, Coleman felt his heart might explode. He considered smiling back, but smiling wasn't his thing. It made him look like an idiot. Shirley walked past and shot them a poisonous glare. 'At least, I think most of them are.'

'Don't worry about Shirley,' he said. 'I've known her a long time. She's a good person.'

Lara smiled again, but tightly this time, and raised her eyebrows so that her face said 'Really?'

It was disloyal of him to entertain this kind of banter with one of the floor girls but he just wanted to be near her.

'Leave Shirley to me. She'll come round.'

Lara had heard that Coleman got around Shirley quite a lot in the past. It put her off him a little bit. Coleman was only in his mid-thirties but he seemed much older to Lara, almost from another generation. He was handsome and enigmatic which made him attractive, but something made Lara nervous around him. Coleman was secretive and cagey and lived on the edge of the law, although he had been good to her, fixing up the flat upstairs and giving it to her at a peppercorn rent. Lara could see why the other girls swooned over him but he was certainly not her type. Lara was an artist, a designer, a beatnik. She could never, truly, be part of that outdated gangster scene, where men were men and women were there just to serve them.

'Well, the main thing is that she looks gorgeous in my design.'

Not as gorgeous as you. Coleman felt cheap even thinking it.

That night, watching the girls enjoying themselves in her dresses, Lara felt the beginning of her design career open up. She spent the evening basking in the glory of her work, then, when her shift was finished, ran straight up to her studio and frantically started sewing. By dawn she had made a sample of a baby-doll dress, the first of many she planned to sell in Kensington Market, starting that very Saturday.

Over the next few weeks, Lara fell into a routine.

She worked all night, and sewed all day. On Mondays she took the bus to Berwick Street in Soho and haggled with the fancy haberdashery shops and street traders alike for the best prices on the finest materials she could afford.

On her way back to Piccadilly Circus Lara would walk through Carnaby Street, visiting each shop, picking through the rails end to end, reassuring herself that her own designs were unique, more special than the grooviest gear on offer in the coolest shops in London.

With two hours sleep, and putting in a nine-to-five working day, Lara was able to make fifteen dresses a week. On Saturday mornings, she got up at five, boxed up her week's work and was down at her stall in Kensington Market. Her first stall was tucked away in a corner at the back. This crammed shopping emporium was the epitome of London cool and was jammed every Saturday with young hipsters. It seemed that everybody knew everybody else, and, at first, nobody paid any attention to the Irish new girl in the corner with her dozen minidresses. On the first week Lara sold three baby-dolls and a blouse. The stall was cheap, but she still made a loss. But two of the three girls she sold to came back the following week with three friends. They all bought a dress each and she broke even. The following week she had sold all of her stock by lunchtime, snapped up by friends of the girls from the previous week.

She ran back to the flat and immediately started sewing to catch up for the following Saturday.

'You look terrible,' Annie said when she found her that evening in her studio. 'Let me get you something to eat – then you need to get some sleep.'

'I'm not hungry.'

'Well at least go to bed for a few hours.'

'I need to get this one finished before nine when my shift starts.'

'You can't work again tonight, Lara, you haven't had a break for...'

'Just leave me alone, Annie,' she snapped. 'I'm not a child! Stop fussing over me!'

Annie was thick skinned when it came to being snapped at. She knew Lara was just overwrought and tired, and didn't mean it. Only those who have experienced genuine cruelty can be that magnanimous.

After two months selling in the market, Lara had built a reputation. She was selling out every week. People started asking, 'Who's that girl in the corner stall?'

Lara put the prices of her dresses up to a hefty £15 to slow sales, but she was still selling out each week. She got to know a few of the other designers and their photographer boyfriends and model friends. Fascinated that the enigmatic Irish girl worked nights in the infamous Chevrons, they followed her down there. Men in frilly pink blouses and girls in jeans, the gangster crowd didn't know what hit them, but before long, the hip street crowd were bringing in a smattering of pop singers and everybody loved a bit of celebrity. Coleman, noticing that Lara was at the forefront of this change, promoted her from floor girl to a hostess. This meant she didn't have to wear a uniform, and she looked after a roped-off area of the room dedicated to the hip crowd. Shirley, of course, was not happy about the change, but Coleman reminded her that fashion-crowd money was as good as anybody else's.

✿

Annie persisted in looking after Lara as if, along with Fred and Giuliana, she was her family. Lara had saved Annie's life on that first day and now, as the designer worked herself into a state of ill health, Annie insisted on doing the same for her.

She pressured Lara to eat, leaving food out for her while she was at work. Sometimes she made Lara sit on the sofa while she served her, then watched as she fell asleep over the plate. Annie would arrange her on the cushions and put a blanket over her. Lara was always cross at her when she woke up, but was usually better for a few days. Nonetheless, as the weeks past, Annie began to really worry about her.

Lara was so determined to succeed she was putting her own health at risk. Compounding this, things had not been working out as Lara had planned. In fact, far from being separated from each other, Lara's worlds were feeding into one another. She was selling plenty of dresses and garnering a fine reputation, fast. However, this was not enough to set up on her own. Lara knew she would never be able to grow her business, buy fabric in bulk, or employ seamstresses, as long as she was working as a waitress. On the other hand, her Chevrons wages were the only thing enabling her to continue making clothes. Plus, as long as she stayed working there, Lara had a free place to live. The only way that Lara could see of opening her own boutique was to work every hour that God gave her. So that's what she did. Until, one night, she couldn't.

Chevrons late evening shift started at 9 p.m. Lara had worked straight through for forty-eight hours. Annie had been keeping different shifts at the cafe and had not been at home to stuff food into her or arrange naps.

Lara was out on the floor serving a gang of regulars who were hanging on from the lunchtime stripper shift. Even by her own standards, Lara was exhausted. Most days, she ran on pure adrenalin, fizzing and buzzing. One of the girls had given her a blue diet pill to try one day, but Lara found that it made her nauseous and her heartbeat sped up too much. Work was usually enough in itself to keep her going. But this evening her limbs felt like lead. She decided, as she was carrying a tray of pints across the floor, that perhaps Annie was right and that she needed a proper night's sleep. As soon as this shift was over, Lara decided, she would take herself home to bed. At the corner of the stripper's floor stage, she passed Shirley and a couple of the girls on their way to the dressing room and she tripped. Except, this time, it wasn't them. This was off her own bat.

As she fell to the ground Lara felt a strange relief wash over her that at least she could lie down. The last thing she heard before her head clipped the side of the stage and she fell asleep was Shirley shouting, 'Stupid bitch! Ethel, get the mop!'

Coleman came out of his office just in time to see Shirley give Lara's unconscious body a nudge with the tip of her stiletto.

'What the hell is going on here?' he said. For an awful moment he thought there had been a fight. He knew Shirley could be a bit rough.

'She tripped up then just – collapsed,' Shirley said, adding, quite matter-of-factly, 'I don't think she's dead,' as she nonchalantly lit a cigarette.

Coleman's stomach lurched. He knelt down beside Lara to check she was alive. As he felt her breath on his ear and saw her chest rise he felt a mixture of relief and arousal. Strange though it was, she was simply asleep. By now the girls had gathered around them.

'You,' he said to Ethel, 'go across to Fred's and get Annie. The rest of you,' and he looked pointedly at Shirley, who was watching him with hawkish eyes from behind her cigarette, 'get back to work.'

Shirley shrugged, giving him a nasty look as she dropped and ground her cigarette into the lino as close to Lara's head as she dared. Turning towards the bar, she saw Coleman pick up Lara's body with careful tenderness and carry her towards his office. She felt a pang of bitter jealousy.

When she woke Lara was lying on the sofa in Coleman's office. Annie was on the edge of the arm and Coleman was sitting at his desk. Part of her knew she should sit up, but her body simply would not let her. Her limbs were made of iron and her eyelids, lead. Every part of her was screaming to be left alone. So Lara kept her eyes closed and listened to them talk in low concerned voices.

'She's exhausted. I'm worried about her, Coleman.'

'Why is she like this?'

'She's working, selling her clothes in Kensington Market every Saturday.'

'I know that.' Coleman was privately jealous of Lara's fashionable friends. They reminded him of how far away he was of ever getting near her.

'When do you think she's making all the clothes she sells?'

Coleman muttered something conciliatory, as if this was his fault. Annie could be surprisingly strident when she was defending a friend.

'During the day! When she's supposed to be sleeping! Coleman, Lara's working twenty-four hours a day. Literally getting no sleep and she eats nothing...'

'Why?'

'Because she wants to be a fashion designer not a...' *waitress all her life*, thought Annie. Coleman knew what she was saying.

Even from her virtual coma, Lara had enough. She yawned noisily and forced herself to sit up.

'What happened?'

'You collapsed in the club,' Coleman said.

'I tripped,' Lara said. 'I must have banged my head.'

'Don't sit up,' Annie said.

'Stay in here for as long as you need,' Coleman said. But it was too late. Lara was already up.

'I'm fine.'

'You are not fine,' Annie insisted. 'Coleman?'

'Take the rest of this shift off...'

Lara began to insist.

'...no buts. Sick leave. You still get paid.'

Annie took Lara upstairs.

When they had gone, Coleman locked the door behind them then sat at his desk for the next hour, smoking and thinking.

Bobby Chevron leaned back in the booth and surveyed his domain. The club hadn't changed much since he opened it ten years ago. The plush velvet booths had held up lovely and the little electric lights with dim bulbs in the middle – state-of-the-art they were. The purple carpet wasn't as thick as it had been, but he reasoned that nobody in here was looking at the floor. Not unless they were in big trouble, in which case they'd be too close for comfort. No, the main thing in here was the girls. Good looking, friendly. One or two of them were new. He hadn't been in for a few months because Maureen had dragged him off to Spain, again. There was something different in here tonight, but he couldn't quite put his finger on it. A slight change of atmosphere, maybe. Whatever it was, it was working. Bobby was in a good mood. And when Bobby was in a good mood – everyone was in a good mood.

Chevron's nightclub was a drop in the ocean now in terms of Bobby's business portfolio but he was fond of the place. He had enough property in London and Spain to never need to work another day. Not that he had done any actual work in years – he had Coleman running the club, and loyal Arthur looking after him. Chevron didn't really have to do anything here at all, except sit back and enjoy the fruits of his labours, as he was doing now. Maureen was tucked up safe at home so he was out for the night looking for a bit of fun. Not that there was much fun to be had out of the club these days. Coleman, if the truth be known, was a bit of a dry bastard when it came to tasting the wares.

'I told you I wouldn't run Chevrons as a knocking shop. If the girls make the first move, that's fine. Just remember, Bobby, you're a powerful man. It's not right to put them under pressure.' Coleman talked some right shit sometimes; he couldn't help it if girls liked a powerful man. But for the sake of the business he was right. He knew from his early days, when he kept knocking shops in Stepney, that running girls was profitable, but it was also complicated. Boyfriends, husbands – then some Charlie would go and fall in love with one of the girls and start following them around. It could get unpleasant. Coleman persuaded him that there was plenty of money to be made out of the bar and a little bit of gambling in one of the back rooms, all very hush-hush, regulars only – no trouble. At least, no more trouble than Ironing Board Arthur could handle on his own.

'In the long run, you're saving money,' Coleman said. And he was right. It just meant that Chevron found that while the girls were polite, and sometimes even flirty with their big boss, they weren't as forthcoming as he would have liked.

Still, there was only one of them he was really interested in.

Chevron had had his eye on Shirley for years, but kept his distance after she married that north London psycho, Handsome Devers. Handsome was small time. A bully boy, flitting about doing jobs for the big boys, but no firm wanted him full time. Handsome was a nobody but he could be dangerous, and no bird was worth risking a beating for.

Coleman came over with a bottle of whisky and two glasses. He put them down in front of them, pinching the fabric on his suit trousers before sitting down.

Chevron smiled. 'I taught you that,' he said. 'Bought you your first suit. Remember?'

'Yeah,' Coleman said, embarrassed. 'I remember.'

Bobby would never let him forget.

Bobby Chevron found Coleman stealing from a bin in Stepney at the back of one of his knocking shops. The scrawny thirteen year old had been moved from orphanage to foster home. He was nicknamed Coleman, after the mustard, because his punch was like being hit with a hot poker. Chevron took the kid home, fed him, cleaned him up and introduced him to his mother, Molly. For the next eight years Coleman slept on a chair in Molly Chevron's small kitchen and ran errands for Bobby. Bobby cast himself as Coleman's hero – a father figure.

Bobby had made good on his promise that young Coleman would never go hungry or homeless again, but he was no hero. Coleman was nonetheless loyal to him, but he understood that their relationship was conditional on him staying grateful. Sometimes that was difficult. When Bobby acted like a prick, it got even harder.

Bobby lifted the glass to his fat lips, took a sip, and sighed. 'Where's Shirley tonight? God, I'd give that woman one if she wasn't with that tosser Devers.'

'They split up,' Coleman said, looking out at the floor, always working, ever watchful for trouble.

'Nah? Gave her one hiding too many?'

'I suppose.'

'Yeah, I can imagine she's a bit feisty alright. Well, you tell her I said if she ever needs protection, or him sorting out – she only has to ask.'

Coleman nodded but said nothing. Bobby wriggled with frustration. Coleman's enigmatic, hard-man demeanour made him an ideal club boss. He had natural authority and that kept the action down. Less action meant less mess and less cleaning up. But it didn't always make for great conversation.

'Well, tell Shirley I was asking for her won't you?'

'I will,' said Coleman.

Bobby chewed on his cigar and let his eyes wander over the club. It was different in here tonight. A new crowd. Younger, fresher. A few women punters out there, and not just the regulars' wives. A couple of girls in short skirts with short hair were standing at the bar, like blokes. Pretty girls always kept the punters happy, waitresses or not. He liked it. Something else had changed too, but he couldn't quite put his finger on it.

'These floor girls all new?' he said.

'No,' said Coleman, 'but their uniforms are.'

Bobby clicked his fingers. 'That's what it is.'

'Everything all right, gentlemen?' Kim, their youngest waitress came over with a bowl of peanuts.

'Lovely, darling, thank you,' said Chevron with a flourish. He could be a gentleman when he wanted to.

As she walked off he took a good look at her back and said, 'I like them. Draws the eyes to all the right places.'

'We had them designed especially. One offs. No other club has them.'

'Exclusive,' Chevron said. 'I like it.'

'The designer works here. She's brought in a lot of new punters.'

Bobby perked up at the mention of business.

'They cost a fortune?'

'Cheaper than the bought ones, and good quality. And the girls love them.'

'Fuck the girls, what about the punters?'

'Look at it, Bobby,' Coleman said, nodding out at the packed room. 'The place is buzzing.'

'Don't see many of the old faces.'

As if on cue, Chevron's old pal, Derek Malone walked past and nodded. He knew not to interrupt Bobby when he was talking business.

'They're all here,' Coleman said, 'just brought in a few new ones as well. Mixing it up a bit with Lara, and these new uniforms attract the fashion crowd in. Nobody's complaining. Matter of fact, the books are well up on last year. It seems like everyone wants a piece of the action when it comes to fashion.'

Chevron shrugged his approval.

'You've got to move with the times. I've always said that.'

He had never said any such thing. In fact, Chevron despised newness – men dressing like nancy boys in jeans and blouses. It was disgusting. He was pleased that Coleman was making him money but at the same time it was important that he was seen as boss. When a right-hand man got up himself and thought he was in charge... that was how trouble started.

'Yeah.' Coleman kept his eyes looking out at the club, into the middle distance, as if making a throwaway remark. 'That girl Lara has got talent. A good eye. She's hardworking. I was thinking of backing her,' he looked over at Bobby now, right into his eyes, 'in a shop. Starting a fashion label.'

He took a sip of his whisky. He knew Bobby wouldn't like that. He did not like people that worked for him getting involved in other ventures. He also did not like anyone coming to him directly asking for money to back anything that was not entirely his own idea.

When Coleman said he was thinking of backing her, he knew Bobby would take it as an invitation. Coleman didn't have the money to back her, and if he did? That meant Chevron was paying him too much.

On the other hand, Bobby was no fool when it came to business. He liked money too much to look a gift horse in the mouth.

They sat, looking at each other for twenty seconds or so. Long enough for a waitress to swerve past their booth, and for Derek Malone to nudge his drink aside to look over and smell the tension.

Finally, Bobby said, 'Talk to me.'

Coleman was prepared. He talked about how the women that worked in the club used to buy a new dress once or twice a year. Now they were buying a new outfit every week. Styles were changing so fast and people were spending their money just keeping up. They wanted the latest trend, the shortest skirt, the coolest cut of jacket. Fashion was a growing industry but you had to know what you were doing, and this girl really did. Mary Quant, Biba – these birds were making a fortune and those arty types were usually out of bounds to businessmen like them. But now, this girl was in their club. She made her scene their scene. This was their chance to cash in. Coleman told Chevron, he really believed that this chick, Lara, had what it took to make a fashion label work.

'Now, that,' Chevron said, pointing his cigar at Coleman's face when he was finished, 'is a very good idea, my son.'

Coleman nodded. Inside he was smiling. Despite himself, part of him still craved Chevron's approval.

'What's it gonna cost me?'

Coleman had the whole thing worked out and ran through the figures. There was a place available on the Kings Road, a few doors down from the club. It was the wrong end of the street for fashion retail but with the right clobber, it could become the right end. He cited kids currently flocking to a far-out boutique called Granny Takes a Trip around the corner on World's End. Bobby would come up with the start-up money for kitting it out and stock. After two years payback (quicker if they could) Bobby would own 20 per cent of all profits as a silent partner.

'Well, I want in,' Bobby said, smiling a broad grimace punctuated by frantic puffs of cigar smoke. 'But you know I can't take that deal, Coleman.'

Coleman knew Bobby would negotiate the hell out of him so he had started low. Apart from the fact that he wanted to help Lara, Coleman saw this as an opportunity for him too. He had been running Chevrons for ten years. Bobby spent most of his time in Spain these days. He didn't need the club or its money any more. But, equally, Coleman knew he wouldn't let it, or Coleman, go out of sentiment or stubbornness. At least if Coleman could carve out a business interest of his own, it might give him a better chance of breaking free. He might even earn a bit of Chevron's respect, which, despite everything, was still important to him.

'The way it is, Coleman, is this. I put in 100 per cent backing, I own 100 per cent of the business, I take 100 per cent of the profits.'

He was stabbing the dead cigar across the table at him. Coleman felt bile rose in his throat.

'You get a salary and so does your...' He was going to say 'slag'. He felt like shouting it. SLAAAAAG! See how Coleman liked his new girlfriend being called that? Chevron took a deep breath and calmed himself down. There was no point in getting upset – this was business and there was money to be made. No sense in losing the rag. Not with Coleman. Not with his boy.

'Your designer lady. Big salaries, Coleman. You name your price. Whatever you like. I won't quibble.'

Coleman felt sick. Sicker than he had ever felt in his life. If he had felt trapped by Chevron before, he had tightened the chain himself. Worse, he had made Lara a part of it.

'You know me, son. I don't do partnerships. Never have. Never will.'

Chevron's tone was conciliatory, almost apologetic.

'I'm a lone wolf. I can't help it. But, if I was ever to go into partnership with anyone, my son,' and in the moment he said it, Bobby's voice softened as if he believed what he was saying, 'it would be you.'

'Maybe we should forget the whole thing,' Coleman said. The thought of Lara being implicated so thoroughly into Chevron's grubby world was too much. This had been a bad idea; he should have foreseen it. He should have known better than to ask.

'No, no, son,' Chevron reassured him. 'It's a good idea. Plus, it's good to diversify, you know? You go ahead. Set it up. Good lad.'

The partnership suggestion was forgotten. Coleman had found a way of making him more money; all was good in Chevron's world again. He relit his cigar, poured himself another whisky, then picked up the bowl of peanuts and poured them directly into his mouth.

'Call that sexy blonde bit over again. Tell her I need some more nuts.'

Business always gave Bobby an appetite. For everything.

11

'Your salary, both our salaries, will be small, initially, but once Chevron's initial investment has been paid off, we can look at restructuring.'

Lara could not believe her luck. When Coleman asked to see her in his office a few minutes ago, she thought he was going to fire her. He had been quite distant and standoffish since that evening when she collapsed and woke up in his office. She thought that maybe he was finally giving Shirley her way and getting rid of 'Irish.'

Instead, with an inscrutable look on his face Coleman had told her that he would like to back her in starting her own boutique on the Kings Road.

'Mr Chevron has agreed to put up some seed money to fit out the shop and buy the initial stock.'

Lara was utterly dumbfounded. It was a dream come true. Of course, she could not let Coleman see that. He was a gangster, and would surely walk all over her.

'I'm interested,' she said, keeping her voice as steady as she could. 'What did you have in mind?'

He told her about the premises and outlined the deal. She

could have her own shop! All the work she had done over the past few months, working around the clock, her hands turning to callouses from all the sewing. She would be able to employ people to sew for her, maybe buy in some stock from abroad to supplement her own designs. She could hardly believe that this opportunity was falling into her lap. The premises they were proposing were just around the corner from Granny Takes a Trip, which was bringing the in-crowd up to World's End in their droves. It couldn't be more perfect. She could have got up and kissed her boss on his handsome, grumpy face over and over again. At this stage, Lara didn't care a jot if she didn't make a penny out of it. Just to get her designs out there and have the space to display them properly was beyond her wildest dreams. However, she couldn't look too keen.

'Why do I only get 30 per cent if I'm doing all the work and providing all the expertise?'

Coleman sighed and raised his eyebrows. He had worked it all out so carefully. There would have to be two sets of books, one for Chevron – which was the real story – and one for Lara – which was the pretty fiction. By forgoing all of the large salary that he would claim for himself and altering Lara's salary from high to low – he would be able to fiddle around with the figures so that it would look like she was taking a percentage share of the profits. He would get nothing out of it at all, except the pleasure of knowing he had done this for her. Coleman had been hoping that Lara might fling her arms around him in a display of untrammelled joy and gratitude. Instead of which, she was breaking his balls.

His new partner was going to be more on the ball about that side of things than he had been banking on. Another thing he might have foreseen before he went jumping in.

'Mr Chevron is a shrewd businessman who doesn't give his

money away easily. In addition to loaning the setup money at a percentage payback, he needs to take a cut of the profits to make it worth his while.'

When you are lying, it's best to stick as close to the truth as possible.

'And the same goes for me.'

Although – it's still a lie.

Lara looked at him and, for a moment, wondered if this was a good idea. By his own admission, Coleman didn't know anything about fashion or retail. In addition to that, his personality and demeanour were impossible to read. Was it a good idea to go into business with someone like that? Bobby Chevron, whom she had never met, was an established gangster. That meant that her business would probably be founded on criminal money. For a moment Lara wondered if it was a good idea. However, before her conscience took over, Lara's heart lured her back to a shop front on the Kings Road, with a glittering display of her fashions in the window.

'And when do you hope to start?'

'The lease on the premises is ready to sign.'

When the landlord heard that Bobby Chevron was interested in leasing the premises, he shaved 20 per cent off the rent, without being asked, and had the papers drawn up immediately. You didn't mess with Chevron, and the handsome henchman who managed the club for him drove a hard bargain.

How thrilling! Lara felt like jumping up and punching the air with delight.

'You won't move on the 30 per cent?'

Coleman gave another, exhausted sigh. Had Lara no idea who she was dealing with here? Was she that stupid? He knew she wasn't. Just feisty and determined, and prepared to dig her heels in. Irish.

'We can look at it in a year's time if Chevron's part of the loan is paid off.'

'When it's paid off,' she reminded him. Then she smiled and reached over the desk for his hand. 'It's a deal. Do I call you partner?'

Coleman's lips hesitated on the word, then he nodded and said, 'Partner.' She thought she saw light flicker across his dark eyes. Then, it was gone.

12

Cork, Ireland, 1966

Noreen felt quite certain she had just had an orgasm. It was not what she had been expecting from only her third time making love with John. The first time had been somewhat uncomfortable and awkward, as they had both been expecting. The second had been pleasant enough but really they were just getting into the swing of it. Then today, their third time. Well, it had been something else altogether. An orgasm. What else could that mighty, shuddering, glorious cacophony of ecstasy have been?

Noreen flopped across her fiancé's chest, smiled broadly and laughed a little. After a minute she leaned on one elbow to look at him. John was looking very pleased with himself indeed. As well he might.

'Ouch,' he said, 'that elbow's sharp.'

Her elbow was the only thing about Noreen that was angular. Fully dressed, she had a broad, traditional build, which, while it didn't suit all of the fashions of the day, made her perfectly delicious when she was naked. At least John thought so. She was boundlessly sexual, with mound after glorious mound of flesh, as white and soft as powdered sugar. Irresistible. John considered himself something of a saint to have held strong as long as he had. Nearly a whole year ago they got engaged and, in the end, they were only here on her insistence. With broad features in an honest, open face Noreen wasn't considered the most beautiful girl in Carney but John didn't care too much about that and neither did she. She was clever, funny and kind. She was all he ever wanted. Noreen was John's girl. And now she always would be. She gave him a playful dig with the offending elbow and reached across him for the cigarettes.

'Just tell me. Did I have an orgasm, John?'

'Jesus, Noreen. Isn't it enough for you to be doing the thing without talking about it as well. Who cares?' Sex had been Noreen's idea. Of course, John had wanted to do it. He was a man, after all. But sex before marriage was a risky business. She might get pregnant, too early to pass it off as post-marital.

She gasped with exaggerated horror. 'I can't believe you just said that. Everyone cares. Every woman is entitled to an orgasm every time she has sex.'

'Who says? I never heard that.'

'That's because you never read the Yanks.'

'Ah, that's grand. It wasn't Father Carney then. Phew. Thought I'd missed something there.'

'Well, did you feel anything?'

He laughed. 'I surely did.'

'I mean from me, not you.'

'I dunno, sure didn't I pull out before… Ah Jesus, Noreen, you have me at it now as well.'

'It's just that if we are going to have sex…'

'Make love. Noreen, please. If we are going to commit

mortal sin before marriage can you at least put a nice name to it?'

'And do this terrible thing that'll have us in purgatory for all eternity...'

'That is correct.'

'Well, then, at least I want to be sure I'm getting the most out of it. It says here,' she pulled a copy of *The Feminine Mystique* off her bedside table, 'that every repressed housewife in America feels they should be having orgasms while waxing the family room floor. They're having orgasms all the time. It's all they're doing. American women are not fulfilled because they're not allowed to work. Only do housework and have sex. And orgasms are mandatory.'

She took a pull of her cigarette and blew smoke up at the ceiling. 'I wish I wasn't allowed to work. Da has me killed out in that pub. I'm on again tonight.'

'Ah no, I thought we'd go into Fermoy and see a movie.'

Noreen tried to look disappointed. Truth be told she preferred real life to the movies and would actually rather be in the pub. Catching up on local gossip and dealing with rowdy drunks was better than chewing on a bag of Emerald toffees and cooing over some soft, romantic Hollywood nonsense with every other couple in town. John was so predictable. Life was so predictable. At least in the pub there was usually a bit of trouble on a Saturday.

'Old Kathleen Molloy passed on this morning, so Da has to get her ready for the wake.'

'At least he hasn't got you fiddling with dead bodies.'

'Yet.'

Noreen knew that her father wanted her to take over the funeral home as well as the pub. Once she and John were married, Frank Lyons would be getting a replacement son.

His own, Noreen's brother Matthew, had run off to become a priest halfway through his arts degree in Dublin, leaving a perfectly good girl, Lara Collins, behind him. Frank had been disgusted until he realised that Noreen was a whiz behind the bar. Even without the addition of fiancé John, she was twice the man her fanciful, holy brother would ever be. Although, she could be flighty too. Noreen liked getting out and about and in among people, and Frank lived in fear of her taking off to London or, worse, New York. While his wife worried about Noreen's moral capacity for withstanding a long engagement, Frank was anxious to get her properly married and settled so that he would be able to take a back seat. His business would be safe in the hands of his daughter and her solid, sensible guard of a husband. However, in the meantime, he had to handle the dead bodies himself and, whenever he could, leave the bar in the hands of his twenty-year-old daughter.

'Besides, I prefer the live bodies,' Noreen said, running her hands down the front of John's bare chest.

'Will we go again? Just so I can be sure?'

'Ah, Noreen. Now, we have to put a stop to this carry on. Honestly. We'll be married soon and then we can be at this whenever we like.'

His voice was saying one thing, but his body was saying quite another.

'Noreen, stop now. You're a desperate woman altogether. Really, we can't be at this messing.'

But it was too late. She had already clambered on top of him and he was drowning under a mound of sugar.

'She looked just like herself.'

'I never saw her looking as well.'

The three Marys were the first of a large, mixed crowd in Lyons's small bar after the removal.* A good funeral was the only circumstance that would bring these respectable women into a public house and, lucky for them, there had been plenty of funerals this year. The smart ones had given their condolences to the family at the house during the day so they could sneak out of mass early and be up at the pub to get a seat before the hoards arrived. You could catch up on a month's gossip in Lyons's in less than an hour if you knew who to sit next to.

'A glass of black and one whisky and red, there's a good girl, Noreen. Your father played a blinder today. Small sherry, Mary?'

'Go on, but make it a large one. One is my limit, as you know, and I had one back at the house earlier, but I'm that upset about Kathleen.'

The Mary who was buying winked and nodded at Noreen. One was her cousin's limit alright. One bottle. It was going to be a long night. Although, if Sherry-Mary did get hammered and started to cause a fuss, she couldn't be in safer hands than young Noreen. She had such a good head on her shoulders it belied her young years.

'What would Frank do without you at all?'

'She's a great girl altogether,' said Whisky-Mary, 'letting her dad off to tend to the dead when she could be off gallivanting with her handsome guard.'

'Fine thing,' Black-Mary butted in. 'When's the big day?'

Noreen smiled and said, 'Next month, Mary.'

'Not long now, just four weeks to wait. And we all know the men don't like to be kept waiting too long.'

---

* Irish catholic 'removal' of the remains to the church, usually the night before the funeral mass.

'Mary!'

The three of them shared a scandalised laugh. Noreen joined in although, truthfully, she was starting to get fed up of people asking her about the wedding. Her father was an important man and her family so well known that people talked about her and John as if they owned them. How she longed to confess to them all that she had already made love to her fiancé, that only that afternoon they had snuck up to the spare bedroom where she had seduced him into giving her an orgasm. An ORGASM! She felt like shouting it out loud in the bar, ringing the bar closing bell and hollering, at the top of her voice, 'ORGASM! ORGASM! ORGASM!' She wondered if any of the three Marys had ever had an orgasm. It was doubtful.

She reached to the back counter and topped up the ladies' round. Next to them were four pints already lined up for the men that came in the door. She knew every customer and their preference. The regulars, all men, liked when she knew what they wanted and ordered with the barest of nods. After the delay of standing around after a funeral, having a pint ready to lift to their lips with one hand, while the other removed their cap, was exactly what they needed. The women, in contrast, made a big fuss over ordering their drinks. They did not like to be kept waiting either, but at the same time, it was important not to assume. That might imply that they drank on a regular basis, which, as witnessed by Sherry-Mary, would not do at all.

The same regulars had been coming in here since Noreen was a child. The same crowd after every funeral. They didn't change what they drank. Habits remained the same through a lifetime. All of these people... they were so predictable. They went to the same masses, ate fish on a Friday, ham and potatoes for tea on a Saturday and, for those that had a chicken to kill, chicken on a Sunday. If somebody got a new coat, it was cause for speculation. When they got married, the town celebrated and the men commiserated in the pub. When the first baby was born, they wetted its head in Lyons's. When they died, the town mourned them the exact same way. And always Frank there, behind the ancient oak bar. The crooked shelves behind his head were lined with bottles of spirits that sat alongside sliced bread, flour, sugar and teabags that gave a husband sent on an errand an excuse for being there. Frank even kept a few bars of chocolate under the counter so that a late-drinking husband could bring back something to appease an angry wife.

Noreen noticed Finbar Fuller nodding off into one of his drunken afternoon stupors and made a note to pop a bar of Dairy Milk in his torn overcoat pocket for poor Deirdre later. On the house. Goodness knows the poor man put enough business their way.

'Who'll be next?' Sherry-Mary said.

'Well, young Noreen here if her big day is next month.'

'No, not that,' Sherry-Mary said, waving her second (or maybe sixth) glass of sherry in the air.

'Who'll be the next to, you know...' and she nodded behind her then, for good measure, squinted and stuck her tongue out of the side of her mouth, adding in a dramatic whisper 'to go.'

Whisky-Mary winced. Black-Mary took up her glass of stout and, taking a sip, said quite matter-of-factly, 'That'll be Joe Gilroy. He's above in Castlebar with a tube the size of a hosepipe draining his gullet and his face is yellow as a sheep's stomach. He looked dead already to me when I was in on Tuesday visiting Kathleen. They're saying he won't last the week.'

'Could be giving us another day out next Sunday then, ladies.'

'And Noreen's big day after that.'

'You never know when the good Lord is going to take you.'

'Thank goodness some things never change.'

'Like a good glass of black. Throw us up another one there, Noreen, like a good girl.'

But Noreen was stood stock still staring past Sherry-Mary's shoulder.

'Noreen?' It wasn't like Frank's daughter to be so inattentive. She was usually dying to hear all the news. 'Noreen, you look like you've seen a ghost.'

And she had seen a ghost of sorts. In the form of her Big Day.

As the women talked Noreen saw her life flash in front of her. In a month's time she would marry John Connolly, their local guard. She would wear the puffy white dress that her father had paid a fortune for, currently hanging in the spare room wardrobe.

She would continue to work in the bar until the children came. At this time her father would retire and enjoy his grand-children, and John would begin to take responsibility for the pub. Having gone through the ordeal of childbirth and becoming a mother, Noreen would then be considered mature enough to work in the funeral parlour, tending fully to the dead. The three Marys would be at their funerals, her parents then and eventually, after a long, long time it would be her turn, and one of her own children would tend to her.

That was going to be Noreen's life. Book-marked by two big days out – her wedding then her funeral. Marriage then death. Her life mapped out for her in a monotonous, straight line for the next fifty years. Sixty if she was unlucky. Was this it?

Noreen had always been a home bird. She had never thought about what she wanted for the rest of her life. She loved Carney and its aul' ones and the gossip. She was great behind the bar. Noreen was fun loving, while her brother Matthew was the sensible one, the priest in training for the last six months. Yet he was the one who had moved away from home to start a life in Dublin. Noreen liked her life in Carney too much and had always been happy to stay at home. She liked the familiarity of her family, the comfort of home, the craic in the bar. Then, when John had come along and showed an interest in her, it seemed that life was complete. But standing here, in this moment, as these three Marys predicted the next death in their small, sleepy town, Noreen found herself infuriated by the idea that her own life was so predictable. Even her boring, weird brother had done something unpredictable by leaving art school to become a priest, by leaving Noreen's best friend, Lara Collins, high and dry. Noreen had been furious at his ruining their friendship, and also mortified by how stupid he was. Most lads his age would have chopped their arm off to get at Lara. Most lads knew they wanted to be priests before they left school. Noreen thought Matt was an idiot for changing his life course last minute. She had always been clear about what she wanted. But now... she wasn't so sure.

As these thoughts ran through Noreen's head she grew more and more indignant. Here she was, stuck in Carney, living out her parents' life. Supposing they knew what she had been up to that afternoon. Sex before marriage. Orgasms. Of course, it didn't matter. None of it mattered really because she and John would be getting married in a couple of weeks. Once they were married the status quo would be set. She would wear through her orgasm quota and become an old Holy Mary like the three standing in front of her. Goodie-two-shoes Noreen, who never put a foot wrong. Here minding Da's pub for him. Orgasms were supposed to be gloriously sinful, but they were only a real sin, a proper sin, if they were with people you weren't going to marry. When was that ever going to happen now? Matthew might even go off travelling the world in the missions, having all sorts of adventures. She would get married in two weeks and...

'NO!'

She shouted it out so suddenly that the three Marys, who had been watching Noreen in bewilderment, all jumped. Sherry-Mary dropped her glass and found it was already empty.

'No, what?' Whisky-Mary asked.

But Noreen didn't reply.

Instead, she went to the back of the bar and shouted up to their barman, Pat, who was in the apartment kitchen, to come downstairs. She untied her apron, went to the end of the bar and lifted it.

'Where are you going?' Black-Mary called.

Noreen pushed past the funeral crowd and said, more to herself than her puzzled audience, 'I'm going to London.'

13

Leaving John was hard. Harder than Noreen thought it would be.

'Does this mean the wedding is off?' His face was full of pained panic. Noreen felt a stabbing in her stomach just looking at him.

'Of course not, John. Don't be ridiculous! I'm just delaying it by a few months.'

That was a lie. Noreen had no intention of coming back any time soon. As soon as the decision had been made Noreen had been able to think of nothing else but getting away. She loved her family, and she loved John but the big lights of London were calling her. It was as if the idea had been there in her heart all along, and it had taken the engagement to bring it to life.

'I need to go away and be independent for a while before I settle down. You understand that, don't you? You had your time off training with the guards in Tipperary.'

'That's hardly the same thing as running off to London to do God knows what!'

'It's something I need to do, John. I've never been outside

Carney in all my life. I just need to have my own adventure. Then I'll be back.'

John didn't look convinced.

'What do you mean by adventure?'

He knew exactly what she meant and so did she. Afraid she might actually put words to it, John changed the subject.

'London's a dangerous city. You won't be safe.'

It was an unconvincing argument. Noreen was the most capable person he knew. She would be fine without him. They both knew that, too.

'I'll be grand. Lara's there. She can show me the ropes.'

'Does she know you're coming?'

It would not have surprised John for Noreen to go chasing off to London on her own. Despite seeming like a sensible girl, his fiancée was prone to giving in to flights of fancy – like making love before they were married. That was when this whole going to London nonsense had started. It was his fault for showing her what lay ahead. They should have waited until after the wedding. He should have held off. He should have said no to her. He was a weak fool, no wonder she was running from him. Thank goodness her father had tipped him off the day before. He was worried, John supposed, that he might lose his temper, although John would never have done that. He imagined Frank had been furious, but he was as wrapped around Noreen's finger as much as John was. Frank had promised he would cancel the priest to spare John the embarrassment. Really, it was Noreen he was sparing.

'We'll defer it for a few months anyway, John. She's her mind made up, and you know what she's like. Best let her go. She'll be back soon enough.'

John consoled himself that Frank knew his daughter. Then

remembered that Frank didn't know they'd had sex. He certainly didn't know about the orgasms.

'When will you be back?'

Noreen looked at John, and her heart filled up. Was she crazy, leaving this fine man?

John's physical strength and practical approach to life made him an excellent guard. The week before, he and Sergeant Gerry had been on patrol and found Skinny McHale, who had drunkenly fallen off his bike a mile from his own house. Inaccessible by car. Gerry told Noreen how John had thrown Skinny over one shoulder, his bike over the other and walked them both across the bog. Skinny's wife had been in the next day complaining that they hadn't left him to rot in the ditch so that she could claim a lucrative widow's pension. Gerry, who had trained and lived for a while in New York, confided in Noreen that it broke his heart seeing John's talents going to waste in this rural backwater.

John himself didn't seem to mind. He did not have any illusions about his job or his life. John knew he was good at his job because he was strong, sensible and reliable. The same qualities that would make him an excellent husband. Of course, like all country guards, he said he would love a good murder or some proper crime to sink his teeth into, but he didn't have any notions about going abroad looking for it. John was happy enough with his life: picking up drunks from the side of the road, ushering people around funerals, checking up on car tax for the five people that owned cars in the village, bothering the odd illegal pitching distillery that operated in the mountains and making sure that the local publicans were discreet enough not to get caught after hours of drinking. If it seemed pedestrian to some, well then that was fine by him because, to be honest, he got all the excitement he needed being engaged to Noreen Lyons and keeping her out of trouble.

And now, Noreen knew she was taking that away from him.

Why was she doing this to lovely John? Sitting in her parents' kitchen, with a mug of tea on the range beside him and his guard cap in his lap, he was clearly sorry for himself. All six foot two of him was sagging, his long limbs collapsed into her father's chair, the fine square head and big chest all crumpled up. Part of Noreen longed to curl herself up into his lap and stay there forever. But her mind was made up. This was something she had to do. The ticket was booked. She was going. If she had to look at John's face for much longer she was in danger of changing her mind, so she drew a deep breath and said as coldly as she could.

'I don't know.'

She would not be pressured to stay. This was her decision, her life.

'Noreen.'

He said her name like a poem, searching her face. His eyes were begging her to stay without saying anything out loud. She could reach out, take him upstairs to the bedroom and make all this go away. But Noreen was determined.

'I see,' he said. She could have reassured him. But she couldn't lie.

John stood up, put his cap on and reached the door. 'Take care of yourself, Noreen.'

Noreen heard the subtext – 'Because I won't be there to take care of you'. The snide implication ignited a small spark of fury. It gave her the determination she needed to face the gruelling coach, boat and train journey that would take her to London.

✸

Noreen arrived at Euston station in the late afternoon. As she walked through the station concourse she found herself among hundreds of people rushing past each other in straight lines. Each person was different from the next: a man in a pinstripe suit with a bowler hat and briefcase, a young woman in a skirt so short it looked like she was running about in her pants, an older woman wearing a smart suit with a pillbox hat and gloves like she was going to a wedding. A cockney man was shouting, 'Ee'ning Stannit!' while he waved newspapers in the air at passers-by. Some handed him a shilling and snatched a paper out of his hands with scarcely an acknowledgment. A man with coal-black skin wearing a bright orange suit sauntered across to the huge clock hanging over their heads. A tall, beautiful woman with long, brown arms in a brightly printed dress ran towards a platform. Noreen stood in the middle of this extraordinary, exotic scene, astonished by the activity around her. All these people, all in a rush to get somewhere, each and every one minding their own business. None of them talking to each other. She had never seen anything like it. There she was, a suitcase at her feet, clearly a stranger in town, yet nobody stopped to ask if she was alright. The very idea was ludicrous. For the first time in her life, Noreen was invisible. Anonymous. It was a strange feeling. She wasn't sure if she liked it.

Noreen hadn't eaten since a rather unpleasant sandwich on the boat and was absolutely starving. She thought about finding a cafe and having a fry up but then decided against it. She had best go and find Lara first.

Noreen had not contacted Lara and told her she was coming. She was afraid Lara might have moved from the address she had from her last letter six months ago. They had been great friends while she was dating Matthew and for a while after he had let her down, Lara had stayed in touch regularly. When she arrived in London Lara had taken great care to let Noreen know how well she was doing. She wrote her long letters telling her about her exciting new life and glamorous job.

I'm working in a nightclub – can you believe it? You should come over, Noreen! Coleman is always looking for good people to work behind the bar.

Noreen had paid no notice then but the seed had been planted and now she had come to reap the harvest. Lara was always going to do well for herself, Noreen had never had any doubt about that. Lara just had that ambition in her. She always pushed Noreen as well, reading between the lines of her chirpy letters. Noreen was well aware that this was partly in hope that she relay the message to her brother; that he would know how well Lara was doing, that she was utterly over him. But Noreen could tell Lara wasn't happy without Matthew. Not really. Because Lara had been head over heels in love with him. Literally daft about him. It was painful to watch. Publicly, Noreen crucified her brother for dumping such a brilliant, attractive woman. Privately, she knew her twin brother better than he knew himself. Lara was not his soulmate and never had been. Lara was fantastic, but she was too much for Matthew. Too passionate, too artistic, too ambitious – too much of everything. She dwarfed him. As much as it pained Noreen to admit it, the love had never been mutual. Matthew had been right to leave her when he had before getting shoehorned into a marriage that would have made him unhappy. Although the priest thing? That was something else. Matthew's vocation was still a mystery to Noreen. In truth, it was that which had driven a wedge between them more than his leaving Lara. Noreen liked to know what was going on. She certainly didn't like being kept out of the loop with people she was close to. Not knowing something so fundamental about her own twin, being told about his vocation alongside everyone else, had been humiliating and hurtful. She was still furious with him. Not calling Lara to tell her that she was coming was more a reflection of her estrangement from Matthew than her fear of being rejected by his ex-girlfriend.

She dug Lara's letter out of her bag and checked the address.

Kings Road, Chelsea. She had no idea where that was and did not feel like asking anyone, so she walked out of the station and hailed down a black, London taxi.

Driving through the London streets, past the Houses of Parliament and Big Ben, made Noreen feel like she was in a film. Her excitement peaked, shredding into nerves as the taxi driver let her off outside a huge, red-bricked building. A glossy, studded black leather door had a gold plate to the side of it that read CHEVRONS.

'Do you know where you're going from here?' the cab driver asked. He seemed somewhat sceptical when she gave him the address. Now he seemed a little nervous about leaving her here.

Insulted by his assumption that she didn't know where she was going, Noreen snapped, 'Of course.' She threw two pound notes in his tray, then said with a great flourish, 'keep the change!'

When he drove off, she stood for a few moments outside the ridiculous-looking door looking for a bell or a knocker. She found neither. She knew that Lara lived above the club, but the building seemed vast, with dozens of windows, and she had no idea how to even get upstairs. She checked her watch and saw that it was seven o'clock. The club had to be open. Anywhere that sold alcohol would be up and running by six at the latest. So she started to bang.

Ironing Board Arthur was stuck on his own in Chevrons. All the staff, even Coleman, had gone to the opening of Lara's new boutique. The shop was sure to be filled with beautiful women and Arthur was left behind holding the fort. As usual. The wiry, balding forty year old was Coleman's muscle. Anyone who didn't know him might have mistaken Arthur for a fool. He wasn't pretty and his overly polite, convivial manner tended to earn him mockery from those who did not know him. Customs had already been in today, sniffing around, asking questions about the provenance of the whisky. Coleman was not happy – and if Bobby Chevron found out, there would be big trouble. Drawing attention to the little things was how you got caught for the big things. Coleman liked a handy price but the goods had to be above board. The bloke that had been supplying them with their cut-price spirits needed the frighteners put on him and he was due in that afternoon to get his cash. Brian, the bar manager, had been sent home. They didn't involve him in any dirty work. That's the way it was at Chevrons. Everything above board. Everything nice and tidy. Unless you were in the know, and then things could get a little messy. That was what Arthur was there for. Cleaning up the messy stuff.

Arthur heard a banging from upstairs. Stupid prick was early to collect his money. Quickly, he chose a cricket bat from his collection of weapons behind the door at the bottom of the maroon-carpeted staircase that led down from the club. With a bit of luck the sight of the bat, in addition to Arthur's mad face, would be enough to get this guy to talk. He wasn't in the mood for a fight. It was a bit early yet. Arthur did a bit of fast, shallow breathing – in out, in out – to get himself worked up. Then he ran up the stairs, pumping up the adrenalin. That fella was pounding at the door. The police would be coming if he got much louder. 'Shut the fuck up,' Arthur hissed as he opened the door, reached out and pulled in... a bird.

Not a bird like Shirley or Ethel either. But an actual woman-bird. Like an ordinary bird. A wife-type bird.

Arthur yelped and his hands flew off her as if she was emitting electricity. Which, with the unexpected sudden man-handling he had given her, Noreen practically was.

'Hey!' she said. 'There is no need for that!'

Arthur was speechless with embarrassment. 'What do you want?' he demanded, angrier than he intended.

'Well you're a charmer aren't you? Planning a game of cricket?'

Here was a real live cockney gangster, brandishing a cricket bat. How thrilling! It never occurred to Noreen that she should be scared. She had been manoeuvring large, gun-toting alcoholic farmers out of her father's pub since she was fourteen. This odd-looking whippet and his cricket bat were no problem to her.

Arthur mouthed soundlessly at her. Noreen shook her head.

'Not much of a talker, are you? Didn't your mother teach you any manners?'

He found his tongue. 'Don't have a mother.'

'Don't be ridiculous. Everyone has a mother.' Arthur gave her a nasty, dead-eyed look then shrugged. He had torn through a man's skull for saying less. With an ironing board in the prison laundry. It was where he got his unique handle.

'Somebody should teach you some manners. Your father?'

'Don't have no father either.'

Noreen tried to look him straight in the eye. Arthur looked away and she followed his head around as he avoided her. No mother? No father?

'Siblings?'

'No.' Arthur was feeling uncomfortable. What sort of a game was this?

Noreen sighed, giving him a steady gaze. 'That is terrible.'

Arthur agreed. It was terrible. He suddenly had an overwhelming urge to cry but swallowed it back instead and barked, 'What do you want?'

'Are you Coleman?' she asked.

'No,' he said. Arthur felt a small delight at being mistaken for his suave boss. 'He's not here.'

'Never mind. I'm actually looking for my friend rather than him. Lara?'

A friend of Lara. She must be alright then. Some of the English girls took Lara as a bit snooty, but Arthur liked her. She was posh, and Irish, which was a weird combination, but there was no point in holding either of those things against her. Also, Coleman was in love with her. He never said it, but he was. Arthur watched. He could tell. But it wasn't fair to hold that against her either. It wasn't like she was asking for it. Since she had started working there, about six months ago now, the place had changed. The fashion crowd had started frequenting Chevrons. Men in polo necks and brightly coloured trousers. It wasn't Arthur's scene but the arty crowd were no trouble and that made his job easier. Also, Lara was nice to him. She treated him like a proper person, not like some of the other girls. They knew he was a bit soft with women so they took the piss. Especially Shirley, who looked down her nose at him and made him run about, getting her fags, picking up her washing and that. Lara was running a business, making clothes as well as working in the club, and she never made him do anything for her. She even offered him cups of tea, and sometimes that nice girl she lived with, who worked in the cafe across the road, gave him free dinners. Now Coleman had given her money to open one of them fashion boutiques. Shirley was jealous but it served her right. Lara deserved some success. She was a bloody hard worker.

'Lara's not here either. I'd take you over to her but...'

'You're expecting someone.' Noreen smiled and nodded at the cricket bat. *This is so bad*, Noreen thought, being thrilled by the certain knowledge that a terrible act of violence was about to be perpetrated. *He 'ad it comin'* she said to herself.

Really, it was like she was in that film, *The Wrong Arm of the Law*, that she had seen in Carney picture house last week. This little man was a crabby version of Peter Sellers. Well. That may be a stretch – but still – she was in London! It was all so exciting.

'Lara's having a party down the road,' he said. 'I can tell you where it is but like I said...'

'You've got business to attend to.'

She said it gently. Mocking him a little, but in a kind, soft way.

Arthur beamed at her, which was actually a little terrifying. He then explained how to get to Lara's new shop, That Girl, which was just a few doors down on the Kings Road.

He noted that Lara's friend wasn't exactly dressed for a party but she didn't seem to mind. The suitcase meant she would be hanging around for a while, maybe staying with Lara in the flat upstairs. Arthur didn't know if that was a bad or a good thing. As he watched her portly frame disappear down the Kings Road, he decided on the latter.

14

Lara Collins looked around her shop. Her shop. It was the opening of That Girl, the Kings Road's latest and, she hoped, hippest fashion boutique. People would be arriving in less than an hour and everything had to be perfect.

Hip-skimming miniskirts in brightly coloured leatherette were arranged on a pegboard display at the door, pages torn from *Vogue* magazine scattered between them. In front were rails, neatly hung with her designs – brightly coloured floral and sexy baby-doll micro dresses. There were a dozen pairs of white and yellow ankle boots that she had to have shipped over from Italy, and a long wooden table piled with candy coloured twinsets and jazzy hand-printed silk scarves neatly folded into their necklines. On another rail she had set up twenty see-through plastic mac coats which had a customised That Girl logo emblazoned across the back.

Lara felt confident that her relationship with Coleman was on firm, business grounds. In providing backing for this Kings Road boutique venture, he was her business partner. The deal worked both ways. Coleman was not a fool who would give money to a girl because he fancied her. Lara knew he felt he was lucky to have her to run this business for him. She had brought the fashion crowd into his club. The designers, photographers and models had given Chevrons the kind of clean, glamorous image that its grubby gangster notoriety needed. Now Coleman was going to make plenty of money out of her shop with his and Chevron's 70 per cent cut. Lara had been delighted with the offer at the time, but now that the novelty had worn off and after a few months of putting in such gruelling work, it was beginning to smart that two men who had contributed, essentially, nothing (except money) owned such a big part of That Girl. Regardless of that, it was still her shop. Right now, her pipe dream was finally becoming a reality. And dreams, she was discovering, lost their soft edges when reality hit.

Lara's large eyes narrowed in concentration as they ran across every inch of the freshly polished linoleum floor, checking for stray sleeves, dropped hangers or fallen labels. Everything was riding on the next few hours. The broken heart she had left behind in Ireland, the promise she had made to herself never to fall so hard or to love like that again – led her to this moment. Everything had to be perfect.

Lara walked to the back of the shop, where she had hung up a selection of exquisite bouclé suits in shades of candy pink and green. While she was confident that her groovy, eye-catching window display would bring customers in the door it was also important that the more sedate, conventional women were catered for. Not all women wanted to show off their bodies or be so overtly mod, and having been raised an Irish Catholic, she understood that better than anyone. Some women wanted to be Jackie Kennedy. She had decided that some of the shop should reflect that vibe, and so the dressing room was deliberately old-fashioned in a lavish Hollywood style, with gilt mirrors, silk curtains and chaise longues. It was deliberately anti-unisex hip.

The sixties had heralded a trend in fashion which allowed women to show off their bodies. They were no longer expected to look demure and sophisticated, but could be young, sexy and free. Lara enjoyed the freedom that gave her as a designer but she also saw a harsher side emerging through Chevrons. While the waitresses enjoyed wearing the short sexy costumes she had designed, they were no less susceptible to the gropes and leering of the men. If anything, short skirts were giving a certain type of man permission to take any girl he fancied. Unisex boutiques were currently all the rage, and with so many tailors in the area it would have made sense to go down that route. But Lara wanted That Girl to be a place of glamorous refuge as well as an up-to-date boutique. A place where women, whether they were confident or shy, could enjoy dressing up and being 'That Girl' without men looking at them.

Lara moved across to a rail of her trademark miniskirts and, for the hundredth time, carefully adjusted the last hanger, checking it was exactly three finger widths apart from the one either side. As she did she spotted an infinitesimal thread from the edge of a cotton label and yanked it away. The labels had been a week late, only arriving in the workroom late yesterday afternoon. She had cut them off the roll herself and stayed up all night sewing them onto every item. Her fingers were calloused and pin-pricked to ribbons. But it had been worth it. Her brand. Her label. 'That Girl' it read, in flowery, italic script.

She smiled to herself. Soon, every fashionable hipster in London would be wearing a That Girl mini. She was sure of it.

She was still shocked that she had pulled it off. A girl from Cork city, who had arrived in London with nothing but broken dreams and a sewing machine. She had made it, although, admittedly, Coleman had more than helped. Still, fashion was big business these days and he would get his cut back in no time.

'Why don't you call it Lara Collins Ladies' Fashions?' he had asked her.

'Don't be ridiculous,' she had laughed.

Coleman flinched. He didn't like it when she stood up to him like that, but then, Lara believed, that was the only way to be treated with respect by these English tough guys. You had to put them in their place. Besides, while she dressed all the It girls in Chelsea, Lara did not want to be one herself. She was an artist, a fashion designer and now, with her own shop, a business woman.

She rearranged the price tags making sure that they were all facing outwards. £23.60. Was it too much? Everyone would be coming to this opening. Ladies from the club, models, photographers – all the fun fashion crowd she had brought to the club. Bobby Chevron would also bring the Fleet Street press in full force – hopefully a couple of fashion editors too.

She walked past the refreshments table, laden with pineapple, cheese nibbles, stuffed celery sticks and bottles of Mateus rosé, with a pyramid of TAB cans for the figure conscious. Her flatmate, Annie, had played a blinder. At least the food was a guaranteed success.

Lara walked over to the back wall. It was painted with a huge mural of semi-nude models dancing in silhouette. It was well done and a very up-to-the-minute image but for some reason, it just did not sit right with Lara. It wasn't a proper representation of what she was trying to do with her designs. The creative part of her was so irritated by it that she actually thought of cancelling the whole event for a split second, locking the doors on everyone and starting again. But that was impossible.

'I hate that image,' she said to Annie, who had appeared behind her.

Annie was always as quiet as a mouse. You never heard her come into a room. In the past few months Lara had come to look on Annie as the sister she never had. Annie had created a beautiful home for them both and encouraged Lara in her fashion endeavours in a way that was selfless and sweet. Nonetheless, Lara understood why everybody else found Annie a bit odd. She was old-fashioned, secretive. Demure to the point of nunnish. Despite having the slim figure of a fashion model, she favoured frumpy, old-fashioned clothes that covered her up. She was happier in her grubby fry cook's work tabard than any of the minidresses Lara was always trying to persuade her into.

Annie had come to the opening straight from work, through the tradesman's entrance at the back, placing two trays of Fred's mushroom vol-au-vents down on the refreshments table near the entrance before joining her friend.

'I like it,' disagreed Annie, gazing up at the dancing silhouettes.

'You like everything.'

'That sounds like an insult more than a compliment.'

'It is! You're far too nice. You should be more discerning.'

'We can't all be artistic and brilliant like you, Lara. Some of us have to be content with duller activities, like cooking.'

'Alright, alright. You win. I'll shut up about you having a career and you keep cooking my dinners.'

Annie laughed. She didn't have confidence in many things about herself but she knew that she was one hell of a cook. Since coming to London, Annie's cooking portfolio had expanded from traditional French and now included exotic food like curries and pasta.

'What do you want me to wear?'

Lara looked at her, blank, before remembering that she had asked Annie to model for her that evening. Annie had such a fantastic figure – tall and slender and very much the look of the day. The problem was that she didn't do anything with herself and had no interest in clothes and fashion. Annie's passion was cooking and what she called homemaking. Lara continuously tried to shake her out of her old-fashioned attitude, trying to convince her that modern women didn't cook. Although she also had to admit that it was nice living with somebody who kept the place spotless and cooked delicious meals for her.

In any case, despite having a good face and figure Annie's personality was so awkward and shy that Lara knew she would make a dreadful model. For that reason she had already booked three smashing girls to model for the opening party. They would get paid in dresses and were currently doing their hair and makeup in a local hair salon. In the midst of the craziness over the past few days she had completely forgotten that she had asked Annie to model for her. After all it had been in a throwaway panic a couple of weeks ago.

Annie, however, had not forgotten. She had been terrified at the prospect but Lara had been so kind to her and she was prepared to make the sacrifice for her friend. She owed her that. In fact, she owed her a lot more. No amount of cooking and cleaning could ever repay Lara for the friendship she had extended to her. She had taken her into her home, got her a job and treated her with such kindness – with no questions asked.

So Annie stood expectantly while Lara felt a pang of guilt at having forgotten her offer.

'Put this on,' she said, grabbing a bouclé suit from a nearby rail. Annie rummaged in her bag for some lipstick and Lara stiffened. With horror she realised that in the flurry of preparing the shop to perfection, she had not done the same for herself. She looked up at the large clock above the front counter – it was time! The models would be coming up the steps to the door any second, and the press would be right behind them.

She grabbed another jacket from one of the bouclé suits for herself, throwing it over her pedal pushers and sweater, quickly shaking her freshly bobbed hair into place. Then she ran to the door to open it for her first guests.

Annie watched from the dressing room, wondering at the confidence and capability of her beloved friend. Thankfully, nothing more seemed to be expected of her than to wear this lovely suit and stay in the background.

The launch went better than Lara could possibly have expected. The place was thronged with people, the models looked great and she could hear the till pinging as That Girl bags went flying out the door. For the first half hour Lara was so happy with the response and the crowd that she could not stop smiling. But as more and more people arrived she started to worry that they would run out of food – and clothes! A vague panic began to wash through her smile. She had already run out of cigarettes and now needed a drink as well. She had seen Annie passing around refreshments five minutes earlier, but she couldn't spot her, likely hiding somewhere in the background as usual. Although it was her party, Lara suddenly started to feel alone in the big crowd. This was her night, but at the same time, it was all on her head. It was somewhat overwhelming, and there was nobody there to share that with. Of course, she and Annie would talk about it later but it wasn't the same as having somebody there to share the moment itself. Whenever she felt alone in London, Lara's thoughts wandered in only one direction... home. And to only one person. Matthew. 'I love God more than I love you.' What did that even mean? Not just pain. Rage.

But, no. Not now. This was not the time or the place for her fury at Matthew to surface. She took a deep breath, shook her head and brushed the thought aside. She would not let the past ruin her big night. She was a different person now. She had a different, better life.

Lara looked around for Coleman but he was nowhere to be seen. What kind of a useless business partner was he? He always had cigarettes on him and she was the hostess and couldn't be seen getting her own drinks. She should have hired two more waiters. It was stupid to think Annie would be able to handle all this without more help.

As she moved towards the door, Lara noticed that the front two rails, the ones featuring her signature baby-doll dresses, were already empty.

One of them was in the bag of the woman walking towards her. With dawning fear Lara saw it was Penelope Podmore, Women's Editor of the *Daily Mail*, and terror of the London fashion scene.

'I love your work.' Penelope Podmore held out her hand, cooing at Lara.

She was intimidating, an elegant woman well into her forties, whose weekly fashion column could make or break a designer. She had a photographer with her. A small, wiry man whose camera looked like it was weighing him down.

'Alex is from our newsroom,' she said with great disdain. The small man smiled at Lara and shrugged apologetically. 'He has been going around taking shots of the models for our weekly page – but we'd like to get a picture of you as well.'

'Of course,' Lara said, nodding and smiling as best as she could manage. She was terrified. Utterly overawed. A picture for Penelope Podmore's page! Was she even wearing lipstick?

'Just let me call one of the models over to stand with me.' Lara quickly looked around the room for Annie. She was wearing one of the pink suits – she would be perfect.

As Alex fiddled with his camera, loading film and making a great fuss of checking the lens, Penelope lit a cigarette and smoked, seemingly bored waiting.

'I love the name – That Girl. But who is she exactly? There are a few rumours flying around about this place. About where exactly that Irish girl got the money to open a big shop like this on the Kings Road?'

Lara was only half listening, her eyes frantically scanning the room. Where was Annie? Had she gone out for more food? Lara's eyes moved across the shop, her head craning through the crowds, then – stopping dead at the door in a sudden shock.

'Is there a rich Paddy daddy? Or, my editor wants to know if Bobby Chevron himself is behind the whole thing?'

Penelope's words receded into background babble. Lara didn't hear a word. Standing at the door of That Girl, suitcase at her flat feet, plump legs poking out from the bottom of a worn, brown coat, looking around her in awed wonder was Noreen Lyons. Matthew's twin sister.

15

Coleman adjusted his tie and ran his finger under his crisp white spread collar so that it sat neatly just inside the lapel of his grey worsted suit. The shirt was homage to his new position as a fashion impresario. The infinitesimal nod to changing fashions was unlikely to impress Lara, but there was only so much he could do.

Coleman did not like change.

He was often courted by rival gangs; some said he was a fool to stay working for Chevron. Coleman was the one with the smarts and the natural authority. Bobby was a nutter. He should go out on his own. But he was loyal. Coleman carried Molly Chevron's coffin shoulder to shoulder with her son when she died three years ago.

Bobby had turned nasty after his mother passed. Beat Maureen so badly he put her in hospital, twice. He was sorry afterwards. Chevron was always very sorry. Coleman could not turn away from him. The Chevrons had given Coleman stability and he had come to value that above all else. Coleman kept things the same. He slept in his office in the same spirit with which he had slept in Molly's kitchen; it kept him alert, watchful.

No. Coleman did not like change.

Finding true love with Irish Lara would be the biggest change of his life. He could not let himself fall.

Coleman had been fighting back the impulse to take Irish Lara into his arms and hold her there forever for the last six months. But even if he had the courage, he didn't have the will. Lara was educated, beautiful – she was no gangster's moll. She deserved better than him. Once, he had heard, she had been engaged to a priest. Even if he could find the courage within himself to make a move, she would never consider loving a man like him. It would be wrong to even try.

And so, Coleman kept his feelings under wraps. In her company, Coleman showed no signs of having any feelings for her whatsoever.

He took a last drag of his cigarette and, grinding it under his Grenson brogue, was opening the door to go in when he heard a call from behind him.

'Coleman!'

Ethel and one of the younger girls were running up the road, their high shoes clicking on the pavement, making a beeline for him.

Both women sighed inwardly as they saw their handsome boss wait – chin set, eyes narrowed against the smoke of his cigarette, an impervious rock of be-suited masculinity outside the frivolous, pink-fronted shop front. The words 'That Girl', in large, italic type sat directly above his head like an invitation.

Ethel was glad Shirley wasn't here to see this. As soon as news hit that Coleman was opening the boutique with Lara, Shirley booked a holiday. She didn't bother telling Ethel where she was going. She hardly told her anything any more. Ethel had been on Shirley's side for ages after Coleman dumped her. She felt so sorry for Shirley married to that brute of a husband, coming into work with bruises, always covering them up and smiling for the punters. Even though all the girls fancied Coleman, she had been glad when Shirley hooked up with him. However, the affair had only lasted a few weeks. That was a shame but, afterwards, Shirley just would not let it go. She kept blaming 'that Irish bitch,' saying she was trying to get Coleman off her, when she never really had him in the first place. Not that Ethel would ever say that to her face. Shirley could be as dangerous as any man if she had a few drinks and a broken glass in her hand. Ethel got sick of Shirley's complaining about the same time Shirley started to pull back from everyone. She went pure hard at work. Came in, did her job and that was it. The only person she spoke to at work was Brian. That suited Ethel. She would never be stupid enough to go near Coleman herself and if he fancied Lara? So what. Lara was all right. And her clothes were great.

'Ladies,' Coleman said to them, treating them to a rare smile. Both women shivered with desire, then they took an arm each and marched him into the shop.

Once inside, Coleman let go of the girls' arms, delivering them chivalrously to the racks and rails of clothes. He looked around the room. Coleman could speed read a room in one sweep. He was anxious to check that Bobby Chevron had not heard about the party from his holiday villa in Spain and turned up, unexpectedly. This was Lara's night and Chevrons larger-than-life owner had a way taking over. Although, Coleman had other more serious reasons for not wanting Bobby here tonight. Coleman had negotiated a cut of the shop from Lara and given her the impression they were partners; Chevron had provided the setup money and the building. Technically, Bobby Chevron owned That Girl. There was no other way Lara would ever be able to afford a shop on the Kings Road.

So, Coleman had approached Bobby. He did not think of it as a lie. He had simply seen a way of making Lara's dream happen for her and gone for it. There was nothing wrong with subterfuge when your motives were clean. Coleman had made Lara happy and that made him pleased. She need never know any different.

Once he established the coast was clear, Coleman's eyes searched for Lara. She was standing by the back wall, surrounded by people. He barely had the chance to appraise her when Lara looked towards the door and their eyes locked. He read her expression and saw that there was something wrong. Coleman's stomach tightened as he immediately set off across the room towards her. Had someone said something to her? Despite his worry, Coleman felt a tinge of satisfaction that, despite the crowds hanging off her tonight, Lara had been looking out for him.

When Lara saw her old friend Noreen standing in the door of her new shop, she froze. Worlds collided; the grey, black and white world of her past, her ordinary childhood in Cork, her first kiss, with Matthew, at the Town Hall dance, college in Dublin all led to that awful evening, with Matthew standing on the steps of her student hostel. In that moment of seeing Noreen in her drab, brown coat, the technicoloured joy of Lara's sparkling new life seemed to drain out of her.

But then a most unexpected thing happened. As larger-than-life Noreen launched herself across the room and hugged Lara, lifting her slightly off the ground, the painful memory evaporated as quickly as it had come.

'Yay – Missis – it's good to see you!'

'Noreen.' Lara tried not to sound shocked or look too upset then remembered, with a smile, that it didn't matter. Noreen had skin as thick as a bull's hide. 'What are you doing here?'

Noreen looked fit to explode.

'I've moved to London! Can you BELIEVE IT?'

'How did you find me?'

'With your address, stupid! Actually, I called into Chevrons,' Noreen said it like she had lived here all her life. 'A man with a face like a spanner told me about the party.'

Ironing Board Arthur. It felt strange hearing Noreen reference her world. Funny, outspoken, resolutely Irish and deeply unfashionable Noreen was really here. In London. Smack, bang in the middle of her new life. This was the thing she had most dreaded and yet, it didn't feel as bad as she had feared it would. Still, Lara and Noreen had not seen each other since before she and Matthew broke up. They exchanged letters but their deep friendship seemed to dissolve in the back draft of Lara's heartbreak. What was she doing here?

Noreen noticed Penelope Podmore who was standing with her arms crossed, smoking intently, eyes narrowed as she looked Noreen and Lara up and down, drinking it all in. Lara grimaced inwardly. She had forgotten where she was. This was why she had wanted to keep the past at bay. Before she had the chance to rectify the situation Noreen stepped in.

'I'm Noreen,' she said, holding out her hand, 'this wan's oldest friend. Who are you?'

Penelope raised her eyebrows in answer.

'This is Ms Podmore,' Lara said. Penelope's haughty expression glittered with furious shock as Noreen vigorously shook her manicured hand. 'Penelope is the fashion editor of the *Daily Mail*,' Lara added hopefully, trying to keep the note of desperation out of her voice.

That meant nothing to Noreen. This was a disaster, after all.

'Well, if it's fashion you're after, Lara here is yer only woman. What's a girl got to do to get a drink around here?

I don't suppose there's any grub to be had. I'm famished. All I got was a pork pie on the boat and it was red-rotten.'

Penelope bared her teeth in an attempt at a smile and was clearly about to move on. She didn't 'do' gauche and she certainly didn't 'do' gauche Irish.

Lara looked around desperately for a distraction and saw the answer walk in the door. Coleman had just arrived. Lara felt a snap of irritation tinged with an irrational feeling of disappointment as his eyes scanned past her across the room, before resting back on her face again. He acknowledged her signal and by the time Lara had said, 'Ah, Penelope. I'd love you to meet my business partner,' he was already walking across the room towards them.

'Hot to trot!' Noreen said, barely under her breath, but Penelope didn't notice. She was already adjusting herself. Her hands raised to smooth the hair at her ears, her lips parted, her back straightened and the fashion editor's eyes widened with flirtatious delight as Coleman joined their company.

'Coleman, this is Penelope Podmore from the *Daily Mail*.'

'Please to meet you, Penelope,' he said. Unsmiling but not unfriendly.

'So, Coleman, tell me,' Penelope leaned into him, blowing a stream of smoke just past his ear, 'are you the rich Paddy daddy behind That Girl? You're certainly not Irish in a suit like that.'

Noreen was waiting for her introduction but Lara dragged her off to the bar.

'This is Annie,' Lara said, introducing her, instead, to her flatmate. 'Your boss for the evening. Take off that horrible coat and put this on.' She thrust a bouclé jacket in an unfashion-ably large size at her.

'Does this mean I have a job?' Noreen said.

'No,' Lara answered firmly. 'This is you singing for your supper and earning the right to crash at our pad tonight.'

Noreen grinned, forced her arms through the narrow sleeves of the jacket and grabbed a tray of canapés before the second arm was through. Lara could not help smiling. Why Noreen was here didn't matter. Their friendship had never ended, after all. Only paused and in less than ten minutes they were back where they started.

Lara was pleased to see Noreen but she had to get back to business. She had a clothes line to get into the paper!

The photographer, Alex, was hovering near the door looking like he was running out of things to snap. Lara frantically searched the room for one of the models but could not see one. Checking her watch she realised they had been booked for an hour and the party had been underway for over two now. Lara's eyes moved across the room, and finally fell on poor Annie, invisible to all, just heading off with a tray. She was wearing one of the pink suits – she would have to do.

Annie did not want to have her picture taken, but Lara made her stand beside her for a few shots. When they were done Alex insisted on taking Annie over to the wall with the logo on it and arranging her in front of it, encouraging her to pose this way and that. Considering how much she loathed being photographed, Lara thought she did quite a good job. The whole process took less than ten minutes.

Alex left, saying, 'Good luck with Po-faced Podmore!'

Annie went back to her catering duties.

When Lara returned to Coleman, he was still struggling to make conversation with the aloof Penelope although there was a lascivious edge to her eye that told Lara she was enjoying Coleman's rugged charm and proximity to his suave appearance, if nothing else.

'Well, dear Lara – it seems you have fallen on your feet with this delightful man. He was telling me all about how clever and talented you are. He quite thinks the world of you.' The implication being that she was still somewhat less than impressed herself.

However, as she said it, Coleman took a sip from his glass, looked Lara straight in the eye and smiled. There was not a hint of irony. Only intent. Despite herself, Lara shivered. She shook it off. Not Coleman. No way.

'I'm afraid I'm not in with a chance,' Penelope purred, looking pleadingly at Coleman, willing him to contradict her. He gave the editor a noncommittal smirk that could be taken one way or the other.

Penelope, hot under the collar now, put down her glass to light a cigarette. Lara felt slightly giddy. With Penelope distracted, Lara gave Coleman a look that said, 'You're good.'

He gave her one back that said, 'I know.'

Then he smiled at her and she smiled back, and there was a moment when it felt as if they were alone in the room.

Both were grateful when Penelope returned to the conversation with her lit cigarette.

16

Back at their flat, the three girls celebrated That Girl's success. Lara had finally relaxed after the adrenalin of the launch and, as the wine took over, felt the warm pull of home from her old friend.

'Do you remember that time we climbed over the wall to the Bishop's palace?'

'Stealing apples and they were pure sour!'

'We never got caught though.'

'And the old sod glaring at you under the mitre during your confirmation then? I swear he recognised you.'

'Stop! I pure bust myself laughing at it in the back of mass for weeks afterwards!'

Annie was amazed how Lara's accent became more pronounced when she was talking to Noreen. They spoke in the same voice. Like real sisters.

She might have been jealous but in fact was simply a fascinated audience to their stories about teenage parties – skinny dipping in the stream at the back of Lara's house, boys they liked, pranks they played – the fun to be had being young and carefree! It was something that Annie had never experienced, but in the delight of listening to these two entertaining friends, she felt happy and grateful to be experiencing it, now, through their telling.

Lara, too, was enjoying Noreen's company. So much so that she forgot she was Matthew's sister. But then that was the way it had always been. She had known and loved Noreen even before she and Matthew had fallen in love, aged fifteen. When Matthew's name did come up that night, briefly and anecdotally, in the minor role he had played in some prank, Noreen was careful to shut it down.

Lara was grateful for her sensitivity, but at the same time could not help wondering if there was a special reason behind her doing that. Because, of course, a part of Lara wanted to know where he was and how he was doing. Did the priesthood suit him? Had he asked about her? Did he know that Noreen was coming to see her in London? Noreen volunteered nothing, which Lara read as polite discretion. Not a usual trait of Noreen's, but it reflected how deeply she knew Lara felt her brother's loss. Lara did not like to think Noreen felt sorry for her so she made a point of not asking and revealing herself as caring about him. Because, Lara had stopped caring. At least she thought she had. Hoped she had. And finally, was determined to have done.

'You must stay here with us,' she said, after it was way too late for Noreen to find anywhere else.

'I fully intend to!'

'For as long as you like.'

'Of course!'

Annie flinched and hoped that Noreen didn't notice. She was still nervous of meeting new people, especially people from Ireland, always fearful they would make some connection with her past. But she liked Noreen, and she loved how the ebullient

Cork girl had shown her a different side of her beloved Lara. Reluctant to talk about herself, she had never asked Lara about her life and so knew very little about Lara up to now.

Late in the evening Noreen finally turned to Annie and said, 'Look at us, babbling on. Tell us about you. Annie what? Where from? How, who, where etc?'

Annie gave her the brief information she had carefully rehearsed.

'My name is Annie Austen. I'm an orphan. My mother was Irish – my father English. They died in a car crash. I was raised in a convent and I came to London a few months ago.'

Noreen smiled, waiting for her to continue. But she didn't.

'That's it?'

'That's it.' Annie smiled awkwardly, trying not to look nervous.

'Seriously?'

'Yes. That's all there is.'

'Right. Fair enough, so,' Noreen said. 'That's you done; let's get back to talking about us. Do you remember the time Buckly cycled across the bridge wall...'

Annie felt a surge of gratitude to Noreen for letting her off the hook. She was so much fun and Annie decided she liked her as much as she liked Lara.

When they had worn through their entire childhood Lara and Noreen agreed that the past was gone.

'The future!' Noreen said, raising a glass of Blue Nun.

'The present!' Lara chimed with a bottle of Cinzano.

Annie knew she was part of their present, pouring out their wine and bringing them food. She felt the privilege of new friendship warm her.

'I'm here to stay,' said Noreen. 'I'm fed up with Carney. Too small. I want to spread my wings,' she said flailing her arms around drunkenly. Annie laughed, and moved the Blue Nun bottle before she tipped it over. 'I want adventure, excitement – MEN!'

'You'll find plenty of them in Chevrons,' Lara assured her, 'but not one decent one.'

'Good. I'm fed up to the back teeth with decent men. I want some INDECENT ones!'

Then she looked over her glass directly at Lara and said, coquettishly, 'Coleman seems very nice.'

Lara flinched. Did she mean for Noreen or her? Noreen was too drunk to notice her friend's discomfort, but Annie did. Coleman liked Lara. She had seen it in the way he looked at her. Would they ever get together, she wondered. What would happen if they did? What would happen to her?

Lara changed the subject by looking at her watch.

'Jesus Christ, it's two o'clock in the morning. I have to get up in a few hours to open the new shop.'

'I'll sleep here.' Noreen lay down, drunkenly, half-asleep already.

'You can stay in my room,' Annie said.

'No,' Lara said. 'She's my friend she should have my room. I'll kip in the studio.'

'Your friend is my friend,' said Annie. 'This is your apartment; you need your own space. Come on,' she said looking across at lumpy Noreen, open mouthed and snoring on the sofa, 'help me get her into bed.'

Alex Cohen took the final print out of the fixer tray, clipped it onto the print line and sighed miserably. More pictures of some pointless party to add to his growing collection of rubbish work.

Alex had been trying to break into the fashion world for a year now, with no success. His erstwhile contemporaries, Donovan, Duffy and Bailey had it all sewn up. They had the models, the agency contacts, the press in their pockets and the talent. Alex badly wanted to join them, but loathe though he was to admit it there was still something missing from his work. He knew it lacked that special something, he just didn't know what that something was, or how to get it. So while The Black Trinity (as his feted photographer mates had been named by Norman Parkinson) were busy being celebrities and socialising with actors, musicians and royalty, Alex was scrabbling around for features work at the *Mail*. The news editor had been sending him out to cover glamorous events (at which he always hoped he wouldn't bump into one of the lads) and the closest he got to a fashion shoot in months was this boutique opening with Po-faced Podmore. As he picked the first of the dry prints to check over, he could not have felt more thoroughly miserable. The picture was, as he was expecting, a perfectly competent capturing of a girl in a minidress. The next one, two girls in minidresses standing next to a rack of clothes. Next, Penelope Podmore draped over some good-looking gangster in a suit. (It was her good side. That would guarantee him the next gig, whether he wanted it or not.) Three little-known pop singers drinking wine, the girl who owned the shop standing next to her shy, skinny friend then a print of the friend posing in front of a logo wall. Alex stopped. He looked at this last picture again. The girl had an expression on her face that he could not identify. She looked soft and vulnerable but there was something defiant – not in her eyes, but behind them. He tried to remember what she was like, but all he could drum up was that she was unremarkable. Shy. A reluctant model. Alex had to push her to move at all in the suit. But looking at her now he could see that this girl was astonishingly beautiful. Perfect, in fact. Large, doe-like eyes, long, thick auburn hair, a button nose, high cheekbones, a sharp chin, flawlessly symmetrical features. She could certainly give Jean Shrimpton a run for her money. Alex carried the picture into another room to check that his hunch was not simply some darkroom trick. As he looked at the picture under daylight, adrenalin began fixing through him. This picture had the thing that had been missing from his work. The girl in the picture was That Girl, alright. Alex carefully placed the picture of the girl in his satchel, then gathered up the other prints and threw them on the picture editor's desk on his way out the door. With a bit of luck, he wouldn't be back here again.

'He's dead. He's dead.' Five months later, that single thought still woke Annie up every morning. The words were still in her head but had she said them out loud? In a panic she looked down and saw that her new bed mate, Noreen, was still snoring. She had not thought about the danger of this happening when she offered to share her bed with Lara's old friend. During the day, these days, she did not think of Dorian at all. When Irish Hanna became London Annie she forced herself to forget what had happened. Her happy life here, living and looking after Lara and her work at Fred's helped her forge a new identity. But the truth of what she had done persisted. It revisited her while she slept and Annie woke up, every morning, filled with that same hellish dread of being caught out. And so, every day she re-ran the scenes in her head. Reassuring herself. Remembering. Annie learned how to lie to other people. Dorian taught her that. But she could not lie to herself.

She got out of bed and walked over to the window to look down onto the early morning quietness of the broad street. With a deep breath, she closed her eyes and took herself back to that day, five months ago in Ireland.

Dorian's lifeless body. Lift his hand, check he's dead. Blind panic. Suitcase. Desk. Running through the bog. All the way to Fred's cafe and her new family. Although they would never be her family. Not truly. Because she was a liar. Lara had given her a life. The life of Annie Austen. It wasn't her real life. Not as long as she had to reassure herself by remembering. With every passing day, she hoped to belong to it more. But hope, she learned long ago, in the days when she hoped the nuns, somebody, anybody, would come and rescue her from Dorian, was sometimes little more than an empty promise from a cruel God. Nonetheless, she had learned to live in the moment. And in this moment, she was in London and safe.

Annie opened her eyes and checked her watch. It was just gone six thirty. London was still asleep, but Annie's early morning customers, the builders from the nearby World's End building site, would be in before eight looking for their fried breakfasts.

She looked over to check that Noreen was still asleep. She was snoring. She smiled and went downstairs. Debris from last night's reunion was on the coffee table. Overflowing ashtray, three empty bottles of Blue Nun and an empty platter that had once contained sandwiches left over from the party. Noreen had polished off the lot exclaiming in her loud, somewhat drunken voice that they were, 'Delicious! The best sandwiches I have ever eaten!'

As Annie cleared away the table she smiled to herself. She had not just one friend now, in Lara, but two. She liked Noreen instantly. There was a warmth and an openness about her that was irresistible. Annie knew that sometimes she came across to other people as awkward and secretive. She could never be totally free and always had to be guarded in what she said, because of what had happened. Being around Noreen's chatty indiscretion was like a breath of fresh air to her.

As Annie stepped out into the dewy, early morning air to walk the few hundred yards down the Kings Road to work, she was feeling, she was surprised to note, happy. Like an ordinary girl, on an ordinary day, going to work. She was Annie Austen and she had a new friend. Another small triumph. Another piece to add to the jigsaw of her new, invented life. One day, perhaps, there would be enough pieces to make it real.

Fred's cafe was busy that morning. She barely sat down before eleven. As she had already done four hours, Giuliana, her boss, told her that she could go home for a couple of hours and come back for the early evening shift if she wanted.

As she was leaving she bumped into a young man coming in. She recognised him and, assuming he must be a customer, she smiled and said, 'Hi.'

'It's you,' he said. She was suddenly gripped with panic. He knew her. Who was he?

'I'm Alex,' he said. 'From last night? The party? I took your picture for the paper.'

'Oh,' she said. 'Yes. I remember now.' She smiled.

God – she had an amazing smile. Hell – she was the most beautiful thing on the planet. This was unbelievable. A poor waitress working in a cafe and he was discovering her. Right here. Right now. Standing in front of him was the new Shrimpton. Shrimp? Hell – this girl was LOBSTER! Every model in town would be wiping down cafe tables once this kid hit the scene. Bailey would be a has-been shooting Jewish weddings in Hendon. How had he not seen this last night?

HOW? He was snapping this chick up and out of here, right now, in case Duffy came wandering down the Kings Road and decided he wanted a bacon butty for his lunch.

'I want you to take a look at this,' Alex said, taking the print out of his bag and laying it on the table.

Annie looked at the picture. It was her at the party last night. Her hand was on her hip and she was staring at the camera. She remembered him asking her to 'put your hand on your hip love – strike a pose' and feeling uncomfortable and silly. But she did not look silly in this picture. She looked like the girls in the magazines. She looked London cool. Was that really her?

'It's very nice,' she said. But Annie felt excited. Slightly giddy.

'It's more than nice, darling. It's bloody fantastic! I want you to model for me.'

Annie laughed. 'I'm afraid not,' she said. She was flattered but there was no way. 'It's just not me.'

'Don't be daft, girl. Can't you see from the picture? You've got "it".'

Annie laughed and looked at the picture again. In front of her was the girl she wanted to be. Confident, smiling – eyes sparkling. The picture looked more alive than she felt. Alex could see from her interest that he nearly had her. He just had to close the deal.

'Come on, love. You are That Girl. Trust me. Let me make you a star. You'll make a fortune.'

Trust me. Let me do this thing. That's what Dorian said when her mother was sick. Hanna crept up on Annie and reminded her she didn't need a fortune. She had all the money she had stolen from Dorian, and his mother's jewellery, hidden in a locked case under her bed. The apron she had not been able to burn. With no access to a fire, she had left it in there. She felt sick at the thought of it. She looked at the picture again. That girl wasn't her. Not at all. *Don't tempt fate, Hanna. Somebody might see you. Somebody knows. Keep a low profile. Keep yourself hidden.*

'I'm afraid there's no way,' Annie said. Her face was hard and determined.

'Come on love,' said Alex, genuinely surprised. What girl turned down the chance to be a model? She must be kidding, leading him on.

As she walked out she turned to the diminutive photographer and, looking down on him said, 'I am not your love.' She said it with such venomous disdain that Alex felt as if he had been slapped sharply across the face.

God – but she was gorgeous. He simply had to get her in front of that camera again.

17

Coleman was regretting his agreement to take Noreen on for an afternoon try-out in Chevrons.

Lara had a job persuading him. 'Noreen is the best barmaid in Cork. I swear she won't let you down.'

'Chelsea is not Cork,' he said, looking across at Lara's plain-faced Irish friend as she ran around the room with a tray of cheese and pineapple nibbles, one of Lara's expensive bouclé jackets straining around her back.

'Please, Coleman,' she said. 'For me.'

The launch party had been in its final dregs and Lara was a little drunk. Her eyes were full of flirtation. She touched the arm of his jacket. He smiled at her, despite himself. Business and pleasure was a bad mix, he told himself. And Lara was more than pleasure. Way more than pleasure. The fact that she was drunkenly flirting with him made it even worse.

Shirley was on holiday for three weeks. Visiting friends in Spain she told him. Not that Coleman had been interested. Shirley had been angry with him since he made Lara hostess, calling it a betrayal. He thought sometimes that Shirley could sense that he was in love with Lara. Women had intuitions he could never hope to understand. He avoided Shirley as much as he could these days, and was frankly relieved when she announced she was going away for three weeks. However, Shirley was still his most senior waitress and with Ethel gone after her recent marriage, Coleman was very short staffed. So, he agreed to give Noreen a trial on the lunchtime stripper shift the following day. Mistress Molly was on and some of her regulars were seedy weirdos. Things could sometimes get a bit grubby so Coleman was very particular about what women he let work the shift, and Arthur was always out front to make sure the audience never got physical with Molly. It was a mean trick, but if this nice Catholic Irish girl could survive a Chevrons lunchtime stripper shift, and if Brian was happy with her, he might be able to find her a spot before Shirley came back.

Noreen was not impressed with the setup behind the bar. The taps were dirty and the shelves were a mess – bottles everywhere, different brands with bits taken out of them – some on optics, some not. Brian was equally unimpressed that Coleman had sent a bird in to work behind the bar. An ugly one, too, who was looking around with a beady eye.

'Will I take out these?' she offered, lifting a bucket of empties from next to the full sink.

'Put them down,' he barked. 'I'll take them out later. Look, this is my bar, yeah? I know how things work back here. If you want to be useful, just wait the tables for me.' Then, remembering she had been sent in by Coleman, he added an afterthought of chivalry, 'There's a good girl.'

Noreen said, 'Yes sir!' and clipped her forehead, which only riled him more.

However, Noreen didn't mind. She had the best four hours of her working life. The windowless club had a plush, red interior and a small stage with a gold tinsel curtain at the back. When Molly came out in her minuscule bikini, Noreen was initially shocked, then almost instantly thrilled by the near nudity. The men were muted, some pretending not to look but glancing up furtively, others just talking among themselves. Arthur was sitting at the front of the stage looking out into the crowd, obviously guarding Molly. Noreen thought that was very chivalrous of him, and nodded across with a smile. She would not disturb him with chat while he was working. That would not be professional and it was important that she make the right impression on her first day. So Noreen did as Brian told her – waited the tables and tried to keep the customers happy. The men looked a bit awkward, some of them, so she went out of her way to put them at ease, letting them know there was nothing wrong with looking at a bit of flesh. They were paying customers. Worthy of respect, always.

'There's your drink now, sir, and if you want another just give me a wave.' Within half an hour, the men felt like she had always been there and were ordering more drinks to flirt with the new Irish barmaid.

'Wish I had breasts like that,' she said nodding at Molly.

'So do I,' said prison beefcake Dennis Rogers.

'Dennis already does!' his friend quipped.

'Go on,' she said, 'show us your tits Dennis.'

Noreen couldn't believe what was coming out of her mouth. She would never get away with language like that at home. Nobody ever heard her say things like that, except John. But this was London and she was in a strip club. She could say what she liked!

Dennis pulled up his sweater and the whole place briefly erupted in hilarity.

When Molly was finished and leaving the stage, she initiated a large round of applause among the men, issuing a loud wolf whistle herself. For the first time in her ten years, Molly came out and did an encore, inviting Dennis up onto the stage to go topless and giving him her nipple tassels, which he did a pretty good job of jiggling himself. Noreen would have got up and joined them, but it was her first shift and she didn't want to be presumptuous. Besides, there was a lot of clearing up to do. All in all Noreen was confident that her first afternoon had been a huge success. The customers were all waving and cheering at her as they left. There had been some quantity of drink consumed. Noreen knew that good chat made heavy thirst.

'See you next week, Noreen,' Dennis called as he went out the door.

When the last customer left and she was wiping down the tables Noreen was on a high.

'How do you think I did?' she asked Arthur, as he was locking the door.

'Brilliant!' said Molly, butting in. 'Breath of fresh air! If things don't work out here, I've a regular gig at the World's End. They'd love you.'

Noreen beamed, but she wanted to stay here. She liked the atmosphere, and she already felt like she'd made a good friend and ally in Arthur. And as for Coleman? She'd like to get to know him better. What a dish!

However, Brian was already in with Coleman, telling him that Noreen had to go. 'She drove me mad, fussing about behind the bar. And the state of her, Coleman? The men weren't happy.'

Coleman had stuck his head out earlier and seen East End hit man Tippy Fleming and huge Dennis Rogers roaring their heads off laughing.

'They seemed happy enough to me.'

'Yeah well, she nearly caused a riot. She got the men all riled up. She threw a punter out earlier. He wasn't happy, Coleman.'

'Who?'

Brian didn't want to say, but Coleman stared at him.

'Whazzer Phillips,' he eventually said, under his breath.

Coleman laughed out loud. Whazzer was their resident pervert. Even Shirley had been afraid to get rid of him. Brian's chin set with irritation.

'I want her out, Coleman. I can't work with her. And Shirley will go mad when she gets back and finds her here.'

He was right about that. Shirley was bitchy enough these days without adding more fuel to the fire.

'Alright, alright – send her in.'

Noreen stood in front of Coleman, beaming.

'I'm afraid I can't take you on.'

Noreen's face collapsed.

'Why not?'

'Well, you're just not... right for Chevrons.'

Noreen felt sick. She got it. This place employed beautiful women. Women like Molly, and Lara – even mousey Annie had worked here for a while. It was because she didn't have the right figure or face. She wasn't glamorous enough. Well, stuff him. She wasn't going to stand for it. Noreen knew she had been red hot out there that afternoon and if Coleman didn't want her, well then, she didn't want to be here.

'That's OK – Molly already offered me work at World's End and, oh, by the way? Your barman is on the take. Good luck!' She headed for the door.

'Woah. Wait a minute.'

Noreen stopped. She knew that would get his attention.

'What do you mean?'

'The World's End pub? Maybe you've heard of...'

'Not that. Brian.'

'Oh that. So you're not in on it?'

Coleman glared at her to continue. Angry. Brooding. Grrrr – what a hunk.

'Well – when I was in earlier, cleaning up, I found a funnel under the sink with the cleaning gear. Just a regular, plastic, kitchen funnel. But who keeps a funnel in a bar unless they're siphoning off drink? Then, Brian got all defensive when I asked if I could take out a bucket of empty bottles. He was most insistent I didn't go near it, so when he was down in the cellar, I checked through and found these.' She went outside the door and brought back in four full bottles of liquor she had hidden there earlier. 'He's been siphoning off stock and selling it back to the supplier,' she said. Coleman looked furious. She could not be sure if he was angry with her or Brian. She didn't care. He was pure gorgeous! 'And he's taking cash too. I saw him. Rang the till, put a twenty to the side of it.'

'And I'm supposed to believe you over my barman of five years?'

'I don't care whether you believe me or not. I'm just letting you know that I served over £200 worth of drink on that shift. If that's what Brian put through the till – I stand corrected. But I saw him pocket cash hand over fist and I'd say you'll be lucky to see £100 of it.'

The lunchtime stripper shift had been underperforming for months. Fifty on average, just under a hundred on a good day. And Brian liked the gee-gees. Coleman had had his suspicions but Shirley had said there was no way. She had her eye on him and there was no way he was ripping him off. Coleman probably should have followed it up but the truth was he had been distracted. By Lara, the shop. He had taken his eye off the ball. People didn't rip off Bobby Chevron. Not if they wanted to stay alive. It was Coleman's job to make sure the books tallied. This was bad news.

'Brian said you insulted a customer earlier.'

Noreen flushed.

'He was interfering with himself. It was disrespectful to Molly. The rule is "no physical contact". I saw him making physical contact with himself so I kicked him out. No fuss. Just told him I knew what he was playing at and quietly showed him the door.'

'He was still a customer.'

'Not much of a customer. Any man who spends that much time with his hands in his pockets isn't drinking.'

Coleman raised his eyebrows. That was true. And they'd been trying to find a way of dealing with that weirdo Whazzer for months. None of the muscle would go near him. They were afraid to touch him. This girl, it seemed, wasn't afraid of anything. Coleman liked that.

'Alright. You can come back for the evening shift. Can you really run a bar?'

'If you pay me you might find out.'

'I'll start you on the same wage as the floor girls to see how you do. Then we'll take it from there.'

'How about you start me on the same wage as Brian, and I don't rob you blind?'

She was standing there, directly eyeballing him with more honest hutzpah than any man he had ever faced down. Coleman pursed his lips then reluctantly nodded. He had no choice.

'Good,' Noreen said. 'I'll be back in two hours to clean up that bar before opening time. Arthur can help me do a proper stock take so we all know exactly where we are.'

She held out her hand, like she saw her father do with his business associates, and said, 'Coleman. You can trust me.'

Coleman shook Noreen's hand and after she had left, lit a cigarette, drawing the smoke down deep into his lungs.

Although he didn't like to admit it, Coleman trusted Noreen already.

Which was more than he could say for his other female manager. Because, if Brian was scamming the bar in such a stupid way, there was no way that Shirley didn't know about it. She must be in on it too.

18

Lara unlocked the front door of the shop, then made herself a coffee before laying the newspaper out on the counter. She turned with great expectation to the fashion pages and her stomach sank when she saw – Quant. This season's staple pieces. Again. Resigned, she turned to the society page. Sure enough, there was a large shot of Penelope posing next to an awkward looking Coleman. The caption read 'Chevron's nightclub manager, the dashing Coleman, at the opening of his new business venture – a boutique on the Kings Road.' No mention of Lara or That Girl. After all that fuss, Penelope had obviously decided that Lara wasn't the next big thing after all. She just fancied Coleman. Although, Lara mused, he wouldn't be happy seeing his face in the paper like that. Coleman liked things to be kept low key. She wasn't even supposed to tell people that he was involved in the business at all. Only for Penelope being so damn nosy, she wouldn't have.

Lara downed her coffee and decided to shrug it off. She had no choice. There was a business to run and she wasn't about to let one disappointment upend her dream. Lara had a busy morning in the shop, setting everything straight after the party and taking in new stock.

At lunchtime, her thoughts turned to Noreen as Lara wondered how she was coping with the stripper shift. She smiled to herself, knowing her old friend would be well able for it. A little part of her wondered if Noreen's abrupt and inelegant entrance had foiled her chances of getting onto the fashion pages, but then she pushed the thought aside telling herself it didn't matter. Lara had known, last night, that Coleman had not wanted to take Noreen on, but Lara knew he would love her once he saw her in action. Coleman didn't bother nearly as much with glamour as he let on. He inhabited a world where men were men and women were pretty, but it wasn't who he was. If it was, Lara could never be his friend. And they were friends. She liked and respected Coleman, and believed the feeling was mutual. That was why she agreed to letting him put up the money for her business. Had she flirted him into taking on Noreen? She had been quite drunk at the end of the night. A picture of leaning her face into his shoulder as he helped her out the door flashed into her mind, quickly set aside by a customer coming up to the till with the last of the pink baby-doll dresses.

Despite the lack of publicity, the shop continued to tick over, with customers wandering in and out all day and a healthy take on the till. Then, late afternoon, a familiar face walked in and marched straight up to the cash register.

'Ah,' Lara knew him straight away. 'The great photographer. I can't remember your name but gee thanks for the great spread in today's paper.'

'Alex. And you'll thank me when you see what I've got here.'

He reached into his satchel, pulled out a black and white print and laid it down on the counter.

'*Voilà.*'

It was a picture of Annie in a suit. From the party last night.

'Well thank you, Alex, for this very lovely print, but frankly I would prefer if it was printed in the actual newspaper. Where people could see it.'

'When you look at this picture, what do you see?'

Lara gave him a bored look that said, 'Are you still here?'

'Please. Just look.'

She picked up the print. 'I see a picture of my flatmate posing in a suit, which, despite my best efforts, was not in the paper today.'

'No,' Alex said. 'This is a picture of That Girl. The coolest chick in London. Internationally famous superstar model Annie...'

Lara picked up the picture, eyed him sceptically, then looked at it again.

'Austen,' she said. 'Annie Austen.'

'Exactly. Annie Austen. That Girl.'

This time she looked properly – and she saw it.

Annie in reality was beautiful, but she was no It girl. In this picture, however, she was. They said the camera never lies but in this case it most certainly did.

'She's got it,' Alex said. 'Now you've got to persuade her to give it to us.'

Lara looked past him so he added, 'If I take the pictures...'

'No,' she said. 'I get that. She's coming in the door now.'

Annie spotted Alex and the picture straightaway. She marched up to them both. She was angry and afraid. Annie was so secretive that she could not bear other people keeping secrets from her. She had to know what was going on around her at all times. Her life depended on it.

'It's not what you think,' Alex said. Then turned to Lara and explained, 'Annie has already said she won't be photographed.'

'Well then,' Lara said to Annie, 'it's exactly what you think.

You said no to him and now, this sneaky worm has come to try and persuade me to persuade you to model for the shop.'

Annie breathed a sigh of relief. Her friend was not betraying her.

'Do you want me to?'

'Well,' Lara said, 'Alex said he has already asked you and you said no.'

'I know,' she said. 'But I would do it for you.'

Her voice was almost pleading. What she meant was, 'I would do anything for you, Lara. You rescued me. You are my best friend in the world.' Lara heard that and flinched. Annie's neediness could be grating at times.

'Look. Annie. This picture is amazing.' Lara handed her the picture. 'You are, and you know this because I've said it to you before, extraordinarily beautiful but – if you don't feel comfortable...'

Annie held the glossy print in her hand and looked down at it again. Lara's words faded into the background. Was that her? Could that be her? Not Hanna. No, someone else. It was the girl she wanted to be. The girl she was trying to be. Perhaps it was possible to change, after all.

'I'll do it,' she said. Alex raised his eyebrows in surprise. 'I want to do this. I'm going to do this. Not for you Lara – or you,' she said, looking vaguely at Alex, 'but for me.'

Inside her head she said, *Annie Austen. It's time to bring you to life.*

19

Annie arranged to meet Alex at his studio later. Lara locked up the shop and they went back to the apartment. They found Noreen there, slumped on the sofa working her way through a packet of Ryvita.

'There's no food in this house,' she complained.

'There's food in the shop,' said Lara. 'They work the same way as the shops in Ireland.'

'I've been too busy managing strippers,' said Noreen, dropping a chunk of crispbread on the carpet. She eyed Annie as she leaned down to scoop it up, then carried it over to the kitchenette where she immediately busied herself with the carpet sweeper. 'I didn't get the chance. I just can't believe you haven't got anything in. Two women in a flat and no food!'

'Sorry,' Annie paused her wiping. 'I should have brought some supper back from the cafe. I didn't think. And with the party and everything I didn't have the time to shop for us.'

She seemed genuinely upset by her mistake.

'Don't apologise,' Lara said.

Noreen raised her eyebrows and smiled knowingly. Clever, popular Lara had got herself a skivvy. It was a role Noreen herself had inhabited as a small child, but tired of by the time they were ten.

'It's not your responsibility to feed us,' Lara said to Annie, a little too firmly.

She turned to Noreen. 'And we don't have a Mammy looking after us here, so you had better get used to fending for yourself in the kitchen. Anyway, Ryvita is food and by the way, they're expensive and they're mine.' She snatched the packet off her and flounced into the kitchen. Noreen laughed. Annie was in awe of the easy way Noreen and Lara were with each other. The pretend anger. Saying awful things without reproach. Fearless.

'Well, fear not, I'm not eating any more of this shite,' Noreen said, waving her last crispbread in the air before stuffing it in her mouth. 'This is paper. I want some spuds. I haven't had a proper feed since I got here.'

'Did you not have anything at the club today?'

'Just peanuts and crisps. Arthur was supposed to go and get me a plate from the cafe but he couldn't leave Molly. The lads got a bit rowdy today.'

She said it like she had been working there for ten years.

'You plied them with drink and wound them up, I suppose.'

'I do recall having a laugh and flirt with one or two of them. In the interest of pint sculling, of course. By the way – why do they call Arthur 'Ironing board?' He wouldn't tell me.'

'I have no idea,' Lara lied. She knew. She had heard the story from Shirley, then wished she hadn't. She supposed Noreen would know everything about everyone by the end of the week, but she wasn't going to enlighten her. In Noreen's own interests she added, 'And just let me tip you off. Coleman likes people who mind their own business.'

'Well actually,' Noreen said, with a little hint of spite in her voice, 'Coleman was very happy when I didn't mind my own business today. Brian, the bar manager— '

'I know who Brian is.'

'Yes, well, he was ripping Coleman off.'

Lara had suspected Brian in the past, but had never done anything about it. It was best not to get in between these gangster boys. But there was no point in trying to explain that to Noreen. It might frighten her or, worse again, encourage her.

'So Coleman sacked him on the spot and I got his job.'

'Good for you,' said Lara.

She felt a little spit of envy. Was Noreen muscling in on her territory with Coleman? After just one day?

'Anyway, it means I need something glamorous to wear on my first night behind the bar.'

Before Lara had time to comment, Annie, who had finished tidying, piped up.

'I'll find you something.'

'I don't think your clothes would fit me,' Noreen said, then with a dramatic sweep down her body adding, 'I am an exceptionally voluptuous woman.'

Noreen remembered how John had described her as that the first time they had sex together. Noreen had taken it as the compliment it was intended to be, and used it to make her even less apologetic for her curves than she was already. She pushed the thought of John aside.

'Nonsense,' Annie said, smiling. 'You're not that big. I'll find you something.'

Noreen raised her eyebrows at Lara as Annie scuttled off to her room.

'She's trying to be nice,' Lara said, 'so be nice back.'

Noreen let it go. She had other, more pressing matters to attend to with her best friend.

'Talking about being nice,' Noreen said. 'I think Coleman fancies me.'

Lara got a fright. She consciously readjusted her face from shocked amusement to vague interest.

'Really?'

'I know. He's gorgeous and I'm... voluptuous. But I felt something from him. I think we made a connection.'

Lara was sure they had. Coleman was a hard-headed businessman and she knew that Noreen's business acumen would be immediately apparent to him. But fancy her? She supposed it was possible.

'You've been here less than a day, Noreen.'

'No point in letting the grass grow, Lara. It's the sixties. I'm a sexual adventuress! I'm here to have new experiences. London experiences! Orgasms! And Coleman looks like the kind of guy who knows all about that. Oh God,' Noreen suddenly thought of something awful, 'you're not after him are you?'

'No.' Lara said the word quickly and firmly then wanted to grab it back straight away. Was it kind to let Noreen go through an attempt at seducing Coleman when she had seen so many other, more experienced woman fail? Although, she could see Noreen had her mind made up and there would be no stopping her. In any case, Coleman was a gentleman and would find a way of putting her off. Unless...

'I thought so. Because I figured if you had wanted him you'd have taken him by now.'

Lara shook her head and said, 'No. Not interested. Go right ahead, Noreen, just...' she wanted to say be careful, but then another question opened up inside her. Suppose he said yes? Suppose Noreen seduced Coleman and...,'just have fun.'

'Oh I will. Glad I've got a clear run at him, so.'

Annie came back in holding up a dress on a hanger. 'I thought this would be perfect for you for tonight.'

It was a navy A-shaped smocked dress with a high, round, light blue collar. Annie bought it two weeks ago and was keeping it for special occasions. Because of its loose shape, it would fit Noreen and give a serious, professional look for her first day at work. Also, crucially, it would cover her up so that the men weren't giving her lots of unwanted attention.

Noreen's lips tightened with offence.

'Are you joking?'

Annie looked crushed.

'I'm working at a strip joint. As a barmaid. That's like something a nun would wear.'

'Noreen!' Lara could see Annie was hurt.

'Sorry. It's a nice thought, Annie, but, well, I just want something a bit more sexy, you know?'

Annie didn't know. Her demure nod and querying eyes made Noreen want to give her a smack. She didn't come all the way over here from holy, Catholic Ireland to be judged by some skinny strap who wanted to dress her like a bloody nun.

'I'll go down to the shop,' Lara said.

None of her own clothes would fit Noreen. Lara knew that Annie had dug out the big frock to make Noreen feel better. To help Noreen believe she was thinner than she was. Noreen didn't care about that. If clothes didn't fit her, it was the fault of the clothes, not her body. The kind thought had backfired.

'I'll bring you back something a stripper would wear. A voluptuous stripper.'

'Classy though,' Noreen called after her. 'I wouldn't say Coleman goes for anything trashy.'

When Lara was gone, Noreen found Annie looking at her in wide-eyed horror.

'What,' Noreen said, unable to help herself, 'is the matter with you?'

Annie replied with uncharacteristic force.

'Leave Coleman alone. He's in love with Lara.'

Noreen took a breath. It was a small shock. On the other hand, everyone was in love with Lara.

'Lara's not interested.'

'She is. Everyone sees it. It's just...'

'Just what?'

'Well, Lara is reluctant. Nobody knows why. She's just – I don't know – but she should be with him. That's all.'

'Oh really?'

Even as she snapped her disbelief, the germ of an idea formed in Noreen's head. Maybe Lara wasn't over her brother. She had not, by the sounds of it, been out with anyone else. Coleman, if he did fancy her, was pretty irresistible.

Plus, while Matthew was a subject non grata with her, Lara had not exactly asked where he was or what he was doing. If she had, Noreen might have told her that he was in a London seminary, on a six-month academic bursary, researching religious art. Something to do with restoring some old paintings for the seminary, unimaginably boring. Her parents had asked Noreen to leave Lara's address with them so they could forward it on and have him call on them when he got there. Checking up on her and upsetting Lara at the same time! Noreen had destroyed every shred of evidence of where she was going before she left. The last thing she needed was Matthew turning up here, cramping her style. By the look of things, Lara would certainly not be too happy to see him. How awful if she wasn't over him? Although, how stupid too, when she had a dreamboat like Coleman after her. Still. Noreen was no competition to her. Noreen wasn't interested in love. She had that at home with John. In fact, she had come here to get away from it. All she wanted was a bit of modern fun. She'd be in and out of Coleman like Flynn. Lara wouldn't even notice she'd been there.

'Yes really.' Annie was standing in front of her staring. She looked angry. In fact, in that moment, Noreen felt a little afraid of her.

The pub had taught her that sometimes it was the quiet types you ought to be afraid of. Aggressive people blew out a lot of hot air. It was the ones in the corner, quiet as mice, nursing their drinks, who could be unpredictable – even dangerous – when they blew. *What is your story?* Noreen said to herself. *No family, no friends, apart from Lara. There's something amiss here. Something creepy. Something I really don't like.*

'Alright so,' Noreen said. 'I'll keep my hands off him.' And she raised them in the air just to make a point.

'Good,' Annie said. 'Thank you.' And she smiled a beatific, glittering smile.

Noreen flinched.

'Now,' Annie said, 'excuse me. I have to go out.'

'Where are you going?' Noreen asked, trying to end their exchange on a relatively normal note.

'I've got my first modelling assignment,' Annie said. Then, not even bothering to put on lipstick she grabbed her bag and called back to Noreen, 'Wish me luck!'

'Good luck!' Noreen said, her voice brittle with irritation.

As soon as Annie had gone Noreen headed into her bedroom. There had to be something in here. Some evidence of who Annie was. Where she was from. She was a liar, Noreen knew that for sure. Lara said she thought she was from Leitrim, but Annie had implied to Noreen the night before that her mother was from Cork. Noreen had been quite drunk but she remembered that contradiction, and used it to justify opening and closing all of the drawers in Annie's room. She looked for letters, diaries – but there was nothing. Only carefully folded, plain-coloured clothes. Everything she had looked new. There was no evidence here of a family, no memorabilia, no ornaments, no photographs or trinkets. Nothing that would even put her in Ireland. Noreen knew that Annie was pure Irish. Despite her best efforts to hide it, Noreen could hear the accent behind the fake, English twang, although she could not place it by county, which frustrated her no end. But she could find no evidence of Irishness in her drawers, not even a set of rosary beads. Noreen's mother had stuffed one into the pocket of her coat, which she had found on the boat, and hidden two in her case before she left. If Annie was Irish there would be a miraculous medal on a vest or a pair of rosary beads somewhere in this room. Eventually, Noreen pulled back the valence sheet, got down on her hands and knees and looked under the bed. And there it was. Right in the middle under the bed almost beyond reach. She leaned in her hand and managed to pull it towards her when she saw there was a big padlock on it. Noreen's stomach lurched. Why would somebody padlock a suitcase?

'Noreen!'

Lara was back. Noreen shoved the case back towards the middle of the bed and gathered herself.

She wouldn't say anything to Lara about this. She didn't want to explain to Lara why she had been snooping. But there was something very wrong here. Until she got to the bottom of this mystery, there was no point in worrying her old friend.

20

Alex rang one of his friends and begged him to lend him his studio on Cheyne Walk for the evening.

'I'm impressed,' Lara said when she turned up at the address and found the lights and backdrop all set up, along with a box of cigarettes and a plate of biscuits.

In the past six months, Lara had been courted by several photographers, but none whose work had especially impressed her and none of the big ones. Chevrons was developing a name as a cool underground hang-out spot for some of the photographers and their models, and although she knew them in her capacity as hostess there, she was still not established enough on the scene to approach any of them about photographing her work. In any case, ambitious Lara was learning that in sixties' London asking wasn't cool. Blowing your own trumpet was considered crass and uncool. The polite thing was to wait to be discovered. Lara had been hoping Penelope would do that for her. When that fell through, this unknown press photographer was a pretty poor, but possible, second bite at Podmore's fashion page. He had taken some knockout shots of Annie so the least she could do was give him a break – and hope she might get a break out of it too.

When Annie sat down in front of the photographic studio's dressing room mirror, with a dozen bulbs illuminating every crevice of her being, she regretted her decision.

'God – you are so beautiful,' Lara said, putting her small makeup bag down in front of her.

Dorian used those exact words to Annie before he defiled her. The memory made her feel sick.

She looked at herself. She was beautiful. Even she could not deny it. Nonetheless, with her perfect skin and her high cheekbones and her large, soft green eyes and doleful expression, Annie hated the beautiful girl in the mirror. Her extraordinary, ethereal face had led her into years of abuse and finally driven her to murder. That face was her enemy. Annie rarely looked in a mirror and now, here she was, staring at her vulnerable self under a dozen spotlights and inviting other people to do the same.

Sensing her despair, Lara grimaced and said, 'Ugh – everyone looks bad under these lights,' and spun Annie's chair around so that she was facing away. Spilling out her small bag of cosmetics, she started applying makeup. Lara patted the Max Factor panstick onto Annie's cheeks in thick, beige stripes then began to gently blend it into her skin, covering the smattering of light freckles on her otherwise perfect, pale skin. With her eyes closed, Lara's gentle, feminine touch reminded Annie of her mother and her nerves began to recede.

As she worked Lara thought, not for the first time, what an unusual girl Annie was. Secretive and unworldly, she didn't even know how to apply makeup properly. It was not common for any woman, certainly not a model, to allow other women to do their makeup for them. Every woman, even the plainest girl, knew how to make the best of themselves. Applying makeup to another woman's face felt like a strange intrusion, but as Annie closed her eyes and yielded to the touch of the brushes and sponges, Lara decided to use the beautiful bare face as an artist's canvas, to create a modern masterpiece.

When she was finished Lara spun Annie around to look at her reflection in the mirror. Her long red curls were flattened down under a hair net and her face seemed like a shocking, exaggerated version of itself. Her skin was mask-like pale and her eyes were contoured in black and white with long spiky lashes, looking enormous and staring back at her, blankly. Annie's lips were powdered and painted, pouted in a seductive way that a good, Catholic girl could never have intended them. She was just taking in the strangeness of this new self when Lara, securing her grip by pinching the middle of her forehead, slid a short blonde wig over Annie's head. Wig on, Annie stared at the reflection in awe. She could not see any part of herself looking back. Who was this blonde, seductive, confidently modern girl? Not her. Not Hanna.

'Annie? Are you ready?'

Every trace of Hanna was gone now. Not just in her name but in her face too.

Annie Austen had finally arrived. She was blonde, mod and brand new. She was That Girl! Vulnerable, abused Hanna was gone. Hidden so far under this new disguise, that Annie could not find her. She was free.

'I'm ready,' she said.

A sheet of thick white paper hung from a scaffold and rolled onto the floor in a carpet. As she stepped onto the pristine background Annie willed herself to enter this new life.

She moved, this way and that, showing off the cut of the A-line minidress Lara had picked out for her.

Alex spoke in a stream of instructions. 'Now you're working. Good girl. Move forward. Come on. That's it. Now –

hand on hip, right side to camera.' Encouragements and chides came flowing out of him, filling the awkward space between camera and model. Disguising the intrusion of capturing a human moment by assuming ongoing permission.

As Annie moved in front of the camera, the movements began to feel natural to her. She became aware of how these new, painted-on features might look to the camera, how the most minuscule flick of an eyebrow or curve of the lip would alter the mood of her face. 'Centre it up a little now sweetheart – perfect! To the left? Loving it – loving it. Good girl – there you are. Look at me. Over here. Look to your right, now. Lovely. Eyes wide. No blinking, naughty girl…' She was aware of her tall, slim body making shapes.

'Wardrobe! Wig!' With every fresh outfit she projected through her facial expressions and the placement of limbs a new story, a new mood. She altered the light in her eyes, acting out the part of the girl she wanted to be. The girls she read about in books, sewing magazines. Pretty, carefree girls, free without burdens. The girl she might have been before she knew pain. The girl her father would have loved if he had stayed alive. The girl that her parents wanted her to be. The girl her mother thought she would create with the help of a loving stepfather.

In front of the camera Annie was no longer a prisoner of the beauty that had inspired the savage love of a dangerous man. This was a new beauty, defined by Alex's camera and her kind friend's skilful makeup. This was a beauty that she was in control of. Annie would dictate the effect that her looks had on the world around her, not the other way around.

She modelled as if her life depended on it. In that moment, it felt as if it did.

Alex and Lara watched as the transformation came over shy, reticent Annie. From mousy beauty to powerful supermodel.

They knew they were watching something extraordinary. The special quality that Alex had seen in the earliest photographs, with her reluctant moves and her barely made-up face, were hugely exaggerated, not just with Lara's clothes and wigs and makeup, but, more importantly, in Annie's willingness to be there. Her hunger for the camera was insatiable as she moved, in small, confidant flicks of limb and hand. Placing her body in awkward, interesting shapes, throwing Alex sly side-glances one minute, then shocked seductive looks the next. He started off by guiding her, but after a few minutes, Annie was in charge and she was loving every moment.

After two hours Alex called it a day. Annie threw herself down on a large, round plastic chair, legs akimbo. She was utterly exhausted and, yet, felt calmer and happier than she had felt in a long time. If she had to put a word to it she would have said she felt – reborn.

Lara and Alex stood and looked at each other for a short moment. They both suspected they had unearthed something extraordinary, but neither felt able to put words to it. Certainly not until the pictures were developed. Alex went straight into his friend's darkroom and began processing. Lara, saying nothing, went across and peeled the wig from Annie's head then began to massage Ponds cold cream into her skin, removing it, and the makeup, with tissues. Annie's face yielded to her friend's touch and she smiled gently in a kind of peaceful reverie. It felt right to be pampering her in this way. Annie had cast herself in the role of house servant to Lara since they had met, and Lara had not objected as much as she should have. In the past few hours something changed. It was as if Annie herself knew she was a star.

The half hour that they spent waiting for the photographs to develop was the longest of Lara's life.

Eventually, when Alex emerged from the darkroom, he looked more shocked than happy as he handed the printed sheets over to Lara.

She had been expecting a set of great pictures but nothing like this. She had never seen such breathtakingly beautiful images. Comparable to Shrimpton but with an even wilder, untamed energy. Alex looked at Lara's face as she studied the pictures. He could see from her eyes, eagerly scanning the images, that he had been right. She saw what he saw. Annie was not simply beautiful or different – she was extraordinary. They had, in their hands, a revolutionary new look.

The naming of Lara's clothes line had been a random idea, but Annie brought it to life. She was That Girl. Not just a dress, a handbag or a cute short plastic mac – but a live woman. A way of life. Penelope Podmore was now, they knew, merely a given. Alex and Lara had a *Harper's* cover girl on their hands.

In the meantime, Annie had not joined them. She lay snoozing peacefully in the big yellow chair. Sated. Happy. Deep in the dreamless sleep of the innocent.

21

'The boss wants to see you,' Ironing Board said to Brian as he arrived at work the next afternoon. Brian didn't bother answering him but as he was taking off his coat Arthur added, 'Don't bother with that. He wants to see you straight away.'

'Jesus,' he snapped, and gave Coleman's idiot lackey a savage look. Coleman probably wanted to talk to him about that new Irish girl again. He hoped he had got rid of her like he told him to. The last thing he needed was that nosy cow sniffing around behind his bar. Especially with Shirley away, he couldn't be sure his back was being covered. Coleman was going soft, especially on the girls these days. As Brian walked into Coleman's office he noticed the moron had followed him in.

Coleman was standing with his back to the door and didn't move.

'What the hell is Ironing Board doing in here?' Brian said, flicking his head behind him.

He turned and saw Arthur locking the door behind him, then popping the key in his handkerchief pocket before walking across the room and standing, legs apart, arms behind his back, next to Coleman. He adjusted his neck in his collar. Loosening himself up.

Brian felt sick.

'I'll tell you what Arthur is doing in here,' said Coleman, turning around. 'He is here looking out for an old friend. Isn't that right Arthur?'

Coleman never called him anything but Arthur.

'That's right, boss.'

Arthur didn't look like such an idiot now. His eyes were narrowed, like he had business in mind. Arthur looked hard and mean, like a man who could beat another man close to death with a prison-issue ironing board.

'Arthur and I have known each other for a long time, haven't we?'

Arthur nodded.

'Arthur is a man who understands the value of friendship.'

'Yes, I do.' Arthur nodded.

'And loyalty.'

'Loyalty is very important,' Arthur agreed, casually picking up a paperweight from Coleman's desk and testing it in his hands for weight before placing it back down, ever so gently, as if afraid of scraping the leather.

'And respect.'

'Respect is very important,' said Arthur before turning to Coleman and saying, 'I respect you, boss.'

'Thank you. And I respect you too, Arthur.'

Arthur closed his eyes in deferential thanks then the two men looked across at Brian.

He was hanging tough, keeping his mouth shut, inwardly praying that this banter was perhaps, just banter. Waiting, hoping against hope. However, both Coleman and Arthur could see from his saucer-like eyes and slack, slightly shivering jaw that he was not in good shape.

'Coleman?' Arthur said.

'Yes?' said Coleman.

'Have you by any chance seen my cricket bat?'

'Is that it there by the filing cabinet?'

'Why, I do believe you're right.'

Neither men took their eyes off Brian. As Arthur moved towards the filing cabinet Brian shouted out in a high, terrified voice.

'It was Shirley! It was all her idea!'

Coleman felt disgusted that Brian had snitched Shirley out so willingly and so quickly.

Coleman, unlike his friend Arthur and boss Chevron, rarely laid a hand on anyone. Certainly never gratuitously. He worked with the truth that there was nothing to fear but fear itself. Once you started hurting a man you had lost him. Mostly though, if a man gave in to those urges, he lost himself. Coleman's suave suggestion of violence was usually enough to get the truth out of people. If a man was sufficiently frightened, he would make himself disappear with no need for bloodshed. However, there were times that Coleman had to hold Arthur back. This, he knew, was going to be one of those times.

Arthur was shifting from side to side, his hands opening and closing in angry fists.

'She put me up to it! Fixed everything up with the suppliers, everything. I didn't mean to. I—'

Arthur was furious. 'How dare you say that about Shirley. Blaming a woman? Shirley wouldn't never do nothing like that. Shirley's a lady...'

Brian let out a laugh. He couldn't help it. Then, Arthur lost it.

'You fucking scumbag! I'll rip your fucking head off.' As Arthur lunged across the room, Coleman pulled him back, wrapping both arms around his friend's chest. Arthur's weight was strained against him. He was furious and strong.

'He's not worth it,' he said through gritted teeth. Then he whispered in his ear, 'Come on mate, pull it together.' These histrionics would get them nowhere. This was turning into a bloody shambles. 'You OK?' Coleman asked. Arthur nodded. Coleman loosened his grip, patted him on the back and said, 'You go out and get the doors open. I'll deal with this scumbag.'

Arthur's outburst had frightened Brian, but the fact that Coleman had protected him gave him pause. When Arthur had gone, Coleman looked Brian in the eye and said, 'To be honest, I'm not interested in what Shirley did or didn't do and I'm not interested in you either. I just want you out of my club, today.'

That was true. Coleman already knew all he needed to know. Shirley had betrayed him, but she was angry with him, and although he would never have assumed that she was in love with him, he understood that she was a woman scorned. Brian, on the other hand, was a gambling, cheating, ill-mannered, lazy and – now it turned out – robbing scumbag. He had already wasted enough time on him. The best thing Coleman could do now was make sure that the club was run tight to try to make up the money they had lost, and keep this incident from Bobby Chevron. God knows what he would do to Brian, but more especially Shirley if he found out he'd been betrayed in this way. Coleman didn't think it was worth anyone getting hurt over.

'That it?' Brian said. This was a lot easier than he had thought it would be.

'That's it,' said Coleman. 'Make yourself scarce, keep your mouth shut, and never come back. Ever.'

Woah, Brian thought, *Coleman really has gone soft. No wonder Shirley was able to scam him. No comeback.*

'Keep my mouth shut, eh?'

'That's right,' Coleman said. 'Get out, stay out, keep your mouth shut about all of this and you'll be safe.'

Brian looked over at him, a sly expression crossing his flabby features.

'I suppose Bobby would be very upset if he found out what Shirley's been up to.'

Coleman's stomach tightened. The stupid idiot. He had really hoped he wouldn't have to do this.

Coleman leaned across his desk and opened the top drawer. He could hear his own heart pumping as he reached in and slid out the Webley shotgun, sawn down to the size of a large handgun.

'Jesus Christ!' Brian shouted as Coleman lifted the weapon, pointed it directly at his face and began to walk towards him. Coleman's face was as calm as it had been at the beginning of their encounter, before Arthur lost his rag.

'Coleman, I – Jesus – don't shoot me!'

Coleman kept walking until Brian's back hit the door of his office then slid down the oak panelling until he was lying on the floor in a snivelling ball.

'Please,' he said. 'Please. I won't tell anyone.'

Coleman knelt down beside him and gently placed the cold barrel of the gun under Brian's chin, then pulled it around, forcing him to look into his face.

'I can't trust you, Brian. I can't trust you to keep your mouth shut, can I?'

'You can trust me, Coleman, I swear. Please don't kill me.'

'Do you think I'm a fool?'

'No, no, of course I don't.'

'If you think there will be any comeback on me for this, Brian, you'd be very wrong about that.'

'I know, I know.'

'If, IF, I decide not to shoot you, Brian, do you know what I am going to do?'

'Please, Coleman, please don't shoot me I—'

'I'm going to call Bobby Chevron and tell him what you did – on your own – and tell him you tried to blame his old friend Shirley. Do you understand?'

'Jesus, Coleman, don't tell Bobby.'

'Then, I'm going to get word out to Handsome Devers and tell him that you were banging his ex-wife, while they were still married. You understand?'

Brian wished, in that moment, that Coleman would shoot him.

'I don't like getting angry, Brian, but Handsome and Chevron, well, they're men who enjoy getting angry. You understand?'

Then, Coleman stood up and brushed down the front of his jacket with the gun.

'I like this suit and I don't want it messed up today.' He gave Brian a small kick to the leg to indicate it was safe for him to stand up.

'I'll give you a twenty-four hour start before I make those calls, Brian. Now make yourself scarce. And I mean invisible. Like you never existed.'

Which, Coleman thought to himself, I really wish you never had.

When Brian was gone, Coleman put the shotgun back in his office drawer. He smiled to himself. It was unloaded. A man was only as dangerous as he was convincing.

Nonetheless the encounter had pumped him up. Coleman could almost feel his veins harden with the surge of adrenalin and testosterone running through them. He still felt angry. He put his feet on the desk, leant back and took a few deep breaths to try to slow the beating of his adrenalin-fuelled heart, but it didn't work. His limbs were fizzing. He was tight, agitated – all wound up. He needed to wind himself down, relax. So he decided to take a shower.

22

L ara couldn't wait to show the pictures of Annie to Coleman. Alex had taken them to Penelope at the *Mail* straight from the shoot, and Lara was surprised to note that the first person she herself wanted to share them with was Coleman. She told herself that his charming handling of Penelope on the night of the party had gone a long way towards cementing their relationship as business partners. He had proven himself to not simply be the money behind the shop by playing such a pivotal role in supporting her at the launch. Or, perhaps, now that she was working in the shop and not in the club, Lara needed an excuse to see Coleman. Perhaps, too, there was a frisson of wondering if the conversation she'd had with Noreen making a play for Coleman the night before had come to anything. She had not seen Noreen since she came in from her late shift.

Either way, Lara tripped down the stairs of the club and, knocking on her way in, opened the door and marched straight into Coleman's office, just as he was coming out of the shower, a towel secured around his waist.

The shower had not done much to loosen Coleman's mood or his muscles, so when he came back into his office and saw

Lara standing there, the door open behind her, and a small
amused smile on her face, he felt irritation more than surprise.
The first time he had met her had been like this. Months ago.
How many months was it? Six? Seven? Who was he kidding?
Six months and five days. He'd been counting. What a fool!
And just like that, Coleman decided that, today, he had had
enough of being a fool. He brazenly looked Lara up and
down. The long curve of her neck beneath the triangle of hair
cut tight into her nape, her small breasts tapping at the front
of her thin, white blouse, her brown eyes gazing across at
him from a bare, pale face and those lips curved into that
mocking smile. The disappearing curve of her thigh up into
the micro-mini she was wearing made his decision for him.
Coleman walked past her then closed and locked his office
door. He grabbed both her elbows in his large hands and
manoeuvred her across the room. Initially taken aback by the
manhandling, Lara staggered along with him until she caught
her breath, then pushed back at him until he fell onto the sofa
and was seated in front of her. Towel miraculously in place,
but otherwise, naked. She looked at him, looking at her. His
eyes were drinking her in, as if she was the naked one. This
wasn't the fool in a towel she had first encountered six months
ago. The cool, debonair club manager had disappeared too.
Here was a savage, his eyes filled with defiant rage. Waiting.
For her. By the weight of the fast, heavy breathing that was
ripping across his broad chest he wouldn't wait long.

This was not a good idea. Lara knew that. All the times she
had not allowed this to happen in the past had been for very
good reasons. However, Lara's reason had been hopelessly
weakened by the desire that had systematically set fire to
every sinew of her body the moment she had seen Coleman's
wet, naked body walk towards her with such intent.

Lara shook out her bob, unbuttoned her blouse and allowed herself to fall into him.

As his mouth opened in answer to her kiss, Coleman closed his eyes and became utterly lost.

Noreen got all dressed up that morning in a sexy rig-out – a black skirt, high boots and a striped Bardot top. This meant she couldn't wear a bra, which as she had quite large breasts wasn't ideal, but then, she didn't plan to be wearing it for long! Noreen had heard London was swinging and she was planning to swing it clean off its hinges – starting with heartthrob Coleman. She even played out some possible scenarios in her head. Noreen had seen the smutty seaside postcards and the Carry On films. She knew all the double entendres. *You've done such a good job, Noreen – I think it's time I gave you a bonus.*

Noreen adjusted her bosom and smiled as she headed for Coleman's office to report for duty and was just putting her hand on the heavy, soundproofed door when Arthur called out to her, 'I wouldn't go in there if I was you.'

He had seen Lara go in there just after Brian fled. The prick had lost his cocky edge alright. He was such a shaking mess, Arthur was pleased to note that he hadn't even bothered to give his arse one last boot out the door. That had been just over two hours ago and Coleman hadn't stuck his head out the door once. Arthur knew his friend. When a man was that hyped up and there as a woman on hand – there was only one thing to be done. It had only ever been a matter of time between him and Lara anyway. Still. In the middle of the day? It didn't seem entirely right to Arthur. Especially as he now had to find a way of explaining it to Noreen.

'Why not?' Noreen turned around too quickly and her breasts, two loose cannons under the tight, striped top, followed her torso with an unseemly slap. Arthur's eyes nearly popped out of his head as she shamelessly grabbed them in her hands to steady them.

'Oh, for God's sake, what's he doing in there that's so important?'

'Attending to some business,' Arthur said.

'I've got some business for him to attend to.' Noreen smiled. When she was feeling this frisky, there was no stopping her. She was not silly enough to believe that Coleman would seduce her there and then. It would take weeks, perhaps, for her to get him into bed, if ever. It might not lead to anything more than a fling. It's not like Noreen could see herself settling down with an Englishman. Nonetheless, she was enjoying the thought of it. The freedom of being away from home had given her a sense of optimism. Anything was possible. As she began to rattle the locked door, Arthur quickly stepped in front of her, gently but firmly taking her hand off it.

'Your friend Lara is in there with him.'

Arthur shuffled awkwardly at the door, not knowing what to say. He was worried that Noreen would be shocked at the idea of her friend making love in somebody's office during the afternoon. Despite her bawdy antics behind the bar, Arthur struggled to consider Noreen anything other than a nice Irish, Catholic lady. However, seeing his bashful demeanour, Noreen immediately assumed that Lara must have said something to him. Told him that she fancied Coleman. Otherwise why would he not have told her straight away?

It wasn't the fact that Lara was with Coleman that upset Noreen. It was the fact that she had told her she wasn't interested in him. Letting Noreen go ahead and make a play for him then getting him for herself was humiliating. She'd probably had a good laugh telling her new friends, Arthur and Annie, about her stupid, fat friend from Ireland who was so randy she went for men who were out of her league.

Noreen was so upset, she felt like turning on her heels and running out of there. But, she reminded herself, that was not what the Lyons' were made of. You didn't sit around boo-hooing over a foiled seduction. Not when there was a bar to be run, girls to be feted, drinks to be served and money to be made. Business took precedence over pleasure, always. The dead don't book in and they don't bury themselves, her father used to say. The bar is always open, was his other one, and, as long as there was a bar open, Noreen was compelled to be behind it.

'Where's Brian?' she asked Arthur, letting him off the hook.

Much relieved he replied with a huge grin. 'Fired!'

'Excellent,' she said. 'I assume you came the heavy and saw him off?'

'If you're asking if I took care of business? Then, yes.'

Arthur felt a little bad about exaggerating his part in Brian's shakedown and realised, then, that it was time to be honest with himself. He was trying to impress Noreen. Coleman liked Lara and he liked her friend. That's just the way it was. Unlike Coleman, he would never be able to do anything about it. Arthur had never found a way of seducing women and no one had ever bothered seducing him. It was because, he knew, he wasn't good enough. To entertain designs on Noreen was beyond his wildest dreams, given she was such a lady, a goddess with her magnificent bosoms and firm, capable manner, so far above him in every single way. Nonetheless, it was important to Arthur that he put his services, such as they were, at her disposal.

'If there's anything else you need me to take care of, Noreen,' he said, 'anything at all – you just let me know.'

Noreen wasn't sure that she liked the anything at all implication. But she smiled and said, 'Thank you, Arthur. Changing over those two barrels from last night for me would be a good start.'

It was another hour before Lara emerged from Coleman's office. Noreen was standing to the side of the bar, collecting some spirits from a locked cupboard, and watched Lara as she sneaked out. It was obvious from the furtive way she checked the bar that she was hiding from Noreen. Noreen felt hurt.

Nonetheless, Noreen was too busy to worry about it and found she had a great evening after that. The bar was buzzing and she was utterly in charge. The girls on the floor had taken to her, no dropped trays, one punter had his wrist slapped with no hard feelings, and everyone had a ball. Coleman did not offer her a 'bonus' at the end of the night but Noreen had long since decided she didn't mind. Lara had opened the door for her but, already, Noreen felt like she owned this place, this job, this new life. Sure, she fancied the pants off Coleman but, hey, so did everyone. She could probably have more fun leching over him in the changing room with the waitresses than actually having sex with him. She would never have put them together, but from the way he was mooning about the club that evening, Noreen assumed he was in love with her friend. Every man in Carney was a little in love with Lara. That was the way love worked. You never knew who you were going to fall in love with. Who would have thought she'd end up with John? For a moment, Noreen forgot she wasn't with him any more, then remembered and felt sad. She reminded herself that their adventure ended because it became predictable. She could not begrudge Lara her romantic adventure.

Not when she had left so much love behind to come in search of it herself.

However, after Noreen had packed up the bar, said goodnight to Arthur and headed back to the flat, she could not help but feel a little sad. Lara's deception had been a betrayal, however unintentionally. The old friend she trusted had let her down. There was no harm done and Noreen certainly would not let Lara and Coleman spoil her plans to stay in London. In any case, Lara might have just been biding her time. She could be planning to explain to her later on that evening. At this very moment she could be upstairs waiting to tell her all about it.

23

When Bobby Chevron got back to his flat in Knightsbridge after doing a deal on the fashion shop with Coleman, Maureen had said, 'Was Shirley lording it up, then?'

'What d'ya mean?'

'Well – her and Coleman. They're seeing each other ain't they?'

Bobby was pissed off that Coleman hadn't mentioned it to him. Especially after what Bobby said about wanting a go at her. Although, if he was seeing her, it might have been awkward to mention it.

A week later, Bobby walked into his villa in Marbella and found Shirley sitting in one of the white leather sofas in his sunken lounge.

Maureen was beside her, with one of those grim smiles on her face she used when she didn't like someone. She was a bad liar, Maureen. That was why he stayed married to her.

'Maureen invited me over on a holiday any time – so here I am!' Shirley snapped brightly. Shirley was a good liar. Butter wouldn't melt. That was why he fancied the pants off her.

Maureen smiled and said, 'You're very welcome, Shirley.' And she made them all a drink.

Chevron told Coleman to offer Shirley protection after her divorce from Devers, hoping she would never need it. This unexpected visit was nothing to do with that, he could tell. The cool way she was looking at him suggested that perhaps Devers was the one who needed protecting.

'I want that slag out of my house before I get back from the hairdressers,' Maureen spat at Chevron when Shirley left to powder her nose. 'This is family time. No business for the next three weeks. You promised.'

'Another drink, Shirley?' Maureen asked when she came back in.

'Thank you, Maureen,' Shirley said, all smiles.

While his wife was at the drinks cabinet with her back to them, Shirley leaned across and pressed a small, soft package into Chevron's hand.

Puzzled, he looked down and saw it was her panties. He barely got them into his pocket, managing to smile up at Maureen, benignly, as she passed him a drink.

Maureen knew Bobby and, usually, she could smell the interest of other women, but Shirley was as cool as water, admiring the furniture and complimenting Maureen on her good taste. By the time she had left, Maureen was almost regretting her suspicions.

'Why are you here?' Chevron said when his wife had gone.

'Why do you think I'm here?' she cooed, uncrossing her legs.

The sex was fantastic.

The next day, Chevron put Shirley into an apartment he owned in a neighbouring complex. He told Maureen he was going on a fishing trip in Torremolinos with the boys.

They barely got out of bed for five days.

Bobby was beginning to think he might be in love. He was certainly in trouble.

Shirley stood up after giving him the blowjob of his life. Bobby watched her walk across the room, naked, except for a pair of frilly, pink panties. Her breasts were firm and heavy; he could almost feel them pressing onto his face again. Her bouffant was dishevelled, sliding out of its pinned scaffolding in bleached mermaid tails.

Bobby Chevron turned on his side and reached for the cigar which he had left balancing on the marble locker beside the bed. Sometimes he liked to smoke at the same time but Shirley was too good for that. She had a way of keeping him on edge and it didn't do to get the 'big surprise' if you were holding a lit cigar. Bobby once set fire to a bird's hair. He managed to put it out by spraying her with soda water from the bar, and they both laughed about it afterwards. (Well, he had.) But Shirley wasn't the type who would laugh off a burning bouffant.

'It's gone out,' his voice was whinging, expectant. 'Pass me my lighter, Shirl, it's in my jacket pocket, hanging behind the door, there's a good girl.'

Looking back at him through narrowed eyes, Shirley moistened her lips with her tongue, then slowly slid her long manicured nail into his suit jacket. Chevron could feel himself getting hard again as she rooted about in his pocket, then lifted the solid gold lighter up to her shoulder and threw it straight at his head. 'Shit!' Chevron shouted and, in one swift move, barely dodged the lump of metal as it embedded itself deep into the pillow beside him.

'Fucking hell, Shirl. You could've killed me!'

She shrugged. 'Well, I didn't, did I?'

Her body tensed as she studied his face, eyeballing him coldly so he wouldn't read her shaking hands.

Shirley had thrown the lighter at Chevron so he would see she wasn't afraid of him, but she was afraid of him. Any woman would be a fool not to be. Short and solid with a flat head and a thick head of wavy hair tortured into a neat side parting, Chevron was physically unimpressive. However, every pore of him exuded the kind of casual violence that was immediately apparent to a woman like Shirley who had grown up around violent men. Charm and smiles, drawing you in, making you believe you were the woman who could change everything, the one who would make them soft and safe. They want to believe it themselves, but one joke, one wrong word, a look across the room at another man and – BAM – you never saw it coming. Her father had been like that. As Shirley got older, she thought her mother a weak fool. Then she married Handsome and got a taste of it. She knew from watching her mother that crying and pleading made men like that worse. So, when Handsome knocked her down, she stood up, wiped the blood from the side of her mouth and carried on like nothing had happened. But, when the bruises came out she never covered them up. She let him read his shame across the breakfast table and met his snivelling apology with cold indifference. These men always said they would never hit a woman. But they did. They also said they would never betray a friend. But they did that too. When they didn't lie directly in their words, they lied in their actions. Shirley wore Handsome's bruises like a badge, and they won her the sympathy of the only decent man she knew, Coleman. Coleman comforted her and offered her protection in the club, and when their friendship led to bed, Shirley believed they were together. Then, after only a few weeks, he started to make excuses. He said it was because they were working together and he wanted to preserve their friendship.

It turned out that was a lie too. Over the past six months

she watched him fall for the Irish girl. He tried to hide it but Shirley knew what it was like to love somebody and not have them love you back, and that's the way he was with Lara. Shirley was convinced he must be sleeping with her on the sly. Otherwise why would he have first made her a hostess, and now buy her a boutique? He was a liar. A man doesn't do all that for a woman for nothing.

Men like Coleman, Chevron and Handsome lied and lied and lied to get what they wanted.

So Shirley decided to lie too. Skimming a few quid off the bar was her way of having one over on them all. The extra money was nice, but it was never the point.

Rage flashed across Bobby's eyes and she thought he was going to snap, but then he smiled and shook his head, as if dealing with a bold child, before flicking the lighter open and puffing his stogie to life.

If she wanted to get my attention, he thought, *she's got it.*

'So tell me why you're really here, Shirley?'

'I told you, Bobby, I just fancied a few days away and...'

'Cut the crap girl. What happened to Coleman? I'm not shitting on my boy's territory am I?'

It's a bit late now if you are, thought Shirley.

'No,' she said, looking up coyly. 'Me and Coleman are over. Well – we never took off.'

Something in her voice, something uncharacteristically sweet made him curious.

'What do you mean?'

'Well...' her eyes flickered up at him. For a second he thought he smelt fear, then it was gone.

'Coleman just didn't turn out to be who I thought he was.' Shirley looked down quickly. Bobby saw she didn't want to diss Coleman in front of him. That was fair enough.

'You know what they say about love and war, darling.' He didn't like talking about Coleman in this context. Knowing he'd been with her. It didn't feel right. It was like sleeping with family or something.

'It wasn't that.' Her voice was barely above a whisper, as if he wasn't intended to hear it. Then she started fussing about finding her cigarettes on the floor and looking for a lighter. She was trying to put him off. The bird was hiding something. Chevron didn't like being lied to. And he didn't like birds playing games with his head.

'Wasn't what?'

She pretended she hadn't heard him.

'Why did you break off with Coleman? What happened?'

Just saying his name out loud reminded Chevron that Coleman was like a son to him. Here he was doing the dirty with some slag who, for all Bobby knew, Coleman might be in love with. It wasn't right.

He puffed heavily on his cigar, letting a huge plume out of the side of his mouth and nearly choking himself. Sitting up, he threw his legs over the side of the bed, reached down for his trousers and asked her again.

'What happened, Shirley? Did he break it off?' Then in his gentle voice, cunningly added, 'Did he hurt you?'

'No,' she said. 'He didn't hurt me.' But that wasn't the end of it. She seemed to think about continuing but then said, 'It don't matter.'

Bobby started to get impatient. Her voice was quiet and vulnerable; not like Shirley. Was she playing him? Or was she scared? What Shirley didn't realise was that everything Coleman did mattered to Chevron. He ran his business for him. He had taken him on as a kid, so in a way he was like a son. He had carried his mother's coffin. But mostly, Coleman was Chevron's representative. If something was going down with Coleman, it was Chevron's business. Who he slept with, what car he drove, what Coleman fucking ate was Bobby's business if he chose to make it so. He owned Coleman. He owned this bitch too – even if she didn't seem to know it. Yet.

'Oh go on,' Bobby said, then in a mock posh voice, 'do tell.'

He was turning nasty. She could hear it now. She just had to hold her nerve.

'It's none of my business,' she said pulling on her cigarette, trying to hold tough.

'Everything is my business,' Chevron said, clicking on his Rolex watch, not looking at her. Throwing a lighter at his fucking head. She could have killed him!

'I'm no snitch,' she said. That was the trigger.

He reached across from where he was sitting on the edge of the bed, grabbed Shirley's ankle, then stood up, jerking her body down so that it fell to the ground like a thrown doll. She heard a loud thud as her head hit the floor. It was carpeted. She'd been hit harder. It was a warning.

She gathered herself up, but he pushed her back.

'What do you mean?' he roared at her.

'Your fucking precious Coleman,' she shouted back, trying to keep the shake out of her voice, 'is scamming you!'

He was astride her now, his fat thighs sandwiching her torso, trapping her hands by her side. She could feel the weight of his muscular body bearing down on her through his groin. He could accidentally crush her to death by simply sitting on her organs if he was careless about such things. But Chevron wasn't careless when it came to hurting people. He knew exactly what he was doing.

'What are you fucking talking about?'

A gob of furious spittle hit her face. His right fist was pulled back. Shirley kept her face forward and held his raging, red eyes. If she turned her face and the punch landed on her cheek, her face was spoiled forever. If he hit her nose, she could get it fixed. Either way, it would hurt like hell. But, Shirley reminded herself, you don't mess with men like this and expect it to be easy. If you can't take a punch, get out of the ring.

'He's siphoning off booze from the bar and selling it back to the suppliers!'

'You're LYING!'

Bobby drew his hand back higher and she could feel his weight bearing down on her chest. Her breast was pushed painfully up under her chin and she strained to breathe as he pressed his knee hard into her abdomen. With every bit of strength she could find in her lungs she screamed at him.

'GO ON – HIT ME THEN!'

Then Shirley surprised herself by starting to cry. Not the pitiful, please don't hurt me cries that sent men like Bobby into a blind rage. These were tears of frustration.

'I swear, Bobby, I'm telling you the truth. Why would I lie? I didn't even want to tell you.'

That was true. Maybe she was telling the truth. Maybe. He lowered his fist but kept her locked to the floor with his legs.

'Why would my boy cheat me in such a stupid way? Why would he want to cheat me?'

'How the hell would I know that?' she said. 'I just know he is, that's all.'

She felt the weight of Bobby's body loosen.

'How?'

'If you get your fat arse off me and give me a cigarette I can tell you.'

Bobby stood up, ending the assault with the casual ease of a man turning away from his wife in bed.

She told him the details of her and Brian's scam, replacing her part with Coleman's. It was true what they said about lying: stay as close to the truth as you can.

'Why would he want the money?' Bobby said. 'I pay him well, don't I?'

'His girlfriend's shop,' she said.

Was there a note of bitterness in her voice? Was that what this was all about? Bobby shrugged it off. Nah. No woman would risk his ire for some petty jealousy.

'I paid for that,' Bobby said.

Shirley shrugged. She hadn't known that. A slither of regret slid through her, then was gone.

'Well whatever it cost, he's pumping everything out of the club into it too.'

She could still be lying but Bobby didn't care so much any more.

Everyone lied. He had taken all he needed from her now, and a bit extra with that information. He'd take some time on his own now to think about what to do next. Because, something would have to be done. He didn't like it, but these things could not be let lie.

As for Shirley? Sure, she'd done him a favour, but no matter how hard the facts were, a snitch was still a snitch.

Nonetheless, they ate a pizza, then Bobby initiated sex and Shirley went along with it.

He asked, out of politeness, how much longer she was staying and she lied and said her flight home left that evening. Bobby knew she was lying but seemed relieved anyway.

After sex, Shirley quickly rearranged her bouffant, then picked up her handbag at the door. As she turned to say goodbye Bobby was standing by the bed, and she thought she caught a look of sadness cross his face. That 'hard man broken' thing.

For a moment she thought she should walk across to him and tenderly kiss him goodbye.

Then he looked at her coldly, his vole-like eyes nonetheless pleading as he said, 'No harm done – eh doll?'

The good gangster code: I'd never hit a woman.

'That's right,' Shirley answered. I protect your reputation and you protect my life. She smiled as convincingly as she could then closed the door softly behind her.

Two days later, Maureen was rifling through a copy of the *Daily Mail*. Her sister posted them over to her in Spain every few days.

'Look at this,' she said to Chevron, who was lying mooning on the sofa. 'You didn't tell me Coleman's opened a boutique!'

'He never. I bought it,' Bobby said, sitting up.

'Well, it says here... dashing Coleman, at the opening of his new business venture – a boutique on the Kings Road. Big picture of him with some posh bird. He looks very—'

'Show me that.'

'Very good indeed. Hmmm.'

He snatched it from Maureen's reluctant hands.

'You're disgusting – you know that? You stupid birds you're all the same,' he said. 'Go and get me some lunch, woman.'

Maureen laughed. Bobby was so easy to wind up when it came to good-looking men. All the power in the world couldn't buy you a Coleman face.

When she left the room, Bobby made a phone call to London.

'Coleman's getting too big for his daisies,' he said to the person on the other end. 'I need someone reliable to sort him out.'

'He don't fright easy, boss.'

'Let's hope it don't come to that. Just keep a quiet eye and let me know if he goes off road.'

Then he called out to Maureen for his lunch. Although, in truth, Bobby felt like he had lost his appetite.

24

The restoration room in the bowels of the National Gallery was crowded. Ten students, six young men and four young women, were gathered around a broad table as their professor delicately manoeuvred his scalpel. Their tutor was working on a torn corner of a Rosa Bonheur rural scene, carefully scraping along the square inch he had just waxed and soldered to exactly replicate the texture of the brush strokes around it. It was intricate work and intimate too, and the students needed to get right up close to see what he was doing. The room was warm and the tension palpable. Matthew felt a drop of sweat trickle from his forehead onto the inside of his glasses and managed to mop it up before it fell onto the painting beneath. Shaken, he stood back a few inches, and a heavyset girl who had been standing behind him immediately pushed into his place as if she had been waiting for the opportunity. Matthew was uncomfortable with his proximity to all these other bodies and also in his stupid outfit. He ran his hand under the collar of his soutane. The full-length garment was made from heavy wool and, try as he might, in the past six months of his religious training, Matthew could not get used to it.

When his Irish seminary, Maynooth, agreed to allow Matthew an internship at the National Gallery in London, attending their painting restoration classes, he held out great hope that he would be able to do so in ordinary trousers and shirts, given the messy nature of the work and the fact that he was in London. However, Matthew discovered, while London was swinging in the newspapers it certainly wasn't swinging in the Catholic Church. The rector in Allen Hall, Chelsea, where Matthew was lodging while he completed his studies, was every bit as vigilant in his governance as his masters in Dublin. More so towards Matthew because he had been forewarned that the keen young art student needed a firm hand. Irish schools were ardently Catholic and ensured that the church got the pick of their male graduates. Monsignor Hoban, the rector at Maynooth, had taken him with great trepidation after learning from the young man's father that Matthew had broken off a marriage engagement to take up his vocation. Such displays of artistic temperament were not conducive to religious study. However, at his interview, the young man showed an impressive flair for Latin and Greek and a true passion for religious artworks, especially Caravaggio and da Vinci of whom his knowledge was encyclopaedic, so the rector had taken a chance.

The twenty-first ecumenical council of the Roman Catholic Church, or Second Vatican Council as they were calling it, had begun in 1962 and it looked as if it was going to revolutionise the church. The possibility had been mooted that one day priests would be able to get married, and there was talk of them doing away with the Latin mass as early as next year. The liberalising influences of the Second Vatican Council were having their own, small effect on certain sections of the Irish religious and Monsignor Hoban didn't like that. What better time, he decided, to accommodate a student with such a passion for languages and art forms that might soon be done away with and sold off altogether, if this wretchedly progressive Pope and his band of groovy clerics had anything to do with it? That was why the university agreed to fund Matthew's restoration course just six months into his training. Having somebody trained in art restoration would be a feather in his biretta. Monsignor Hoban just had to make sure Matthew didn't run off and get engaged to another woman in the meantime. He could not have imagined how far that idea was from Matthew's mind.

When Matthew saw the female students in his class, their bare legs shockingly exposed in their short skirts, all he thought of was how much better off they were than him. He craved a day out of his own, wretched long frock, longing to work in a light shirt and trousers like the other men in his class. However, it would have meant applying to the rector at Allen Hall for special dispensation and Matthew knew their view of his vocation was on shaky enough ground without applying to go about London in mufti. He could have removed the soutane and worn the trousers and shirt at the National Gallery, but was afraid of upsetting his tutors. They all loved the novelty of having a priest among them. Sometimes they addressed him in Latin, which made him cringe.

'That's all for today.'

Matthew ran his sweaty palms down the front of his painter's apron, and found the letter from his father that he had shoved in there earlier. His mother wrote to him every week. Adoring pages in her flowery scrawl, infused with pride and, more recently, an undisguised delight in his celibate state, which he found a little distasteful. Letters from his father contained the opposite sentiment. Short memorandums, usually with instructions for Matthew to post him some special tobacco he could not source in Cork. Often, his father appended his request with pointed barbs: news of his friends' sons excelling in the GAA and getting their young wives pregnant, to which Matthew longed to tell his father what he could stuff his pipe with! But he didn't. Because, now that he was a priest in training, he had to be good and respectful towards his father. Matthew longed for a light-hearted letter from Noreen, but she still wasn't speaking to him. Noreen was mad at him for leaving Lara, and his sister was as stubborn as a mule and slow to forgive. Knowing Noreen, she had banned her parents from mentioning her in their letters. Perhaps she had married John? No. Surely they'd not have a wedding without him? (Ruefully, he reminded himself that his mother would never let the family have a religious service without him. She'd probably want to wait until he could do the honours!) If Noreen was still raging at him for breaking it off with her best friend, well, he didn't blame her. He was still mad at himself.

Truthfully though, he had no choice. For a long time, the past year at least, since the issue of sex had reared its ugly head, Matthew had known there was something missing. Lara was his childhood sweetheart. He loved her. Of course he did. Lara was his best friend. His soulmate. She shared his love of art. They admired each other's talents and were supportive and excited by each other's work. Now, there was nobody to share this extraordinary experience at the National Gallery with. Not a day went by when something didn't happen; a funny anecdote about some doddery old tutor, the revelation in some painting he had always admired revealing itself anew. He missed Lara whenever he wanted to share those moments with her. Each time, he made a mental note, *I must tell...* then remembered that he had screwed his life up and left her.

Except, he knew it could not be any other way. Everything in their relationship had been perfect except the one thing, which, it seemed, was prized above all else: romantic love. He loved her but he was not in love with her. On the few occasions they made love, Matthew became aware that he was simply going through the motions. Sex had been an enjoyable, satisfying experience but Matthew knew it should be more than that. It was for Lara. The first time they made love she cried afterwards. She curled herself into his chest like a vulnerable child and wept with emotion. 'I love you,' she said.

'I love you too.' It was the first time he had lied to her. The other times he said it he had meant it. He loved her like a sister, like a friend, like a childhood sweetheart should. But he couldn't love her like a man should love a woman. With his body, he could do a good job of pretending. But he did not feel the love for her with his heart and soul. Lara was his friend. Clever, capable, kind-hearted Lara. She loved him and he needed her. But that wasn't enough. Not for him and, he knew, certainly not for her.

It was then that Matthew knew he wasn't enough. It wasn't Lara; it was him. Lara was perfect in every way. She knew him, she loved him – they had everything in common. She was beautiful, accomplished, sweet natured, strong. She took his worries away and made everything alright. If he couldn't love Lara Collins, then surely he couldn't love any woman. Didn't deserve to love a woman.

As one of the cleverest boys in school, the priesthood had always been an option for him. He had never considered it because he had always loved Lara. The church offered the best education and could open doors in the field of art that fascinated him. If he could not live his own life, the life Lara had planned for them both, he would immerse himself in history. Live among books and paintings and take refuge from the world by absorbing the legends of saints and scholars. The priesthood was an ideal option. Except for the long, woollen dress.

The students dispersed and ran towards the door, anxious to get out of the claustrophobic room and back to the freedoms of their own lives.

The professor looked up at the lonely priest taking off his apron and said, '*Vere Fratis* Matthew'.* Matthew smiled at him weakly and headed out the door.

Sometimes, Matthew would wind down with a visit to his favourite room at the gallery: the pre-Raphaelite room. The medieval revivalism of the mid-eighteenth century was Matthew's favourite period in art. With its red-haired, pale-skinned maidens, it was unapologetically populist, and, although he could scarcely admit it to himself, the women, with their pale skin, long, luscious hair and soft, sensual poses reminded Matthew, however briefly and inappropriately, that he still was a man. Today, Matthew was too anxious to get into the fresh air to look at paintings, however beautiful. Outside, Matthew walked down the grand, pillared steps of the gallery and into Trafalgar Square. The scale of the gallery and the huge lions that flanked it always cheered him, reminding him that he was in London, a place where history was all around him. In the monuments, the architecture, the galleries and museums – art and history were everywhere. They had galleries and museums in Dublin, of course, but not as many and not nearly as magnificent. History in Ireland was a small, personal affair. The past always tinged with the regretful consequences of famine and revolution. All caused by the

* Translation from Latin: Goodbye Brother Matthew.

English, and although Matthew felt he should have cared about that as deeply as his republican countrymen he found he didn't. People died for causes, men were slaughtered on battlefields. Art outlived them all. You died anyway; nothing could make a man live forever, but these monuments were as much a testament to eternal life as the Holy Trinity. Matthew wasn't 100 per cent sure that he believed in God – but he believed in art. And through exposure to all this beauty he was beginning to believe it might be one and the same thing. If these monuments were for dead soldiers, Matthew thought, even if they weren't for his soldiers, or his dead – did that really matter? What was left here was simply the unapologetic magnificence of these gargantuan lions, glaring proudly into the lunchtime crowd, the sun glinting off their metallic coats.

In the midst of his philosophical reverie, Matthew opened his father's letter. It was brief, one side of a single writing pad sheet in large, round handwriting.

I won't beat about the bush, I'm worried about Noreen. She took off over to London a month ago, for no good reason, leaving poor aul' John in a desperate state altogether. She said she was going to work in a bar with your old beau Lara Collins, then hid the address on us. So I telephoned the Collins and got the details off them which, as you might well imagine, they weren't too happy about giving me! I don't mind telling you, I don't like all this coming and going. First you and now Noreen. So, as you started all this nonsense, will you go and find your sister and tell her to ring home. Her mother is gone demented. And don't even think of giving me any of your nancy-boy shite about upsetting Lara. It's high time you paid a call to that young woman and gave her a proper apology after leaving her high and dry.
Your father

P.S. And when you do see Noreen, ask the selfish strap why the hell she needs to go working in a bar in London when there is a perfectly good bar here? Tell her I'm killed out!

Attached was a card with the name of a club, Chevrons, and an address on the Kings Road.

His father's admonishing tone was no great shock to him but the Lara news was a bombshell. Lara was in London. He had suspected as much over the months since they had parted but had made a point of never asking. Nobody volunteered the information. People were always very careful what they say to priests. It was one of the things he didn't like about becoming one. One of the many things. However, in this case it had been useful, as he had spent a great deal of the past few months trying not to think about Lara. Of course, everything his father said was right. It was time to face up to what he had done. It was time for him to act like a man, even if the very idea of it already made him feel like a foolish, chastised little boy.

Matthew folded the letter over the small card onto which his father had written Lara's address without looking at it.

Then he packed it back into the pocket of his soutane and headed towards Westminster.

A walk back to Chelsea along the Thames was what he needed to clear his head.

25

Chevrons was, at most, a twenty-minute walk from the seminary. Not, indeed, that Matthew ever had much cause to wander the Kings Road. Certainly not in his soutane. In any case, the Kings Road was the heartland of modernity. People his age embracing sex and drugs and a new kind of freedom which, while he could see it was progress of a kind, did not interest Matthew one jot. The modern world had been Lara's domain. She had the sixties' obsession with fashion – brightly coloured clothes, loud music and that new kind of simplistic, stick-on art which he, frankly, found offensive.

Over the past few months Matthew had missed Lara, but he did not miss the progressiveness she had sometimes foisted on him.

'She loves you, yeah, yeah, yeah…' His ears were assaulted by loud music blaring from a shop selling Groovy Denims. Although the greater part of him wished he was wearing denims instead of what he had come to think of as his 'hot frock', Matthew admitted to himself that, while they had been together, he had feigned more interest in Lara's artistic efforts than was entirely honest.

He had been a hypocrite in pretending to think of fashion as a viable art form. Another thing to feel guilty about. Another thing to apologise for when he saw her.

Matthew was dreading meeting both Lara and his twin sister. Noreen had barely spoken to him since he left her friend, and was a fierce adversary at the best of times. She would not be pleased to see him. However, being a priest was all about punishment and discomfort and, of course, martyrdom when you got good at it. Matthew could only hope his furious sister wouldn't turn him into one of those this afternoon. It never occurred to him to pray.

Chevrons, with its battered, black door and tarnished gold plaque looked like a shady joint. More so when the door half opened and an angry, wiry man peered out at him.

'Is Noreen Lyons here?' Fierce as his sister was, Matthew knew it would be easier to face her before Lara.

'Who wants her?' the man asked. He looked Matthew up and down as if he was concealing weaponry under his skirts, before stating the obvious. 'You're not a regular.'

'I'm her brother Matthew,' he said.

The gangster (he could not be anything else) looked at him warily.

'You a Catholic?'

There were several replies Matthew felt like giving to this question, but the funny little man didn't look like he was joking.

'Yes,' he said calmly then indicated his collar and skirt. 'I'm training to be a priest.'

Arthur raised his eyebrow and nodded sagely, as if conferring his approval on a good career choice.

'Follow me.'

Matthew followed him down stairs covered in a plush purple carpet until they reached a long, dark room filled with the quiet murmur of lunchtime drinking.

'Hang on here,' the gangster said then, seeming to think again, turned to Matthew and rather formally held out his hand, saying, 'I'm Arthur... erm... Father.'

Matthew took it and said, 'Just Matthew. Not a priest yet.'

Arthur seemed confused by this assertion, as did a few of the customers who, Matthew noticed, were looking over at him. The bloody soutane. Matthew didn't want to be seen going up to the long bar. He would be less conspicuous sitting down, so took a low seat near the stage. Almost as soon as he did his ears were assaulted with loud music, 'Louie, louie – whoa baby...', the lights came on with a loud snap then, directly in front of his face, from behind a tinsel curtain, a girl emerged wearing a minuscule gold bikini. As she snaked around the stage, frantically shaking her hips, the bikini was revealed to be nothing more than a handful of lightly strung beads, which flicked away from her body revealing absolutely everything. Matthew did not know where to look. Nudity did not bother him. If you were shocked by the human form, you had no business studying renaissance art. What did bother him was being seen dressed as a priest at a strip show. It was already a source of great amusement to the men behind him.

'Go on, padre!' he heard somebody shout behind him. 'Show 'er what you've got under that frock!'

He turned around to give the men a good-humoured smile, shaking his hand to indicate he wasn't here for the stripper, but as he did he felt himself being jerked back by the shoulder.

'What the hell are you doing here?'

Noreen.

'I could ask you the same question.'

'Don't be such a sanctimonious goshawk. I'm working. Something you've never done a day of in your life.'

'At least I'm not hanging out with lowlifes in some dirty den of iniquity.'

'Try telling that to the lads.' She gave her customers a cheery wave. 'They're getting a great kick out of you.'

'That's not my fault.' Even though he was the good one, the moral one, the priest for goodness sake, somehow Noreen was taking the moral high ground.

'Coming in here dressed up like that. They think you're part of the show! I'm trying this new girl out – seeing if we can bring a bit of class into the lunchtime strip – and you're making a mockery out of it!' Then she prodded him, hard, in the top of his arm and said, 'Come on. Up with you!' When Matthew stood up the whole room cheered, and Noreen gave a little bow and a flourish of her hand before handing him over to Arthur, who had been standing on guard ever since she'd admonished him for letting her stupid brother cross the threshold at all.

'Take him out back while I calm this lot down.'

Arthur escorted him to an empty store room where he sat on a barrel and waited for his sister to come and tear strips off him.

She did not disappoint.

'Mam and Da are really worried about you,' Matthew said.

'They're in their hole. Da just wants me to go home and run the business for him so he can swan off and play golf, or whatever. Failing that, he wants to get you back in touch with Lara so that you'll give up this stupid priest business then go home and, presumably, also try to make yourself useful.'

'But Mammy...'

Even as he said it, Matthew could hear how whiney and pathetic it sounded. A nancy boy. That's what his father called him.

Noreen softened. Their mother was a good woman. But not strong.

'Mammy is fine,' she said. 'It's better she doesn't know where I'm working. I'll write to Da tonight and tell him I'm working in an Irish bar. You tell him you saw me and that I'm fine. Tell him I'm busy making a small fortune for a landlord from Longford. That will get his goat and put him so high up on his horse he won't bother us again for a while.'

'What about Lara?'

'What about her?'

'I should see her...'

'Why?'

'To say sorry.'

'For what? Breaking her heart? Deciding you'd prefer to be a stupid priest than be with her? She's over you, Matt, or, at least, she's getting over you.'

Noreen thought about Lara sneaking out of Coleman's office. Noreen had expected, or rather hoped, Lara would tell her about their encounter afterwards. Fill her in on the gory details of her new romance, but she didn't. Whatever Lara's reason – guilt, embarrassment – Noreen was hurt by her silence. It seemed her old friend was becoming as secretive as their strange flatmate, Annie. Was it a good idea for Lara to see Matthew while she was starting a fledgling romance with Coleman? Probably not. But then, that wasn't Lara's call because, if she wasn't going to tell Noreen what was going on with her, then there was no need for Noreen to fill her in on her brother's sudden appearance.

'Leave her alone, Matthew. You turning up on her suddenly would just upset the applecart.'

'I need to make amends.'

'Not always about what you need, brother dear. You're

a priest now – you're supposed to think about what other people need. Lara's moved on.' Shuffling him towards the door she added, 'Speaking of which, you need to move along yourself now. This shift won't manage itself and I don't want those boys upsetting the new stripper – erm, dancer.'

As Noreen walked Matthew to the door she felt a pang of pity for her poor brother. In his seminarian dress he looked out of kilter – not just with the seedy environs of Chevrons, but with himself. While Noreen had the confident bluff of Frank in her bones Matthew had always been less certain of himself and his place in the world. He would make a terrible priest, and the last thing the world needed was more terrible priests. She hoped he wouldn't make it that far. That he might give this priest business up before it gave up on him. As she gently encouraged him out onto the Kings Road, although he didn't say anything, she could sense he was vulnerable and lost and Noreen felt as if she was throwing him to a nest of vipers. At the door, she pulled him back and kissed him, assuring him that she would write to their parents and promised to contact him at the seminary to meet up again before too long. Unseen, from the bottom of the stairs, Arthur witnessed their tender moment, and a lump caught in his throat.

Back in the bustle of the Kings Road, Matthew did not have to be back in the seminary until evening prayer. He had expected that Noreen and Lara would keep him busy for the whole afternoon. Certainly, at the very least, cook him his dinner. Hungry, Matthew wandered into a small, working man's cafe across the road from the club, feeling a little hard done by that his sister hadn't dropped everything to feed him.

Lost in resentment he sat by the window and picked up the plastic covered menu. He had barely begun to read it when he sensed the waitress standing over his shoulder. Another woman come to annoy him.

'I'm not ready yet,' he snapped.

'In a minute, so.'

Something in the soft, smooth timbre of her voice, the barest hint of an Irish accent, caused him to turn around. When he saw her, a feeling came over him like nothing he had ever experienced before. Looking at the girl's face Matthew felt as if he was looking into every painting he had ever admired, all at once. She was every white-skinned, crimson-haired maiden he had ever fallen in love with. In an instant he relived those stunned moments when he first stood in the National Gallery gazing at the sublime originals of his painter heroes, Rubens, Raphael, astonished by their ability to capture the mysterious beauty of women onto canvas. This feeling, he realised at the time, was the closest he'd ever been to falling in love. Now, this feeling was back but it was happening with a real woman. Although, in some sense, her beauty was so otherworldly Matthew felt as if he might be gazing at an illusion, the feeling he had ran deeper than for her beauty alone. Although she was a complete stranger to him, Matthew felt he knew her. He instinctively understood things about her that he knew were true. Even though he had no evidence whatsoever to suggest it, he could see in her eyes that she was vulnerable. She had been hurt. Without her saying a word, he could see in her beautiful eyes that she was carrying something that did not belong to her. It was a lifetime in a moment; this was the world standing still.

Matthew was at a loss for words but he couldn't let her go so he said, 'Erm, mixed grill please.'

'Are you sure?' she said, writing his order down. 'It'll be about twenty minutes – to make sure the steak is well done.' Then she smiled.

Even though he was sitting down, Matthew felt his insides collapse. Unable to speak, he nodded in reply and she went off to the kitchen with his order. Matthew pinched himself for being so useless, then braced himself for the longest twenty minutes of his life.

26

Coleman and Lara made love for nearly two hours. No words passed between them. It was such an instant, instinctive, intense experience that afterwards Lara did not know quite what to make of it. Lying on his office sofa, the weight of his relaxed, heavy arms resting on her naked breasts, Lara became enveloped by the rhythm of their breathing, and a slow panic began to rise up in her. They weren't even in a bed. Lara was no prude. She and Matthew had made love (although it had been a tame, cautious affair compared to this), but they had known each other for years and were getting married. This man was her boss. A London gangster. His role as Lara's friend and business partner had been burned out of her by the passionate heat of what they had just experienced. What was he now? What was she to him? Lover? There was still enough Irish Catholic in Lara for that to sound cheap. Boyfriend? Coleman was no boy. Maybe it was nothing. Just sex. A sixties moment. Coleman was desired by every woman he met. Maybe it was just her turn. Whatever the case, this was all a horrible mistake. She was naked, on a sofa, in the middle of the day, in the aftermath of lovemaking with a handsome Englishman she should be maintaining a business-like distance from. What had she been thinking? Lara was about to make a move to go when she felt the heat of Coleman's breath on her neck. Her eyes closed involuntarily. Despite herself, she was unable to resist even the smallest advance from him.

Then, he moved his mouth to her ear and said, in a coarse whisper, so small it was barely audible, 'I love you.'

Lara got such a fright she thought she mustn't have heard him right. But she had heard him perfectly.

She managed to stop herself from saying 'Sorry?' to buy time out of her shock, and instead did the only thing she could do in response to such a momentous statement. She pretended not to have heard him, extracted herself gently from his arms and started to get dressed.

'I'm sorry,' she said, keeping her voice as light as she could. 'I have to get back to the shop. They'll be wondering where I am.'

She smiled at him, but knew it looked awkward and contrived.

'Of course,' he said, reaching for a cigarette. His eyelids dropped with disappointment and his jaw hardened. He was hurt. But there was nothing she could do about that except the one thing she would not do, which was tell him she loved him back.

Lara managed to sneak out of the club without anyone seeing her. Especially Noreen. The last thing she needed was her ex-boyfriend's sister grilling her about this. Especially after she had expressed an interest in Coleman – although after this encounter it seemed even more unlikely a scenario.

✻

Annie was cleaning under her bed when the carpet sweeper hit something. Her case. She felt slightly nauseous at the memory of its existence. Then, even sicker at the realisation that the carpet sweeper had touched it. It had never happened before. The sweeper didn't reach that far under the bed. It must have been moved. Annie got down on her knees to check and nearly threw up when she saw the angle of the case askew and the padlock facing her. Her first thought was maybe somebody else had moved it while cleaning. But nobody cleaned except her. Somebody must have been snooping. Not Lara. Noreen? But why?

For a moment, Annie wondered what she should do for the best. She took out the case and reassured herself that the lock had not been tampered with. They had no reason to suspect her of anything. Why shouldn't she have a locked case under her bed? She was a private person.

Annie decided the best thing to do was to be open about it. Well, open about the case's existence, if not its contents. So, when the three of them were gathered in the living room that evening she said, quite matter-of-factly, 'Did anyone move my case under the bed?'

Lara vaguely said, 'What case? What are you talking about?'

Noreen blurted out, 'Pfffft. No? Why?'

'Only I was cleaning earlier and I have a suitcase under my bed. It's locked because it has a lot of precious, private things in it and somebody's moved it.'

Lara looked aghast.

'Why would anyone go under your bed?'

'Well, they could be cleaning,' Annie said, looking at Noreen.

Noreen laughed awkwardly. 'That's weird. Who keeps a locked suitcase under their bed?' Noreen said, looking away as she refilled her glass from a can of TAB.

'I do,' said Annie.

Lara took the can off Noreen and took a swig from it.

'Snooping again, Noreen?'

She nodded back at her and said to Annie, 'Don't leave anything private lying around with this one about, she's nosy as all hell.'

Normally, Noreen would have taken the slagging. She knew she was nosy but this was different. If Lara had been on her own and said it, she might have taken it but in front of Annie, it felt like a betrayal. A double betrayal as she was also holding out on her over Coleman. In any case, she knew her instincts were right and that there was something fishy about Annie. Her cheeks burned with fury.

'I'm sure that's not true,' Annie said, not getting the joke, which made Noreen hate her even more. 'I just wouldn't like to think of anyone going through my private things.'

Noreen was speechless with rage but could hardly defend herself, so she stood up and said, 'I've left something in the club.' Then she went downstairs.

She found Arthur and the two of them had a whisky and a fag, and she made him tell her the story of his nickname again. His company and anecdotes reminded her that she was on this great adventure, and that Lara was her oldest friend and they would get over this misunderstanding. Annie was a different kettle of fish. She would have to bide her time, but by God she was going to find out what was in that padlocked case.

After Noreen left, Alex turned up at the door full of beans.

'You are not going to BELIEVE who just called,' he said, the moment he stepped into the living room.

'Amaze us,' said Lara.

The day after the shoot, when Alex's pictures had appeared on Penelope Podmore's page, Lara became inundated with requests from magazines for her clothes. Things were flying. Every model agency in town wanted Annie.

'*Vogue*.'

Lara raised her eyebrows. That was big. Annie was in the kitchen, distracted.

'I said *VOGUE*,' Alex shouted at her but she only smiled politely.

'They want me to take some test pictures of Annie – try us both out. Like Bailey and Shrimp. They think we have a vibe.'

'I can't ask Fred for time off,' she said, wiping down the kitchen counter. 'We're short staffed at the moment and the builders are keeping us really busy.'

Alex thought she was joking. He nearly swallowed his own teeth. He looked at Lara. 'Is she serious?'

Lara nodded. Despite her modelling up a storm on the day of their shoot, Lara could feel that Annie was stalling on starting a modelling career, for some reason. Maybe it was her whole secrecy, privacy thing that drove Noreen so mad. Maybe she just had cold feet about the modelling business. Maybe that wonderful flowering they had seen was a one off or maybe, just maybe, she wasn't interested in being a fashion model.

'Lara!' he pleaded. 'Talk some sense into her.'

'If she doesn't want to do it, she doesn't want to do it,' Lara told him. 'It's up to Annie.' Annie was cleaning and cleaning, wiping and polishing. Lara could see she was agitated; whatever was the matter with her there would be no use talking to her when she was like this. She was gentle, but Annie could be as stubborn as a mule.

As he was leaving, out of Annie's earshot, Alex pleaded with Lara.

'Please talk her around. This is my big break. And yours.'

'I like my job,' Annie said, when Lara came back in.

'You know this is a once in a lifetime opportunity, Annie? *Vogue* don't ask twice,' she said. 'You'll never get this chance again.'

'I already earn more money than I need,' Annie said. 'I'm happy at Fred's. I don't need anything more.'

'But you were good at it,' Lara said. 'The pictures look great. It's such a waste not to do it.'

'It's just how I look, Lara. It doesn't mean anything. Being beautiful isn't...' Then she got a faraway look in her eyes. 'It's not good. It can be – a curse.'

Lara could see that Annie was overwhelmed and not being disingenuous about her beauty. She seemed, if not unaware, then at least genuinely uninterested in the power of her appearance. Everyone in London was all about the look. Annie had it but she wasn't interested in using it. Lara sometimes wondered if there was something fundamental missing in her friend.

It was almost admirable enough for her to let it go. Except that Lara had a vested interest in harnessing Annie's beauty to promote That Girl. Bigging this up was getting them nowhere. So she played it down.

'Look,' she said, 'there's no big deal here, Annie. And there's certainly no need to leave the cafe. Just take one afternoon off, we'll take a stroll up to a quiet part of Kensington Gardens, and Alex can just take some snaps of you. No fuss. I'll do your hair and makeup and put you in one of my frocks.'

Annie still looked uncertain.

'Please, Annie. It's the only way I'll get the fashion editor there to take notice of me.'

'But you're a brilliant designer. They should take notice of you anyway.'

'I need a face, Annie. And I'm afraid you've got it.'

Annie looked at her and Lara put on a pleading face. She had her.

'Just this one time? Please? I promise I won't put pressure on you again.'

Annie nodded.

It wasn't the modelling she minded. But the possibility of curious Noreen snooping around in her room had unnerved her. Her past would make anyone want to keep a low profile and becoming a fashion model was the opposite of that. She'd enjoyed being photographed but she got a fright seeing her picture published in an English newspaper. However, she owed it to Lara to help her in any way she could. And these pictures, Lara assured her, were just for the fashion editor's eyes and not for publication.

Alex was a nervous wreck when Lara called and told him her plan. He told her that *Vogue* would be expecting him to put together a big studio shoot. However, Lara told him there was no way Annie would agree to that and persuaded him to call the picture editor and stand his ground. 'Tell her you work better on location and one to one,' she told him. 'Which is true. You call the shots – they'll respect you for it.'

In the end, they were charmed and a date and time was set, much to Alex's irritation, around Annie's work schedule at Fred's.

Days passed, Coleman had not gone near Lara in the shop, or the flat. Lara felt annoyed about that. Although she knew it was an irrational expectation, part of her wanted Coleman, a proud, macho man, to risk almost certain rejection by telling her he loved her again with such brute force it would quieten the uncertainties she had been feeling since their encounter.

Although the very idea of it terrified her too. What would be the consequences of being with him? An English gangster. What would it mean? He said he loved her – did that equate to marriage with a man like that? Lara was a free spirit but she was also an Irish Catholic. How did that work?

She was so confused. First by her own behaviour. That sudden, passionate letting go she had experienced in his office was very unlike her. Then – with Coleman? And his declaring he was in love with her like that. So soon? It didn't seem possible and yet, in some small part, she felt as if this was something she had really known. Was this what she wanted? Had she wanted it all along? Her and Coleman? She was a middle-class Irish girl from a good family and he was a cockney orphan who had grown up to be a gangster. Lara winced at her own bourgeois sensibility and, yet, it didn't seem possible that she could be in love with him. And how could you not know if you loved someone or not? Surely love was the great certainty. She had never been uncertain about Matthew. If anything, she had been too certain. The more she thought about it, the more of a puzzle it seemed to become.

After a few days keeping herself distracted by the buzz of the shop, Lara decided to lock herself in the studio. Doing some practical, creative work was the best way she knew to give her some space to take it all in and decide what to do about Coleman and the business because, after all, the two were intertwined.

Lara pulled her apron down from its hook behind the door and, placing the plain, navy rectangle over her head, walked across the bare floorboards to her cutting table. Reaching into the pocket for a pencil, Lara found a letter from her mother that she had stuffed in there a few days ago. Lara's mother sent her long gossipy missives about what was happening back home in Cork, every week. Her mother was never short of news, much of it about the state of their neighbours' health and of little interest to Lara. Lara wrote back sporadically, brief notes giving her mother the bare facts about where she was working and what she was doing, but always the impression that she was busy, and happy and getting on with her life, which was all her concerned parents wanted to know. Her mother's letters were important to Lara because they were the only thing connecting her to home. She had thrown herself into London life so hard that sometimes Lara felt she was in danger of forgetting who she was. Marian's letters grounded her, reminded her where she was from and stopped her from becoming completely lost in this new, English world she had chosen. Lara grabbed the envelope and tore it open. One of her mother's silly, light-hearted gossipy letters was just what she needed to escape this jittery, uncertain feeling that was taking her over since she and Coleman made love.

Dear darling Lara,

Just sending you a short note to alert you to the fact that Frank Lyons was onto us by telephone just now. He said himself and Patricia are worried about Noreen. Apparently, she left for London a month ago and hasn't been in touch. She told them she was staying with you. I told him that was news to me. I wouldn't put it past the strap to lie to her parents while she went off gallivanting. That said, she will never be as deceitful as that vile brother of hers. Sorry to preach darling, I am your mother, after all!

I'm afraid I had given Frank your address before he informed me that Matthew is also over in London at present (studying or something) and that he might call on you. I was most insistent in trying to put the man off but you know

what he's like. Very brash (I never liked him). I am so sorry.
Just thought I had better warn you in case Matthew turns
up at your door and gives you a fright!
  All my love, Mam.
  P.S Bridie Bannagher has pneumonia! More next week.

Lara stood, paralysed. Matthew was in London.

In a moment she realised that everything had changed. Rather, the confusion that had been building in her the past week climaxed and spilled over.

When Noreen went for an afternoon nap in preparation for the evening shift she found Lara waiting for her.

'Why the hell didn't you tell me Matthew was in London?'

Noreen's stomach sank to the ground. How did she find out? Oh my God – had he been to see her? Lara was waving one of her mother's letters at her. It was so stupid of her to think she could keep a secret from anyone in Ireland. No matter where you were in the world, word got around by letter. In just one short week, everyone would know your business.

'I didn't think it was important. I didn't think you'd want to know. You hadn't asked after him.'

That was all true. She was out of it now.

'Of course I didn't ask after him. Why would I? After what he did!'

Noreen felt a pang of defensive anger rise up in her. After all, Matthew was still her brother. Bad and all as he was, blood was thicker than water. Normally, it would be in Noreen's nature to lash out and give as good as she got. But something in her held back. Some survival instinct, perhaps a maturity brought on by being away from home, reminded her that this was Lara's flat she was living in. And, she was working for a man who was, almost certainly, Lara's secret lover. Plus, she was annoyed now. In not talking about her brother she had been simply protecting her old friend. Her silence had been motivated by kindness rather than deception. How dare Lara accuse her of keeping secrets when she was, after all, an open book? Even going as far as expressing an interest in Coleman when Lara had, clearly, set her sights on him herself. This small humiliation rose up in Noreen now as a petulant swipe.

'Exactly,' she said, breathing in slowly, turning her anger into haughty reason. 'I didn't want to add to your upset.'

'Well you've bloody well added to it now by lying to me,' Lara shouted at her.

Noreen took another deep breath, closed her eyes and said, 'I'm so sorry, Lara. I didn't mean to upset or offend you.'

Both of them knew Noreen well enough to know that she wasn't one bit sorry. However, fiery, impulsive Noreen had never held the moral high ground before. When it came to losing her temper, she was generally the first to blow. She found she was rather enjoying this new, passive aggressive Noreen and the obviously disquieting effect it was having on Lara. She felt more in control of herself. She was using her annoyance to better effect.

'Would you like me to give you the address where Matthew is staying?' she asked, plastering a look of genuine concern on her face which, as the person looking at it, Lara found barely convincing.

Lara wanted to kill her. But this new, conciliatory Noreen had discombobulated her. Plus, she had no other way of finding out where Matthew was. And, in the past hour since she read her mother's letter, Lara realised that she did need to see him, very much. She was still confused about Coleman, but the letter from her mother, as well as being shocking, revealed to her that the past might hold the answer to her future.

She had not got over Matthew and needed to see him before putting their relationship, and all the anger and hurt it had caused her, to rest. Seeing him, she decided, was a necessity, and she could not bear the idea of sitting around waiting for him to call.

'I haven't even been to see him myself,' Noreen went on. That was true. She hadn't, technically been to see him. Noreen didn't mention that he had been to see her. She hoped to hell if Lara did go and see him (which she probably wouldn't. She'd have to be some eejit to pick her wimpy, priest brother over a hunk like Coleman), he'd have the good sense to keep his mouth shut.

'To be honest, Lara, I really didn't think it was such a big deal, but if it means so much to you, of course, I'll see if I can dig out the name of the seminary where he's staying.'

'Thanks,' Lara said, plastering a grateful and apologetic smile on her face, which to Noreen didn't look the least apologetic or grateful.

Their stand-off was interrupted by Annie who came tripping in the door with a bag of food.

'I just saw Coleman on the way up,' she said. 'He was asking if you were going down to the club this evening, Lara. Said he had something he wanted to talk to you about.' Then she winked – a cheeky wink. It was most unlike her to joke around like that, but Annie had changed a little. Nothing dramatic, just a lightness had taken her over, making her feel like making a cheeky comment about Lara and Coleman. Not, for one moment, did she think it might be considered indiscreet, or that Lara might worry that Annie knew something that she shouldn't know, or was wondering if Coleman had said something to her. Opposite her, Noreen was quietly fuming, convinced that obviously Annie knew about her friend and

Coleman. Lara had confided in Annie and not her, and now, the sly cow was teasing them both with it.

'I've got spaghetti for dinner,' Annie said and, oblivious to the flatmates' anxiety and anger, walked towards the kitchenette.

'Lovely!' the two Cork girls said in unison.

Except, in truth, neither of them felt it was very lovely at all.

27

Annie had finished her morning shift in Fred's and was getting ready to go home when she noticed the young seminarian who had been in a few days before that, taking the window seat again.

When she first saw him, she thought he looked nice. He had been painfully shy, barely able to look at her when she delivered his mixed grill. She had assumed he was a one-off customer but here he was, back again. And, my, but he was handsome.

It was strange for Annie to notice a man in that way. She could not remember ever having looked at a man that way before. When she first met Dorian she thought him handsome and kind. As a child, she had been charmed by him and fallen a little in love with him. That piece of love made Annie feel that, somehow, she had invited him to 'love' her that way. It was what he told her. When he abused her, and she saw the extent to which his appearance was the worst kind of lie, he robbed her of any interest she might have in boys and young men. Not that she ever came across any, but now that she had the opportunity, the freedom to love, she felt too tainted to even consider it. Men were a threat, or not a threat. And yet, here she was, looking at this man, this stranger, in a way she had never considered looking at a man before.

Some of the breezy attitude she had in front of the camera followed Annie home, and over the next few days she found she was feeling somewhat lighter in herself. Her pictures came out in the paper, and everybody made a great fuss of her. Fred told her she was 'sex on legs', which made Giuliana hit him across the back of the neck with a tea towel and Annie laughed until she thought she might be sick.

While she enjoyed the experience, she hadn't really wanted to take it much further, but when Lara and Alex insisted she do some more pictures with them, she said that she would. Perhaps it would be fun to become a model, but for now Annie was happy to enjoy the small feeling of freedom that the one appearance in the paper had given her. She had been hiding for so long it didn't do to rush into anything.

Perhaps it was because he was a priest, but there was a quiet, thoughtful air about him that made her feel safe.

He seemed to have more confidence today. When she brought out his mixed grill, he looked up at her, smiled and said, 'Thank you,' as if it held some significance. He had refined, delicate features for a man and his eyes were shining with kindness. He liked her. She could tell. Yet, she didn't mind.

Annie felt the eyes of men on her all the time. Even if she dressed modestly, she felt herself being leered at, appraised. She always felt nervous in the company of men she didn't know. Even with men she knew, Coleman, Arthur, Fred and Alex, she kept part of herself apart. She closed herself off from every man she met. No matter how nice they appeared, there was always the possibility that a savage demon might be lurking in their psyche. She would not be taken in again.

Sometimes, when she was serving a customer in the cafe,

or simply talking to a man she knew, an image of violence would flash through Annie's mind. A fist. A curse. A slash of pain. Somewhere between memory and fear, Annie lived with the intrusion of these momentary waking nightmares since Dorian first started abusing her. She hoped they would disappear with Dorian, but they returned in small, random shocks, like a trapped nerve jolting her when she least expected it. She believed this was God's way of punishing her for killing a man. Dorian had been her abuser, but it was still a crime against God. Thou Shalt Not Kill. Annie had learned to clamber over these thoughts, not allowing them to paralyse her. But she knew they would never go away. Not as long as she carried the shame of what Dorian had done to her and the guilt of having taken his life.

The memories usually happened when she was in the company of men. It was why she insisted Lara come on photo-shoots with her. Even though Alex was nice and certainly only interested in her modelling capabilities (she wasn't sure that Alex was interested in girls at all), she did not feel safe alone with any man.

While God had not protected her from Dorian, Annie could not help thinking that perhaps He had sent this young priest into her cafe. There was something so delicate in the young man's eyes that she noticed them as soon as he walked into the cafe. It felt almost as if his eyes mirrored her own. Was that God sending her a sign? Or could it be something as human as attraction? That seemed the more likely option to Annie but either way, even though she had finished her shift, she felt herself drawn over to him to take his order.

When she delivered his mixed grill, she took the unprecedented step of sitting down with him, rather in the same way Lara had done with her when they first met.

'May I join you?' she asked, putting down his plate while adeptly balancing a cup of coffee for herself in the other hand.

'Please do,' he said, and his face lit up in a smile that was, to her eyes, almost beatific. She smiled back, put the coffee on the table and sat down opposite him. The two of them sat smiling stupidly at each other for a second, before she nodded at his mixed grill. He quickly picked up his fork and pierced a large sausage, sending two squirts of fat flying – one across the table onto her coffee saucer and the other onto his hand.

'I'm so sorry!' he said, horrified.

She laughed and handed him a napkin.

'Thank you,' he said. He put it aside and put down his fork, confessing, 'Actually, I'm not that hungry.'

'That's a big meal for someone who's not hungry.' And she felt emboldened. Playing her part in the photo shoot the day before gave her confidence. Maybe she could be somebody else. The girl who makes jokes. The girl who flirts. The girl who isn't afraid.

'I guess my eyes are bigger than my stomach,' he said. 'I'm Matthew, by the way.' He held out his hand.

'Annie,' she said, looking at his oily fingers, then at him, and they both laughed again.

Giuliana was watching this exchange take place. A good Italian Catholic, she was delighted to see her young waitress flirting with the handsome seminarian, so she quietly removed his plate and slipped a cup of coffee in front of him.

Neither of the young couple noticed. They were utterly enraptured with each other, and seeing her sad young Irish waitress so happy made Giuliana go out to the kitchen and give her husband Fred an uncharacteristically tender kiss on his bald head.

Matthew and Annie talked about everything and nothing.

Mixed grills, the smell of rain after a sunny spell, and how long it took to walk from Sloane Square to World's End. She asked if he had ever eaten pasta and he said, 'No.' Then he asked her if she had been to the National Gallery and she said she hadn't.

'I could take you there,' he said. When she blushed and looked away in response he added, 'If you would like that.'

She turned her head towards him again and smiled and took his breath away. 'I would like that very much,' she said.

Every vein in his body, from his heart out, was fizzing. He felt so full of energy, he feared he might have to get up off the chair and jump with joy.

Was this God?

Even as he asked the question, he knew the answer. He knew the answer with every inch of himself. He joined the priesthood in search of his soul and found it in the paintings he studied. But he had never experienced that Godliness, that spirit, in himself. And yet, here in this girl's face and the warm, teasing way she was looking at him, he felt something lift from deep within him. It seemed as if God had gifted his soul to this girl and she was returning it to him in her smile. Annie was the most beautiful piece of art he had ever seen. More beautiful than any painting because she was real. She was here. She was God's art, the reason men painted. It was not simply her physical beauty, the pale skin and the curve of her neck, Annie was beautiful in every possible sense of the word. She was sweet and innocent, a rare example of untouched, untouchable perfection. Her warm, gentle manner lit a fire in him and made him feel alive. It seemed impossible to Matthew that this sublime creature, who seemed carved from another, better, age – an age before miniskirts and free sex and fashion – could be sitting here, in the flesh, in an ordinary cafe drinking coffee with him.

No. This was not God. Matthew was in love.

The exchange had not been at all what Annie was expecting. In some part of her, she had sat down to give a confession. She thought that, perhaps, she might be able to give an account of herself to this young man of the cloth. Seek some solace from simply being in the company of a good person. She could not give a full confession of what she had done. At least, not here in a cafe. Although it was something that she had considered and perhaps this young priest would be the person she could tell all to. Perhaps God had sent him in here to help cleanse her soul. But, instead of all that, Annie found herself laughing and flirting with him. She was unable to help herself. It was as if some strange force had taken her over. The groovy chick that had invented herself in front of the camera, That Girl, had tapped her on the shoulder, interrupted her melancholic thoughts and taken over the conversation. Annie would never have considered herself capable of deliberately trying to capture the heart of a priest. Such wickedness! Yet, she could tell he was attracted to her and the thought of that excited her. Even though, or perhaps because, she knew it could never go any further. It was almost as if in knowing that this young man could never be available to her, she was willing him to love her.

'I could take you there tomorrow,' he said. Then in a blaze of courage added, 'We could have tea afterwards. I know a good cafe around the corner.'

She beamed and he felt as if a thousand angels were singing, then her face dropped.

'Oh,' she said. 'I can't.'

The tea had been too much. He should never have suggested it.

'No,' she said, reading his mind, 'I mean, I would really love to but I've made a prior arrangement.'

'No that's fine, really.'

'I'm meeting a man.'

That sounded bad.

'I'm modelling for him.'

Worse again.

An irrational surge of panic flooded through Matthew. Another man was painting her! Of course he was. A creature like this could not go unnoticed by the art world. Who was he? Some lecherous cad no doubt.

'It's for a magazine. *Vogue.* The photographer is nice and I promised my flatmate I would do it for her boutique. I don't want to let them down.'

The realisation that this girl had a life beyond here, beyond this moment, brought Mathew back down to earth with a bang. How had he ever thought she might be interested in him? He didn't even look like a real man – he was just a wimp in a dress.

'Why don't you come along?' she said.

'No really, I don't think it would be...'

What was he doing? Say yes! Say yes!

'...appropriate.' *Oh my Good God and Holy Saint Joseph,* Matthew thought, *did I just actually say that?* The ritualistic indoctrination of his training was taking over. Human passion was no match for the judgemental monsignor that was meticulously inserted into the psyche of every Catholic seminarian. Matthew's eyes tried to plead with her. Ask me again! Ask me again!

Annie was crestfallen. Imagine thinking a priest, a good, kind man like that would be interested in her. He could probably see what she was. And yet, he looked different and there was such warmth in his eyes. So, Annie took a chance. There was, after all, nothing to lose.

'Well,' she said, 'if you change your mind we'll be meeting at the Peter Pan statue at two o'clock.'

'Thank you,' he said.

As he stood up to leave, she stayed seated. Her smile was small and timid. Matthew felt mortified, and he was not even sure why. All he knew was that he had blown it. Embarrassed the most glorious woman in the world. And himself.

'It was nice meeting you,' he said and held out his hand.

She took it, and when he felt the gentle touch of her warm hand in his, he thought he might cry.

'You too,' she said. She tried to smile, like before, but it wasn't the same. That girl from the photo shoot had forsaken her. She was not appropriate.

All the way back to the seminary, Matthew cursed himself. And God. And, tripping twice in his rush to get back for evening prayers, his wretched frock. He was stuck now. There was no two ways about it. He had fallen in love and blown it in one afternoon. He was a worthless wimp of a man, good for nothing, only saying mass. He didn't deserve to be with a woman. And even in thinking that – he knew the church had him now. The way the 'appropriate' had tripped off his tongue like that. He had said it – nobody else. He was that mimsy, judgemental, pinky-raising priest old women invited around to tea. If he wasn't, he would have scooped that girl, Annie, up in his arms, skirts and all. But he hadn't. And he never would.

Arriving back at the seminary, Matthew immediately got the smell of lunch and was furious to note that, having not eaten his mixed grill, he was starving and would get nothing again until after evening prayer. He wished he was more resourceful like some of his fellow seminarians in Dublin who hid food in their rooms.

The pastor suddenly appeared at the door of the drawing room.

'There is someone here to see you,' he said, his face bent with distaste. Irish priests expressed moral disapproval more vocally, sometimes with a curse, often with a stick. The English clergy expressed it with a dry coldness that Matthew found infinitely more disturbing.

'She has been waiting for quite some time.'

She? For a split second, Matthew thought it was Annie. Without thinking, he marched into the room.

Standing by the window, looking out, was an elegant woman whose raised elbows indicated she was holding a china cup and saucer in her hands. She turned when she heard him come in.

It was Lara.

28

Mrs Clarke left the pile of recent English newspapers on the good doctor's desk.

He smiled across at her. At least she thought he was smiling. It was hard to tell since that terrible incident. A burglar brutally attacked him in his own home, one lunchtime, a few months ago now. They left him for dead, but his nurse came looking for him and called an ambulance. The hospital doctors saved his life, but his once handsome face had not survived the attack. The left side was completely paralysed with one eye lost and permanently sewn shut. He wore a patch over it now and held a handkerchief in his hand to wipe the drool from the side of his mouth in which he had lost all feeling. Such a tragic shame. Mrs Clarke and a few of the other church ladies had stepped in to make sure Dr Black was looked after. Up in that big house, a man on his own, there was every danger his house would go to rack and ruin. After all, poor Dr Black was widowed and that ungrateful strap of a stepdaughter had run off to America and not bothered to come back to nurse the unfortunate man. After all he had done for her.

'Thank you,' he said, 'you are so very kind to think of me.'

The interfering old biddy owned the local newsagents and always brought the papers in for him, a day late, when she came in with her myriad of complaints du jour.

He only ever read *The Irish Times*, but it was handy to leave them there in the surgery for what patients he had left to pick over.

'And I have something for you,' he said, handing over her prescription. He reached across and she lingered, for a delicious moment, before pulling it from between his perfect, manicured fingers.

Always so charming. Such a gentleman. Even with half a face.

'How is your lovely daughter?' he asked. 'Darina?'

'Davina,' she corrected.

'Of course,' he apologised. 'How old is she now? She must be twelve? Thirteen?'

'Fourteen. Oh, she's quite well thank you, Dr Black.'

'Quite the young lady by now, I'm sure. Is she still playing the piano?'

'She is – although she's getting very cheeky.'

He smiled, in that pitiful crooked way.

'Oh, I know all about cheeky daughters…'

His one good eye, as blue as ever it was, glittered. He reached up with his handkerchief. Was he weeping with sorrow, or simply leaking? The poor man. Missing his daughter and no sight or sign of her since the robbery. It was heartbreaking.

'I'll bring her with me the next time I drop out to the house,' she said. 'She can play piano for you again.'

'I would like that very much,' he said.

The truth was that pretty, young Davina had objected the last time, saying she found the doctor creepy. Bridget had given her such a whack around the head.

'The poor man can't help being deformed. He's had a terrible life and he misses his daughter. It's not much to give him an afternoon of your time. It's your Christian duty.'

Davina had made a face. She'd send Davina up there on her own the next time – that's what she'd do!

When she had gone, Dorian checked his book. He had an hour until his next appointment. He had let his nurse go since the 'burglary'. The surgery wasn't busy enough to justify employing staff any more, but, truth be told, Dorian wanted to be rid of as many chattering women as he could in his everyday life. Dorian had enough money to never need to work again. He had woken in hospital with such terrible pain, and not just physical. The trauma of finding his face missing paled against the heartache of realising what Hanna had done to him. The shock of her betrayal. The brutality of her actions against him. He was mystified. How could she have done this to him? Had he not loved her? Given her everything she wanted? In the weeks that followed, Dorian wanted nothing more than to be left alone. He could have locked the doors of his large house and stayed within its walls forever. But, after a few weeks, when his body began to recover, Dorian realised that he was still a man and he had needs. Dorian's need for love could only be fulfilled by the very young, and he understood this was unconventional, and frowned upon by the ignorant (which was most people). So, he had to exercise caution in getting his needs met. With the added complication of his ghoulish visage, he had also to be patient. Although he secured the pity of their mothers, daughters were not so easy to reach when you looked like the bogeyman under the bed. It would take time, but he would get there. He had to. He had to love again.

Dorian went back to work because he needed to be

connected with the local community. He became more active as chairman of the board for the local convent where, ironically, his disfigured face earned him even more trust among the already ludicrously trusting nuns. But, he had yet to find himself another Hanna. On good days, he mourned her by thinking about what might have been. Dorian hoped he might be able to stay loving Hanna beyond her girlhood. He hoped that she might have been the woman who would satisfy him and make him like other men. Being with Hanna into her adulthood might have sated his desire for young flesh by tricking his mind into believing that she was forever young. She was so beautiful, it was hard to imagine her never being so. On bad days, he hated her for what she had done. Hurting him, destroying his face, leaving him for dead, but, mostly, leaving him to his own desires again. Forcing him into this situation of desiring what he could not have. Of being loveless and alone.

The injustice of her escape was infuriating. She was out there, somewhere, but Dorian could not get the police to help him find her because the world did not understand men like him. If she had been an old woman, like her mother, he could have done what he liked with her and it would have been nobody's business but his own. If she had been a grown woman she would never have got away with what she had done. Instead of going along with the clumsy lie she left behind for him (the fake letter, the bungled burglary), he would have told the police the truth, that his young 'wife' was greedy and insubordinate, and had run away because she didn't want to toe the line. The police would have helped him hunt her down then brought her home to justice.

Hanna had committed this crime against him and yet she would never be punished because of the small matter of her age.

He was angry with himself, too, for not seeing it coming. Hanna was an evil, conniving bitch. He should have been harder on her. She had deliberately and systematically stolen his heart, his money, his mother's jewellery and the good looks that she knew he needed so badly to replace her. When he thought like that Dorian became so enraged that all he could do was replay the punishments of the past that he had given her, and end them with her slow, torturous death.

It was close enough to lunchtime to justify going home for a sandwich. Dorian had learned to fend for himself, somewhat, although his housekeeper had grudgingly come back, out of pity more than need. There was some cured beef, which he ordered from a delicatessen in Galway and a loaf of brown bread, which one of the church ladies had left for him in one of their insufferable charity baskets he was obliged to accept. How he hated those women, but Dorian had to be smart and play the long game. He had to earn the affection of the dry spinsters and their flabby, fecund sisters if he was to, eventually, enjoy the fresh beauty of their offspring.

As he was leaving the surgery he grabbed a *Daily Mail* from the top of Mrs Clarke's pile and it fell to the floor, opening on a page that caught his eye. Leaning down he saw the headline: Who's That Girl? He collapsed onto his knees beside it. Caked in makeup, wearing a blonde wide, legs akimbo in a short dress, Dorian saw immediately that it was Hanna.

She was in London. The little bitch had been in London, all this time.

Dorian sat for a moment, hardly able to believe she had dropped into his lap like this. Hanna was a model. Showing herself off to the world. He was the only one who used to enjoy her, now she belonged to everybody. The slut. Did she not think he would find her? Did she not know he read the

English papers? Perhaps she was sending him a message. Who's that girl? Inviting him to come and get her. Teasing him. Or – perhaps she thought he was dead.

Either way, Dorian wasted no time.

He carefully tore the cutting out of the paper, folded the edges of it neatly and placed it into the inside pocket of his suit jacket.

The following day he took a flight from Dublin to London where he booked himself into Brown's Hotel in Mayfair.

After dropping his bags he took a taxi to the *Daily Mail* offices on Fleet Street where he asked to see Penelope Podmore, the woman who had written the ridiculous fashion article accompanying Hanna's photographs.

He was not taken into a private office but left standing at the reception desk while someone went to get her. She was a lanky woman and her eyes opened wide in barely disguised alarm when she looked at his face, making her appear rather like an angry ostrich and inspiring Dorian to spitting-point hatred.

'I'm her father,' he said, trying to looking charming and pathetic at the same time. 'Her mother and I are worried she's been led astray so I have travelled over from Ireland to see her.'

Penelope looked at him, more coldly than most women looked on a poor cripple. She had considerable experience of men, and there was something in this one's eyes that told her he was lying.

'I have no idea who the girl is,' she said. When he didn't move she reasoned that it wasn't her job to protect models. Alex could play the hero if he wanted. 'You could try the photographer,' she said and gave him Alex's address.

Dorian took another taxi to an utterly inferior end of town called Fulham, where he knocked on the door of an ordinary house, unearthing a very seedy looking individual who, he surmised from appearance and name, was Jewish. Was Hanna sleeping with him? Probably.

'I am so sorry to trouble you, but I am looking for my daughter.'

Dorian hunched his shoulders, apologetically, trying to make himself look as affable as he could. A harmless cripple in need of help. Suspecting she may have changed her name, Dorian handed the cutting straight to the photographer.

'Where did you get my address?' he asked.

'A nice journalist, Ms Podmore, at the *Daily Mail* was kind enough to pass on your information. She said you might be able to help me where she couldn't. I'm just trying to find my daughter.'

Dorian tried to keep his voice steady and his eyes soft, but he was fuming. Who the hell did these English bastards think they were? He was an educated man. A doctor. And yet they wouldn't just give him what he wanted.

Alex had already had three rock and roll singers and a seedy film producer looking for Annie that week. Magazines were like catalogues for these men. They saw a pretty face and they fell in love. This guy did not look like he was in love with Annie. He looked like one creepy dude. And not just because his face was bent out of shape. Annie had told Alex her parents were dead. Whether that was true or not, and he had no reason to disbelieve her, this guy did not look like her father, no matter what he said. And if he was, Annie did not want to see him. That was certain.

'What's your daughter's name?' Alex said. 'I work with a lot of models you know, they come and go.'

Dorian coughed. Rage burned up in him.

'Hanna,' he mumbled.

'No,' Alex said, 'that's definitely not a Hanna. Sorry I

couldn't help you.' And he closed the door on the guy. Good for Penelope referring these creeps on to him. If he was going to keep Annie on side, he had to keep these weirdos at bay. The chick spooked easily enough as it was.

From out in the suburbs, Dorian had to walk for nearly half an hour, as far as the Kings Road, before he could get a taxi back into town.

29

'Will you do a few extra hours again for me tonight? Alice's brother is coming across from Fermoy and I said I'd take him up to Lyons's for a few.'

'Not a bother,' said John, gazing mournfully out the window of their one-room barracks. 'Sure what else would I be doing?'

Sergeant Gerry Nolan looked pitifully at his colleague. The two of them had been keeping law and order in the village of Carney together for the past five years and Gerry didn't know a better man. The sergeant was a good deal older and had gone soft about his edges. But he had worked in New York in his youth and, as a seasoned cop, he knew John Connolly was the real thing. He hated to see him like this.

In the past fortnight John had begun to worry that Noreen was not planning to come back and marry him. He had been concerned, of course, from the beginning. John was no fool. He had always worried that he was not enough for her. But then, any man who loves a woman properly, as he loved Noreen, knows he is not enough for her. No man, no matter how fantastic he is, is enough for any woman. Women need other things apart from men. Children, furniture, a sense of purpose – even work. Women didn't need men for anything, apart from for the money they earned and the work they did. Noreen did her own work and earned her own money, so John was utterly surplus to requirements. John understood, always, that Noreen was only doing him a favour in being with him, so he sang for his supper. Proud, intelligent women like Noreen liked to live on a pedestal. Her father had built the pedestal for her already, and she was sitting pretty on that by the time John came along. So he simply raised the pedestal up higher. So high, in fact, that she had decided to use it as a springboard to propel herself over to London and start a new life. Without him.

John did not know what to do with himself without her. The natural order, as he understood it, was that your mother looked after you until you reached adulthood. Once there, a man did whatever he needed to do to get himself a woman. Got himself a job and kept himself neat and clean, went to dances and maintained a temperate relationship with drink. Once you found a woman you liked you did whatever it took to get her to marry you, short of pulling her by the hair into a cave. But that too, if it worked. Once you had a woman, you kept her up on a pedestal and did whatever you had to do to keep her there. Because, John believed, as long as a man had a woman, he could do anything. Without a woman, a man was nothing. If he found a woman he loved and one who loved him back? Jesus – that was great stuff altogether. John had never dreamt of meeting a woman he got on with as well as, and loved as deeply as, Noreen Lyons. Perhaps that's what the problem had been. It had been too good to be true.

When Noreen left, she promised it was not a permanent thing. 'I'll be back,' she said. 'I love you John Connolly. We will get married; I just need to do this. I need to get away and, you know—'

'Spread your wings,' he said, quickly interrupting her. He didn't want her to spell it out for him, and he was afraid she might.

In the weeks since she had gone, John had clung to Noreen's promise like an emotional life raft. In the past few days it had begun to sink.

He was heartbroken. He lost his appetite. He began to feel worthless, despairing and lonely. He was nothing without her. John wished he could get angry or indignant with her for ditching him like this. Robbing him of his future, but he couldn't. He understood why she had gone. She wanted to break free – taste life. He got that. John just missed her. That was all. Talking to her. Sharing the gossip and the craic at the end of each day. Putting his face into her soft hair when she embraced him. The secure, happy feeling that each embrace would soon be a daily occurrence, affection on tap. And the rest of it. The 'bad' thing would become the 'good' thing. He couldn't wait for that, although he knew, too, that Noreen had an appetite for being a bit bad. That would be their challenge, coupling her impulsive nature with his own need for routine and certainty. Although it seemed now, along with the joy of marriage, there would be no challenges to face either.

Noreen had been gone almost a month now, and there hadn't been a peep out of her. Not a letter, a phone call to the pub looking for him – nothing. Frank, her father, was furious with her for leaving her fiancé in the lurch, but John knew that didn't help either. He didn't need Frank's approval to win Noreen back. In fact, Noreen was so contrary that her father's blessing would almost certainly turn her against him.

'Come into the house before the shift,' Gerry said. 'Alice says she'd like to throw a bit of dinner into you.'

Aside from the heartbreak the worst thing about being abandoned by Noreen was having every wife and mother in the village trying to feed him.

'Ah no, Gerry. Tell Alice thanks. Mam has a bit of bacon and cabbage left out for me from yesterday.'

There was a pause, into which John sighed. Gerry watched the now familiar look of broken misery flatten his usually jovial features, as he lifted the mug of tea to his lips and took a small sip.

Big man broken.

He couldn't take it any more.

'Oh for God's sake, man, just go over to London and see her.'

'Who?'

'Are you really going to make me spell it out?'

He put the mug down and gazed out the window. A big, strong man mooning over a dame. If there was anything more insufferable, Gerry didn't know what it was.

'She won't want to see me.'

'Of course she will.'

Then he sighed again and said, 'She's moved on. She doesn't love me any more.'

'To hell with it,' Gerry said. 'I'm sick of looking at you like this.'

John raised his eyebrows and, for a moment, Gerry caught a glimpse of the old John and thought he might give him a belt round the head. But Gerry liked him too much to let it go.

'As of tomorrow you're on four weeks' leave.'

'But...'

'No buts. I can manage. Skinny will have to get himself across the bog, or rot – and his wife will get her pension.'

'I don't think…'

'You're going to London, John, and that's an order. Have some fun. Take your girl to a show. Take her out to dinner. Win her back, for God's sake.'

John's eyes filled with tears.

'I don't know if I can.'

If there was one thing a New York cop found unendurable, it was grown men crying and acting like wimps.

He stood up, pushed a couple of inches of his barrel-like stomach into his trousers and said, 'You're no use to me like this Guard Connolly. Be a man, for God's sake. Now – go and get your girl and bring her home. London. Tomorrow. And that's the end of it.'

The morning Shirley got back from holiday Coleman called her into the office. He didn't dress it up.

'You're fired.'

Her face set and her lip quivered but Shirley didn't do vulnerable. She looked more angry than upset.

She didn't ask Coleman why, but he told her anyway.

'You've been scamming the bar with Brian.'

She stood staring at him silently for a moment, then lit a cigarette.

'Aren't you going to say anything?'

Even by Shirley's standards this aggressive silence was unnerving.

She took a long drag of her cigarette, blew the smoke in his direction then narrowed her eyes and pointed at him saying, 'You'll regret this,' before turning on her heels.

Although you would never have seen it, as she walked out the door of the club where she had worked for over ten years, every inch of Shirley's heart wished it had turned out differently.

Men.

Even the good ones made things bad.

While her relationship with her flatmates was falling apart, Noreen's career was taking off. Coleman had put her in charge of the bar and all of the floor girls at Chevrons. She didn't ask what had happened to Shirley. The woman was history that was all she knew. There was no announcement made. Shirley simply did not return to work after the holiday she had been on when Noreen started. Noreen figured that Coleman had fired her. Although nothing was said, Noreen thought it was probably because she was in on the bar scam with Brian. In any case, Noreen assured Coleman she could run the whole lot if he allowed her to recruit her own bar staff. That was how she met Handsome. Quite by chance, he came in one evening looking for Coleman.

The place was starting to fill up and Noreen was getting prepared for a busy shift when he marched up to bar and said, 'Is the boss in?'

The dreamboat had jet black hair slicked back from a brooding brow with dark, perfectly trimmed eyebrows and piercing, hypnotic blue eyes that sparkled careless, macho ice. His nose was Roman, his jawline sharp and chiselled. He was the most beautiful man Noreen had ever seen. She knew at once he was a gangster by the casual way he carried himself and the way he asked to see the boss.

'I'm looking for a bit of work.'

Coleman had asked not to be disturbed so Noreen said, 'I'm the boss.'

He leaned back and smiled at her. Sardonically, although she doubted if he would know what it meant. She wriggled in her mini.

'Have you got a problem with that?' she said, baiting him.

'Nah,' he said, popping a cigarette in the side of his mouth. 'I like strong women.'

'Good,' she said, a thrill rushing through her, 'because I need someone to start behind the bar right now. If you can pull a pint it's yours. You got a name?'

'They just call me Handsome,' he said, in a smooth, cockney drawl.

A gangster called Handsome. Not Ironing Board after the laundry-as-a-weapon or Coleman, like the condiment. Just an accurate testament to good looks. Noreen's dangerous-bad-boy radar went red. He was hot stuff alright. In fact, Handsome was way better looking than Coleman. Nonetheless, professionalism took precedence and she made him pull a pint for her. She could feel him tense when she stood over him but it was important, with all men, to let them know who was in charge. He took it because he had to and, with a bit of guidance, pulled an adequate pint. In any case, she reasoned, his bar skills didn't matter. His divine looks would keep the customers and the girls happy. She put him to work, there and then, on the lunchtime shift. It was not until later that Noreen discovered Handsome was Shirley's ex-husband. If anything, the girls seemed nervous of him. Noreen put that down to Shirley's fierce reputation. Handsome liked strong women and she and Shirley had that in common. If the pretty waitresses were scared to go near him because of Shirley, then that was less competition for her. Coleman, too, didn't seem thrilled to have him there when he stuck his head out the door and saw the place flying.

'I don't like that guy, Noreen. Why did you pick him?'

'He's an excellent barman,' she lied. 'Anyway, I've hired him now, and we're out the door so you'll just have to put up with him. Don't worry, I'll handle him. He won't bother you.'

'It's not me I'm worried about,' Coleman muttered, but not loud enough for Noreen to hear. She'd find out from the girls soon enough what Handsome was like. What the hell was Handsome Devers doing around here anyway? This wasn't his patch. Maybe he'd run out of people to annoy or maybe he thought he had some edge over Coleman. Something to do with Shirley perhaps? Coleman's head hurt trying to figure it all out. Anyway, he didn't want to unsettle Noreen. He needed her out there running the club for him. Noreen keeping the place ticking over was the one thing he could rely on these days.

While the club buzzed, Coleman sat in his office, as he was in the habit of doing lately. He was feeling confused and kept going over and over his experience with Lara.

Lara had seemed to want him. She made him feel complete. For the first time in his life, he knew he was somewhere he utterly belonged. Surely that meant something to her as well as him? It could not have just been him. Otherwise he would never have done what he did and said what he said.

'I love you.' The three words had slipped out of his mouth before he was even aware he wanted to say them. It had been a physical, emotional reaction. A thoughtless instinct, a knee jerk. If he had thought about it, he wouldn't have said it, of course.

As he sat smoking at his desk, pretending to file papers, a memory kept floating to the surface of his mind. Unwanted flotsam from a painful childhood he had tried too hard to forget. He had said those words once before. He was eight years old and in the infirmary of a children's home, one of the rough ones, being treated for measles. She was a nurse and he could not remember her name. More likely, he was never told it but he remembered, now, that she was Irish. She nursed him in the infirmary and wasn't like all the other old bitches. She was young, fat and kind. She bathed him in warm water using a bar of lavender soap she smuggled in from home. 'That aul' carbolic is rotten,' she said. He remembered the funny way she spoke and her gentle hands holding the sponge to his skin. The sweet, feminine smell. He cried as she washed him. She thought it was because he was sick, but it wasn't that. He was upset because he was getting better and would soon have to leave the infirmary, and her, behind.

Afterwards as she dried him with a towel he said, 'Please can I stay with you?' .

'I'm sorry,' she said, her jolly face suddenly older and serious, 'but you have to go back.'

He put his arms around her waist and said, 'I love you.' He just said it to try to get her to let him stay. She sent him back anyway. If she had loved him, she might have taken him home.

He thought Lara was going to take him home. Perhaps he had fallen in love with her because she was Irish like the nurse. Although, why did you fall in love with people? Was there a reason? He wished there was, because then he could make it go away and stop this torture. Then again, now that he had tasted her love, all he wanted was to have it back. Maybe it was because he had waited so long for her, the moment of their being together had felt finite to him. He had made love without caution, or the performance of sex for the sake of it. He had moved around and into her without thought or hesitation, but then, his guard down, he had stupidly allowed his heart to speak in the same way. Coleman had not even been sure that he had said the words out loud, until she stiffened in his relaxed embrace and made her excuses.

Coleman had been avoiding her ever since. It seemed the only thing he could do. For both of them. She clearly didn't feel the same way about him, although he found that hard to believe. When they had been making love, he was never more certain of anything in his life; they were not simply meant to be together but together already. Coleman had made love to a lot of women but he had never felt that raw, that vulnerable and yet, that safe with a woman. There was a certainty in her eyes when they met his, as she bore down on him. No pretence, just an honest coupling.

For the first time in his life, Coleman felt what it was not to be alone. And yet, after that – she had left him.

He was sitting in his office, feeling confused, trying to distract himself by playing around with some papers for the accountant when the phone rang.

It was Chevron.

After a few pleasantries, Chevron asked to speak to Shirley. Coleman took a deep breath and said that he had fired her.

'I know it's shocking Bobby, but she'd set up a scam with Brian. Siphoning off drink and selling it back to the suppliers. I didn't want to believe it, but it checked out and she more or less admitted it to me when I confronted her after she came back from Spain.'

Bobby didn't respond so Coleman added, 'She was on holiday.'

Nothing.

'I thought she might have visited you and Maureen while she was over.' Wrong thing to say. Shirley and Bobby were old friends. The news had obviously silenced his usually loquacious boss. 'Maybe I should have called you earlier but I wanted to talk to her first. I had no choice, Bobby. I have to protect the business – you know?'

Then there was another pause before Bobby said, 'Strange timing.' Pause. 'Why did you wait 'til she got back from Spain?'

Coleman was confused.

'Because I only found out what was happening while she was away.'

'I see.' Another pause. Coleman looked across the empty office at the closed, black leather door. He hated the phone. Bobby was a strange fish. Coleman could always read him. Since he was a young man he had learned to read his mentor's moods, see when he was getting wound up, anxious, agitated. Coleman could always appease him, calm him down. But when he wasn't in the room, Coleman felt powerless. All he could do was sit and wait for him to respond to the bad news.

'So, how's the boutique going?'

Coleman breathed a sigh of relief.

'Yeah, good. Doing some business, you know.'

'I'm going to come over. Take a look at my new venture.'

Shit! Panic. Coleman had been intending to break it to Lara that the business wasn't strictly set up like he had promised. She was making a name for herself, that was the main thing. Lara wasn't a bread head. She just wanted to make dresses. The arrangement he set out with Chevron giving backing for a high profile premises on the Kings Road to be opened, more or less overnight, helped him do that quickly. At some point down the road, Coleman had planned for himself and Lara to buy him out. He had been going to fill her in, just the time had not been right. He thought their afternoon of lovemaking was signalling a new, intimate beginning that would have enabled him to tell her. But now that was gone. This was not the time for Lara to find out she was on the payroll of Bobby Chevron.

Bobby found his voice again.

'Maureen needs some new dresses. To be honest, I'm getting a bit bored over here. I quite like the idea of getting stuck into a new venture. I always fancied myself as a bit of a fashion impresario. What do you think, Coleman? Have I got what it takes to be one of these nancy-boy designers? Poncing about in a blouse? Ha, ha.'

Did his laugh sound brittle and forced or was he being serious? Without seeing him, it was impossible to tell. It was impossible to know what to say for the best. All Coleman knew was he had to put him off. And quickly. Chevron was an impulsive sod. He could be on a plane from Spain by the end of the week. Earlier, if there was one.

'Probably not such a good idea, Bobby. Having a few teething problems. Late stock, a few dodgy designs and that. I'd rather wait until everything is just right before giving you the grand tour.'

It didn't sound convincing, even to him. But, after another of his pauses, Chevron took a sharp breath and said, 'Yeah. You're probably right, Coleman. I'll leave you to it. I'll tell Maureen she'll just have to hold out for her new gear.'

Coleman had an idea.

'Tell you what. Why don't I get Lara to send Maureen over a package? A few bits and pieces. Got to keep the ladies happy.'

There was a break into which he heard Chevron's heavy breathing. Lighting a cigar, probably.

'Now that,' Chevron said, 'is an excellent idea, my son.' Then his mouth stuffed with the stogie he added, 'Nothing too fancy mind. Don't want to keep the good stuff from the customers.'

'Nonsense,' Coleman said, feeling relieved, 'only the best for Mrs Chevron.'

'Coleman,' Bobby said, 'a pleasure as always.' Before hanging up he added, 'You do know you is like a son to me?'

'Thanks,' said Coleman. He never knew what to say when Bobby said that. He certainly didn't feel like his son. Or even his brother. It felt like he was just saying it to keep him on side. Keep him in check.

In any case, the call had ended well, and he was relieved about that.

When he put the phone down, he also made a decision.

I love you. That could not happen again. Ever.

However this panned out, Lara, the business, Chevron – love had to be taken off the agenda.

There was a reason he had never let himself fall in love before, and Coleman had allowed himself to forget what that was.

Control. The business was sliding, Noreen was good but she could not be expected to run Chevrons on her own. She had just employed that lowlife Devers, and he had let it happen by taking his eye off the ball.

Lara didn't love him back. That's what happened when you took the risk of loving people and it was too big a risk for Coleman. If you were stupid enough to fall in love, as he had been, the least you could do was be a man about it, and not go around snivelling 'I love you'. He cringed just thinking about it. Never again. Ever.

Coleman was going to toughen up.

If Lara wanted him, she could come and get him. He was happy to oblige, but otherwise, he wasn't going to make a fool of himself. A man had limits, and Coleman had reached his.

Her silence had spoken for itself. Now he was going to do the same thing. He had lived without love for thirty-four years of his life. He wasn't going to go whining about it now.

He put on his jacket and went out to the club where he found Noreen pushing the last of the customers out the door. He looked around and checked that Handsome was gone. Arthur had taken a rare night off, otherwise the psycho would never have got one foot inside the door. Coleman made a mental note to tell Arthur not to kick him out straight away, but to put up with him for a while, until Noreen was ready to get rid of him, which she would be soon enough, he felt sure.

'You alright locking up on your own Noreen?' he said, double checking.

'Not a bother,' she said. 'Go on, I'm grand here.' She ushered him out and locked the door behind him.

Then Noreen headed out to the back stock room where Handsome was changing a barrel.

She stood at the door and watched him roll the heavy, wooden casket across the stone floor. He had rolled up his sleeves and she could see the muscles on his arms hardening.

She leaned against the wall and arranged her legs in a seductive V.

'Need a hand with that?'

He turned and looked across at her. In that moment, there was something in his expression that Noreen didn't like. Something unpleasant. She couldn't put her finger on it. Disdain? Arrogance? Whatever it was, it killed the fantasy she had been harbouring of seducing her new charge in the stock room after hours.

'If you was offering more than a hand I might take it.'

The niggle grew to a no. Not tonight. Maybe tomorrow. If he behaved himself.

'Now, now, Handsome. You just change that barrel for me like a good lad while I go upstairs and settle the bar.'

Handsome took two long strides towards her and said something, almost under his breath. It sounded like, 'You fucking tease...' But that couldn't be right. Before it had time to register, however, Noreen felt her body being pushed to one side, and as Handsome looked behind her, a shocked expression slapped itself across his pretty face.

Before she turned, a big booming voice with a heavy Cork accent said, 'Oi! Take one more step towards my woman, you filthy hound, and I'll rip your head clean off your shoulders!'

30

'You filthy hound?'

'I know,' John said. 'It was the first thing that came into my head,' he added, stuffing another one of Annie's vol-au-vents into his mouth. 'I just saw him coming towards you and I snapped.'

'Well, I think you overreacted a bit.'

'That's what you say but what would have happened if you hadn't left that service door open and I hadn't arrived at that moment?'

John finished chewing and swiped a few crumbs off his bare chest before delicately wiping his mouth on the corner of the sheet. 'No – don't answer that question.'

'Well,' she said, 'I won't be leaving it open again. The place could have been robbed! Anyway – what the hell are you doing here?'

They had just made love. Twice. Once in the store room after Noreen calmed down a terrified Handsome and again, just now, in the flat, after she introduced him to Lara and Annie. Annie offered John and Noreen her bed after a short and rather embarrassing exchange in which Annie acknowledged that John might wish to sleep on the sofa for propriety's sake and John looked in danger of conceding.

'For goodness sake, Annie.' Noreen had snapped. 'We haven't seen each other in nearly six weeks. We want to have SEX!'

Lara would normally have laughed delightedly at Noreen's forwardness, but there was still a distance between them. She excused herself to go to her studio where she had been working through the night lately. Noreen tried to assume that it wasn't her fault and had something to do with Matthew. She couldn't do anything else as Lara had stopped confiding in her altogether. Noreen was feeling the strain between them terribly. She used work to distract herself and today she thought she might have found another distraction in her new barman. While John turning up to check on her, then muscling in on her new life was very annoying, Noreen had to admit it was a huge relief to see him.

So had the orgasm been. It felt like ages since she had enjoyed herself as much. Which was also annoying.

'I'm on holiday,' he said.

She looked at him sideways.

'I came over for you. I missed you.'

'I know what you missed,' she said.

'That too,' he said, grinning.

Noreen felt a flood of love for him. But she couldn't give into it. This was her great adventure and this Cork lutherum* following her across was not part of the plan. Even though, in her heart, she knew she was glad to see him. Even though seeing him had chased away the loneliness and made her feel complete again.

---

* Irish slang for big, awkward man

Noreen rolled over in the bed and reached across John's naked stomach for the last mushroom and cream cheese vol-au-vent. Annie had sent them into bed with a tray of them. It was an eccentric offering for a lovemaking couple although, Noreen had to admit, it had been equally eccentric of them to accept. Much as she mistrusted the source, Noreen could never refuse Annie's offer of food.

'She's a great cook, your flatmate.'

'Yeah. She works in the cafe across the road firing big breakfasts into big hairy lads, like you.'

'I like her already.'

'Yes, well I don't. She's weird.'

'How so?'

'I don't know. I don't trust her. She's hiding something.'

'What's she hiding?'

'I don't know. Just something. Like her family. She's cagey – you know? Doesn't like talking about her past.'

'Maybe she's just a private person.'

Noreen waved that off as if the notion was ridiculous.

'I'm pretty sure she's lying about where she's from.'

'God, Noreen, can you not mind your own business... what are you doing?'

Noreen was down on her hands and knees rummaging under the bed.

'She keeps a locked case down here. Who hides a locked case under their bed?'

'Jesus, Noreen, get up out of there at once! You can't go opening other people's private—'

The brown leather case was already up on the bed and Noreen was securing the bedroom door with a chair under the handle.

'You're right. I can't open it. I've tried. You do it.'

'Jesus, Mary and Holy Saint Joseph. No, Noreen! Now, you've gone too far!'

Noreen was standing looking at him.

'I know you can open it, John. You told me you can open any lock.'

The moral argument was already over. There was no sense in even trying once Noreen had made her mind up. But he had to try.

'It's a padlock. There's no way.'

Noreen handed him a hair grip.

'You told me Curly Boland taught you how to open any lock that time when you had him in custody.'

Then she pouted at him.

'Please? Are you not just a tiny bit curious?'

He took the grip off her. 'No, I'm not.' He began to fiddle with the lock adding, 'I can't believe you're making me do this.' He easily removed the padlock and said, 'This is illegal, Noreen. You know that?' and clicked open the case.

Noreen threw open the lid and flung her hands in.

'Oh. My. God. Look at this.'

Noreen was pulling out jewellery in clumps and sifting through them: pearls, gold bangles and a choker with tiny diamonds. As she put an emerald ring on her finger John reached over, snatched it off her and started returning the stuff as quickly as she was taking it out again.

'Noreen, this is wrong.'

'She's a robber, John. A jewel thief!'

'This is a suitcase in a person's private room, Noreen. You have no evidence of that whatsoever. Lots of people keep their valuables locked up; if anyone's committing a crime here it's us.'

'Nonsense. What woman keeps her jewellery locked up?

Anyway, she's not a jewellery person – so what is she doing with it? Aha,' she said, taking out a diary and opening it.

'Put that down, Noreen. Are you really considering reading another person's private diary?'

'Of course not,' she said, flicking through it. John snatched it from her and put it back in the case, although not before Noreen had made a mental note of the name in the front, Hanna Black, Killa, County Sligo, Ireland. A different name. Her diary or somebody else's. She recognised Annie's writing.

'She's changed her name. Well if that's not suspicious, I don't know what is.'

'Changing your name is not a crime,' John answered as he frantically tried to arrange the jewellery and diary back in place.

'What's this?' Noreen said, reaching across his work to grab a piece of old fabric. As she pulled it towards her it unfurled into a filthy apron. Dried flakes of large dark crumbs fell onto the bed.

'Argh!' she cried out. Then threw the apron down.

'Shhhh,' John said, his voice rising, 'they'll hear you!'

'Oh my God, John,' she said, looking at him, stricken, 'it's blood,' she whispered. 'We have to go to the police.'

John grabbed Noreen by the shoulder then looked her straight in the eye and said in a low, firm whisper, 'Listen to me. I am not going to the police, Noreen.' She opened her mouth. 'And neither are you.'

'But—'

'No buts, Noreen. There's probably some perfectly reasonable explanation for this.'

'What is it then?'

'She could have been butchering a pig or something.'

'Usually you wash a bloodstained apron – not hide it.'

'The point is we're now breaking the law, right now this minute, in opening her private property. Whatever is in this suitcase cannot be used as evidence of crime. Even if there was a crime. Which there probably wasn't.'

'So I could be sharing a flat with a murderess and you don't even care?'

If that slip of a girl Annie decided to come at his hefty Noreen with a knife, John thought, she would want to be very fast indeed, and even then, he didn't fancy her chances.

'I would worry a lot more about that cad you work with coming at you.'

'I bet you would,' Noreen said. 'Jealous?'

'Yes!' John said. Then, more quietly, 'Of course I am.'

Noreen felt a terrible pang of regret at having hurt him. Then remembered he wasn't supposed to be here.

She let John lock up the case and put it back under the bed. She had what she needed anyway. A name. Hanna Black.

When he was done and the truce set, John propped himself up on the pillows and turned himself into a sofa for Noreen. She leaned back onto his chest, lit a cigarette and looked out of the long Georgian window at the Kings Road. It felt so good, to be just lying there with John, in London. But then, she remembered, she could be doing this at home. Lying there, on his chest, in between lovemaking bouts, eating sandwiches, smoking fags and talking aul' rubbish. This intimacy and affection was so nice. It was what it would lead to she didn't want. The whole 'forever' thing. John wasn't here on holiday. He was here to try to drag her home to Carney. Shove her in a pinny, get her up the duff and trap her there for the rest of her life. Still, she would enjoy this while it lasted.

After a few moments John broke the silence.

'Noreen, can I ask you a question?'

His voice was soft and Noreen felt a shiver of dread.

'Are we still engaged?'

There were so many things that Noreen wanted to say in that moment. 'Marriage is so bourgeois.' 'Why can't people just live together?' 'This is the sixties. Chill out, man. Live a little.' She wanted John to stay. She wanted to make love with him. She missed him. She knew, too, that even though she was playing the big strong girl in London, she needed him. More than all of that, she loved him. But did she want to marry him? Noreen had been hedging her bets, distracting her family, her fiancé, but also, herself to try to hold off the inevitable. In that moment, being asked directly, Noreen knew that she owed it to John to give him an honest answer.

'No.'

Even though she said it in an apologetic whisper, the tiny word filled the room, as if she had shouted it out in a loud, angry stab.

John paused. She felt his hurt move across his chest in a sharp breath.

There were things she could have said to try to explain herself. Can't we just go along as we are for a while? Just because I don't want to marry you that doesn't mean I don't love you. But she knew they were pointless. John was a devout Catholic and a deeply conventional man. He needed to get married. He wanted to get on with his life and have a wife by his side, producing children for him. Noreen knew she had already forced him to break with his traditional values by being with a woman who worked, luring him into having sex before marriage and now, running off to London to spread her wings. There is only so much a man could be expected to tolerate. John was a good man who deserved to settle down with a nice girl. Noreen didn't want to be nice any more. Or good. She wanted to be free. She wasn't entirely sure what that meant. But she knew what it didn't mean. And that was getting married.

'That's it then,' he eventually said. 'It's over?'

Noreen felt the awkwardness of their naked skin pressed together and wished she could take the words back. Or rather, make them not true. But she couldn't.

It doesn't have to be. I don't want it to be.

But what was the point? She'd only be dragging things on longer. Leading him on. Ruining his chances of meeting somebody else. Living happily ever after with a sensible girl. God knows, they'd be lining up for him. The thought of that sent a little shard of rage through Noreen. Kitty Molloy would be first on his doorstep. With a stupid bow in her hair and a plate of scones. Maureen Munnelly? She'd be delighted to hear he was back on the market – so would her mother. Then, Oh God, there was Sheila Nolan. He'd taken Sheila to a dance in Fermoy the week before they got together. She was a proper dolly bird now, since she had the hair dyed. John would probably call on her straight from the boat.

Feck it – I'll marry you!

Noreen could not bear the thought of him being with anyone else. But she couldn't just marry him to keep him off the market. Could she? Maybe that was what everyone did. You had no choice but to marry the man you loved. If you didn't get married you couldn't be loved.

It was very confusing. Except for one thing. Noreen knew that she did not want to get married. The more she thought about it, the more certain she was that she could not, would not, make the commitment to one person for the rest of her life. It just didn't feel right.

As John hurriedly got dressed, Noreen stood watching him in agony, knowing there was nothing she could say to keep him with her. Nothing that wasn't an outright lie or a shallow piece of plámás* that would fall flat on its face later.

He looked at her as he left, his face pleading with her to say something.

'Please don't go,' she said. 'Not like this.'

John looked at her and, while he loved her, he knew he couldn't do this any more. Noreen had to belong to him. Only to him. Whether she had, or hadn't slept with another man since she had been here, the mere threat of it was intolerable.

'I can't go on pretending all this is alright, Noreen, because it isn't. I'm just an ordinary Irishman. All this – it's just not for me.' And he walked out the door.

Noreen cried for an hour.

Then she went and rummaged in the kitchen for some comfort food. She didn't have to look far. Annie had left out a selection of cut cheeses and crackers in case they got hungry in the night. With a snap of irritation, Noreen noticed Annie's new, French wooden-handled cheese cutter was hanging neatly on its hook by the bread bin, and wondered why any woman would want to spend their hard-earned money on such pointless cooking appliances.

After stuffing back a dozen cheese-loaded crackers, Noreen pulled herself together. She had work tomorrow, and an exciting life to lead. She had scarified the love of her life to be on this adventure and to hell with John, and her father, and the wretched Catholic Church and its institution of marriage; she was going to make this adventure happen by being utterly wicked and naughty.

But before she let go of her goody-goody self entirely, Noreen decided to do one last good deed.

* Flattery

She picked up her letter pad and started writing.

Dear Mr and Mrs Black,

*My name is Noreen Lyons and I share a flat in London
with your daughter, Hanna...*

31

Lara had experienced a sick dread in her stomach all the way down to the seminary. She had been greeted by a cold English cleric and taken into a small wood panelled room, which smelt of furniture polish and incense. A large crucifix hung above the mantelpiece. Carved from light wood, Jesus looked merely mournful, a far cry from the agonised bloody Sacred Heart pictures she had grown up with at home.

Lara had been given a cup of tea and left on her own for almost an hour. While she waited, Lara had wondered how she would feel seeing Matthew again. Did she still love him? Was that why she was here? Should she even be asking herself these questions?

Finally, Lara had heard a voice in the hall. It was the same cleric that had seen her in, saying rather crossly, 'The young woman has been waiting for quite some time.'

She had frozen for a second and then, Matthew was there, standing in front of her.

As soon as she saw him, Lara was flooded through with an old emotion. The delight and excitement of seeing somebody familiar that you have not seen for a long time. He looked shell-shocked, so she smiled and walked across the room although the cleric was still standing there so she was unsure what to do when she got there. So she just stood and he said, 'Lara. What a surprise!'

'Don't forget, evening prayer is in less than half an hour,' the priest said before closing the door on them.

'Yes, Father,' Matthew said. He seemed embarrassed.

Perhaps the priest thought they were going to fall on each other the moment he left. Her last encounter behind a closed door, with Coleman, flashed into her head.

'So,' Lara said, 'I heard you were in London and I thought I'd come and see you.'

It sounded so hollow.

'Well,' he said, 'it's nice to see you.'

That sounded equally small, and yet all the things she had imagined saying to him in this moment, the angry accusations, the incredulous fury at being abandoned, were gone. In their place was a vague feeling of familiarity, barely bordering on friendship. There was the same familiar, handsome face, the eyes shining with a mixture of sensitivity and vulnerability that she knew so well and yet the feeling she had been expecting, the overwhelming sense of loss, love – something – just wasn't there. Lara was surprised to realise that she felt less joy in seeing Matthew than she had when his sister bounded unexpectedly into her life a few weeks ago. In fact, with the great love of her life standing in front of her, all Lara felt was guilt at having fallen out with Noreen over – well this 'nothing' moment.

She looked around the room at the life Matthew had chosen. This rarefied world of men in frocks and musty, cloistered martyrdom. The opposite of the modern, liberated, adventurous path she was on. The fact that he had chosen this over her was annoying, but no longer the point. They had shared a life together, but today they were worlds apart. Lara felt a little sad, but mostly she was surprised to find she felt relieved.

However, she had to make some effort so she asked, 'How is the training going?'

'Well,' he said. 'I'm enjoying the restoration work but I'm thinking of leaving the priesthood.'

The words just came out of his mouth. When he saw a wry, amused smile barely disguising her disgust, Matthew realised he was done with this. The pretence. The gradual, brainwashing slide into sanctimonious bachelorhood.

Lara looked interested now.

'Oh?' she said.

'Yes,' he said, matter-of-factly. 'I've met somebody.'

Lara reeled as he explained, quite unnecessarily, 'A woman.'

As subtle as a bullock's bollocks, Lara remembered Noreen once saying of her often stupidly blunt brother.

He didn't care. His mind was made up and he was saying it like it was. It was true. He had fallen in love with a woman.

It was in that moment that Lara realised Matthew hadn't decided he loved God more than he loved woman. He just loved God more than he loved her.

Lara's hackles rose. Leaving her for the priesthood was one thing. Leaving the priesthood for a woman, another woman, a better woman, a woman he…

'I've fallen in love,' he said to himself more than her, adding, 'for the first time.'

For the first time. Had he never been in love with her? Clearly not. Well, that was a humiliation just too great to bear.

What about me? Weren't you in love with ME? The words formed in her head but pride prevented her from saying them out loud. Instead, quite out of the blue, she found herself saying, 'Me too.'

'Really?' Matthew said, without a hint of jealousy in his voice.

'Yes. I've met somebody too.'

'Well, I'm happy for you.'

Matthew expressed no curiosity about who it was because he felt none. He was just delighted that Lara was beyond his hurt. Lara was longing to tell him she had spent a whole afternoon having wild, passionate sex with a gangster but the other, greater part of her felt that would be disloyal. To Coleman. Not him. She certainly did not want a description of the woman he had fallen in love with over her, but not because she wasn't curious or didn't care.

Lara felt discombobulated and angry. She was confused and had no idea what might come out of her mouth next so she picked up her bag from the table and said, as breezily as she could, 'Good for you. I'd better be going.'

Matthew raised his eyebrows at her quick departure.

'Is that it?'

'Yes, Matthew, that's it.'

'Well, phew. I thought you'd come here because you were cross with me or something.'

'No, no,' she said, her voice clipped. After putting her through all that to become a priest and now he had fallen in love and was walking away from it. The stupid, featherheaded, half-witted idiot! She wanted to kill him. 'Why would I be cross?' she said, opened the door and left. Then, unable to help herself she shouted, as loudly as she dared (which was quite loudly), 'Enjoy your evening prayers, everyone!' hoping it would get him into lots of trouble.

Outside the seminary, she lit a cigarette and started towards the Kings Road at full speed, marching off her rage.

Clearly, Matthew had never been in love with her. But

knowing that made her feel angry, not sad. Not heartbroken. Then, a storm of emotion broke inside her and she began to think. Had she ever been in love with him? She had loved Matthew, although she wondered now, had she ever loved him more than Noreen? What she had fallen in love with was the idea of being with him. Two artists studying in Dublin then moving to London. Perhaps what she had really fallen in love with was the security of knowing who she was going to spend the rest of her life with so that she could get on with the important thing at hand, which was designing clothes. Matthew had simply gone along with her; she could see that now. She willed him into an engagement and he joined the priesthood to get out of it. The priesthood enabled Matthew to escape her plans for him and now, ironically, he was free to fall in love.

As the terrible truth of that settled inside her, a thunderbolt hit.

'Me too.'

Was that the truth?

Could she be in love with Coleman, after all? Coleman was not a sensible option, the preferred option, the smart option. But then, you didn't choose who you fell in love with. Perhaps the passionate attraction she had for him meant she was in love, but Lara was a pragmatist and artist. She loved people, of course, but she only fell in love with clothes. Perhaps that was by choice. She certainly wasn't choosing to be with Coleman, not by any means. That would be reckless. Although, she had chosen Matthew even though he had never inspired the kind of dark passion that she had experienced with Coleman.

As Lara reached Sloane Square her anger towards Matthew abated and gave way to a more thoughtful train. She joined the evening crowds crushing along the pavements, city gents in bowler hats and cool cats in miniskirts weaving in and out of each other, bright red buses trundling past – somebody had painted the word LOVE in bright pink and parked it on the pavement outside C&A. Lara never tired of London, its energy and its style. She may have grown up in Ireland and been educated in Dublin but London felt like her home now, and Chelsea was her patch. The past really was gone for her now, inside and out. In truth, Matthew had given her a gift by leaving her. Would she ever have come here with him? Having seen him in the dry environment of the seminary, wearing his soutane and the serious, slightly worried expression he adopted whenever he was forced to come into contact with modern life, she doubted she would ever have got him to London. Not her London anyway. This crazy, swinging, beautiful place. In truth, Matthew leaving her had been the best thing he could ever have done for her. Maybe, just maybe, he had known that.

When she got back to the flat, Annie was in the kitchen and she was singing.

'You're in good form.'

'Oh Lara,' she said, flinging herself down on the sofa and flicking her tea towel in the air.

'The most wonderful thing happened today.'

'You're in love?'

Annie giggled. 'Well I don't know about that but...' Then she laughed again. Lara had never seen her so happy. 'How did you know?'

'Call me psychic. I can tell.'

She stood up and went over to the kitchen. 'It probably won't come to anything. I just met somebody in the cafe today that I liked, that's all.'

This was the first time she'd shown any interest in a man. *There must be something in the air*, thought Lara.

'Well, you're so gorgeous, I'm sure he'll be back.'

'Oh,' she said sadly, 'I don't think he's really interested. He thought my modelling was inappropriate.'

Annie didn't mention to Lara that he was a priest. That would just confuse things.

'He'll definitely be back then,' Lara joked

'Do you really think so?'

'Of course,' Lara said, slightly irritated by her coy innocence.

'Maybe,' she said. 'I invited him along to the shoot tomorrow.'

'That's great,' said Lara. But it didn't feel great.

Noreen had John and now even innocent Annie had met somebody. Lara had had enough of this day.

'I'm going downstairs,' she said. 'If anyone comes looking for me, tell them I'm in a meeting with Coleman.'

Then added with a small smile, 'And tell them not to disturb me.'

Annie, lost in her own delicious thoughts of a handsome Priest Charming was only half listening.

Lara and Coleman had been avoiding each other. She, because she needed to process his action and he, she presumed, to give her time to do that. Or, more likely, she thought with a shiver of excitement, because he would be unable to keep his savage hands off her. To be doubly sure, she hoiked her skirt up a few inches, ruffled her intimidating bob out of symmetry and smeared on some candy pink lipstick to create a fashionably dry pout.

As she stood at the door of his office, Lara's hands paused in anticipation before she knocked, and her stomach leapt when she heard his familiar grunt, imagining what might be awaiting her.

When she stepped inside, Coleman was sitting behind his desk filling in an accounts ledger.

'Hi,' he said, not looking up.

'Hi,' she said.

When he did look up his eyes were cold and querying.

'How are you?' he asked with disinterested distance.

'Fine.' Her stomach started to knot. Maybe he was mad at her for not saying 'I love you' back. She forced warmth into her voice and asked, 'How are you?' It sounded patronising.

'Good,' he said, then nodding towards the ledger, 'busy.'

Coleman was so hard to read. He was showing no signs of loving her now. None. Maybe he was hiding it, for pride's sake. Or maybe...

'Was there something in particular?'

'Yes,' she said, smiling and taking a step towards him. 'I was hoping we might go through some figures? There's some new stock I'm interested in getting, but I'm not sure how to balance the takings with—'

'Sure,' he said cutting her off as if in a tremendous hurry. 'Do you have them with you?'

Maybe he had gone off her.

No. Surely not.

She opened her palms to show her hands were empty and, trying to sound coquettish, said, 'Oh dear – I seem to have left them upstairs.'

She was taking the first step in sashaying towards his desk when Coleman looked down at his papers, again, and said, 'Did you do up those dresses for Maureen Chevron yet?'

Coleman had told her that she needed to put together a few special pieces for Bobby's wife, to keep her and her crazy husband sweet. Lara had started a few drawings but then got too busy with the shop. Anyway, why couldn't the woman just come over and pick some pieces herself?

'Haven't got round to it yet.'

He looked up at her briefly. 'Well make sure you do. It's important.'

Normally, she would have given him a mouthful for using such a patronising tone but she was bruised and felt more hurt than angry.

'OK,' she said.

When she didn't move to go he said, 'If you want to go and get those papers now, I can give you half an hour.'

Really? Is that it?

Lara stood for a moment and looked at him, waiting, willing him to look up again and see that she was on the verge of tears.

He didn't.

'Shall we leave it for another time?'

Coleman ran his finger from side to side across the lines in his ledger.

Was he avoiding her deliberately? Simply trying hard to resist her? She checked and saw that his eyes were following the figures. It seemed like he was genuinely involved in his work. If he was avoiding her because he felt awkward, he was doing a very good job. Too good a job.

'Perhaps that would be best,' he said looking up briefly, holding her eyes in a harsh stare.

'Perhaps it would.' Lara tried to regain some dignity. And failed.

After she gently closed the door of Coleman's office, she stood with her back against it and took a deep breath. In just one day she had experienced the indifference of two lovers. One had hurt her pride, the other her heart.

32

'I don't want you going near the bloke again.'

Noreen was having a bad day. Arthur had just got wind of the fact that she'd employed Handsome in the bar.

'He is bad news, Noreen. Baaaad news. Do you hear me?'

'I hear you, Arthur,' she said, driving the drying cloth so far into the glass, she nearly broke it. 'I'm just not listening.'

'This is stupid, Noreen, he's a daaangerous character.'

Noreen thought that was pretty rich coming from someone who nearly killed a man with an ironing board.

'You'll find I can be pretty dangerous myself if you don't shut up!'

Arthur muttered something about 'aving words with Coleman and sloped off.

Noreen picked up another glass from the draining board and felt a bit sick. Not eaten-too-many-biscuits sick. Emotionally-upset sick. Noreen could not remember ever having felt this way before. A kind of empty, hollow dread, as if something rotten was around the corner. Or worse, nothing at all was around the corner.

As she was putting the glass on the shelf she saw Lara come down the stairs.

With nobody else there she had no choice but to address Noreen. She left a large envelope marked 'stock receipts' on the bar and said, 'Would you give these to Coleman please?'

Coleman was in his office and there was no reason that Lara could not give them to him herself. However, Lara and Coleman had not spoken, at least not that Noreen had observed, since that afternoon when she had seen her come away from what she assumed was a passionate encounter.

Noreen was finding the coldness between her and Lara increasingly painful. The resentment she held towards Lara for keeping her Coleman affair a secret from her had gone. Especially as it seemed that Coleman had been using Lara, after all, in which case, Lara had been right to keep quiet about their encounter. However, Noreen could not seem to find a way of breaking the ice.

'No problem,' she said, her eyes down.

'Thank you,' Lara said in a clipped singsong tone, before heading straight back up the stairs.

As she watched her friend leave Noreen felt impossibly sad. It wasn't just Lara. It was a lack of contact. No how are things? What are we having for dinner? Any news chitchat. The only people she had to talk to now were the punters and Arthur. Handsome had turned out to be a useless barman and a worse conversationalist. He was pretty but boring as all hell. Plus, Arthur's dark warnings had taken any sheen off her fancying him whatsoever.

She craved John. He was the one person she could tell everything to. Had she been wrong to let him go so easily? It seemed that everything had gone wrong.

For the first time in her life, Noreen suspected that the empty feeling she had was loneliness. So she decided to go and visit her brother Matthew.

She called the seminary and they informed her that he was at the National Gallery.

As her bus trundled along the Embankment, Noreen looked out the window and realised that she felt better already. She wondered how she had managed to be in London for this many weeks and never been into central London before. The only places she had been since arriving here were Chevrons, the flat and Fred's cafe. Yet, now that she was here, looking out on the River Thames, seeing Tower Bridge, Big Ben, Noreen did not have any great sense of adventure or excitement about being near the famous places she had seen in films and read about in books since she was a little girl. For Noreen, the kick she got out of life was from the people around her. What they were doing, who they were having sex with, who they wished they were having sex with.

Perhaps her motives in seeing Matthew were not entirely familial loneliness after all. Noreen knew that Lara had been to see him. After all, she had given her his address. She was not in a position to ask Lara how the visit with her brother had gone but she was longing to know how they had got on.

She managed to locate Matthew after traipsing around room after room, until she finally found somebody who unearthed him from the bowels of this huge, ancient place. This one building was the size of the whole of Carney. It was massive. Rather than be impressed or amazed, she felt rather uncomfortable in its grand, imposing environs.

'Isn't this the most amazing place?' was, annoyingly, the first thing he said to her. 'Have you been to see Caravaggio?'

As much as she hated being in this huge, cold place filled with ancient old stuff, Matthew loved it.

'Never mind that,' she snapped. 'Did Lara come to see you?'

Matthew squirmed.

'Yes she did. Last week.'

'And?'

'And what?'

'And what did she say? What did you say? And don't skimp. I want to know every minute detail.'

'Mind your own business.'

'She told you to mind your own business?'

'No. I'm telling you to mind your own business.'

'Don't be ridiculous. I'm your sister. You are my business.'

'No I'm not. I'm my own man, Noreen, and it's time you realised that.'

'That's even more ridiculous. You joined the church so you wouldn't have to be your own man and make your own life – and now they own you.'

Noreen knew it was a bit harsh but she had to put a halt to his gallop. Except, Matthew threw his head back, lifting himself up a few inches above her and said, 'Actually, I'm leaving the church.'

She was not expecting that.

'Oh really? And where are you going?'

'I don't know, but I've fallen in love and plan to leave as soon as I've finished this restoration course.'

Noreen laughed. The soft eejit. He must have read something into Lara's visit. It wouldn't be the first time her stupid brother had picked up the wrong end of the stick.

'Look,' she said, trying to sound kind. 'Whatever Lara might have said to you, Matthew, take it from me, there's no way that she's intending to take you back.'

'It's not Lara,' he said, a hint of sheepishness creeping into his voice. 'It's somebody else.'

Noreen reeled. He had met somebody else. How? When?

'Who?'

'You don't know her.'

'What's her name?'

He opened his mouth to say Annie's name then looked at his bossy sister and realised she was right. He had to make his own life. Starting right here, right now, by holding his ground and telling his interfering sister to back the hell off!

'Does Da know?'

'I said, mind your own—'

'Did you write to Ma? She won't be happy.'

'Noreen.'

'If you tell me who this girl is then maybe—'

'NOREEN! Will you please mind your own bloody business!'

Cursing. From a priest. Well, nearly a priest. Noreen got up on her high horse.

'Fine!' she said. 'Be that way but don't come crying to me when...' she couldn't think what that 'when' was. Matthew was leaving the priesthood, as she always thought he should, to make his own life, as she has advised. She should be pleased. 'Oh never mind!' she finished then turned on her heels.

As she flounced off across Trafalgar Square, Noreen wasn't sure why she was so upset or crying as bitterly as she was. All she knew was that she was hurt by the fact that nobody – nobody – was confiding in her any more. She felt shut out of everybody's life. Even her own brother was telling her to mind her own business. The problem was, Noreen realised, she still didn't have any business of her own to mind. She had lost her lover, her friend and now, it seemed, a brother. The only business that was hers to mind was Chevrons. And, if she wanted to spend her life managing a pub, she could have stayed at home.

As Matthew watched his sister bumble across the broad, magnificent square with her capable, mannish stride he could see from the hunch of her shoulders that she was hurt. He felt regretful about that. He also felt like a stupid fool for telling Lara, and now blabbermouth Noreen, that he was planning to leave the priesthood for a woman he had barely met. One who, in actual fact, he had blown off in that stupid, clumsy way of his.

As Matthew watched his sister disappear behind the great lions onto the Mall, he checked his watch. What time had Annie said she would be at the Peter Pan statue?

What was the point though? Yes, he told those two he was leaving the priesthood for Annie but, in reality, it was simply that meeting her had given him clarity that it was the right thing to do. He didn't actually stand a chance of being with her. Especially after acting like such an idiot.

Matthew looked down at his soutane. It felt not just uncomfortable any more, but wrong. His contemporaries all complained about the comfort of the soutane, but never about the symbolism of wearing a uniform that marked them out as God's army. Most of the men he was in the seminary with were good men. Well-intentioned, honourable men. They struggled with their faith and their vow of celibacy, but they did so gracefully, manfully. Had Matthew ever been a proper man at all, he wondered? Certainly, he knew he was a fraud. And with that certain knowledge, his mind was made up. The pretence stopped today. Now. He would have to give up his studies and return to Ireland, in all likelihood alone, with his tail between his legs. There would be shame and recriminations, but the lying had to stop.

Matthew was wearing a priest's black trousers and white shirt under his soutane. He reached up to his neck, unbuttoned and uncoupled his priest's collar and stuffed it into the deep pockets of his skirt, pulling out his wallet from the same pocket. He had been to the bank the day before and counted through twenty-five pounds.

Enough money, surely, to buy a pair of jeans and a colourful shirt, something that might send the right message to a girl. If he moved quickly, he might get up to Oxford Street, kit himself out and get to the Peter Pan statue in Kensington Gardens to meet her by 2 p.m.

33

Alex picked Annie up from outside That Girl. Framed against the backdrop of the unapologetically modern shop front, she looked curiously old-fashioned, but stunningly beautiful. Lara had dressed her in a simple shift dress in cream silk. Lara, herself, had been held up. She was waiting for an order to come in from Wales and had called Alex to ask if he could collect Annie from That Girl and assured them both she would be there as soon as she could get away.

Annie waved at Lara before climbing into Alex's convertible. There was, Alex noticed, an air of confidence about her. They whizzed through London, the wind whipping Annie's long hair in fluttering tendrils across her face. She could not help but smile. *This*, she thought, *is what freedom feels like.* Alex parked up on the pavement outside Lancaster Gate tube station and they walked through the gate and past the lawns and colourful, gaudy flower beds towards the statue. Alex was weighed down with his huge camera bags and Annie was swinging her arms by her side; they were an odd couple. Annie's dress was light and the day was breezy, although warm. As they walked, Annie could feel the air lift the light down on her arms and legs. There was only one thing on her mind.

Would he come? Was Lara right in what she had said yesterday? '... you're so gorgeous, I'm sure he'll be back.' Annie had no idea but she did know that she wanted him to and, in that sweet longing, was happiness already. Dorian had taken so much from her but now, she knew, he had not taken everything. He had not taken her love. Not all of it. There was still a little trust left in her heart. And from a little, planted well and tended, more could grow. She wanted it to be with the priest, but if not him? At least in liking him she had hope there might be somebody, someday.

These unspoken thoughts settled across her face in an almost unworldly glow. Alex put down his camera beside a large oak tree on a quiet piece of lawn, near, but not at, the statue itself and arranged Annie on a rug at its base. The afternoon sun dappled through the leaves and sent shards of soft light down on her. She looked like the most beautiful girl in the world. Alex's stomach contracted with excitement. Not for the girl herself, but her beauty, and for what it would help him achieve.

Matthew could have worn his own trousers. They were black and perfectly functional. He could have simply removed his soutane, bundled it into a bin somewhere, and gone collarless. Nobody would have known. But, stupidly, recklessly, he now realised, in his despair at not wanting to be dressed even remotely like a priest, he had cut things too fine. You don't mess about with time because, if you do, God might decide to have a laugh at your expense. Walking into a hipster jeans shop on Oxford Street wearing a soutane was not an option, Matthew decided. He would look less conspicuous in a large department store. So, he had gone into Dickins and Jones on Regent Street and run straight up to the menswear department.

Faced with racks and racks of clothes, he realised he was in the wrong place and was about to leave when a middle-aged assistant slithered up to him and, bowing slightly said, 'Can I help you, Father?' Eugene, as his badge said, was so painfully deferential that Matthew found his obligation to be priestly outweighed his urgent need to get out of there. 'Are we looking to go mufti, Father?'

Matthew gave him an awkward smile, which Eugene took as 'yes' and set about measuring him from head to toe. He kept him for an age in the changing room when he came back with essentially the same outfit he was wearing – black corduroy trousers and a white shirt, albeit with an ordinary, attached collar and a ludicrously frilled cuff. Eugene then folded the soutane, wrapping it in tissue paper with great care, before finally placing it into a Dickins and Jones bag. This process took just short of an hour and cost Matthew all of the money he had on him, which put a taxi fare out of his reach and meant he had to run to Kensington Gardens.

By the time he got there he was in a terrible state. The corduroy trousers had heated up to oven levels and the white shirt was sticking to his chest with sweat. When he finally managed to locate the Peter Pan statue, it was nearly 2.45 p.m. and there was no sign of Annie. She must have gone already. There was certainly no reason for her to have waited for him. If, indeed, she even remembered who he was, which he doubted. Still, he cursed Eugene for holding him up, but mostly himself for being such a weak-willed, pathetic creature, for joining the priesthood in the first place, and then imagining he could extricate himself when he couldn't even assert his secular status with a shop assistant.

This whole thing had been ridiculous; imagining a girl like that would be interested in him.

'That's lovely, sweetheart. Smashing. Now move that left arm over to the right a tad – no – too much, too much – that's it, just there. Good girl. Lovely.'

The inane banter was coming from behind him, on the other side of a tall, ornamental hedge. Curious, Matthew walked across and as he looked behind the hedge his eyes took in a tableau that took his breath away.

Annie was sitting under a tree, surrounded by heather and bluebells. She was wearing a cream dress, like a bride. Her long auburn hair curled around her shoulder in unkempt flicks and her bare legs were arranged in a provocative curl to one side. When she saw him, her mouth opened in surprise, and she pressed her pinky finger to her pale, full lips. Matthew's heart was in his mouth as he saw the recognition glitter across her eyes.

'Oh yes. Loving that look – good girl – you've seen something over my shoulder.'

The photographer didn't know he was there and Matthew didn't want to disturb the view. It was as close to a Raphael painting as he had ever seen. He had never in his whole life been as bereft of sketchpad and charcoal as he was now.

Matthew gave a small wave, and Annie waved cautiously back.

'Clever girl – you're waving at somebody over my shoulder. Loving it. Good girl – keep your eyes off camera just like that! You're on FIRE now. Keep that look in the eyes. Look at you, girl – you're GLITTERING! Loving this look, lady – glowing from the inside out. Damn – hang on.'

As he was quickly and expertly loading film into his camera Alex looked up at the sky, always checking cloud cover, then saw Matthew and jumped.

'Christ! Who the hell are you?' he snapped.

For the first time in his life gentle Matthew had a manly desire to punch somebody. It wasn't rational; he knew that. The photographer was a friend of Annie's and was just doing his job. Still, it was a job that involved capturing the extraordinary beauty of this woman who Matthew, also irrationally, loved beyond all measure. Matthew felt, even if he didn't entirely understand, that this should be his privilege, not that of this impolite little English squirt.

He gathered himself and said, 'I'm a friend of Annie's.'

'Well,' Alex said, looking him up and down then quickly snapping shut his camera and raising it to his eye again, 'whoever you are, just stand there and keep doing what you're doing because she's clearly loving it and it's working a dream.'

Alex went from being a class A rotter to an angel of mercy.

Matthew beamed and waved at Annie. Annie beamed and waved back.

Both were thinking the same thing. Matthew – the very moment this is over I am going to take that woman in my arms and kiss her and to hell with all propriety. Annie – the very moment Alex is finished, I am going to fling myself into his arms and kiss him – to hell if he's a priest.

Neither could barely wait.

Although, in truth, Alex knew in those last few frames he already had everything he needed. Annie had given him as much beauty and mood as any editor could possibly want; he might as well keep it going as long as this soft light from the cloud cover held.

'Alright you two,' said Alex, 'pull back on the smiles, Annie – keep it small and subtle like before. Let's not lose that vibe. It's a wrap.'

When she heard Alex say the words, the excitement she felt

reached a crescendo as she saw Matthew walk over towards her. She knew it was going to happen. She had been antici- pating it since she first saw him standing over at the hedge, watching her, then every moment since. Still, when Matthew leaned in and kissed her, Annie felt as if she was floating, transported, lifted to a place so glorious that she never wanted to come down. And for the rest of the day, they didn't.

They left Kensington Gardens, hand in hand, and walked and talked their way around the London streets. Every now and again, they stopped and kissed. He would stop, lean down and kiss her, then she would stop, reach up and kiss him. He told her a bit about himself but it was all so pointless, so pedestrian that all he mentioned was that he had a sister and that his father owned a pub. He told her the most interesting thing about him, which was that he had been engaged once, and broken a girl's heart when he joined the priesthood. He regretted it now. They settled on a bench under a tree in Hyde Park as the early evening sun was setting, and she told him her story. How her father died when she was young. Then, her mother moved them both to Mayo where she met a rich doctor and remarried. Matthew could not help thinking how his marrying a doctor's daughter might soften the blow for his own mother when he told her he was leaving the priesthood. She was too perfect. Then, she paused.

'I need to tell you something,' she said.

Matthew could tell she was uncomfortable.

'Something bad happened.'

'You don't have to tell me if you don't want to.' He wouldn't coax her.

'I do want to tell you but I never told anybody any of this before.'

'Not even a priest?' he said.

'No. I've been too ashamed. When I tell you, you'll understand why.'

Matthew felt a little afraid, but he knew that no matter what this girl told him, he belonged to her. Perhaps that was the most frightening thing of all.

'Matthew, I want you to know who I am. I want you to decide for yourself if you can be with me. But first you need to know everything.'

So she told him. Everything.

Right up to the point before she killed Dorian.

'Then,' she said, 'one day, I just packed up my things and ran away.'

Matthew was enraged, disgusted, horrified that such a thing could happen. But, more than that, he was filled with admiration for her strength and tenacity.

'So you see,' she said, 'I'm broken.'

'You're not broken,' he told her. 'You're the most beautiful person I've ever known. Beauty like yours is unbreakable.'

Annie's face darkened.

'He told me I was beautiful. That was why he did what he did to me.'

'You're beautiful on the inside too, Annie. Beauty isn't in the body; it's in the soul. Men like that have no soul. If he had, he couldn't have done what he did. A man like that is not a man at all, Annie. You say he was the closest person to you for most of your teens, but he never knew you. Not like...'

It seemed too forward to say it.

'I want you to know me,' she said. 'If you'll let me.'

He held her, and kissed her until she felt tears pouring down her face in a flood of relief.

'Something else,' she said. 'Something I left out.'

Could she tell him? Should she tell him? Murder. He would leave her. If he left her she would die.

'Anything,' he said. 'You can tell me anything.'

She paused and her courage was snatched away on a summer breeze. 'My real name. It's not Annie, it's Hanna. Hanna Black.'

34

'Will you be able to manage the shop for a few hours, Dolly?' Lara asked.

Dolly was Lara's full-time shop assistant. She had worked in a couple of other boutiques along the Kings Road and was reliable enough, but would only be there until the end of that week as she was heading off to New York. A friend of a friend of hers knew Warhol and said he could get her some modelling work. It was, Lara thought, a silly, pie-in-the-sky idea. Although part of her was envious of Dolly's impulsiveness. In the past few months Lara discovered that the creativity involved in designing and making clothes was the smaller part of her job. Her day-to-day was largely taken up with managing young staff and endless paperwork, neither of which she was good at or particularly enjoyed.

Dolly looked up from the counter where she seemed to be permanently planted.

'And please stop painting your nails, Dolly. I don't want you getting varnish on the clothes.'

Dolly said, 'OK, boss,' pouting sulkily. She couldn't wait to get out of there and over to the laid back, woozy lifestyle waiting for her in Manhattan. Lara was cool but, man, she could be so uptight. Weren't the Irish meant to be all drink and parties?

Lara was a bit worried about leaving Dolly in charge, but the lunchtime rush was over and, between stocktaking and selling, she had barely been out of the shop in the past three days. She was itching to do something creative, even if it was just playing a small part in the shoot with Alex and Annie. She put a couple of jackets and accessories in a That Girl bag and grabbed a black cab, which took her to the Lancaster Gate entrance to the park.

It was nearly three o'clock, but they would hardly be getting started. They had probably moved on from their original meeting place. In fact, knowing Alex's roving eye, they could be anywhere in the park by now, so Lara wandered in the direction of the Peter Pan statue keeping her eyes peeled. All around her were people enjoying the sunshine. A young couple sitting on the grass, feeding each other crackers. A gang of four youths leaning on the railings, smoking cigarettes – too old for school, too young for the pub. An old-fashioned nanny in her smart uniform pushing a pram, a young mother with her two children running in front of her, chasing a ball, and two old men sitting side by side on a bench, watching the world go by. One of them was smoking a pipe while the other raised his hat as she passed and said, 'Good afternoon, miss.'

She smiled back and said, 'Good afternoon, gentlemen.' The woody smell of pipe smoke reminded her of her father and Lara felt a pang for home. London was not just for the fashionable and the frantic. All life was here. She just never got to see it.

A few feet away to her left, she heard a voice.

'Damn this is heavy.'

A familiar face appeared from behind a hedge. Alex was lugging a huge camera bag and muttering to himself, 'No chance of getting a hand here I suppose.' Then, when he saw her, 'Hey Lara, grab this for me?'

'Are you finished already?'

'Sorry, you're too late, love. But wow – we got some great shots.'

'Aw,' she said, holding up her own bag. 'I brought gear. Are you sure you're all done?'

'Oh trust me. We are all wrapped up – in more ways than one.' He nodded behind the hedge. 'Annie's got herself a bloke.'

'NO!' Lara said in a loud whisper. 'I don't believe it!' and she stuck her head round the edge of the hedge. Sure enough, Annie was in a clinch with a big strong man. Lara came back quickly, before they saw her. She was not sure if ingénue Annie had even ever been kissed before. Lara was so excited for her. And dying of curiosity to see this mystery man.

'Give me that,' she said, and dragged Alex's heavy metal camera case over to the side of the hedge. Before he could object, she was standing on it, on tip toes, looking over at the couple, unseen.

'Bloody nosy Irishwoman,' Alex said.

'I just want to get a right look at HIM,' she said. 'The mystery man.'

'Ordinary looking bloke,' Alex said.

'Gah,' Lara complained, 'turn around.'

'You're worse than my mother.'

'I didn't know you were Irish.'

'Jewish. But when it comes to interfering mothers it's the same thing.'

The couple were lost in each other, kissing in a messy,

untrammelled way that made Lara begin to regret her intrusion. She was about to come back down when something held her there. Curiosity was joined by a slight familiarity. Like the answer to a question you didn't know you had asked. The man took Annie's face in his hands and turned slightly to the side. Lara craned her head and fully saw him.

Before she registered him, his name, she registered the expression in his eyes as he looked down onto Annie's beautiful face.

Love.

The soft, pleading, passionate, uncompromising, desperate certainty of true love. The thing she had craved, sought in all their years together, and never seen.

If he had loved her like that, she would have loved him back.

If he had loved her like that…

Lara toppled on the box and Alex caught her.

'Whoops,' he said, 'did you get a good look?'

'Good enough.' She got down from the box and said, without a hint of good humour, 'I'm going to head back.'

God, women were moody. As much as he worked with them, and loved (some) of them, Alex thought he would never understand them.

'You sure you don't want to hang on and interview him, he seems like a reasonable enough bloke.'

'No,' she snapped. 'I have to get back to the shop.'

As she walked briskly towards the gate, Alex thought he saw her break into a run.

She left her clothes behind too. Another thing for him to carry. Or perhaps Annie's boyfriend would give him a hand.

In the end, the couple were so engrossed he left them to it and carried his bags back to the car himself.

As he was loading in the last one he became aware of a figure loitering near the gate, as if waiting for someone. He would not have noticed him except for a sense that he might have seen him somewhere before. When he turned to check, the man was gone and Alex slammed down his boot. The clouds were gathering and the roof was down, so he pegged it back to Fulham before the rain came.

Lara did not know what to do with herself. She needed a drink but did not want to go and sit in a strange pub in London, alone. So she flagged down a taxi and went straight to Chevrons. Lara needed to be with somebody she trusted. Somebody who knew her. Suddenly, nothing else mattered more than that.

She walked down the stairs, swept past Arthur and straight up to the bar.

'I need a drink,' she said to Noreen.

As Noreen opened her mouth to ask what she wanted Lara said, 'Something strong and something fast.'

Noreen poured her a straight whisky and put a bottle of ginger ale next to it.

Laura knocked it back, slammed the glass down on the bar, said, 'Again,' and knocked that back too.

Noreen didn't want to ask what was wrong. She was surprised, but pleased that whatever was wrong Lara was bringing it to her.

Lara nodded at her empty glass and said, 'Three more. One for me, one for the ginger ale bottle and Noreen – I think you're going to need one too.'

'Why? What happened?'

Noreen could not imagine what had happened to bring

Lara to her door like this, but whatever it was she was glad to have her back.

'Annie is seeing Matthew.'

Noreen was measuring out two whiskies and, almost, spilt a drop. She thought she must have misheard.

'When you say seeing you mean…'

'Seeing. Going out. Making love to.'

'Annie?'

'Yes.'

'And Matthew?'

'Yes.'

'My brother?'

'Yes.'

'The priest?'

'Jesus J Christ, Noreen – yes! I saw them,' her voice lowered to a whisper, 'kissing.' She threw down the third whisky.

Lara looked over at Noreen. Her face was defiant and the whisky glint was beginning to enter her eyes but Noreen could see a thread of anger and hurt burning there.

'Matthew never looked at me the way he looked at her.'

Then Lara began to cry. Noreen felt terrible for her.

'It's not even like I want him back, Noreen. Of course I love him, like I love you.' She reached her hand across and Noreen took it. Lara never told her she loved her before. Lara was quite drunk now but, still, Noreen felt curiously delighted.

'It's just, well, seeing him so obviously in love with somebody else like that when it was what I wanted for such a long time.'

'I'll kill him,' said Noreen. 'And then I'll kill her.'

'No, no, no, Noreen,' Lara shook her head. 'If you had only seen them. They were so in love.'

'Nonsense,' Noreen said. 'I'll make mincemeat of the pair of them so I will, for hurting you like this.'

Noreen could not imagine how she would feel if John fell in love with somebody else. Certainly, if she caught him kissing anybody else, ever, she would shoot him on the spot and as for the strap that got him...

'If John did that I'd—'

'But you and John broke up didn't you?'

Lara was not being mean. She said it quite matter-of-factly but Noreen felt it like a blow to the head.

John could go with anyone he liked now. He had sometimes threatened her with it as a joke when they were together.

'If you don't hurry up and marry me some girl might get her claws into me.'

'Sure who'd have you?' Noreen would quip back.

She looked around the club at Chevrons' clientele. Rough gangsters with their cauliflower ears, their flat heads and their bent noses. No need for one of them to go home alone tonight.

John could be one of them. He could get snapped up and carried away from her.

It was one thing sending him away, but the possibility of never getting him back was quite another. Noreen did not want to think about it, so she pushed the thought aside and concentrated on comforting Lara on her romantic misfortune.

They moved into a booth and floor girls picked up the slack to allow Noreen and Lara to chat. Coleman had been in but locked himself in his office when he saw Lara was there for the night. Lara was smarting about the other man in her life and felt curiously triumphant in not caring about Coleman. She had enough whisky in her not to care. When they ran out of man-talk, Lara and Noreen talked about other things, the shop, the club and everyday gossip that the hiatus in their friendship had missed.

'Who's he?' Lara asked after Noreen had given Handsome a telling off for interrupting them with a stupid question about where to get more lemons.

'The worst barman in the world,' Noreen said.

'Handsome though. I could use a good-looking guy in the shop. I'm selling menswear from next week.'

'You can have him.'

'Will he mind?'

'He'll be told. Anyway. He's always out the back, preening. He'll love it.'

As the two 'Irish' talked and laughed and cried, the floor girls brought them drinks and peanuts, delighted to see their formidable boss Noreen and hardworking hostess Lara let their hair down for a change.

It was closing time when they left. 'I'm kicking myself out!' Noreen said, staggering up the stairs with Lara all but crawling behind her.

Noreen was more sober than Lara and put her to bed, then she sat up and waited for Annie to get in. She was going to give her some piece of her mind. That girl was so much trouble. There was something just wrong about Annie; Noreen could feel it even though she couldn't put her finger on what it was.

And now, this business of her seducing Matthew was more of the same. She must be the girl that Matthew was planning to leave the priesthood for. So now he was turning his life upside down for her. How had Annie even met Matthew?

Had she stalked him? Gone looking for him to cause trouble? Through the fog of whisky Noreen vaguely wondered if she had ever even mentioned Matthew's name in front of Annie. Come to think of it, had Lara even told Annie that her beau left her to become a priest? The thought occurred to her that Matthew may have called to their flat looking for

Noreen that day he called into the club, or afterwards, to apologise for being such a clot. Annie might have opened the door and he could have simply fallen in love with her. Annie had the kind of looks that men fell for at first sight, and her brother was exactly the sort of impressionable eejit that could happen to. If that was the case, she thought, all of this could be her fault. A sobering thought. She swigged back the last of the Blue Nun and reminded herself that, regardless, sneaking about with a man behind your flatmate's back was highly suspicious. Noreen didn't know why Lara was as forgiving and protecting of Annie as she was. Perhaps if Lara knew about the bloody apron and the jewellery in the suitcase she would change her tune. But telling her about that would mean Noreen admitting that she had been snooping around Annie's things. Even though they were friends again, she wasn't sure that Lara would understand. John certainly hadn't.

John. If only he were here. He would know what to do. He would certainly have something to say about Annie going out with Matthew. She tried to imagine what that something might be and realised he would probably just say mind your own business. She wouldn't listen to him, of course, but she never minded John saying those things to her in the way she minded other people bossing her about. She wished he was there to tell her off. She missed him.

Matthew never looked at me the way he looked at her, Lara had said.

John looked at her that way all the time, with that soft, do-anything-for-you look in his eyes. Noreen had never appreciated it before. She liked it, but she always brushed it off. Big strong man going all lovey-dovey – what use was that to a girl? Now that she didn't have it, Noreen knew it was everything. Lara said it was rare, and it was.

Noreen desperately wanted John back.

But was his love worth giving up her freedom for? She thought not and yet this freedom business was proving not to be everything it was cracked up to be. She was essentially doing the same thing she had done at home: working all the hours God sent in a bar. She had a bit of gossipy craic with the gangsters but she had as much craic at home with the three Marys. And as for sex? It turned out it was a lot easier to come by in Carney than it was in London, once you knew where to look – which she did.

A sad feeling washed over Noreen. She knew, without doubt, that she still didn't want to marry John. She wasn't being awkward or rebellious. Marriage just didn't feel as if it was her. However, sitting here in the flat, she knew that she could not envisage a life without him. She had to go and find him and get him back. If that meant marrying him then she would have to do that too.

She drained her glass and decided not to bother waiting up for Annie. She wasn't in the mood for a confrontation. Noreen took off her uniform, went into Lara's room and crawled into bed beside her. The two of them breathed in tandem as they slept. In the early hours, Noreen's left arm threw itself clumsily over Lara's waist, anchoring her on her side. In her sleep, Lara reached across her breast and took her friend's hand. She smiled and dreamt she was loved.

35

'Oi! Noreen! That bloke from the new suppliers is dahnstairs looking for ya!'

Arthur banged on the door like he was waking the dead. Which, in effect, he was.

'Shite,' Noreen said, rubbing her head. 'Early meeting with vintner big shots. I forgot.'

Lara was already up. She might have got drunk quicker but she could weather a hangover better than her friend.

'Better get a move on – here.' She threw a fresh blouse and skirt across at her.

Noreen threw on the clothes, located her sling backs, then dragged a comb through her hair and ran downstairs.

Lara was relieved that she would have the chance to talk to Annie before Noreen got her hands on her.

When she came out to the living room Annie was in the kitchen, making a loaf of Irish brown bread.

Her hands flicked over the floured dough ball gathering up crumbs from the Formica countertop until it was as clean as when she started. Lara never failed to wonder at Annie's talent for domesticity. She gathered up the light loaf and put it on a tray in the oven.

'What's the occasion?' Lara asked.

Annie's naked face was glittering with her secret excitement. She looked as if she might have been up all night. Lara could not look at her beautiful, perfect face without imagining the love in Matthew's eyes.

'I'm off work today so I thought I'd treat us all and have fresh bread for breakfast.' She smiled awkwardly and added, 'I saw Noreen rush off just now. Will she be back before lunch?'

She seemed as if she was trying hard to control her voice and keep calm.

'I doubt it,' Lara said. 'She's very busy today.' It was true, but everything about this conversation was starting to feel like a lie.

'How did the shoot go with Alex yesterday? Sorry I didn't make it.'

That was a lie.

'It was fine. How was your day? Did the stock arrive from Wales?'

'Ah yeah. Fine.'

Noreen's dark warnings about Annie's duplicitous nature began to weigh on her. Could Noreen be right? Was Annie the devil incarnate? Did she even know Matthew was Noreen's brother? Lara tried to remember if she had ever mentioned his name to Annie.

'You were out late last night.'

'Yes,' Annie said, 'I was.'

She wasn't going to say anything. Lara turned away and walked towards the bedroom door feeling hurt and humiliated.

But, just as she was on the point of leaving, Annie shouted out in an excited burst, 'Oh Lara, the most wonderful thing happened last night. The boy that I was telling you about – he came along to the shoot and he kissed me and we're in love!'

Lara was relieved. She put a smile on her face.

'I'm not supposed to tell anybody, because, and please try not to be shocked, but he's a priest. Well, not a full priest, he's training to be a priest. Although really he should never have been a priest at all because he just loves art and old paintings. He's very creative, a lot like you. I think you would really get along.'

Then, something surprising happened. Lara found that the fake smile she had plastered on her face was, in fact, real.

'Anyway, I never dreamt I would meet anyone so wonderful, Lara. We stayed out all night long. We walked all over London and we talked and talked about everything. I told him things, Lara, that I've never told anyone before. Is that wrong?'

She was speaking so quickly and excitedly Lara knew that the question was entirely rhetorical. She could not possibly answer even if she had known what she was talking about.

'No,' Lara replied, and found herself giving out a small laugh. 'That's not wrong, Annie. It's good to share things about yourself with the person you love.'

'Oh, Lara, I do love him. I know that's silly because we only just met but we feel as if we've known each other forever. And – we kissed and kissed and kissed and…'

'And?' Lara asked. She could not believe she was mischievously asking Annie if she had had sex with Matthew! The truth was she no longer cared that is was Matthew. Her Matthew. Because he wasn't her Matthew any more. Any man that could make Annie this happy, who was so obviously, so innocently in love with the sweetest girl in the world, didn't belong to her any more. In truth, he never belonged to her. She knew that yesterday when she saw him kissing Annie. If she was entirely honest with herself, she had known it long before that. Now, the truth closed the circle. She set him free although she knew Matthew had done that for himself when he left her.

'NO!' Annie said, shocked but laughing. 'We certainly didn't do anything of the kind!'

'That would be a mortal sin would it?'

'Most certainly,' Annie said. Then her face dropped into an expression that was so forlorn that Lara was worried she had taken away some of her joy.

'Sorry, Annie, I didn't mean to make light of your feelings.'

'I know. It's just there are things I didn't tell him. Things I can't tell anybody. Bad things.'

Noreen's foreboding tone last night floated up to the surface of Lara's mind. She shook it off.

'There are things about my past that are so terrible, Lara, that I cannot tell another living soul.'

'If this man loves you,' Lara said, 'then he'll forgive you anything.'

Annie's expression did not lift.

'Not anything. This is bad. Very bad.'

If Annie had a confession to make, Lara did not want to hear it. Despite herself, she felt genuinely pleased for Annie, but her lover was still Matthew and the fact was still raw. In any case, she was keeping her own secret now. Try as she might, Lara could not find a way of telling Annie who Matthew was. Perhaps she would leave that up to Noreen. Along with trying to make sure their furious, sturdy flatmate didn't skin Annie alive when she got in.

'Love isn't always as straightforward as it seems, Annie. But it does conquer all in the end.'

It came out as it was intended: a clichéd platitude. But, as she said it, Lara had an epiphany. She had seen that look which she so painfully observed Matthew give Annie in the park.

It had not been as soft or as lingering. If she had not been paying such close attention she might have missed it.

But there had been a moment when they were making love that she had seen that look but not been entirely certain she could trust what it was. Lara now knew with certainty that she had seen that look all right. Just, not from Matthew.

'Sorry, Annie,' she said. 'I just remembered something important.'

Lara ran out of the flat, without her shoes. Barely dressed in a long night shirt that could pass as a mini, she ran down the stairs, banged on the door of Chevrons then shoved Arthur to one side and ran past Noreen and her men in suits until she got to the office door. She knew Coleman might still be asleep, or in the shower but she didn't care. She put both hands up to the heavy door, banged and called his name.

Noreen looked across, curious but also furious at the interruption.

When he didn't come immediately, Lara appealed to his business nous and shouted, 'Open the door now, Coleman. Noreen's in a meeting with suppliers and we're disturb—'

The door opened a foot, and he dragged her in and slammed it behind her.

'What the hell are you playing at?'

He was genuinely annoyed at being disturbed. Freshly showered, he was wearing trousers but was shirtless. His hand held her arm, his fingers digging in to her biceps.

She looked him square in the face and said, 'Say it again.'

'Say what again? What are you talking about?'

'You know exactly what I mean, Coleman. Say it again.'

Coleman felt sick to his stomach. She couldn't possibly mean it. She couldn't possibly expect him to humiliate himself in that way. What kind of sick bitch was she?

'I have no idea what you're talking about.'

'If you really have no idea then I'm wasting my time.'

But she didn't walk away. She just stood there, looked him in the eye and asked, 'Am I wasting my time, Coleman?'

He didn't know what to say. Or rather he didn't know if he could say it. The last time being on the spur of the moment. The words had just come out of his mouth instinctively. That seemed the only way with any of these things. Love, anger – you couldn't make them happen. They just did. You couldn't be deliberate about emotion like that. You could lift the lid off, occasionally, but you could never be sure what would come out. All he could do was tell the truth.

'I don't know,' he said.

Still, she didn't walk away.

'Say it again.'

'I don't know what you're…'

'Yes you do, and I know you do.'

He pushed her arm down by her side. She thought he would walk away but he didn't, he just stood there.

'So, Coleman. Say it again.'

He looked at her and his cold, dark eyes were dead with fear.

'I don't know if I can.'

His jaw set and his words crawled out through lips tight with fury. But Lara wasn't afraid.

'Try,' she said.

'Jesus, woman I—'

'Just three little words.'

'I can't, I—'

'No big deal. You already said the first one. I…'

She smiled at him and, for a split second, he trusted her. He looked at her and could see she wasn't going anywhere.

She wasn't going to leave him alone until he had done as she asked. Coleman hated being badgered and bullied like this. It made him feel angry. But also not. He looked behind her ear, at the side of the door and blurted it out, 'I love you. OK? Happy now?'

Lara reached over and put her hand under his chin, drawing his face over to her until they stood, eye to eye.

'No,' she said. 'Say it again.'

His eyes flicked away but her hold was gentle and persuasive, and her steady gaze drew him back. She wasn't going anywhere.

'Say it again, Coleman.'

'I love you,' he said to appease her.

She reached up and kissed him on the mouth, then pulled back, all the time holding his face in her hands.

'Again.'

What kind of game was this? But her kiss had been tender and real.

'I love you,' he said. And she kissed him.

'Again.'

'I love you.'

She made him say it until 'I love you, I love you, I love you' was issuing out of his mouth so that the words themselves had lost their meaning and Coleman felt he was drowning in the pool of vulnerability left when a man relinquishes his pride.

They kissed then made love. The phone rang out, twice, but they barely heard it.

And, when it was over, Lara lay on his bare chest and said, loud and clear into the still, dead air of the soundproofed office, 'I love you too.'

✻

'Where's that clobber you promised me?'

'Hasn't it arrived yet, love?'

'No it bloody well hasn't and you know it. Have you forgotten, we've got Billy and Sandra's anniversary party on Thursday, in the new villa? I was told I'd have a fabulous new outfit by then.'

'You will, love.'

'It's TWO DAYS away, Bobby. How long has it been since you promised me that new wardrobe? Nearly a month!'

'You've got loads of new outfits, love. What about the dress you bought in that new shop in the arcade? You were a right bobby-dazzler in that.'

'Don't be such an idiot, Bobby. It's not the same as getting something specially made from London, which is what you promised me. No point in turning up in some tat I bought locally. All the girls are expecting me to make a splash.'

'You make everything look special.'

'Piss off. I know your game, trying to wriggle out of it. Have you gone and upset Coleman? It's not like him to break a promise.'

Cheeky bitch. Chevron was itching to give Maureen a swipe but, like she said, they had his business associate Billy Jones's party on Thursday and it wouldn't look good if Maureen turned up with a black eye.

But then, neither did it look good if you owned a boutique and couldn't fix up a couple of new frocks for the trouble and strife with a simple phone call.

He had rung a week ago and left a message for Coleman to call him but he hadn't heard back. It just wasn't on. His 'eye' had been worse than useless. No information had been forthcoming. Coleman was still blaming the whole scam on Shirley. Chevron had fixed Shirl' up with a few bob and a flat in Manchester. Got her a job waiting tables in another gaff he had a share in up there. She seemed happy enough, but, to be honest, he didn't give a shit whether she was or not. He just wanted to keep her away from Coleman until he could work out what was going on. Because there was something going on. He was sure of that.

He tried Chevron's office phone again. No reply. It rang out. Chevron hated when that happened.

Coleman was meant to run the club for him and report back like a good boy. Like he had always done. But now, he was acting like the boss. Coleman was going behind his back, doing naughty things like nicking money and going in the papers pretending to be something he ain't. Pretending to be a big man like him. Bobby did not like that. He did not like it one little bit.

Now, his boy had caused him to get a roasting from his wife and show him up in front of his associate Billy.

Coleman had stepped over the line. Bobby had no choice. Something had to be done.

36

So, the slut had met somebody else. Of course she had. And it wasn't that nancy-boy photographer either. Dorian had been following the runt for two days. He had engaged the services of a reliable taxi driver, telling the fool that he was a private detective from Ireland, sent to find the daughter of a rich client. Alex had taken dirty pictures of the girl and that's why they were following him. Money was no object. Good was on their side, he assured him. The cockney halfwit was delighted and, it turned out, was a nifty driver who successfully followed Alex unseen. After all, who's going to notice a black cab in London? However, it was costing Dorian a fortune. He had followed Alex to faraway Hendon and waited outside a synagogue for hours while he attended a family bar mitzvah. Then there were endless trips to and from Fleet Street and Soho – all the time with the meter running. By far the worst aspect of all this for Dorian was having to make conversation with Bert, the driver, who complained endlessly about the immigrants in London. He occasionally remembered that Dorian was a 'Paddy' then would apologise to him saying, 'The Paddies is alright though. At least you're white – know what I mean? Anyway you don't saand like a

Paddy.' Dorian smiled and nodded agreement. Bert wanted to say 'you don't look like no Paddy neither,' but he didn't want to bring up his looks. To be honest, the poor sod was terrifying to look at, although he didn't frighten Bert. Bert's brother had half his face blown off in the war. It was a nasty business looking so terribly changed when you were the same, good person inside. Bert was glad to be helping this man do his job. It wasn't every driver would pick him up looking like that. Never judge a book by its cover. That was one thing Bert had learned from his brother's ordeal. Sometimes people that look terrible on the outside could be soft as kittens and good as gold on the inside.

But not Dorian. Even by his own standards he was beginning to get very wound up. Despite the ordeal he had been going through he found he liked London better than Ireland. He enjoyed the anonymity here. If people looked at him with pity, they did not end up on his doorstep with a tray of scones. They simply passed him by. Sometimes he saw an expression of fear slide across the face of a shop assistant when they saw him. Dorian found other people's fear upset him less than he might have thought.

Dorian realised that perhaps he had had enough of small town mollycoddling. There was a hard edge to the city and his own edges had hardened to match them. In a big city there was more choice. It was hard work finding love in his small town in Ireland. Over here he could buy girls, locally. He found the idea humiliating. But there were other options too. The evening before he had been taking a stroll through central London and passed by Great Ormond Street Hospital. He had specialised in paediatrics at college. Perhaps there might be a job for him there. It was something to think about while he listened to Bert wittering on.

He had decided to bankroll Bert and give his search one more day. However, when Alex pulled up outside a ladies' clothes shop on the Kings Road Dorian was more or less ready to call a halt.

Then, the name of the shop caught his eye: That Girl. It was beginning to sink in where he had seen it before when out she came.

My God, but she was as magnificent as ever.

She was wearing a short white dress. Sluttish, of course, as were all the modern fashions, but she wore it with that sweet innocence he remembered of the child he had fallen in love with. His sight of her was fleeting, and as the car took off he anxiously told Bert to follow.

'Is that her?' Bert asked.

'Yes,' said Dorian. 'Don't lose them.'

'I won't. Poor girl. Looks so innocent too. Makes you fink dunnit?'

'Indeed,' Dorian said.

The MG pulled up and parked outside Lancaster Gate tube station and the photographer and Hanna walked across into the park. Dorian told Bert to wait then followed them on foot. He stayed a good distance behind and waited until they turned a corner. Dorian looked behind the hedge and saw that the photographer had set up his camera. Hanna was sitting under a tree. He walked around the area until he found a series of bushes on a mound that was large enough to cover him but had a small gap in the leaves that he could look through straight on to Hanna.

It was essential that nobody knew he was there. He could not reveal himself. Not yet. As stealthily as a fox, he bent down on his haunches and watched.

The photographer was blurting out inane platitudes. He

could have killed the little shit and wished he would be quiet but after a few moments in the presence of Hanna's beauty, even Alex's idiotic burblings faded into the background. Unlike the photographs in the paper, Hanna had barely any makeup on. She looked exactly the same as his girl Hanna. Daughter, lover and, as he had hoped, wife. He thought he would be angry when he saw her, but instead he was filled with that feeling he described as love. He wanted her, in the same way that he'd always wanted her. Despite everything she had done, he wanted her back. He would have to punish her, of course. But she would forgive him, as she had always done and he would try to forgive her for what she had done to him. Things would never be the same again but perhaps they could start a new life, here. Jealousy and attraction washed over him. Nobody could elicit this kind of emotion from Dorian. Nobody made him feel the way she did. Most people made him feel nothing except irritation and sometimes anger, if he let them. Hanna drew feelings out of him he did not know were there. She made him feel – human. She made him feel like he thought a man should feel. When she wasn't there he was empty of emotion. Now, seeing her again, in the flesh, it all came flooding back. He had to have her again.

As he watched, Dorian began to fantasise about how he might get her back. She would take some persuading; he knew that. He also knew that they were meant to be together and surely she would know that too. He was lost in that thought when he realised another person had entered the equation. A man. Another man was watching her! Except he was doing it openly from behind the tall hedge opposite. And now, what was this? Alex invited him into the circle as an audience. Dorian felt sickness taking him over. His head began to spin. Another man was moving in on his territory.

Taking over his position as watcher, observer and, finally, sexual predator.

Then it got worse.

As Alex began to put his camera away the young man (he was young, a good deal younger than Dorian) walked over to Hanna then wrapped his arms around her and kissed her. Dorian lost all breath. The shock was terrible. She did not push him away but seemed to respond. Dorian thought he was going to throw up, but at the same time he could not take his eyes off her. She was responding. It was clear what she wanted. Doubly clear because she had never wanted it from him in that way. Part of Dorian wanted to turn away and run but he knew that would be the coward's way out. He had to face this.

So he watched them.

He followed Alex to the gate, knowing they would not be long behind him. He dismissed Bert and followed behind the young lovers on foot for the rest of that day and late into the night. He stood with his head down in bus shelters while they sat on street benches, talking. He dipped into doorways when they stopped walking to kiss. When they went into a cafe in Soho for breakfast in the early hours, he sat on the pavement opposite, pretending to be a poor beggar so that he would not lose sight of them.

As the night wore on the hurt hardened.

At 3 a.m., he sat in the back of a night bus to Chelsea. At this point, even he was wondering how they could not have seen him. How they had not noticed that for most of ten hours a crippled man had been following them. Love is blind. He had heard the expression but never understood what it meant before.

At this point Dorian thought he could go face-to-face with

Hanna and the man and they would neither care nor notice. They were so heedlessly, carelessly in love that Dorian might as well not exist.

Well, he would show them that he did exist.

Dorian followed them as they walked up the Kings Road. When they stopped outside a door, Dorian dived into the yard of a derelict basement flat and watched as the skinny young man took Hanna to the door, where he assumed she lived. He was skinny and delicate looking. A pathetic physique. Dorian was broader and stronger. More of a man than that kid could ever be. What use was such a wimp to a girl like Hanna? After all, she had almost killed a man Dorian noted, almost admiringly now. She needed a man who could keep her in check. She'd walk all over a boy like that. Dorian burned with hate as the young man kissed Hanna on the doorstep. He did not follow her inside, which Dorian took as indication that she didn't live alone.

He allowed himself one last look at her face as she entered the house. She was smiling, beaming like a fool. Dorian had never liked Hanna's smile. He hadn't seen her smile often. It was a cause of annoyance to him that even when he tried to amuse her, he rarely elicited a smile. When she smiled for other people he took it as a direct slight to him. In any case, even as a child, the subtle beauty of her face was more sublime when it was resting. Her face was certainly not resting now as she waved and blew kisses. Her eyes were dancing with joy. Dorian had never hated or wanted her more.

As the young man came down the steps Dorian clenched the iron bars of the basement to steady his anger. He felt one of them come loose in his hand. It was a sign – a gift. He pulled the bar off then, keeping a safe distance, stuck to the shadows and followed the boy. He waited until the boy walked in front of a side alleyway that Dorian picked out when following them earlier.

'Hello,' he shouted to him from a few feet behind.

Matthew nearly jumped out of his skin. Lost in a reverie of love, the voice of this stranger brought him back down to earth. Matthew stopped walking then turned and saw a man running towards him. It seemed like he was in trouble of some kind.

Matthew said, 'Can I help you?' The next thing he knew the man had strong-armed him into an alleyway and thrown him to the ground. He was strong and as Matthew tried to get up he put his foot on Matthew's chest and raised what looked like an iron bar in his fist.

Shocked, Matthew said, 'What do you want? Money? I can get you money.'

The man laughed.

'You have something I want but it's not yours to give – it's mine to take.'

He was talking as if he knew him. Confused, Matthew asked again, 'What do you want?'

As the blows began raining down on his body, searing pain slammed his head, his chest, his shoulder, over and over again until he knew he was going to die and gave in to the pain. Just before he lost consciousness, Matthew's hands fell from where he had been trying to protect his head. It was then that he caught sight of his attacker's face. It wasn't a man at all, but a hideous demon. Perhaps, even the devil himself.

37

Noreen got lost on her way to the north London suburbs. She got confused between the Metropolitan and Circle lines, then, when she finally got off at Edgware Road she got on a bus heading in the wrong direction, and ended up back at Hyde Park Corner. Every time she stopped somebody to ask where she was, they just glared at her as if she was mad. Eventually, more by miracle than design, she managed to get herself to Connolly's pub in Wembley, which was owned by John's brother, Kieran. She walked in the door and she was back home. And not just because of the shamrock banner above the bar and the smell of warm beer and stale cigarette smoke in the mornings. Kieran was delighted to see her and gave her a warm hug. Then, without asking why she was there, he dragged her upstairs to his wife, Sinead. Sinead was so excited that she called the four kids in from the street to sit with her while she called her sister. Maureen arrived within five minutes of the call with her two children, kissed Noreen until she thought she would never stop then used Sinead's phone to call her cousin, Finoula. Finoula wasn't in, her husband said, because she was visiting the sister and their three children with her four children in Cricklewood. They didn't have a phone. So, before Noreen had time to object, or explain that she was simply there to locate John, she found herself being bundled into the back of a Ford Cortina with two adults and half a dozen children then dragged into a small, brand new house in a tidy, suburban estate.

The children were sent to the corner shop to buy Mr Kipling cakes, ham, white sliced bread and Rothmans cigarettes and for the next three hours Noreen was effectively held hostage by the Connolly family.

She learned that they had a great life in London. That the work was easy, the kids were happy and even the Catholic priests were better, with a looser attitude to sex. Maureen confided that after five kids in four years, her parish priest had given her dispensation to go on the pill. A good, convent girl, she had been sceptical but he had reassured her that he would try to fix it for her not to burn in hell for all eternity. Then he said, 'Maureen? By the time you get to hell, you'll have had so much fun you won't care!'

They all roared laughing. It was fun, Noreen had to admit, hanging out with her own but despite the craic, she did not learn where John was.

'I thought he was with you,' Sinead said. 'Sure, we haven't seen him since he got here.'

'What the hell would he be doing up here with this mad clatter of kids when he can be down there living it up in Chelsea with your gang?'

Then, they looked worried.

Noreen lied her way out of it saying there had been a misunderstanding. That she thought he had gone back for a spell and had expected him back. She must have got her dates wrong.

Kieran broke the awkward moment by offering to drop her back to Chelsea in the Cortina.

When they got to Quex Road he said, 'John told me you broke off the engagement.'

Noreen stayed quiet. She was mortified. Upset too.

'He told me it was all off and I told him he was a stupid fool to be putting pressure on you like that.'

Noreen still didn't know what to say.

'You're a modern girl, Noreen, a worker. Not like Sinead. Don't get me wrong, she works at home and that and helps me out, like, but I'll tell you something for nothing – I sometimes wonder if we would have had all the kids if we had our time again. Times are changing, I told him.'

'Where is he, Kieran? I need to see him. Did he go back to Carney?'

'Not yet. He said he was going to hang around London for a bit. I asked him if he wanted to come and work in the pub for a while, stay with me and Sinead. But he said he had met a couple of guys on the buildings and that he was going to take some time for himself. You know John he likes to stay busy. Like yourself.'

'I think I might have broken his heart, Kieran.'

'Of course you did, girleen. But I know my brother and he's a tough chaw. He'll be back. Sure, if I had a pound for every time that wife of mine has broken my heart I'd be a rich man. They're still picking bits of me up off the floor of the Cork ballroom from the time she took off with Mel Murphy.'

Yes, but she married you in the end though, Noreen thought.

Kieran dropped her to the door of the flat and after she thanked him she said, 'Let me know if John gets in touch, won't you? Tell him I'm looking for him.'

'I will,' Kieran said, 'but you might hear from him before I do.'

Noreen smiled but she knew, in her heart, that it wouldn't happen. She had broken her big man. He was gone.

The night porter at Brown's gave a curt, 'Goodnight, sir,' when he opened the front door to the guest and let him go up to his room unhindered. When people came in at 4 a.m. they didn't usually want to chat. This chap was disfigured, so he wouldn't like being looked at, so the porter didn't notice the blood on the edge of the coat cuffs of his dark coat, or that his hands were plunged deep into his pockets. He didn't wonder why the guest did not call the lift even though he was on the fourth floor, but instead shouldered the door to the stairs so that he would not have to take his hands out and risk them being seen.

Dorian had taken his room key with him, thank God. He could not have known earlier that day that he would be killing a man and coming back covered in blood. Had he killed the boy? As near as dammit anyway. He was smashed to bits in an alley, and if he survived, he would be no prettier than Dorian. Although, Dorian had run out of steam after he became unconscious. He had thrashed at his torso a few times but then been aware that, essentially, he was beating a stranger – the type of thing only gutty boys and guttersnipes did looking for money or kicks. He was a gentleman who had lost his temper. When his temper cooled, he stopped. He didn't bother checking if the body was alive or dead. In truth, he didn't care either way. In any case, he was not a murderer. Not like her. She had driven him to it. It had not been a cold-blooded act but a crime of passion. And there was more passion to come.

When he opened the door of his suite he found an envelope

on the carpet in front of him. He opened it and inside was another envelope addressed to him in the handwriting he recognised as the insufferable Mrs Clark's. It aggravated him that he even knew her handwriting so he put it to one side and left it until the morning.

Dorian showered and went to bed. The rigours of walking and beating that he had put his body through caused him to sleep soundly.

The next morning he opened Mrs Clark's envelope over breakfast, which he always took in his room.

This came addressed to you and your wife. It was being kept at the post office with all of your letters but then my friend alerted me. I thought that it might be important so I decided it might not wait so forwarded it across to you.

Then a page of endless guff and gossip along with:

If there is anything I can do for you here.

A barely veiled invitation to tell her what the letter was about. If she hadn't steamed it open already.

When he read the contents he sincerely hoped she hadn't.

Dear Mr and Mrs Black,
  My name is Noreen Lyons and I share a flat with your daughter, Hanna...

It wasn't a long letter, but it was a clear one and the address given was the one he had been to the night before. It was dated a few weeks ago. It had probably been read by every old biddy in Killa by now, but he didn't care.

This was a wonderful, wonderful turn of events.

He was, after all, the civilised person. The gentleman. He did not want to go sneaking around on his loved one. And he did love power. Otherwise why would he have done what he did last night? Why would he have put himself through that ordeal, physically, mentally and emotionally unless he truly wanted her back? He was not a savage. He could forgive her for what she had done. Dorian did not believe in God, but holding this Noreen's letter he felt that perhaps this was the hand of the saviour in action. He went to the desk in his room, pulled out the notepad and wrote a short note.

He took it downstairs to the reception desk and asked if they might be able to get it into the morning post for it to arrive at the Kings Road that very afternoon.

Noreen didn't have to go back to work that afternoon and, feeling like company, she walked straight round to That Girl to see Lara. When she got there she was surprised to find Annie there too.

As soon as they saw her, Lara turned her head slightly towards Noreen then rested her hand on her cheek so that it shielded her face from Annie.

'Annie has a new boyfriend, Noreen. Isn't that great?'

Her expression clearly said – if you say anything, I'll murder you.

'Fantastic,' Noreen said, her face a flat plate of sarcasm.

Annie did not notice.

'I'm so in love,' she said, 'but the best news of all, Noreen?'

She looked as if she was going to explode with excitement and joy. Noreen had an urge to pick her up and throw her out the window. She resisted. For Lara's sake. Although why she was protecting Annie when she should be punishing her for messing about with Matthew was beyond her.

'You'll never guess?'

Jesus, what was she? Ten?

'Try me.'

Annie threw Lara a 'can I tell her' look that Noreen found insufferably offensive. There the two of them were, sharing secrets again.

'Lara and Coleman finally got together. I think they're in love too.'

Noreen did not know what to say. That was how this day was going. People said things to her and she was lost for words. Was this what unhappiness felt like? She thought her and Lara were back on track, but it seemed that weird Annie had pushed her way back in again. Using Matthew. And more fool Lara, getting back with a man like Coleman that had used and abused her already.

'I'm going back to the flat,' she said. 'I have to get changed for the evening shift.'

Noreen had taken the day off but decided she had nothing better to do than work tonight, after all. Neither Annie nor Lara seemed to notice, or care, that she was upset.

In fact, when she was leaving, Lara tapped her on the shoulder and mouthed, 'Thank you,' as she walked out the door. Noreen raised her eyes to heaven but Lara, demented with love, or whatever, didn't seem to notice that either.

When she got back to the flat Noreen found a letter waiting for her. Strange handwriting and a London postmark. She thought it was John, although it wasn't his handwriting. Quickly tearing it open, she hoped something awful hadn't happened to him.

It was a short letter written on headed notepaper from

Brown's Hotel. It looked very posh and was from Annie's, or rather Hanna's, father. He said that he was in London. He explained that his wife had been very sick and died and that, being a doctor and unable to save her, their beloved daughter had blamed him and run away. (Noreen was unsurprised at this. Annie didn't strike her as being very bright and this was typically selfish of these whimsical, overtly feminine types of girls.) Hanna was the only family he had left in the world and Noreen's letter had been like receiving a lifeline. He knew that Hanna would be upset if he got in touch directly, so was there any possibility that she could find it in her heart to facilitate a meeting between them? She would need to keep it quiet from Hanna beforehand, of course, but he felt certain that once she saw him, all would be forgiven and forgotten. 'In the end,' he said, 'we are father and daughter and should be there to comfort each other.'

Noreen thought of her own father, Frank, and of all the times he had annoyed her to distraction over the years – including just a few weeks ago when he had written to Matthew. She could never fall out with her own father to the point of estrangement but she could certainly imagine how that might happen.

Poor Annie, and the poor, poor man. Of course she would help them reunite.

Later that evening Noreen asked Coleman if she could use the office phone. Dorian sounded like a real gentleman. She made an arrangement for him to call at the flat. She reassured him that she would make certain that Annie would be there, alone, for at least a couple of hours.

38

Coleman felt his feet sink into the shagpile carpet as he looked around. Cheyne Walk was one of the most expensive streets off the Kings Road, and this basement bachelor pad was the first place he had seen. It had a kitchen, a bedroom, bathroom and a sunken area in the living room with plush cream leatherette seating built into the shagpile. It was fully furnished with all mod cons, a television and a trouser press.

'Everything a gentleman like you might need,' the girl from the estate agency said. Then parted her blouse with the tip of her nail and said, 'Well, almost everything.' He smiled, curtly, and she dropped her hand and picked up her notes. 'Although it's not cheap.'

'Not a problem,' he said. Coleman never considered getting his own place before and felt curiously disloyal to Chevron to be considering it, even now. However, he couldn't continue to entertain Lara in his office and the idea of booking a hotel room with a girl like that was out of the question.

'Yeah. I like it,' he said. 'How much is it?'

'Too much!' Lara was coming down the steps of the basement and heard him through the open door.

'Excuse me?' Tamara asked in a tight squeal.

'It's OK,' Coleman said, 'she's with me.'

Then he looked at Lara, his eyes slightly quizzical, as if looking for reassurance.

'Arthur told me where you were and I rushed down before you did anything rash.' She placed her hand on Coleman's arm, marking her territory then looked Tamara up and down. She got the measure of her predator. Money or sex – both if she could manage it.

'Could you give us a moment please?'

'Sure,' Tamara said. She knew it was over before it had begun. Wives and girlfriends always wanted two bedrooms.

'There's no need to do this,' she said. 'The rent would cost a fortune. I hope it's not for my benefit?'

'Of course not,' he said, a small humiliation smarting through his cheeks.

'Although,' aware she may have hurt him, 'it would be nice to have some space together. We could book into a hotel?'

He smiled. It looked unfamiliar, therefore silly but, to Lara, glorious.

'I didn't think you were that kind of girl.'

'Well clearly I am,' she said.

Tamara looked at her watch. She had been trying to listen in, and now wished she hadn't.

'Anyway, I'm a grown man, I need my own place.'

'We have my place.'

'And you have Noreen,' he said.

Lara looked around.

'You don't want this place, Coleman. It's tacky and poky and I'm sure,' she looked at Tamara, 'overpriced.'

'But what about...?'

He stopped short of saying 'us'. He didn't want to presume.

'Why don't we see where we are in a month's time and maybe then we can…?'

She stopped short of saying 'find somewhere together'. But only because Tamara was rattling her keys at the front door.

When they reached the corner of Cheyne Walk and the Kings Road, they kissed. It was a soft lingering kiss, not a precursor to lovemaking, but an expression of everyday intimacy. Lara headed up to That Girl but Coleman was too wired to go back to the club. As he walked away his head was full of what she had said. One month. It was a trial, a test, but he didn't care. It was what he wanted. To love and to be loved. In his thirties, to share his life with somebody. Ordinary love. The thing that most people felt entitled to, but not him. Coleman always thought that love was beyond him. Lara was not simply the woman he loved. In returning that love, she was a gift. A miracle. He needed some time alone to take it all in, so Coleman decided to run some messages in town.

First, Savile Row. Standing in front of the mirror in the oak-lined dressing room of his tailor, Sid's, studio he pressed down the front of a blue worsted pinstripe and said, 'My girlfriend will like this one.' He forced the words out awkwardly. It was the first time he talked about Lara to anybody. He was still pinching himself and wanted to tell somebody about the relationship to make it real.

· Sid replied, 'She's got good taste then.'

'I don't know about that, but she likes her fashion.'

'Don't all the girls?' Sid said, smiling.

'She's not all the girls,' Coleman wanted to say. 'She's the only girl.'

On the way back from Piccadilly, he picked up his Karmann Ghia from the garage where it had been for servicing. He would make Lara take the weekend off and drive her down to

Brighton. They could stay at The Grand and walk along the front. They would eat fish and chips on the pier. His stomach was in knots of excitement just thinking about the life they were going to have together.

Although it was going to mean making some changes in his lifestyle, and he was going to have to tackle Bobby about the shop.

With every step she took back up the Kings Road towards That Girl, Lara felt her life fall more firmly into place. Her career was on the point of taking off. *Vogue* loved the pictures Alex took of Annie and offered him a commission. They were sending their fashion editor to look at her new collection and it looked as if they were considering featuring That Girl alongside a small profile on her. In seeing Matthew again, Lara had finally put the pain of her past to rest, and now, her love life had taken an unexpected but perfect turn. She was in love. Unlike the inevitable, brotherly closeness that she had with Matthew, this love was passionate and gut wrenching but no less certain.

It seemed extraordinary that everything in life she had wanted, and failed so spectacularly to have with her childhood sweetheart Matthew: the creative collaboration, the living a free life in London, was now about to happen with this Englishman. Extraordinary and unexpected, but wonderful.

Her mood dipped when she opened the door of That Girl. The place was a mess. At the door was a half-opened box of stock, which she had specifically told Handsome to unpack and hang immediately just before she left an hour ago.

Worse, the shop looked empty of staff. She looked around and saw Handsome preening himself at the dressing room mirror. Squinting at his reflection and smoothing his Beatles fringe into shape, with a cigarette dropping from his lush lips. Lara was furious. She felt a snap of irritation at Noreen, too, for passing her on such a dud.

'Why are those boxes still at the door? I asked you to unpack and hang up that menswear delivery while I was gone.'

She also hated calling him Handsome. He had, on his first day, reluctantly informed her that his first name was Hillary; she felt she couldn't call him that either.

'I was just going to get round to it when I was finished here.'

It was then she noticed that he had changed his outfit.

'Is that from the new stock?'

'Yeah,' he said, patting the collar. 'What d'ya think?'

'You took that jacket out of the box and didn't unload the rest.'

'Thought I'd try it on – to model it, like.'

She looked behind him into the changing room and saw myriad items from the box strewn around the chairs and floor.

'Who was minding the shop when you were playing dress up?'

A nasty look sliced across his face then was replaced by his usual nonchalance. Lara noted he wasn't entirely sure she was being sarcastic. Not even bright enough to pick that up.

'There weren't any customers in.'

'And if a customer had come in?'

'Well they would have rung the bell, wouldn't they? Then I would've come out.'

'But that would have meant walking right through the shop and going up to the counter. With no staff here, they might have left or stolen something.'

Handsome shrugged and continued preening. Half ignoring her, as if she was annoying him.

Lara was incensed. Being short staffed was better than this.

'I don't think this is going to work out,' she said. Seeing the look of vague confusion as he turned around and saw her still there, she added firmly, 'You're fired.'

'What?' he said, pulling the cigarette out of his mouth.

'I said you're fired.'

'You can't do that!'

'I can,' Lara said, 'and I am.' Her heart was thumping. She had never fired anyone before. But there was something else, something nasty in his tone.

'Why?'

She let out a disbelieving laugh then shook her head.

'Look, Handsome, it's just not working out, alright?'

'Well, I ain't going.'

That, she had not been expecting.

'This is my shop and I am asking you to leave. Nicely. Right now. I will pay you until the end of the week and—'

'But it ain't your shop is it? It's Bobby's.'

'I beg your pardon?'

She heard him all right.

'Chevron's. Bobby owns this shop. It ain't yours. You just work for him. Like Coleman.'

She knew she shouldn't question him. He was a nasty bit of work. An idiot, who had probably got the wrong end of the stick. Lara knew she should just ignore him but there was something in his tone that rang true.

'What do you mean?'

'Coleman acts the big man, like it's his business, like he owns Chevrons but, at the end of the day, Bobby don't give nothing away.'

'Mr Chevron is a shareholder in my business. But this my shop.'

Handsome laughed. He didn't look stupid now.

'Chevron don't do sharing. Everyone knows that. Not even with his precious Coleman, I can guarantee you that.' He threw his cigarette on the dressing room floor and stamped it into the carpet. 'You get Bobby Chevron down here to sack me.'

Then, the good-looking boy turned towards the mirror and continued fixing his hair as if she wasn't there.

Lara didn't know what to do. She felt sick. She was angry, of course, but the greater part of her was afraid of what he might do. She could not take him out physically so there was only one thing for it. She would have to leave him there and run up to the club and get Coleman, and maybe even Arthur, to sort him out. As she closed the door behind her Lara's gut tightened as she wondered if Handsome could have been telling the truth. Was this Chevron's shop? The thought of that sickened her but at the same time there was a ring of truth to it.

Could all of this be just one big lie? If that was the case it would mean that Coleman had betrayed her.

Coleman skipped down the stairs of Chevrons. If the floors had not been carpeted he would have slid on his leather-soled shoes to his office like Fred Astaire.

When he opened the door he didn't even want to sit down. He put his feet up on the desk and leaned back. He felt like a king and now he had a queen. There was a bang on the door and Arthur came in, locking the door behind him. He looked shaky and paler than usual. There was something wrong, but the day Coleman was having he could fix anything.

'What's up my old mate? Whoah!'

Arthur had pulled a Walther PP gun on him, and it was

pointing straight at his face. Coleman raised his hands, 'Easy, easy, mate.'

Arthur pulled his face back from a strained grimace. His hands were shaking and his eyes were darting left to right. Coleman tried to lock them down.

'What the fuck is going on, Arthur?'

'Don't move,' he shouted. His finger was lost over the trigger. Arthur wasn't used to guns and the Walther was an automatic. It could go off by accident.

'OK, OK,' he said, raising his hands higher.

'Talk to me, mate. What's going on?'

A bead of sweat fell down over Arthur's eye and he blinked it away. Coleman kept his eyes glued to the Walther. Arthur fought with his fist and whatever came to hand. A gun was a cold-blooded way to kill someone and he wasn't that type. He was a hard man with a short temper. When Arthur lost it, anything could happen. The rest of the time, he was a pussy cat. When Coleman found out who sold Arthur the weapon, he would shoot them with it. But first he had to find out why he was pointing it at him.

'Arthur,' he tried again. 'What's going on?'

There was a knock on the door. Arthur's head turned and Coleman flinched.

The handle turned.

'It's Lara. I need to ask you something.'

Arthur glared at him, wide-eyed, panicked. He nodded and hissed, 'Get rid of her.'

'Not a good time,' Coleman called out, trying to keep his voice firm.

'It's important,' she said, trying the door again.

'Please,' he tried to keep the pleading whinge out of his voice but at the same time send her a message that he did not mean to reject her. It didn't work. He had a gun pointing at him so his voice came out firm and angry. 'I'm serious, Lara. Now is not a good time, alright? Come back in an hour. Please.'

She banged the door with her fist in temper and Coleman heard the muffle of a demure curse as she walked away. He sighed with relief. He didn't know if he would still be here in an hour, but at least she would be.

'Just stay still and stop talking,' Arthur hissed.

'Alright, alright. I won't move. Just tell me where this is coming from.'

Arthur's sweat turned to a trickle and, as he lifted his right elbow to put his face to his shoulder and wipe it off...

BANG!

'Shit, shit, shit...'

Coleman ducked.

BANG. BANG. BANG! A splatter of blood on the parquet floor.

'SHIT! My foot!'

Noreen started banging on the door.

'Is everything alright in there?'

The room was soundproofed but the gunshots sounded as a set of muted thuds that were unmistakable.

'Will I call the police?'

Noreen had no intention of calling the police. She just wanted Coleman to open the door so she could see what was going on.

'Jesus Christ...' Coleman went to the door and opened it an inch.

'No, Noreen,' he said. 'There's just been – an accident.'

'Lara's here she said...'

Arthur groaned from behind the door and Noreen strained her head to look in.

'Is that Arthur? Is he alright?'

'He's fine.'

Another groan from Arthur.

'Tell Lara to call back later.'

He shut the door, and picked the Walther up from the ground where Arthur had dropped it. He carefully emptied the cartridge and put it into his jacket pocket then put the gun on his desk. Coleman felt the adrenalin drain out of his body and his mind fill up on a cocktail of curiosity and anger.

'What the fuck was that, Arthur?'

'I think I've shot myself.' He was trying not to cry.

Coleman knelt down and had a look at the floor – two bullet holes on the floor – God knows where the other two landed. A small pool of blood was gathering at Arthur's foot and the top was torn off his shoe. The bleeding was slow, so at worst he'd taken the edge off a toe.

'Hurts like hell,' he whimpered.

When he lost it, Arthur could drink the blood of a man, but the rest of the time a paper cut made him queasy. That was why his actions were so infuriatingly puzzling. Arthur needed a reason to get riled up and Coleman, as far as he knew, had never given him one.

Coleman took the gun down from his desk and held it to Arthur's neck.

'This will hurt a lot more if you don't start talking.'

'Oh, Coleman mate – you wouldn't.'

'I bloody would and I will if you don't tell me what's going on.'

'You can't shoot me. Look at me. I'm hurt. Coleman, please, this is Arthur – your oldest mate.'

Coleman could have shot him just for begging. The gun

wasn't even loaded. He knew Arthur. He could go on like that all night. Coleman had never killed a man. He had never had to. Half an hour ago he would have certainly said he could never hurt Arthur. But the fucker had nearly killed him – even if it had been by accident. Coleman had smelt death once or twice before and he hadn't liked it. But today. No. Today was not a good day to die.

Coleman pushed the gun into his friend's neck and started counting.

'Ten, nine...'

'Jesus, Coleman, you wouldn't...'

'Eight, five... I never could count... three...'

'Alright, alright. Bobby's got a hit out on you.'

That was a shock.

'Bobby?'

'Yes.'

Coleman stopped himself from saying 'Are you sure?'

They both knew Bobby. It wasn't the sort of thing Arthur could make up.

'Can you move the gun away now please, that trigger has a delicate...'

Coleman threw the gun roughly down on the floor and Arthur flinched, then realised it wasn't loaded. He felt pleased about that, although he was in so much trouble, it might have been better if Coleman had shot him.

'Why?'

'Something to do with some clobber from the shop you promised Maureen.'

'What? He's having me killed over a few fucking dresses?'

He shrugged. 'And some other stuff.'

Arthur looked across at him pitifully, apologetically.

He was broken by the betrayal. Too broken to apologise

and, in any case, for what? Bobby was the boss and Arthur did what he was told. Now Arthur had failed both of them.

'What other stuff?'

'He said you was robbing the bar with Brian.'

'I told him it was Shirley!'

'I said that too, but he didn't believe it was her. He said you set her up. That it was you all along.'

'And you believed him?'

'I dunno.'

Arthur looked away. He wasn't the brightest and when it came to women, he was always inclined to take their side. As, in fairness, was Coleman. He had been as shocked by Shirley's betrayal as anyone and now, it seems, she had set him up with Chevron. That Chevron was willing to sacrifice his 'boy' was a blow, but not entirely a surprise.

'He said you'd been slagging me off to him. He said you told him I was more of a hind... hind...'

'Hindrance?'

'Yeah. That in the club, he said you told him I was too soft with the girls. That I was a useless piece of shit. Good for nothing and that you was going to sack me.'

Coleman's jaw set and he shifted his neck from side to side. That was an outright lie. He wasn't angry about Shirley setting him up – a woman scorned and all that. Even Chevron wanting him dead made a sort of morbid sense to him. Bobby gave him a life, of sorts, now he was taking it away. But lying to Arthur? That was low.

'Did you believe that?'

Arthur shrugged. Arthur loved Coleman and, as much as Coleman was capable of it, he loved Arthur too. They were like brothers. Bobby had brought them together so he knew how to tear them apart.

'He said you told him I'd always been the weak one. The stupid one. He says you told him you wanted the club all to yourself, and that you wanted to get rid of me. He said he was defending my honour as well as his business.'

'And you believed him?'

Arthur looked away.

'Maybe. I know I'm a bit soft on the girls and… well. Fucks sake – look at me. I just shot my own foot! He said he'd put me in charge of the club.'

'Do you think he would have?'

Arthur's face set into a defensive tightness.

'I dunno. Maybe. Probably not.'

'You know I never said that about you? Any of it.'

Arthur looked at him sheepishly, then after studying his friend's face for a moment, he smiled broadly.

'Yeah. You know I'm useful.'

Coleman punched his arm playfully.

'Not useful enough to see me off though.'

'And I shot my own foot. Fuck me but it hurts.'

'I'll get Noreen to come in and kiss it better for you will I?'

Arthur blushed. Then tried to stand up, yelped and flopped back down again.

'Fuck me, Coleman. What are we going to do?'

'How long have we got?'

'I told him I'd do you by tonight. While the club was quiet, like. He said he'd arrange some muscle to help me get rid of your…' It seemed rude to say body.

'Who?'

Coleman was generally well liked. He and Arthur knew that Bobby would find it hard to involve one of his hired hands in this. He could manipulate Arthur because love could be easily turned. Respect was different. Any of the heavies or henchmen they knew would have come straight to Coleman and told him Bobby had the hits out. Several of them had approached Coleman in the past about bringing Bobby down. That was what cut him deep about this hit. His own stupid loyalty. The thing was, Coleman did not want to take out Bobby or even take his business from him.

He didn't want a part of this any more. He wanted no part of Bobby Chevron's world. He just wanted a normal life now. To be with Lara and help her run her business.

'I dunno,' Arthur said.

'What did he tell you to do?'

'He said I was to ring him straight away from the office phone. He said he'd have someone here in ten minutes. That they was very discreet and very effective.'

'He didn't say who?'

Arthur shook his head and ran through some names.

'Not Frankie Nee, anyway.'

'Johnny "Hippo" Johnson?'

'You're joking – he hates Bobby.'

'What about Alexie Smith?'

'Nah.'

'Fingers Malone?'

'Nah.'

'Joey Brennan? Dave Wedgie? Bertie Lazlo?'

'Nah, nah. I can't think of anyone, honestly, Coleman. Who would take you out?'

Then as an afterthought, Arthur remembered himself and said, 'I'm sorry, mate.'

'Forget it.' Coleman waved his apology off. That was ancient history now. It seemed like Bobby was bluffing, but something just didn't sit right.

'He's got no one on side?'

'Bobby has pissed off all the muscle, Coleman. Think about it. And now he's over in Spain – he's not even here to do his own dirty work any more.'

Then Arthur had a revelation.

'I think he's bluffing, Coleman. I don't think he's got no one, except us. We could have him. We could take him out. We could have it all.'

Coleman shook his head. Even if Bobby wasn't popular, he was still a nutter. If Bobby had one person on his side, they would have to find him and take him out first. Then they would have to take Bobby out. And that would not be easy. Not with him being in Spain, and not with him being such a manipulative bastard, either. In any case, Coleman wasn't a killer and Arthur, as he had proven, didn't do cold blood.

'He must have someone, Arthur. Otherwise he wouldn't have put the hit out. He knows you couldn't get rid of a body on your own and leave it hanging around the club. He must have somebody and it has to be someone close. Someone who he can get here at a moment's notice.'

'It's got to be someone that don't like you, don't have no respect, and I can't think of anyone unless…?'

Coleman had exactly the same thought and they both said in unison,

'Handsome Devers.'

'Come to think of it – I haven't seen him for a while,' Coleman said.

'Noreen gave him the heave-ho. Thank God. Said he was going to work in the shop with Lara.'

Handsome in the club with Arthur and the lads keeping an eye on him was one thing. In a ladies' clothes shop surrounded by women was another. Especially when one of them was his girl. Coleman opened the door and shouted for Noreen.

She ran in and, seeing the small pool of blood on the floor, immediately ran to Arthur.

'Jesus, Mary and Joseph!' she shouted. 'He's been SHOT!'

'Where's Lara? She was here a few minutes ago.'

'I knew I heard a gun...'

Noreen was struggling to keep the note of delighted drama out of her voice.

'Noreen, this is important.'

'I think she's gone back to the shop to get rid of Handsome. She tried to sack him earlier and he refused to leave.'

Coleman picked up the Walther and the cartridge from his desk as Noreen continued.

'I told her I'd come and get Arthur but now – look at him he's...'

She looked up but Coleman had already left.

39

'Six pints there, Paddy, and a red lemonade for John.'
The barman smiled broadly at John and he winced with shame.

Since the break-up with Noreen, John had been working on the site of a new tower block in World's End. It was a big job. The concrete foundations for the tower block were going down tomorrow and there had been over fifty good, strong Irishmen preparing the site.

John's brother had been right, John wasn't ready to go back to Carney and resume life without Noreen again. He didn't want to stay with his brother in north London because his wife and kids were a reminder of all he had lost, so he had taken up the building labour to clear his head and keep himself busy. Also, north London was miles away from Noreen. He could have got the same work up in Kilburn, but John had wanted to stay close by, so when he saw the site hoardings, he had just called in and been given work. Noreen told him she could look after herself, and she could, but John didn't believe her. He had not liked the look of that whole set up. Gangster types were in charge of that nightclub where she worked and all those girls running about in short costumes was unseemly and could only lead to trouble.

In truth, there were girls in miniskirts and skittery slips of blouses everywhere you looked in London. John thought they must be frozen. Some of the men would call rude things after them in the street but all John ever wanted to call after them was, 'please put on a cardigan!' There was a place for going about in the nude and it was called bed. God, he missed Noreen in that way. He loved the way she'd be all wrapped up, then step out of her skirt, pull her jumper over her head and suddenly, all would be revealed! Sure where was the fun in seeing a woman naked if they were going about half naked all the time anyway? John didn't see the point in that at all.

John and six of the lads were in the World's End pub. They came here every day, after they finished work in the afternoon. They drank. And drank. And drank. Then they went back to their digs, worked, and drank some more. John had gained weight and felt as if he was walking around with a large dog strapped to his stomach. John was a proud Irishman and would drink alongside the best of them to join in, but these navvies were a whole other kettle of fish altogether. He drank fifteen pints alongside them last night and crawled through the day's work in a haze. He simply could not take any more.

'There now,' said Gerry, a hod carrier from Mayo with a face as raw as bacon, putting the pint glass of red fizz in front of him. 'There's some holy water there for you, Father John.'

They all roared laughing.

John smiled and raised his glass alongside their pints and took the slagging. They were good men and, the drinking aside, he enjoyed their company. But, much as he worked and drank alongside them, this wasn't the life that he wanted. Some of them would meet a girl, go home to Ireland and start their lives after a stint on the sites. Others would stay locked into a life going from work to pub to digs, spending every penny they earned on drink, living in the day. In his hopeless, hungover state, John was beginning to think he might be one of them. He had no girl. She was gone. He stayed in this area so he could be close by if Noreen got into trouble. But the truth was he had not seen her at all. Some guardian he was. If he was honest with himself, he was just afraid of moving on. There were plenty of girls out there he could marry. A lot of them in London; in the dance halls of north London. Fine girls, too, his brother had told him. 'The Galtymore is crawling with women, John. Get over yourself, for God's sake, and move on.'

But he couldn't. John was stuck in no-man's-land. He loved Noreen but she wouldn't marry him and that meant she didn't really love him. She said she wanted to experience life and he knew what that meant. It meant he wasn't enough. It meant other men, and the thought of that horrified him. Maybe she was with one right now. Maybe his girl was off experiencing life with some smarmy, English guttyboy.

John drained the red lemonade and lifted the glass to the barman. 'Send me over a right one, Paddy.' The men all let out a cheer, visibly relaxing now that the big guard from Cork was back on form, and settled down for a gossip.

'Did you hear about the priest got an awful beating down around the Kings Road?' Jamesy started them off with.

'I heard something – go on.'

'A young lad, seminarian. The bin men picked him up in an alley down the road here. Left for dead, it seems.'

'Jesus, Mary and Holy Saint Joseph,' Gerry said, blessing himself. 'A priest. That's shocking.'

'He was in mufti, mind you. No collar on him.'

'Why's that I wonder?'

'Up to no good in all likelihood. Sure all them miniskirts around here would turn a blind man horny!'

'Tommy Malone, that's a terrible thing to say!'

They're like a bunch of aul' women, John thought, *with all their gossipy carry on.* Despite himself, he was grateful when his pint arrived and he gulped it back to drown out some of their nonsense.

'They didn't even know the poor man was a priest until he came to and told them who he was.'

'And how do you know all this – have you been sniffing around the seminary looking for indulgences again Jamesy?'

'Feck off. The cousin is in St. Stephens Hospital down the road in Fulham. She was working the night shift and was with him when he woke up.'

'And did he confess his sins to her? A young priest going around the Kings Road in mufti. I'd like to hear what he was up to alright.'

'I'm sure she looked after him – hey?'

'You'll burn in hell Tommy,' Jamesy said, then nodded at John. 'He was from around your way, she said. Name of Lyons. Martin? No, Matthew. Father Matthew Lyons.'

John spat out a mouthful of stout.

If John had been looking for an excuse to see Noreen, this was not a good one. He borrowed a van off one of the lads and ran across to the club. That rat Arthur wasn't at the door and he told the big henchman in his place, 'I've got to see Noreen. It's urgent,' he said, pushing him out of the way. 'Family business.'

The big man knew better than to stand in the way of a big

Irishman, and let him through. 'She's in the office – second door after the bar.'

When John opened the door he found a Pieta-esque type scene before him. Arthur was lying on the floor and Noreen was wrapping a bandage around his bare foot. Arthur looked very pleased with himself.

When she looked up and saw him, John thought he saw the old love light come into Noreen's eyes. She was thrilled to see him. Then she said, 'Arthur's been shot,' in a dramatic way that suggested whatever pedestrian business John was there on could not compete.

Her face dropped suddenly when he said, 'It's Matthew. He's in hospital.'

'What happened? Is he all right?'

'He's alive anyway. He was beaten up pretty bad. That's all I know, Noreen. I came straight over to get you. I have a van outside.'

Noreen stood up and halted.

Arthur said, 'I'll be fine. Just go.'

John smarted at his permission.

John got directions from Chevrons' doorman before he left, so they sat in silence on the way to the hospital, any potential small talk silenced by their haste and worry. John didn't ask about the shooting, and the fact that Noreen didn't volunteer anything spoke about how worried she was. They pulled up at the hospital entrance and as Noreen opened the van door John said, 'I'll wait for you.' She looked confused and he added, 'In reception.'

'Thanks,' she said, then paused briefly to say, 'for everything,' before running off through the vast, glass doors.

As he drove to find somewhere to park the van, John said the words to himself, again.

'I'll wait for you.'

He wondered if it would be worth waiting for Noreen, after all. However long it took.

The nurses told her that Matthew was conscious but it had been touch and go.

'He was very lucky,' the nurse said. 'It seems like his head injury was caused by a fall more than a blow. His injuries are largely external but he was unconscious for a while and we are not entirely sure how his brain is functioning since he woke up.'

She warned her that he was sleeping a lot and found speaking a huge effort.

'Will he know who I am?'

'Well he knows who he is so I assume he will know his own sister. He's just having trouble speaking. His facial injuries are bad and word loss is not uncommon with this type of concussion. You just might find him a bit – quiet.'

'That'll make a change,' Noreen quipped, trying to keep her spirits up not to look too frightened walking in the door.

As Noreen was opening the door the nurse put her hand on her arm and added gravely, 'Your brother really got an awful beating. If you have any idea who might have done this to him you really should report him. We see a lot of beatings coming in here, and this is not like any I've ever seen. It really looks like somebody was trying to literally beat your brother to death.'

Noreen felt sick. What on earth could she mean? Matthew didn't know anyone in London apart from priests and art academics. For one short, horrible moment, she wondered if the world of gangsters that she inhabited had followed her brother. But how could that be? Nobody knew him. He did not carry much money on him so it seemed unlikely to be a random act of violence. The only person he knew in London apart from her and priests and academics was Annie. And although Noreen still did not know quite how, she knew that Annie was trouble.

Noreen burst into tears when she saw him. Her sweet, gentle brother was nothing more than a lump of bruises and bandages. Unable to move, his arms and legs were bandaged and hoisted up. Whoever had attacked him had broken every bone in Matthew's body. It looked as if they were trying to kill him.

His face was unrecognisable, with his eyes barely visible beneath swollen mounds. His lips were indistinguishable and when he opened his mouth to speak it was little more than a bloody gash. Noreen cried out when she saw he had lost two of his front teeth. His parents had spent a fortune getting him dental treatment as a child to get his teeth straightened.

'What the hell happened to you?'

He raised his eyebrows indicating that she was annoying him already. Noreen didn't care. If he was irritated it meant he was still in charge of his mental faculties. As much as he'd ever been.

He tried to say something and she leaned in to him as he said a single word, 'Annie.'

Noreen shrugged and folded her arms.

'I know you're seeing Annie, and I have to tell you, Matthew, that girl is very bad news. She's a liar. Her real name is Hanna Black, not Annie. She ran away from home and left her parents heartbroken. I'm afraid she'll do the same to you. Her father contacted me a few days ago and...'

Everything fell into place. It had not been a demon that attacked him but Hanna's father. You have something I want but it's not yours to give – it's mine to take. He had appeared to Matthew as a demon because he was the devil incarnate.

He had to get up. Every bone in his body was crying out but he could not move. He had to find that man and kill him, if necessary, to protect Annie. How had he ended up here? How had he let himself take such a beating from that terrible man? If he had known who his attacker was, he would have found a way to fight back. He would have killed him to protect Annie. Because she was Annie. His Annie. Not Hanna Black. Annie Austen.

He opened his mouth to speak but nothing came out.

Noreen saw him struggling; something desperate in his eyes relayed that what he had to say was important. She leaned in and took his hands but still the words wouldn't come.

'I'm broken,' Annie had said. She wasn't broken, but Matthew was and that bastard had done it to him.

'You're not broken,' he had told her, 'because you have soul.'

So Matthew dug deep. He closed his mouth and found he could breathe through his nose. He had breath. He was still alive. He breathed in deeply then opened the gash that was serving as his mouth and pushed out what he needed Noreen to know.

'Annie's father abused her. That's why she changed her name. He's dangerous. He did this to me. Help her.'

Matthew shut his eyes tight with the effort of speaking and Noreen watched, helpless, as tears poured out of the side of them.

He was helpless. Useless. He couldn't even speak any more but he hoped his twin would know what to do. She usually did – even if it wasn't always the right thing, Noreen always did something.

40

Lara was furious with Coleman for fobbing her off. She said it was important and yet heard real irritation in his voice when he asked her to come back in an hour. Who the hell did he think he was? After all that lovey-dovey stuff earlier.

The exchange through his closed door had just confirmed her worst fear – that Handsome had been telling the truth about Chevron. They were all liars and cheats in here. She thought Coleman was different, but it seemed he was worse than the lot of them put together. He had taken an independent, career-minded, creative woman and was trying to trick her into becoming his gangster's moll. Indulge the little woman by telling her she owns a shop, wait for her to get fed up, then move her into a nice flat and wait for her to settle into a lifetime of cooking, cleaning and looking pretty.

Well, he had better think again.

In the meantime, she had to get Handsome off the premises.

'Where's Arthur?' she said to Noreen as she was marching past the bar.

'I think I saw him go into the office,' Noreen said.

Lara's fury rose to its full height. What on earth could

Coleman be talking to Ironing Board about that was more important than her?

Noreen could see Lara was agitated. 'What's the matter?'

'Urgh. That useless article, Handsome. I tried to sack him and now he won't get out of the shop. I need Arthur to remove him.'

Lara realised how pathetic it sounded but Noreen nodded. 'I'll go and get him.'

As she was going Lara realised that, actually, she did not want to take help from either Coleman or his sidekick. She headed for the stairs then dilly-dallied for a moment at the foot, remembering that Handsome was a nasty piece of work. She was about to go back when she heard a bang coming from the centre of the club. A fight breaking out or some kind of man-aggro and Lara did not want to get caught up in the frame – it made the decision for her. She had her own drama to contend with.

As she walked back to the shop, Lara gave herself a good talking to. These gangster types, all of them, were only bullying men. What they needed was a piece of her mind. There was no point in being cowed, especially if you were a woman. You had to stand up to them and show them they couldn't walk all over you. She was going to start with that guttersnipe, Handsome, then work her way back to the other two 'in an hour', as Coleman had said. And what a going over she would give him! Move into a flat with him? Not a hope. And when she had finished she would approach Chevron herself and do some kind of deal with him on the shop. At the end of the day, Bobby Chevron was a businessman. She vaguely remembered promising Coleman to make Chevron's wife some gear and as she reached the shop, she thought, maybe now was the time to make good on that promise.

When she put her hand on the door of the shop she found it locked. She was relieved. It meant that Handsome had left and locked up. Nonetheless, it meant he had a key, which she would have to get back off him. Also, it was a working day and, as she opened the door and stepped inside, she saw that the door still had its OPEN sign up. The idiot couldn't even turn a sign. What the hell had she been afraid of? She reached over to turn on the lights at the door when he emerged from the shadows and put his hand over the light switch to stop her.

'Hello, boss.'

Lara nearly jumped out of her skin. Her heart thumped but she must not show him she was afraid. The key was still in her hand and the door open behind her.

'What the hell are you still doing here? And why didn't you turn the sign?'

She tried to keep her voice hard but her body felt weak and shaky. In the moment that it took her to get the words out, Handsome quickly snatched the key out of her hand and went to lock the door behind her. He had done this before.

She dropped her handbag and the edge of her scarf got caught in the door.

'What the hell are you doing?'

This time the words came out high-pitched and afraid.

'I thought we'd have some fun, boss. Take it nice and slow.'

'Get out of my shop,' she said in a terrified whisper.

But he was already moving towards her.

It took Coleman no more than two minutes from running up the stairs of Chevrons to the door of That Girl, but it felt like an age. His brain had switched off as his body engaged. Lara might be in danger. And if she might be in danger, the need was as urgent as if it were a certainty. The possibility of her being hurt or upset by that creep Devers, in any way, was an anathema. It simply could not happen.

When he got to the shop, it was locked. A split second of relief turned when he noticed a piece of fabric halfway down the edge of the door. He pulled at it and the fine silk came easily towards him. It was the scarf Lara had been wearing earlier.

She was in there.

He began banging on the door furiously shouting, 'Open the door.' When nobody came immediately, he knew there was trouble.

He had to get in but there was no back door to this building. No delivery door, only high windows at the back. There was only one way. Brute force.

He had to stay calm. If he lost it he'd end up taking a run at it and dislocating a shoulder.

Coleman quickly looked to see which way the door opened by checking its hinges. He breathed a small sigh of relief when he saw that the door opened inwards, then gave a forceful and well placed kick to the side where the lock was mounted, near the keyhole. Using a long front kick, he drove the heel of his foot into the door, keeping his standing foot balanced by driving the heel of it into the ground. He was careful not to kick the lock itself and break his foot.

The wood began to splinter and Coleman kept repeating to himself, *stay calm, keep on kicking.* After half a dozen kicks, the door gave way and he ran in.

The shop was empty.

'Hello?' he shouted. Silence. There was nothing untoward, no fallen clothes racks, no sign of a fight. The shop was as neat as ever. Spotless. There was nobody here. Maybe he had knocked the door down for nothing. The beginnings of relief as he thought he might have acted rashly. He looked back towards the door and saw Lara's handbag on the floor, the contents spilling out of it. The beginnings of a sick feeling as he reached into his pocket for the cartridge and loaded the gun. Then he heard a small muffled noise. Barely discernible, like a dog yelping in a neighbouring street.

He called out, 'Lara? You in here?'

Another tiny yelp. It was coming from the direction of the changing room.

Slowly and with great care so that the cartridge did not make a snapping sound he loaded the Walther. Then he took off his shoes and began to walk towards the curtained area.

His heart was pounding; he was almost dizzy with adrenalin. If that creep had harmed a hair on Lara's head – but he couldn't think about that now. He went to the edge of the curtain and carefully snuck behind so as not to make any noise. Inside the dressing room there were four curtained areas, two of them with lavish, full-length curtains drawn across so that he could not see if anyone was behind them.

He put the gun to the edge of the first one and peeked in. Empty.

They were in the next one. Or not there at all.

But when Coleman quickly pushed back the curtain, he was ready for whatever was there.

At least he thought he was ready.

Lara was gagged, stripped down to her underwear with her hands tied behind her back. Her eyes looked at him, gargantuan and terrified. Handsome was behind her, naked. His eyes were darting with fear, indicating he was high, and he had a knife held to the side of Lara's neck.

'I'll cut her,' he said. 'I'll cut her throat.'

'Mate,' Coleman said, 'come on. How about sharing it around a bit?'

Lara's eyes widened and she made a guttural noise.

'She's a pretty girl. I get it...'

'You're fucking with me...'

'No, no, I'm not. I swear.' Coleman lowered his right hand as if putting the gun on the ground.

Handsome smiled and relaxed his hand.

As he did Coleman shot him in the leg and Handsome fell screaming on his side to the ground. Then, before Lara could stop him, Coleman pointed the Walther at Handsome's head and drilled two more into his skull.

41

Annie arranged the cheeseboard on the counter top and polished the six new Babycham glasses she bought as a sort of celebration for today. After their big day together, Annie and Matthew had agreed to leave it a few days before seeing each other again. Matthew wanted to get the whole priest thing sorted out before they moved forward. He did not want the deception to go on any longer than it already had.

'The next time I see you, darling,' he told her, 'I will have rescinded my vocation. I'll no longer be a priest.'

'How do you know if I'll still like you when you're not a priest?' she said teasingly. He looked slightly crestfallen so she leaned in and kissed him and said, 'I can't wait to have you all to myself.'

In the days since that glorious day together, Annie had tried to keep her feet on the ground. She had changed. Her life was changing. When *Vogue* went wild for Alex's test picture in the park, Lara had, finally, persuaded Annie that modelling could be a lucrative career for her.

'You'll need plenty of money if you're going to make a life with an artist,' she cautioned.

Annie defended Matthew's ability to make money as an artist but she thought Lara was probably right. Matthew wasn't a rich man and it would take a while for him to get on his feet. She had not cared about having any more than the bare essentials up to now, but if she and Matthew were to be together, get married, do the things that ordinary people did, they would need money. So she told Alex to go about getting her an agent and already, she had three jobs booked for the following week.

She took three of the glasses and put them back in the press. She didn't want Matthew to think she was having a party although, in her heart, she wanted her friends there to meet him. This would be a celebration of sorts and while she had not specifically arranged for Lara and Noreen to be there, they were in and out of the flat all day and Alex had said he might drop by to finalise some arrangements for next week. How wonderful it would be if they all turned up and met Matthew!

She checked the clock and it was twenty past four. Matthew was late. Her stomach shrivelled with fear that he might not come. Of course he would come. This was Matthew. Although, perhaps something had happened to him. Perhaps he had changed his mind. Or perhaps she had said half-past. Yes. That was it. There were ten more minutes before she should start worrying. To distract herself she checked the cheeseboard again. The big lump of orange cheddar looked unsightly so she decided to dress it properly. Annie took down her new cutter from its hook and began to meticulously cut it into thin slices. Repetitive, meticulous domestic work calmed her down, and sure enough – ding dong, there was Matthew at the door.

Annie threw aside her apron and the cheese cutter and ran down the stairs, then quickly opened the door and...

'Hello, Hanna.'

She reeled backwards. Dorian wasted no time. With great speed he stepped into the hall and closed the door behind him. He cocked his head to one side and said, in a sudden quick voice, 'Surprised to see me? Why Dorian you're looking so well. You haven't changed one bit!'

Annie was paralysed with shock. A ghoul, risen from the dead. Any pretence at handsome charm was gone and in its place was the physical embodiment of ugly anger. It was as if he had been turned inside out and now the world could see the monster he was. As he stood there now, Dorian was her worst nightmare made manifest. She had made him that way and now he was back to haunt her. Was he real or a ghost? Perhaps her love for a holy man had brought God's wrath down on her and He had sent the devil, in person, to claim her.

But he was real, alright. Dorian grabbed her shoulders, spun her around and prodded her up the stairs. Weak with terror, she led him up to her flat. He quickly closed the door behind them, then secured the flimsy bolt lock and pressed a chair under the door handle, 'Just in case,' he said, and smiled at her. Annie felt a chill run through her. Again.

It was going to happen again.

'There now,' he said. 'All cosy.'

He looked around him as if it was the most normal thing in the world.

'This is nice,' he said, as if he were her visiting stepfather, as if he still had his good looks and charm. 'A very tidy arrangement. It's Annie isn't it? What do I call you now?'

As if she still belonged to him.

She opened her mouth but nothing came out. Annie couldn't speak. Annie was gone.

'Hanna,' she said. She pushed the word out, forcing it up from her gut but it came out in a guttural cough.

'Pardon? I'm afraid you'll have to speak up my dear. My hearing is a little off since our little,' and he coughed portentously, 'accident.'

'Hanna,' she said, as clearly as she could.

He smiled. His eyes were as black and hard as granite.

'That's right. You're Hanna – my stepdaughter and you have been a very naughty girl haven't you?'

She felt sick. She could feel bile rise up from her stomach.

'Answer me!'

'Yes,' she said.

As she held back the vomit, Annie's shock began to subside and the reality of her situation started to sink in. Dorian was alive. Here, in the flesh. She had not killed him, after all. She was not a murderer. But – he was. He had cold-bloodedly stolen and destroyed the soul of a child. Her inner child. He had destroyed who she was as surely as if he had killed her.

Now, he was going to rape her and possibly kill her. Worse, he could take her back to Killa and they would carry on as before except this time there would be no escape. This life, Annie's, all of it, would be gone. And Matthew? Love? It would all be no more than a distant dream.

'Everyone had been very worried about you, dear Hanna. All the ladies of the village, Mrs Clarke and the like have been wondering where you were. They are very cross with you leaving your poor stepfather after he was so...' then he drew his hand down suddenly and fiercely on the coffee table, 'viciously attacked!' The glass smashed in one long crack and she flinched.

Then, she remembered. Matthew. He was on his way. The relief subsided as she thought about what that meant. Would he rescue her? Would he be able to get in? If he did, what would Dorian say? He would tell Matthew that she had tried to kill him. That she had left him for dead. Dorian would play the poor cripple and manipulate everyone into his way of thinking. That was what he was good at. Matthew would believe she was lying about having been abused and people would believe Dorian. They would believe him even more now that he was crippled. She would be labelled a wicked murderess and Matthew would hate her. That would be worse than anything.

Her only hope was to stand up to Dorian. To show him that she was a strong woman. To let him see that Hanna had grown up into Annie. Annie was a strong, independent woman with friends and a job and a life of her own. Annie was beyond his reach. She drew herself up to her full height, raised her chin to give herself a haughty look that Alex had taught her, and said in the clearest voice that she could, 'I want you to leave, now. Please get out of my flat.'

'Really?' he said, and laughed. 'Is that the best you can do?'

'My friends will be here soon and when I tell them what you're like, what you've done—'

'Ah, your friends. That skinny Jew that takes those common pictures of you? I doubt he could do me much harm, even if he wanted to. And then there is the lovely Noreen…'

What was he saying?

'Oh, didn't you know? Noreen and I are great friends. In fact, she arranged to keep the flat clear this afternoon so that you and I could have our…' and he sank his head in a dramatic gesture of humility, then looked up at her coyly, 'emotional reunion.'

Annie was shocked but not surprised. Even him following her and all of this set up. She did not feel betrayed. This was how Dorian operated. If he was that determined to get her back, she had to be more so.

'I've met somebody else.'

Even putting Matthew in the same context as Dorian felt wrong, but perhaps suggesting that he once meant something to her might appeal to some shred of normality in him.

Dorian looked at her for a moment and she could see the reference sinking in. Just not in the way she had hoped.

'Ah, the boyfriend. Tall, slender chap. Not bad looking, I suppose. Rather serious though. And not much of a man by the look of him. Rather a lot of kissing and not much else.'

Annie felt the bile rise again. He had been watching them. The whole day she spent with Matthew. The day, which belonged only to them, had been witnessed by this vile man.

'No, Hanna, I'm afraid you won't be seeing that young man again.'

She looked at him and her eyes asked the question that her mouth couldn't.

'Yes, I'm afraid he met with an accident. He came close quarters with an iron bar. Repeatedly. Rather like myself.'

Annie ran behind the kitchen counter and vomited into the sink.

'Oh dear, oh dear, what a terrible mess,' Dorian said. 'I thought you might be disappointed to hear that but you know, Hanna, in life you win some, you lose some. And those who live by the sword, I'm afraid...'

As he talked, Annie's body emptied itself. And when she could feel her body was empty she kept the tap running and imagined she was purging her soul. Everything she had known being flushed down the sink. She did not want a shred of anything inside her. Without Matthew, Annie was as much a painful memory as Hanna was. It was all pointless. Without Matthew, there was no love. She had lived without it for so long, then found it here. Among these people and with Matthew she had started again. But women like her could never start again. If she couldn't have Matthew, if she couldn't have love, then she didn't want anything inside her.

So Annie ran the tap at full speed and watched the water flood down the plug hole. With it she flushed everything she was. The abuse, the shame, the fear, the guilt of Hanna and then, the joy, the optimism, the hope and the love of Annie – all gone.

When she stood up she heard Dorian still talking.

'You couldn't have liked him anyway. Not really, Hanna. A wimp like that? He didn't even fight back. Well, not much anyway. Begged for his life. Pleaded with me. Even I didn't beg, Hanna. Do you remember? I took it like a man and now – here I am! Coming back for more – and where's he? No, only the strong survive, Hanna, and I am strong. This is for the best, Hanna, really. You'll see that. When we get home everything will be different. Although I'm thinking now that perhaps we could stay here in London. Not here of course in this poky dump. Things will be different between us too, Hanna. You'll see. I can make you happy.'

This was what Dorian enjoyed. Making plans for them. Being in control. Lying. He didn't know he was lying most of the time. He just wanted things to be true and thought he could make them that way through his will. He believed he could be kind and loving by simply stating it. He did not know what kindness or love were so he talked about them all the time to try to bring them to life. He was, really, a pitiful creature who could not help the way he was. He was beyond redemption. So, perhaps, was she.

Annie didn't feel angry any more.

The anger was gone, along with everything else.

She just knew that she couldn't do this again.

She turned off the tap, and went over and stood behind Dorian's chair.

Then she leaned down and kissed him on the top of his forehead. Dorian leaned his head back into the chair. She had come to her senses. He knew from the softness of her touch that she was sincere. She stroked her fingers across his neck, then tenderly drew the thick, black hair back from his collar.

Hanna picked up the cheese cutter from the countertop.

'Not like before,' she said, firmly securing the wooden handles in her small fists.

'That's right,' Dorian said closing his eyes, not seeing the wire thread as it whipped in front of his face. He leaned back to her in ecstasy and promised, 'No, my darling girl. It won't be like before.'

42

John almost missed Noreen as she came tearing down the hospital stairs. She grabbed him by the arm and told him to drive her back to the flat urgently. She filled him in on Matthew and the dangerous stepfather on the way.

Noreen could not believe she had got it so wrong about Annie. She felt sick with worry and fear for her flatmate as well as a frightful anguish that all this could be her fault.

'I invited this man back into her life. John, supposing something happens – supposing he...'

'Don't think about that now, pet,' John said trying to sound reassuring. It was the measure of how upset Noreen was that she allowed him to call her pet without violent contradiction. John was not at all sure that this situation was going to sort itself out. It sounded like a very messy business. More messy and violent, indeed, than anything he'd ever encountered in his life as a guard in Carney. Although he would do anything that was necessary, of course, to protect the women, John still rather hoped he wouldn't be called upon to henchman this nasty character into submission. However, with Noreen at the helm of this problem, it seemed highly likely that he would. The woman really did know how to attract bother. He had to bite his tongue to not give her a severe talking to about minding her own business.

When they arrived at the house everything seemed quiet.

'No sign of forced entry,' John said, hopefully.

Noreen looked terrified. 'She would have let him in.'

John walked up the stairs ahead, knocked on the door of the flat then tried to open it.

'It's locked,' he said, 'maybe there's no one in. Maybe they went out or he didn't come.'

Noreen pushed him aside, rapped firmly on the door and shouted, 'Annie! Annie! Open up! It's Noreen.'

A tiny voice came from inside. Like a mouse squeaking. John didn't hear it but Noreen did.

'Matthew?'

'Can you open the door, Annie?' Noreen had her face up to the door and was speaking gently. 'Are you alone? Is there anyone with you? Come and open the door, Annie, please.'

Another tiny whimper.

Noreen turned to John and said, 'Break the door down.'

'I can't just break down a door like that, Noreen.'

'He's probably got her at knifepoint,' she spat in an angry whisper. 'Just do it or I will!'

'Annie,' John called out in his booming voice. 'It's John here. Noreen's erm...' He looked at Noreen and she raised her eyes to heaven.

'Annie, John's going to break the door down if you don't...'

They heard a bolt go back, then Annie opened the door and collapsed into Noreen's arms.

The two women sank to the floor of the small landing and Noreen comforted Annie as she shook and wept in her arms.

'I'm sorry, Annie,' she said. 'I'm so, so sorry.'

Noreen was crying herself, bereft at having caused her friend such pain and trouble. So upset, in fact, that she forgot her own curiosity and did not look beyond the door into the flat before John closed the door firmly on them both.

Not in a million years could he ever imagine the scene before him. Certainly not at the hands of that wee girleen who knew how to make such delicious mushroom vol-au-vents.

Lying on the chair was the body of a middle-aged man, with his throat cut. His eyes were open and looked up as if pleading with his attacker. The back of the chair was covered in blood as was the front of his shirt, but, otherwise, it was not as messy as John would have imagined. Not indeed, that he had ever imagined walking in on such a scene.

The garrotte was still dug into the wound and hanging off the sides of his neck. John observed the cheeseboard on the counter suggesting that the kitchen appliance had come to hand rather than an actual murder weapon. Self-defence. John didn't think there was any doubt about that after what he had heard. But by God, this was going to be something to explain away in a court of law.

He didn't touch anything and went out to the hall to the two women.

Annie had calmed down and found breath through the sobbing. Her head was resting on Noreen's chest and Noreen was stroking her hair.

He looked at Noreen and shook his head to indicate what had happened. Her head craned to look round the door and he closed it firmly. Not even Noreen with her morbid curiosity and strong stomach should have to look at a scene like that.

'I'd better go downstairs and ring the police,' he said.

'You will do no such thing!' Noreen snapped. 'Look at Annie. She's in no fit state to talk to the police. Whatever happened between Annie and that wicked bastard, it was self-defence. He nearly killed my brother remember? Certainly, he intended to.'

'Well, this is really a matter for the police.'

'Well, you're a policeman.'

'I'm an Irish guard, I don't have any jurisd—'

'And I'm telling you we just need to sit on this and figure out what to do for the best.'

'We can't just leave him there.'

'No of course we can't. We have to get rid of the body some-how. I'm going to go downstairs and get Arthur.'

'And by the way,' Noreen turned on the way down the stairs and said to Annie, 'Matthew is my brother.'

'Matthew?' Annie suddenly woke from her catatonic state. Had she heard Noreen correctly through the fog of her shock? 'So he's alive? Matthew's not dead?'

'He certainly is not dead,' she said. 'He's not looking very pretty right now, but he's alive.' Then she sunnily added, 'Welcome to the family!'

Under the circumstances, John thought it sounded rather more like a threat.

Coleman stood in front of the body with his gun pointing at the floor. He had just shot a man. Shot him dead, deliberately – without stopping to think. Now the body was lying in front of him. Two seconds ago, Handsome had been alive and now he was lying there in front of him, lifeless and naked. Coleman focussed on the fact that Handsome was naked and reminded himself that he had been about to rape Lara. The creep would almost certainly have stabbed her, maybe hit an artery and killed her, if Coleman hadn't fired at him quickly.

However, Coleman should have shot him in the leg and left it at that. If the cops had been alerted, they might have looked the other way and put it down to a gangster tiff. Handsome would probably have let it go. He might even have learned his lesson and laid off the women, for a while anyway.

But Coleman had not done that. Rage had taken him over and he shot to kill. He stood there, with the gun hanging limply from his hands, paralysed. He couldn't take his eyes off the man he had just shot. Dead. Alive – then dead. Alive – then dead.

Coleman had seen men beaten, thumped, have their faces smashed in, their noses broken. He'd seen them shot in the leg, the knee, and, as of earlier that day, the foot. He had seen guns pointed at their heads and he pointed guns at the heads of men. He had listened as they begged for mercy, begged for their lives. Once or twice, he had helped lift dead bodies into the back of cars. But, probably more by coincidence than design, Coleman had never seen a man die before. He had certainly never killed anybody himself.

Men got angry with each other and somebody had to win. Coleman understood that as a rule of life. If you wanted to stop a man fighting, you had to hit hard to quench their fire, to bring them down. Now he realised it was quite another thing to put out the light entirely.

Alive – then dead. Alive – then dead.

Coleman had not thought of God since he was a child.

But he thought of Him now that he had killed someone. Nobody had the right to do that except God.

He tried to think of all of the men Chevron had snuffed out over the years. He imagined Arthur there, telling him to pull himself together. Handsome was a scumbag, a rapist – the lowest of the low. He deserved to die. He had it coming.

But still, Coleman could not move or speak. He was paralysed with shock.

Lara manoeuvred herself off the chaise longue and he untied her hands. She unbound herself and said, 'Jesus, Coleman. What the hell are we going to do now?'

Coleman looked at her and then looked down at his hands. She followed his eyes and saw they were shaking. Then she looked back up at his face and saw that he had started to cry.

Lara was in shock, too. She had nearly been raped and killed, there was a dead body on her changing-room floor with blood and brains everywhere, including, she noted with horror, on her half-naked torso. And Coleman was falling apart. What the hell kind of a gangster was he?

She wanted to slap him, bring him to his senses. But then, he looked at her and she saw in his eyes the pain of a small, gentle child. The immeasurable yearning for love in the vulnerable. Something terrible had happened and all he wanted now was for somebody to tell him it was all right. When she saw him shoot Handsome with such certain confidence, Lara had been shocked, assuming this was an everyday occurrence with him. Clearly, by the expression in his eyes, fear, grief, pleading, it wasn't. Coleman was a hard man but he was not a killer. He had just killed a man to protect her.

Lara was terrified. This violence was outside of her experience. Nonetheless, she knew she had to step up.

She put her arms around Coleman, led him out of the changing room and made him sit on a chair behind the till.

'Wait here,' she said. 'I'm going to get Arthur. Don't move.'

Coleman realised that he could not move anyway. He had untied her hands at her request then allowed himself to be guided to this chair but without her hand on him to guide him, he was powerless. He looked up at her, disbelieving his own weakness.

'I'll be back in a moment. We'll sort this out.' She kissed him sweetly on the forehead, and, grabbing a trench coat on her way, ran out the door, locking it behind her.

'So let me get this straight,' Arthur said. 'We've got two dead bodies.'

Lara and Noreen were standing in front of him, both in a state of dishevelment. The left side of Lara's hair was stuck to her cheek with a lump of congealed blood and there was what looked like a small piece of somebody else's brain nestling in her neck, just under her ear. Noreen was in slightly better shape but had blood all over her hands and the front of her blouse.

'Yes,' the two girls said in unison.

'Handsome got shot by Coleman while he was trying to have a go at Lara?'

'That's right,' Lara said.

'Then some scary creep from Ireland was strangled by your pretty flatmate who wouldn't say boo to a goose.'

'Yes,' Noreen said.

Arthur smiled.

'You Irish are some piece of work.'

Truth be told, he was rather delighted with himself. Two damsels in distress and he was the first person they called to sort this out. This had taken his mind right off his foot. And the other imminent problem with Chevron. In fact, he was beginning to think that one problem might just sort out the other.

'We need to get rid of the bodies, Arthur. Quickly.'

'Ladies. I make bodies. I don't get rid of them.'

'Who does?'

'I dunno. Let's have a look and see what we've got.'

First, Arthur went to the shop with Lara.

'Anyone else got a key to this place?' Arthur asked.

'No,' she said.

'Good, because this lot will take some cleaning up.'

Coleman had rallied somewhat but was quiet. Uncharacteristically he allowed Arthur to take charge. Arthur took the responsibility on board without judgement or comment. Coleman had spared his life earlier. It wasn't easy killing people. Death could discombobulate the toughest hard man. Arthur knew that.

They locked up. Lara took Coleman and Annie down to the Chevrons' office to clean up; Noreen and Arthur went back to the flat.

'Shit,' Arthur said. 'Annie did that?'

Noreen nodded. 'Him, I could understand,' he said looking at John. John did not laugh. He was not happy taking orders from Arthur, but Noreen had warned him.

Arthur walked over and examined the body. Looking Dorian up and down. 'Neat job,' he said approvingly, 'although, fuck me, he's one mean looking dude.'

'Language, Arthur,' Noreen said.

'Sorry,' he apologised.

John was not impressed with the familiar talk between this lowdown gangster and his girl.

'I think we should call the police,' John said in his most assertive guard's voice.

Arthur gave him a look that left John in no doubt whatsoever as to his meaning.

'Inadvisable,' is all he said.

'You will in your decking hole,' said Noreen, furious. 'Arthur will sort this out.'

'I'll make some calls,' he said. Now that the problem had come to a head, the novelty of being in charge was beginning to wear off. Arthur was worried. He didn't know anyone who could clean up this kind of carnage. Chevron had hit out on Coleman this very night. If he got wind of this, which with two dead bodies on his premises he would, God knows what would follow. Chevron didn't mind dead bodies as long as they were his dead bodies. This was a right mess and no mistake.

Two dead bodies and neither of them Coleman.

Then it came to him in a flash. Normally, when Arthur had flashes, it meant somebody was going to get hurt. This flash was different. It was a sudden, problem solving idea and it was quite, quite brilliant. If he could make it work. Although, for the life of him he could not imagine how.

'I think we'd be better off keeping this to ourselves,' he said.

Noreen and John agreed. John was still reluctant, but the fewer gangsters he knew in person the better. If he could confine his acquaintance to Arthur and Coleman, he might be able to salvage something of his moral integrity somewhat.

'We need to bury these lads. Deep. Somewhere they can't be found.'

Noreen nodded. John despaired. His life lay in the hands of this half-witted cockney.

'What we need,' Arthur continued, 'is a bloody big hole. Problem is where the hell are we going to find one?'

Noreen looked at John and John looked right back at her.

He was shaking his head but, as always in the company of his girl, John was utterly powerless.

✿

Once they established they had access to the foundations of the World's End site, they put their heads together and refined the plan.

Before they cleaned up the shop, Coleman lay on his side on the dressing room floor and Lara took a photograph of him with Handsome's body.

Arthur borrowed a van from a friend who did not ask questions. Nonetheless, in case Chevron checked in later, he assured him he needed it overnight to transport some stuff from the boutique to a supplier. Handsome's slim body was wrapped in a clothes bag and flung over John's shoulder with a couple of other clothes bags, as if it weighed no more than a shirt. Then, they took Dorian's body out of the flat using the same principle. It was not uncommon for the neighbours to see Lara coming in and out of the flat with clothes bags and she stood outside instructing the men to be careful with her precious collection. That night, Noreen, Lara and Annie set about the two scenes with buckets of bleach. The following day they took turns in the launderette washing soiled curtains and fabrics on boil wash, running in and out of their workplaces keeping everything looking normal. John worked the World's End site and made sure that things were in place before going for pints as usual. While his foreman was in the bathroom John managed to steal the padlock keys from his pocket and handed them to Arthur. Coleman had the van parked at the back entrance of the site. Between them, they managed to get the two bodies into the foundations hole. Arthur took a photograph to show Chevron, of the two bodies in a heaped mash of flailing limbs at the bottom of the pit. They found the two shovels that John left for them and threw sand and gravel on top of the bodies until they were hidden from view.

The following day the concrete went down and Handsome and Dorian disappeared, forever.

Chevron was told that Coleman killed Handsome because he tried to get up on his girl and that Arthur had taken the opportunity to shoot him then. Best to keep the mess all in one place, boss. When you are lying, Arthur found, it was always good to stay as close to the truth as possible.

Chevron asked for evidence. Eventually. 'Not that I don't trust you, my son,' he said. Bobby had never called him son when Coleman was alive. When Coleman was alive he was just Ironing Board. Now he was the boss. The man in charge.

Bobby never questioned why Arthur had taken the trouble of photographing the bodies for him, but it made him think there was more to Ironing Board than he had given him credit for. The way he got rid of Coleman had showed a ruthless streak he hadn't known was there. Honestly, he had not really been expecting him to do it. Shirley had surprised him though. Cried like a bloody baby down the phone to him. She was very cut up saying that she hoped her grassing him up hadn't resulted in Chevron taking Coleman out. Bobby had reassured her that he would never dream of killing Coleman. He never hit women, and he never took out mates. That was the rules.

'He's probably off somewhere living it up and all that. That designer dolly of his moved back to Ireland after I closed the shop. Maybe he followed her?'

Shirley didn't like that.

Matthew recovered and left the priesthood. He and Annie got married immediately. Her modelling career paid for him to finish his studies and get work teaching. Whereupon she gave up modelling and started having babies.

Coleman laid low with Lara's Auntie Una in Cricklewood for a month before leaving for New York. Lara followed him a month later, after organising their affairs so that they could start again. She continued designing, but for other people. Coleman's smart appearance, business nous and a few forged references got him a job on Wall Street where he made a fortune. Lara was sorry to leave Swinging London but discovered, with Coleman, that everywhere swings when you're in love.

Summer 1975

Noreen leaned back on the pink, studded velveteen headboard and lit a cigarette.

'I tell you what, John, you've still got the magic touch.'

'Oh God, here she goes.'

'I mean it. Triple orgasms – here we come!'

'I wish you wouldn't talk like that.'

'What?' she said, swooping her hand down under the bed and picking up a copy of this month's *Cosmopolitan*. 'It says here you're only annoying yourself with an ordinary orgasm and double orgasms are only for beginners.'

'Can we change the subject, please?'

'Oh,' she said, 'I think Father Carr might have figured out we're not married.'

'What?'

'He was looking for certificates for Mary's First Holy Communion and I panicked. Started telling him some long-winded tale about the fire in our last house and that the wedding certificate was in a particular place, blah, blah, blah. Lying through my teeth, you know what I get like when I'm nervous.'

'Yes I do.'

'Do you remember we had the same problem when we were getting her christened?'

'Yes I do.'

Nearly ten years together and John still hated having this conversation. She had not taken much persuading to leave Chevrons after their experiences that night. She started working in his brother's pub in Cricklewood. She loved the craic and the buzz of London so much that they persuaded her dad to put up some money and they bought The Green Boat, an established pub in Hendon. They lied to Frank and told him they were already married. Noreen was pregnant. Frank was furious that they had gone shotgun but not as furious as he would have been if he'd known they had never got married. Noreen just wouldn't do it. Everyone thought they were married anyway, so John was able to forget about it most of the time. Unless she brought it up. Sometimes he thought she did it to hurt him. Or remind him how lucky he was. Perhaps you could not have one without the other.

'Anyway, I was thinking,' she said. 'Maybe we should get married anyway.'

He looked at her. Was she joking?

'Why not?' she said. 'It's no big deal is it?'

She put out her cigarette and looked at him square in the face. Querying but not fighting with him. Motherhood had softened some of her old defiance. Noreen was bigger now, after the three kids. Her white skin was mottled with stretch marks, and her chunky legs were splayed on their eiderdown under the practical candlewick dressing gown she had proudly picked up from a church jumble sale the week before.

She was the most unfashionable, incorrigible, unapologetically insatiable woman he knew and she was his. All his. Yet she did not belong to him – she belonged only to herself.

'Look' he said. 'I'll sort out the padre. Let's stay as we are for a while yet.'

She looked at him sideways.

'Are you sure?'

'Ah lookit,' he said, 'the paperwork, everything, it's too much hassle.'

'John Connolly,' she said, giving him a whack over the side of the head with her *Cosmo*, 'you are the most unromantic man I know. I will never marry you.'

He laughed, then pinned her down on the bed, peeled back the candlewick and said, 'Sure there's no point in rushing these things.'